"I AM NOT A CHARITY CASE, AMANDA!"

Antonio's voice was chilling as he continued, "Perhaps I will be partially blind, but I can assure you I will not be helpless. I do not need your good intentions."

Amanda's anger flared, and she cursed his Spanish pride. "Then Señor Hernandez, you do not need me!"

His eyes glinted dangerously as he moved toward her. "Ah, querida, but you are wrong. I do need you."

In one swift movement he swept her into his arms, claiming her lips with such intense and urgent passion that her anger dissolved, and she clung to him with limitless desire. She could hardly hear her heart's warning—that to Antonio, need was just another word for lust!

THOUGH HEARTS RESIST
MEG HUDSON

A SUPERROMANCE FROM
WORLDWIDE

TORONTO · NEW YORK · LOS ANGELES · LONDON

For Alison...
who just may be even lovelier
than the heart of a hibiscus. . . .

Published May 1983

First printing March 1983

ISBN 0-373-70064-4

CHAPTER ONE

New snow for a new year. Standing at the window of her studio apartment overlooking the Charles River, Amanda felt an odd twinge of wistfulness as she watched the swirling flakes drape Boston in winter white.

Across Storrow Drive on the Esplanade, she could see two children, one wearing a bright blue knit cap, the other a counterpart in vivid red. Long ago she and her brother Keith had romped through the falling snow just as these children were doing now. Watching them, she even imagined a touch of moisture on her cheek, a snowflake dissolving. Except it wasn't a snowflake. She touched the spot, then angrily brushed away a tear.

Annoyed with herself—because this was coming very close to self-pity—she moved away from the window, back into the room she had made so definitely hers via the use of subtle color, clever decorative touches and the careful placement of some of her choicest possessions. She had not kept many things after Gerard's death. She'd felt that most of the contents of the big house in Chestnut Hill rightfully belonged to his son and daughter by his first marriage. They were her contemporaries, really— Gerard had been nearly thirty years her senior. It had been a May-September marriage, and her friends had accused her of wanting to be "an old man's sweetheart, rather than a young man's slave," but this had been far from the truth. She had loved him deeply, and her devotion to him had been complete, even during the last terrible months of his terminal illness. Now, more than a year since his death, she still missed him intensely.

A large portrait photograph framed in silver stood on an end table, and she paused to glance down at it. Gerard Hughes had been a handsome and distinguished man. The photograph had been taken before his illness struck and was an excellent likeness. Amanda's eyes misted as she looked at it, and she turned away, as if by doing so she could shut out memory, loneliness and a kind of despondency that didn't seem to lessen with the passage of time.

Saturdays, admittedly, were bad. So were Sundays. She'd made just a few friends in Boston, most of them people she'd met in the early months of her marriage to Gerard. Many of them had also known her father and were contemporaries of both men. They had been kind to her after Gerard's death, even solicitous, calling and asking her to dinner or perhaps a Sunday brunch. She'd accepted one or two of the invitations, only to find that despite everyone's efforts to be nice to her she had felt very much out of place.

Finally the invitations had abated, and now it was seldom that any of Gerard's friends called her—which was just as well.... With one exception. She would always be grateful to Martha Ferris, also a widow but in her mid-fifties, who had alerted her to the job opportunity at the Cunningham Language Institute.

At first Amanda had not thought she could possibly be qualified for the position Martha was describing since she spoke no foreign languages. As it developed, though, what the institute wanted was someone who could teach English as a second language, principally to people who were either emigrating to the United States or who planned to be in the country for long visits and knew little or no English at all. Even so, she knew most of the teachers at the Cunningham Language Institute had their Master's degrees in the subject, and so the day she set out for her interview Amanda was not overly hopeful.

The institute, headed by Dr. Howard Cunningham, occupied a former mansion on Commonwealth Avenue. The building, a huge brick structure Victorian in design, with bay windows and cupolas and elaborate exterior stonework, was beautiful. It was a perfect setting for Dr. Cunningham, Amanda thought. He was tall and stately with a shock of white hair, and he favored black suits, stark white shirts and narrow ties that were totally out of fashion.

At her interview Amanda had been almost painfully conscious of her youth, even though she was twenty-six and ordinarily considered herself mature for her age. Marriage to a much older man had in a way subdued her. She tended to dress in understated colors, automatically choosing styles that were really too old for her—this from the long entrenched habit of trying to bridge that gap of years between her husband and her. She was a bit taller than average, slim but with all the curves in the right places, as a college friend had told her once, his eyes afire with enthusiasm. Yet her clothes were selected with an eye to camouflaging, rather than revealing, these curves.

Her hair was truly her crowning glory, a deep antique gold, long and naturally wavy. Amanda wore it pulled straight back from her forehead and arranged in a coil at the nape of her neck because the style made her look older. She was slightly farsighted, so glasses were helpful for reading. Even though she didn't need to wear them all the time, she usually did so, having convinced herself this was easier than taking them on and off.

The day of her interview at the Cunningham Institute the glasses had been firmly in place and she had worn a gray suit of excellent quality and very little style. She had felt at least forty—and was sure she looked it—until she was ushered into Dr. Cunningham's decidedly august presence. Then she had the odd sensation everything about her was false, a kind of masquerade. Perhaps it was because Dr. Cunningham seemed such a father figure to her that she'd begun to feel like an awkward teenager under his scrutiny—thus swinging the pendulum from one extreme to the other. She had ruefully decided that he'd certainly never hire her. But she had been mistaken.

For one thing, Dr. Cunningham had known Gerard. They had both been members of the Harvard Club. Also, he had heard of her father, who had been a distinguished professor of literature and an authority on Shakespeare. Martha Ferris had also elaborated on Amanda's qualifications: that she had majored in English in college and had a good grasp of language.

So with very little ado at all she was added to the institute's staff.

She had started work at just about the same time the sale of the Chestnut Hill house had been finalized and the contents distributed, for the most part, between Gerard's two children. There had been an excitement at first at moving into a place of her own and decorating it exactly as she wished, but there was a limit to the amount of time one could spend fixing up a studio apartment, even a spacious one.

As it was, she had more than enough to do to fill her daytime hours. Her job at the institute was fascinating, and she soon proved to have a knack for this sort of language teaching.

She learned that ESL programs—teaching English as a second language—were widespread. Many of them were wholly or partially subsidized by federal or state grants and often offered free of charge to newcomers to the United States who desperately needed to acquire a quick grasp of the strange new language.

The Cunningham Institute was a private language school, but the clientele was sufficiently diverse to make teaching very interesting. A number of students were at the school under scholarships provided by philanthropic institutions. Most of them were younger people who hoped to learn English quickly enough and well enough to secure employment in the Boston area. Then there were a number of women, obviously wealthy, who were attending the institute because their husbands were in the States—often on temporary business—and wanted their wives to learn enough English to be able to enjoy such things as shopping expeditions.

Amanda taught some of her students on an individual basis and she found these experiences the most satisfying even though the classes represented more of a challenge. In the group she had to be sure to give everyone an equal opportunity to learn—not easy when there were such varying aptitudes to be dealt with.

At the institute each day was different—each morning brought new challenges. She had even begun to feel quite close to some of her students. Only the lonely Saturdays and Sundays were difficult to get through, especially at this time of the year, when the weather was apt to be as dismal as her spirits. Today, for instance. She glanced toward the window, to see snowflakes falling more thickly than ever.

Actually winter was only beginning, and she told herself she'd have to face up to this fact—and to a lot of other things as well—and start getting out more. Just scanning the newspaper was enough to give one all sorts of ideas about places to go and things to do; it merely took a certain amount of incentive to translate thoughts into action.

For one thing she could start planning a minivacation in New Hampshire, she reminded herself. She'd have to ask Dr. Cunningham when it would be convenient for her to have a few days off. She had spent the Christmas holiday with her brother Keith and his family at the ski lodge he operated in the White Mountains and had promised to return before long. This time she would take some skiing lessons.

I've got to stop moping around and begin to fill in my time constructively, she told herself so firmly that she wondered if she'd spoken the words aloud.

And at that very moment the telephone rang.

"I don't like to intrude on my teachers' free time, Amanda," Dr. Cunningham said apologetically, "and I wouldn't be doing so now unless I felt it was justified."

"That's perfectly all right," Amanda assured him quickly.

"Do you have guests?"

"No. As a matter of fact, I was about to see if there's a good afternoon movie on television. It's snowing out and...."

"Yes," Dr. Cunningham said a bit absently, his mind clearly not on the weather.

He seemed to be hesitating, and it was impossible not to wonder if something was wrong. Amanda's mind raced back over all her classes of the previous week. In retrospect, however, it seemed to her everything had gone especially well. She'd been extremely pleased with the progress of one young man from the Dominican Republic, and the wife of a South American diplomat sent to the United States appeared to be surmounting the first hurdles of conversational English. Had she missed something, she wondered?

"Is there anything wrong, Dr. Cunningham?" she finally ventured.

"Wrong?" Dr. Cunningham echoed, that absent note still there. "No, nothing at all. I've had a rather unusual request, that's all.... I admit I'm of two minds about it."

"Oh?"

"Selfish of me, I suppose," Dr. Cunningham said, only increasing Amanda's curiosity. "I wouldn't

want to lose you. Not that we'd be losing you exactly...."

"Why should you lose me at all?" she asked, per-
plexed.

"I was approached this morning by the attorney
for a wealthy Spaniard who will be in the States for a
major part of next year," Dr. Cunningham began.
"He intends to have his niece, who is in her late
teens, join him, and she doesn't speak English. As I
understand it, he wants her to obtain an excellent
grasp of the language while she's here. The attorney
tells me this man wants to be certain his niece ac-
quires what he terms a 'proper accent,' as well as
fluency in English."

"I can't see why that poses any particular problem," Amanda answered slowly. "Couldn't she
simply come and take private classes at the institute?"

"She won't be in Boston," Dr. Cunningham said.
"Otherwise that would be the obvious solution—that
or private instruction at her home."

"If she isn't going to be in Boston," Amanda
asked logically, "why is her uncle applying to us?"

"He's in Boston at the moment himself," Dr.
Cunningham replied, "and his attorney, whose office is in New York, tells me he's heard of us. I'm
happy to say that evidently our ESL program has
gained something of an international reputation."

"That's marvelous," Amanda acknowledged.
"Still, if this girl is going to be living in New York
with her uncle, I can't help but feel the sensible thing
would be to look into ESL facilities there...."

"True enough," Dr. Cunningham agreed. "Or it

would be if she were going to live in New York.
You're getting ahead of me, Amanda. The young
lady and her uncle will be residing in Florida.''

"Then I really can't see what it has to do with us,"
Amanda rejoined.

"I wish I could be so definite," Dr. Cunningham
said. "That's why I told you my reluctance regarding
this situation is due—at least in part—to the fact that
I don't like the thought of giving up your services
even on a temporary basis. On the other hand,
there's no doubt this would be an excellent opportunity for you. I've two daughters of my own as you
know, so forgive me if I sound fatherly... but I've
noticed you've been a bit on the peaked side lately,
and we're just into January. The worst of the winter
still lies ahead, and there's no question in my mind
that you could do with some sunshine, fresh air and
the chance to get outdoors. It seems to me it would be
good for you to be with a young person, too, such as
this Spanish girl...."

"My teens are a long way behind me, Dr. Cunningham," Amanda said, her voice tight.

"Only seven years behind you," he surprised her
by saying. "You're twenty-six, are you not? I've
been looking over your file. The Spanish gentleman
had his attorney direct quite a few questions to me
about anyone I might recommend to him."

"He sounds like an elderly despot," Amanda decided resentfully.

"I imagine he may well be precisely that," her
employer agreed. "He's a businessman with widespread interests—a family pearl manufactory on Majorca is but one of many of them. Yet he seems to

have his niece's interest very much at heart. He's her legal guardian.''

Gerard had been her legal guardian, Amanda remembered, and again that bleak sense of loss came over her. Her mother had died years ago—she barely remembered her at all—and so growing up, she had been especially close to her father. She had been nineteen when he died—this during the summer following her second year in college. Gerard had been right there when she needed him—and for the next two years, until she had graduated with honors. He had taken her out to dinner the night after graduation and proposed to her, and she supposed that in a way she had literally fallen into his arms. He had been gentle and loving. . . .

Dr. Cunningham's voice returned her to the present. "Will you consider going that far with it, Amanda?''

Her attention had strayed, and so she had to say, "I beg your pardon. I—I became sidetracked for a moment. Will I consider going that far with what?''

"As I think I mentioned, Mr. Blake, the attorney, called from New York,'' Dr. Cunningham said. "However, his client is at the Carlton Plaza here. He has a suite on the eighteenth floor. I agreed that if you were at all interested in the position, I'd ask you either to present yourself for an interview at four this afternoon or else phone and make another appointment. If you've no conflicting engagement, I'd suggest you be at the Carlton Plaza at four. Our prospective client doesn't appear to be someone who likes to be kept waiting or to have his own plans changed.''

"And you're asking me to seriously consider working for such a man?'' Amanda protested. ''I doubt we'd get along.''

Dr. Cunningham chuckled. ''I sense that Yankee spirit flaring up,'' he said. ''But then I imagine our Spanish nobleman may need someone to stand up to him—in his niece's interest, at least. And, I might add, I noted a long time ago that despite your quiet appearance, Amanda, you have all the spunk typical of New Englanders with forebears like yours. For that matter, I doubt you'd see very much of the gentleman himself. From what his lawyer told me, I gather he has some sort of health problem. In fact, I believe it's a matter of health that brought him to Boston for medical consultation. So probably his main concern—one of his main concerns, at least—is to get his niece off his hands by hiring someone suitable to teach her English.''

''Doesn't he have a wife?''

''If he does, Mr. Blake didn't mention her, and it seems to me he would have. No, from our telephone conversation I'd guess that this man is either an old bachelor or a widower. I rather think, considering his nationality, that we can rule out divorce.''

''His poor niece,'' Amanda mused.

''How's that?''

''I can't help but feel sorry for her. If she's as high-spirited as most teenagers, it must be a rather dismal prospect to think of being under the wing of an elderly ailing uncle for an entire year in America. She'll be leaving all her friends in Spain and—''

''Not Spain,'' Dr. Cunningham interrupted. ''Majorca.''

''Oh?''

"The largest of the Balearic Islands, well off the coast of Spain in the Mediterranean," he elaborated. "The principal family residence is there, though I believe the uncle has a place in Madrid, as well. Mr. Blake said something about the family owning one of the largest Majorcan pearl manufactories."

"Majorcan pearls are famous," Amanda conceded. "I'm rather vague about Majorca itself, though. It sounds as if it would be quite an exotic place. . . ."

"A tourist paradise among other things, from what I've heard," Dr. Cunningham said. "I'm not as familiar with it as I probably should be. Whenever I have the chance to travel, I seem to turn back to France or the British Isles."

"And you a language expert," Amanda teased.

There was a time not too far past when she couldn't have imagined joking with Dr. Cunningham, but now that she had come to know him better, she had seen his wonderful sense of humor displayed on many occasions. He was a fine man; he had been very kind to her, and the more she thought about it, the less she liked the idea of leaving the institute, even though the position she'd be taking would be under its aegis.

She said slowly, "Isn't there someone else who would be better suited for this job, Dr. Cunningham?"

"No," he answered, "there isn't, and more's the pity. No one I've been able to come up with, at any rate. I was tempted to tell Blake to contact one of the language schools in New York with ESL programs, just as you suggested. But then it seemed to me that in all fairness I should give you a chance at this first.

You know, Amanda, simply because you agree to an interview doesn't mean you have to take the job. What I'd do if I were you is keep the four o'clock appointment and take it from there. And I can promise you I will abide by your judgment.

"Don't commit yourself unless you really wish to," he added. "You can simply say you must talk things over with me first. Also, even if the position appeals to you, I would suggest you not agree to a year's contract or anything of that sort. It seems to me a three-month trial period would be fair for both sides. It would mean that if you didn't like the job, you could be back at work with us here in Boston by Easter."

"But suppose I stayed away an entire year?" Amanda asked. "I can't imagine such a thing, but if I were to do so, what then?"

"Your job here would be waiting for you upon your return," Dr. Cunningham assured her. "That, I promise you. You're far too skilled at this sort of work for me to let go of you easily, believe me. In fact, I've a strange feeling I'm making a mistake in urging you to keep this rendezvous at all!"

CHAPTER TWO

THE CARLTON PLAZA was a relatively new Boston hotel, and yet it already had become something of an institution. Designed by a major architect, it was a beautifully proportioned structure combining the best of the old and the new.

Amanda had been told by Dr. Cunningham to take a tower elevator off the lobby, which would lead her directly to Don Antonio Hernandez y Vega's eighteenth-floor suite. No need to announce herself, the institute director had added after carefully spelling the Spaniard's name for her. She was expected.

That was well enough. But now as she stepped out of the elevator, Amanda found her knees were actually trembling, and she knew only too well that while Don Antonio Hernandez y Vega might be ready to meet her, she was not at all prepared to meet him!

She had decided to wear the same gray suit she'd worn when Dr. Cunningham had interviewed her for the job at the institute, and she had kept her makeup to a minimum. Her hair was coiled into a bun, and she wore a waterproof hat that matched her rather bulky, all-weather tan coat. At the last moment before leaving the apartment, she had taken off her leather boots because they stood a good chance of being ruined if she wore them today. The snow had changed to slush, and it was thoroughly nasty outside. So Amanda had dragged a pair of old black overshoes out of the closet, and they completed what admittedly made a very poor fashion picture.

She had called for a taxi from her apartment and had been more than slightly surprised when she was successful in getting one. Now, on the elderly Spaniard's actual threshold, she found herself wishing she had asked the taxi driver to wait; if she had, she would surely have backtracked, and she looked longingly at the self-service elevator, which still stood open just behind her.

She was standing in a small foyer, and the only door in evidence obviously led to the suite she was seeking. It struck her as oversized just now, like a portal leading to she couldn't quite imagine what. It was painted a deep tone of Chinese red and an ornate, highly polished brass knocker gleamed in the center. Amanda touched the knocker with tentative fingers, raised it carefully, then let it fall—and felt as if the resulting clang was loud enough to shake the building to its very foundations.

She waited, but nothing happened, and now she very nearly did take refuge in the elevator, which still offered an escape route. Dr. Cunningham had been right in assessing her New England character. It was her streak of obstinacy, among other things, that kept her waiting. It seemed to her that if she truly were expected, the least someone inside could do was come answer the door.

This time she lifted the knocker and dropped it with determination. Almost immediately the door swung open, so that Amanda, her hand still in mid-air, felt as if she'd been thrown off balance and actually staggered backward. Inadvertently she closed her eyes, and opened them to find herself staring down at two very long legs enclosed in dark brown corduroy pants that fitted so snugly, it was as if calf and thigh muscles had been deliberately contoured, leaving very little to the imagination.

Her eyes traveled upward to a slim waist cinched by a thick cordovan belt with a large buckle of wrought silver. Then they went on, as if moving without any volition at all on her part, to assimilate a broad expanse of chest and wide, beautifully formed shoulders, these dominantly male attributes clothed in an open-necked shirt of loosely woven white material. She noted skin slightly olive in tone, and then inevitably, as her eyes continued their upward course, she came to his face, and the impact of pure shock made her gasp aloud.

Dark brows contorted into a decided frown, and he said, "Yes?" It was difficult to believe that a single word could convey the impression of such coldness! He seemed to draw out each letter and edge it with ice as he looked down at her from a height that at the moment seemed formidable. Most of the men Amanda met were seldom much taller than she was. This one was a notable exception!

She knew she was gaping at him, and the worst of it was she didn't seem able to keep herself from focusing on the black patch that covered his left eye. The elastic from it wound around his head to faintly dent hair that was raven black except for a subtle sprinkling of silver at each temple.

"Did you wish something, señorita?" he asked now, the deep tone of his voice sending a strange little shiver through her. His English was accented, but attractively so. In fact, it seemed to her everything about this man was accented—and in a disturbingly seductive fashion. Even the eye patch did not detract from his arresting good looks. And there was no doubt about this: he was extremely handsome. His features were distinct, chiseled in appearance, from the high forehead to the slightly aquiline nose to the proud, well-formed chin that thrust forward, almost as if he were defying her.

There was mockery to his question, too, and she sensed he knew very well she was curious about the eye patch, curious about *him*. Was he a relative of Don Antonio Hernandez y Vega, she wondered, or did he perhaps work for the elderly Spaniard? If the latter was the case, she knew—this with a sense of something akin to suffocation—that she could not possibly accept the position being offered. It would be absolutely out of the question to try to work in such proximity with this dark arrogant stranger.

Because he was arrogant. This was clear from the thrust of his chin and the way he was regarding her through his one visible eye, which was almost as dark as the patch covering the other one. A velvet black. Could it be as warm on occasion as it now seemed cold, she found herself wondering.

"Señorita?" he asked again with exaggerated patience.

"I'm sorry," Amanda said, and found to her horror she was stammering. "I have an appointment with Mr. Vega."

"Mr. Vega?" The laugh was short but nevertheless managed to be disparaging. His lips curved in a faint smile entirely without mirth, and she found herself wondering if this man ever really smiled. It seemed to her his face was, in a way, a mask that hid honest emotion. Or perhaps at some point emotion had been drained out of him entirely and he had been coated in a psychological sort of porcelain. Amanda frowned, because this was pure fantasy on her part. How could she possibly surmise such things about a total stranger? And intensely aware of his scrutiny, she said, "Will you tell him I am here, please?"

"A moment, señorita," this arrogant Spaniard— for obviously he was Spanish—cautioned. "I think you are mistaken, for Señor Hernandez has no such appointment on his agenda. Yes, señorita, the name is Hernandez. This is a fact of Spanish nomenclature with which I see you are unfamiliar. One takes both one's father's and mother's surnames. Vega is the surname of Señor Hernandez's mother's family, you understand? It would therefore be improper to address him in such a fashion. *¿Comprende usted?*"

"I'm sorry," Amanda said stiffly. "Very well, then, will you tell Señor Hernandez I'm here?"

"It would perhaps be advisable if you first tell me who you are," he countered.

He was taunting her, and there was no reason for it, Amanda thought resentfully, and that New England spirit Dr. Cunningham had spoken of was beginning to stir and simmer. "You may say Mrs. Hughes is here to keep her four o'clock appointment," she said coldly. "It has already gone past the hour—through no fault of my own—and it is my understanding Señor Hernandez does not like to be kept waiting.''

The arrogant stranger disregarded the latter part of this statement—or at least seemed to. Now it was his turn to stare, and there was an intensity to the regard of that one dark eye that Amanda didn't understand.

''I am correct that you said, 'Mrs. Hughes'?'' he demanded.

''Yes. From the Cunningham Language Institute,'' she answered, glad she had worn her glasses as she pushed them firmly up on the bridge of her nose, deliberately being very prim in her manner.

But he disregarded this, too. ''You have credentials?'' he asked.

Amanda frowned. ''Credentials?''

''You have something, do you not, that proves you are who you say you are?''

''I'm afraid I don't understand you.''

He shrugged, then stood back wearily and said, ''Come in, señorita. Clearly there has been a mistake, but there is no need to keep you standing in the hall while we try to correct it.''

She moved past him with a muttered, ''Thank you,'' to find herself in a large and beautifully furnished drawing room that terminated in a floor-to-ceiling picture window at the far end.

Instinctively Amanda moved toward the window, the soft, cream-colored carpet yielding beneath her feet as she did so, and now she stood looking out over Boston in the snow. The Common and Public Garden were spread out far beneath her and the golden dome of the State House was barely visible through the swirling flakes and the growing darkness.

Dusk was giving way to night. The streetlights had been turned on long since, and the big lamps that studded the bridge across the Frog Pond in the Public Garden glowed like oversized pearls matched to make a perfect giant necklace.

"How absolutely fantastic," she breathed before she was sharply aware of the tall man standing close by her shoulder. The scent of the after-shave he was wearing wafted across her nostrils—an exotic yet essentially masculine sort of aroma almost as tantalizing as he was.

Something stirred in Amanda—a twinge of feeling so purely sensuous that she was totally taken aback by it. And when he asked in a curious tone, "What is so fantastic, señorita?" she could not immediately answer him.

He followed her gaze and then said indifferently, "The view? This is what attracts you? I grant you it is interesting—this glimpse of the town that is...what do you call it...'the home of the bean and the cod.'"

Again the laugh was short, disparaging, and now she swung around to face him defiantly, brimming with resentment. "Boston is my city," she said tightly. "For that matter, Boston is much more than a city. It is one of the world's great places, replete with a history and feeling you probably wouldn't understand."

"Indeed?" There was a hint of lazy amusement in his question, and this only added more fuel to Amanda's personal fire.

"Indeed!" she echoed, resenting him all the more, resenting the attractiveness of which he was obviously well aware, resenting his arrogance and his tendency to disparage. "I don't imagine you agree with me about Boston," she added hotly, "but then your opinion really doesn't concern me. Now will you kindly tell your employer I'm here?"

His dark eyebrow rose, as he puzzled, "My employer?"

"Señor Hernandez," she replied impatiently. "He is your employer, isn't he?"

"In a sense, yes... I suppose he is. Another moment, señorita, if you please. Señor Hernandez has an appointment this afternoon with a Mrs. Hughes, that is true. But you cannot possibly be this person. Perhaps she was not able to present herself here and sent you to represent her?"

"No!" Amanda snapped. She marched away from the window toward a large, marble-topped coffee table centered in front of a couch covered in deep purple velvet. Somewhat unceremoniously she cleared a space on the table for her handbag and then opened the bag with fingers that fumbled. Because she was not merely angry—she was furious. Stony-faced, she withdrew her wallet and from it extracted her Social Security card, her driver's license, a Jordan Marsh charge card and her Boston Public Library card, and all but flung them in the tall stranger's face.

Strong fingers caught her hand at exactly the second the cards surely would have slipped to the floor, and Amanda was not at all prepared for his touch. A volt of the kind of current she was not ready to cope with surged through her, and she wondered if he could possibly remain immune from the effect of this supercharge himself.

It seemed to her it was something that must be sweeping through both of them simultaneously, for how could such a current—such a shock—be one-sided? Yet when she glanced up at his face, it was totally impassive. Then, slowly and deliberately, he detached his fingers from her hand and, gripping her identification cards, went to sit down in an armchair next to the couch, thrusting his long legs out in front of him.

"Sit, please," he said to her rather curtly, and she subsided into a corner of the couch, shaken by everything that had been happening to her since this maddening and inscrutable man had opened the door of the suite.

She saw now that he was glancing at the picture on her driver's license, then comparing it with her appearance in the flesh, and he said abruptly, "Take off your eyeglasses, if you please?"

"Why should I?" she asked rudely.

"Because you are not wearing glasses in this picture," he said—again with that air of patience she knew very well wasn't patience at all. "Such things change one's look. You must realize that, no?"

Amanda's lips tightened. "Oh, very well," she said, snatching off the heavily framed glasses and then glaring at him. "Is that better?"

"A matter of opinion," he replied infuriatingly, and shrugged as if her appearance were of no concern to him whatsoever—which, she realized dismally, was probably all too true. "I would say there is no doubt you are the same person who is in this photograph."

"Thank you," she said, her own words rimed now with frost.

"And I see, also, on the license that your date of birth is given. That would make you twenty-six years old, correct?"

"Yes, if you must know."

"Indeed," he said, regarding her levelly, "I must know. But it is quite ridiculous, señorita. Or perhaps I should say señora?"

"I'd prefer you call me 'Mrs. Hughes,'" Amanda told him.

"So," he said, and shrugged again. "Mrs. Hughes, then. The situation is not, perhaps, of your doing, but I cannot understand why you were sent here. I thought my attorney made my requirements very clear to Dr. Cunningham. . . ."

"Your attorney?"

"Yes," he said, and the very slight smile that came to curve his mouth was a study in pure mockery. "I am Don Antonio Hernandez y Vega."

The statement came as a jolt. And although Amanda realized that later she would be chastising herself and telling herself she should have known all along, this didn't help at the moment. She felt a heat compounded of anger and embarrassment coursing through her body. It was as if she had suddenly become sunburned.

"I think," she said, feeling as if she were about to choke, "you could have easily told me who you were right away."

"Right away?" he asked, that interrogating eyebrow rising once again. "Yes, you do have an impatience to your nature, do you not, señorita? *Perdón.* I should say Mrs. Hughes. The way you pounded on my door. . . ."

"I did not 'pound on your door,' Señor Hernandez," she retorted.

"One does not say the *h*, Mrs. Hughes," he protested mildly.

"What?"

"In my name the *h* is silent. For the correct pronunciation you would say, 'Air-nan-dez.' But then who am I to give you a language lesson?"

"I don't find that very funny," she said coldly.

"I did not intend to amuse you. Your Dr. Cunningham extols your qualifications in language teaching—at least he did so to Gregory Blake. He insisted you are an expert in this matter of 'teaching English as a second language,' I believe you call it?"

"I don't call it anything," she said. "That's the name of the overall program."

"I see. An apt term, I would hope. It would be useful to anyone, it must be admitted, to have English as a second language—"

"As you obviously do yourself," she finished for him.

"I would not agree to that," he said. "I attended university in England. Therefore, I do, I suppose, have a certain fluency. However, to master a language one must be able to think in it. I cannot say I think in English, señora. My thoughts are formed in Spanish, so there is always a matter of translation between one idiom and the other—which makes me hesitate in speaking. Then, too, I am aware I have an accent...."

Quite a devastating accent, Amanda agreed silently. Aloud she muttered only, "True." And then added ungraciously, "But your English is quite clear, despite it."

"So," he said, "aside from clarity, I would wish that Cristina—my niece—could learn to speak your language like a proper American. Or shall we say a proper Bostonian? I should like her English to be free of any Spanish accent."

"Do you really think the matter of accent is that important?" Amanda queried, and added without thinking, "Actually, a foreign accent can be quite charming."

"Oh?"

She avoided his discerning gaze. "Anyway," she said quickly, "the basic reason for language is communication. In our teaching of English as a second language this is what we stress, señor. It is first imperative to establish a visual-vocal method of communication. We do this in ways that might, I suppose, seem primitive to you. Sometimes we devote quite a period of time to oral recognition of pictures alone. You may associate such a technique with the teaching of children, but I can assure you adults learn a language very well through the picture method until they reach a level of proficiency at which instruction can become more sophisticated."

"You do indeed sound like a teacher," he said, and she darted a swift look of suspicion at him, feeling he was making fun of her. But once again his face was impassive. "It is unfortunate you are not suitable."

"Not suitable?" Amanda leaned forward, her beautiful large eyes more expressive than she realized. Because she'd forgotten to put her glasses back on, they were fully revealed to this man who sat across from her. They were unusual in color, tending to change from gray to blue to violet not merely because of the clothes she happened to be wearing but often because of the state of her own emotions. She'd been told, in fact, that to those who knew her well, her eyes were a kind of personal barometer.

"I do not wish to insult you," Antonio Hernandez said now almost gently. "But surely you must see it would be out of the question to engage you as a companion-teacher for a girl not that much younger than you? I wish to find for my niece someone she can look up to, someone who can offer her guidance in addition to teaching her the English language. Even though you seem to have done your best to make yourself look—what are the words I want— middle-aged and dowdy—I believe that is what I want to say—I am not fooled by your camouflage, señora. Nor do I admire it. I am not entirely blind, you see," he added, his tone caustic. "Perhaps especially because I am partly so, I do not like to be deceived."

CHAPTER THREE

AN INNER TENSION had been mounting from the moment Amanda had first encountered this arrogant Spaniard, and it was past the point of being suppressed. Now she got to her feet in a swift automatic movement, shaking with rage. And this, too, surprised her. Antonio Hernandez was forcing her to overreact.

The impact he had on her was astonishing. She had never experienced anything like it before, and she felt singularly at a loss to cope with him now. It seemed to her he had her at a total disadvantage, and she could not imagine why both Dr. Cunningham and the lawyer, Gregory Blake, had not been more accurate in telling him about her. Dr. Cunningham had reviewed her file and had even mentioned her age in their phone conversation. Certainly there would have been no point in keeping it from either Gregory Blake or Antonio Hernandez himself. It was not something she could—or would—hope to hide.

His assertion that she had deliberately made herself dowdy to convince him she might be a suitable companion for his niece was galling beyond words. What right did he have to make such an assumption?

"Damn you!" she said hotly. "Let me tell you I was just as fooled by you as you seem to have been fooled by me! I thought you were a sick old man who—"

"A sick old man?" he interrupted, seeming more amused than annoyed. There was that faint hint of a smile again, but this time it was devoid of mockery, and the effect was mesmerizing. White teeth blazed against slightly olive skin, and he actually laughed. "I disappoint you?" he questioned.

"If you must know, yes...you do disappoint me," Amanda said, and certainly in one way this was true. In another way she felt herself overpowered by his attractiveness, by his purely male vitality, which seemed much too tangible to her just now.

He said with a ruefulness she didn't believe in the least, "I am sorry, señora. So you would have preferred I was ancient and infirm, yes?"

"It doesn't matter to me what you are, Señor Hernandez," she said, knowing this for the lie it was even as she spoke. "What does matter to me," she added hastily, "is your suggestion that I—that I came here in an attempt to defraud you."

"I do not think I made that suggestion," he said, "but then it is perhaps my grasp of your language that is at fault. That is to say, I used the wrong words with which to express myself. What I was trying to tell you, I suppose, is that your youth and your loveliness are obvious to me despite—"

"Please," she interrupted. "I think that's enough. There's no reason why we should continue this. Perhaps Dr. Cunningham can find some doddering individual who will suit your needs better. Or perhaps your lawyer can find something for you in New York. There are a number of ESL facilities there, and you have other excellent choices right within the Boston area, for that matter. Whatever, I hope you solve your problem, Señor Hernandez, though I feel very sorry for your niece. And I regret having wasted both your time and mine.''

She was on her way to the door as she spoke and she had just put her hand on the knob, when she was arrested by his voice.

"Stop!" he said, his tone of command making her bristle. "I am not accustomed to having a woman walk out on me, Señora Hughes."

"Then," Amanda said tautly, "I suggest you begin to get used to the feeling. This isn't Spain, señor. Or perhaps I should say Majorca."

She tugged at the door as she said this, and once again the entrance to Señor Hernandez's suite proved to contain a surprise. This time as the door swung open a new man appeared, and she bumped into him with such force that he dropped the brown leather briefcase he was carrying and muttered an expletive.

To her horror Amanda could feel tears brimming, and she knew that if one more thing—just one more thing—happened, she would make a spectacle of herself. She said thickly, "I'm sorry," and started to push toward the elevator, which once again stood open. But this new stranger reached out and somewhat forcibly took hold of her arm.

"Just a minute," he cautioned. "Who are you and why are you here, and where are you going in such a hurry?"

Directly behind her Antonio Hernandez said, "She is the schoolteacher sent by the Cunningham Institute, Gregory. It would seem we were both misinformed. Amanda Hughes, my attorney, Gregory Blake.''

''Mrs. Hughes,'' Gregory Blake said with a slight formal nod, and Amanda found herself looking into deep blue eyes set in a pleasantly rugged face. The lawyer was slightly above medium height, probably in his mid-thirties, with sleekly combed brown hair styled in a manner that conformed with present fashion while managing to remain conservative. He wore a three-piece gray suit that was decidedly conservative, too, with a discreet gold-and-navy striped tie, but she had the feeling this outer facade was for professional appearances only. There was an engaging quality about the lawyer—laugh lines at the corner of his eyes—and it seemed to her even on such short acquaintance that he was an essentially likable person—something she certainly could not say for Don Antonio Hernandez y Vega.

Now he looked from one to the other and said, ''I don't know what's happened here, but couldn't we sit down, have a drink together and talk things over—whatever they are?''

''I think that is an excellent idea,'' Antonio Hernandez said. ''You are being needlessly hasty, Mrs. Hughes.''

''Am I?'' she asked him. ''I don't think so. You've made yourself extremely plain, Señor Hernandez. I really don't think I need to hear you elaborate on why you don't feel I'm suitable for the position you are offering. Your employer can fill you in on this entire encounter, Mr. Blake,'' she added, turning to the lawyer. ''As for me, I'll call Dr. Cunningham as soon as I get home, and I'm sure he'll get in touch with you.''

She left them at that, but as the elevator doors were closing, it was impossible not to catch one last glimpse of Antonio Hernandez's face. She realized anew that the black eye patch was not only distracting but added to his look of inscrutability, making it that much more difficult to read his expression accurately.

Nevertheless it seemed to her his look contained a mixture of surprise, annoyance and something that just might be defined as reluctant admiration.

If she was right about the last, she couldn't help but feel more than a bit pleased.

THE STORM HAD SNARLED Boston's traffic, and Amanda stood shivering on the sidewalk outside the Carlton Plaza for a long time before the doorman succeeded in getting a taxi for her. Then the ride back to her studio apartment was a nightmare. Several times she was certain they were going to skid into either a tree, a lamppost or another car, and it was more of a relief than she could have imagined when she arrived home again.

She changed out of her cold damp clothes into a caftan that was a soft lovely shade of amethyst and brushed out her hair until it fluffed around her shoulders like a deep golden cloud. As she put the brush back on her dresser, she glanced into her large gilt-framed mirror—one of the items she *had* taken from Gerard's Chestnut Hill home—and could not suppress the wish that Antonio Hernandez could see her now.

Dowdy, indeed!

Smarting, Amanda went to her tiny kitchen and took out a wineglass and a bottle of sherry, even though she normally wasn't much for drinking alone. As she filled the glass, the words on the label seemed to leap out at her. *España*—Spain! Spanish sherry, of course. For a moment she thought it was going to choke her!

Nevertheless, as she settled down in her favorite armchair with her wine, her thoughts inevitably turned to Antonio Hernandez, and she reviewed everything that had happened that afternoon over and over again.

She had to admit he was the most physically attractive man she had ever seen in her life. But insofar as personality was concerned, she could give him no points at all. He was rude; he was arrogant, and he had been completely insensitive in his remarks.

He had told her coldly he was not entirely blind, then had added that perhaps because he was partly so, he especially resented being deceived. Now she wondered what had caused his injury. Undoubtedly an accident of some sort. But there hadn't been any scars near the patch—of that she was sure. Could he have lost his eye entirely, or had it only been damaged? She shuddered as she thought about this, and his face seemed to swim before her own eyes with astonishing clarity.

Away from him, away from the undeniable impact he had made on her, she found she was able to think about him more clearly. And she remembered other things—small things—she'd overlooked at the time. For one, he seemed to be exercising a very tight sort of control over himself. She wondered now why this should be necessary. She had thought at one point that there was a masklike quality to his face, and this illusion seemed heightened by the eye patch. But she also sensed this was an inner rather than an outer sort of rigidity. There had been a tautness about that handsome face, with its clear-cut, very Spanish features. It occurred to her he looked like a man who had been through his own kind of personal hell and was determined not to let anything touch him deeply ever again.

She was surprised at this analysis, because there was no real reason for her to come to such a conclusion. Yet there had also been a weariness about Antonio Hernandez, translating sometimes into a seeming indifference that, she suspected, was not really valid. He had accused her of camouflage; she suspected that actually he was the one who was concealing his true self, and her curiosity forced her to think about this.

Finally she poured herself a second glass of sherry and sipped it as she fixed some chicken, curried rice and a small tossed salad for her dinner. She seldom had much appetite when she was alone, but tonight she finished her food without thinking very much about it at all. Her loneliness was forgotten, too, as she continued to dwell upon the mystery of Antonio Hernandez y Vega. For he was mysterious.

After a time she made herself turn on the television and tried to escape in a situation comedy that unfortunately proved to be more silly than funny. But even the best of dramas would have been hard put to hold her attention that night, and although it was unlikely she would ever again see the arrogant Spaniard who had managed both to excite and infuriate her so thoroughly, it was impossible to put him out of her thoughts.

"I'M SORRY it happened this way, Amanda," Dr. Cunningham said when she phoned him. "It's my fault entirely. I should have made it clear you were a young woman. I suppose because I said you were a widow they assumed—"

"It doesn't matter," Amanda said hastily, hoping Dr. Cunningham would believe this. There was no point in telling him it actually did matter—entirely too much.

"Well," Dr. Cunningham said, "it's a pity you had to go out on a day like this when it turned out to be a wild-goose chase. I'm surprised I haven't heard from either Blake or Señor Hernandez."

"I imagine you will," Amanda said dryly. "I just hope the institute's stock hasn't gone down because of me."

"Of course not, Amanda, nothing of the sort has happened," her employer told her. "Now get a good night's sleep and then do something enjoyable tomorrow. Next time I'll screen job opportunities more carefully!"

SUNDAY PROVED TO BE an unexpectedly pleasant day. Sunlight sparkled on the Charles and sprinkled shimmering golden specks over the surface of the snow. During the night the temperature had turned colder and there'd been another brief snowfall, so once again the world was new and white. Amanda dressed warmly, put on her trusty old overshoes and went out, welcoming the touch of the cold bracing air on her cheeks and breathing deeply, as if the deep breaths could snuff out memory.

True, the only memory bothering her at the moment was a very recent one. She had even dreamed the previous night of the inscrutable Spaniard, and now he kept intruding over and over again. Once ahead of her she saw a tall, dark-haired man walking along rapidly, and for a heart-stopping moment she thought it was Antonio Hernandez y Vega. Then he turned at a corner to cross the street, and she saw the profile was entirely different.

She had no desire to return to her apartment that day any earlier than necessary, so finally she went to the Isabella Gardner Museum on the Fenway, where the lovely inner courtyard of a beautiful mansion-now-turned-art-museum was still filled with vivid red poinsettias—these a holiday tradition each year. Next she went to a movie, then had a late dinner at a small restaurant on Beacon Street, where, as it happened, she met two other teachers from the institute. They asked her to go on to a friend's place for brandy and espresso, and though she usually tended to sidestep such invitations, this time she accepted. They were interesting people; it was a diverting evening, and it was very late when she got home. She hoped this would help her to fall asleep without dreaming of Antonio Hernandez, but again the Spaniard, as a tantalizingly handsome and decidedly stubborn ghost, came to encroach upon her subconscious.

AMANDA GOT UP early Monday morning and dressed with more care than she normally did. She found herself reaching for a bright turquoise scarf to twist around the neck of the dark brown dress she was wearing, experimenting with a dash of eye shadow and arranging her hair in a fancy chignon rather than the casual bun that was easier to fix.

Dowdy, indeed!

Her first pupil was a young man from South America who had always been very polite to her, flattering her slightly in the Latin manner. But he had never before looked at her in quite the same way he was looking at her this day.

"The señorita is *muy bonita* this morning," he said finally, and Amanda flushed.

"Thank you, Enrique," she replied, slightly unsteady.

Dowdy, indeed!

It was midmorning when Dr. Cunningham's secretary came to tell her there was a telephone call for her. She took it in the assistant director's office, vacant at the moment since its usual occupant was on vacation, and her pulse pounded as she picked up the receiver.

There was no reason she should expect to hear Antonio Hernandez y Vega at the other end of the line. Yet she was acutely disappointed when the voice that answered her was distinctly American, without a trace of a Spanish accent.

"Mrs. Hughes?" a man inquired.

"Yes," she said.

"Greg Blake," he told her cheerily. "We met Saturday."

Amanda recalled that meeting only too well—the memory was actually painful—but again she said only, "Yes."

"Could we have lunch?" the lawyer asked without further preamble.

An imaginary caution flag fluttered down before her eyes. Its yellow color also symbolized cowardice, she realized. But she wasn't about to try to be daring where the arrogant Spaniard was concerned...and she felt sure he must somehow be involved in this phone call of Gregory Blake's. Certainly it seemed unlikely the lawyer had been so impressed by her in their brief rather traumatic encounter that he'd want to try to date her.

He said again, "Would you be free for lunch, Mrs. Hughes?"

"No," Amanda replied. "I'm sorry. I have a previous engagement," she fibbed.

"Could we meet for a drink, then, after your working hours?"

"I don't think so, Mr. Blake."

"I have the feeling you're telling me you don't want to arrange any sort of meeting with me at all. Is that right?"

"Yes, it is," she admitted.

"Well," he conceded, "that's what I more or less expected. Frankly I wish you would meet with me so I could fill you in about a few things."

"Concerning Señor Hernandez?" she asked coldly.

"Well, yes, concerning Señor Hernandez, of course. But—"

"I don't think I need to know anything more

about Señor Hernandez,'' Amanda said. "He made his own impression.''

"I'm sure he did,'' Gregory Blake said wryly. "Nevertheless, in all fairness—''

Amanda took a plunge. "Are you suggesting I'm being considered as a teacher for his niece?'' she asked directly.

"Not that exactly,'' the lawyer told her. "But—''

"Then I don't think we have anything to discuss,'' Amanda cut in. "Goodbye, Mr. Blake.''

She hung up before he had a chance to say anything further, conscious of the fact this was rude. But then self-defense took all sorts of forms. Before the phone call interrupted her she had been teaching a small class composed mostly of Hispanic Americans at the school under a scholarship arrangement. Back in the classroom again it was difficult to resume or to concentrate on the task at hand, and she was glad when the session was over.

Today she asked one of the other teachers to go out to lunch with her for the first time. It seemed to take a bit of the falsity out of her refusal to see Gregory Blake, and in any event she wanted company.

Several private lessons were scheduled for the afternoon, one with a beautiful Iranian music student who wanted to improve her English, one with a Swedish woman whose husband was in Boston on a long-term business assignment and one with an elderly Frenchman who had come to live with his daughter. She was married to an American, and her father was attempting to learn at least the basics of conversational English, at her insistence.

All these students were interesting, and it was challenging for Amanda to try to introduce them to the concepts of her language, starting in a way that was quite elementary, then moving on into broader fields. Learning to recognize, to speak, to understand, came first. Later came reading. Still later came writing— this completing the circle that was communication. Perhaps the most important thing in the entire world, Amanda found herself thinking as she dismissed her last student of the day. People had to learn to communicate with one another if they were ever to get along. Communication was the hope of the world. It could prevent war, even guarantee eternal peace. People responding to people.…

Her thoughts were interrupted by the buzzing of the intercom on her desk. Answering it, she flinched a bit when she heard Dr. Cunningham's voice coming through the small plastic box, requesting she come to his office. She felt certain this summons had something to do with Antonio Hernandez y Vega.

She was right.

"I've been talking to Gregory Blake, Señor Hernandez's lawyer," Dr. Cunningham began, coming directly to the point. "He says he's been attempting to make an appointment with you and you refuse. Why, Amanda?"

"I should think that would be obvious," she told him.

"Yes," the institute director said, leaning back in his swivel chair and eyeing her carefully. "You've had your feelings hurt—I can see that. But Mr. Blake seems to think there is an explanation, and he'd like the chance to give it to you. It seems to me the only fair thing is to hear what he has to say."

"How can you possibly speak of fairness?" she replied, feeling stung. "Señor Hernandez was about as unfair as anyone possibly could be!"

"Maybe he's trying to make amends," Dr. Cunningham suggested mildly.

CHAPTER FOUR

DR. CUNNINGHAM SELDOM TRIED to force his will upon his subordinates, but he had a very personal technique for bending them to it. Amanda realized this fully as she set out to meet Gregory Blake for lunch the following day. The institute director had blended logic and persuasion with a seemingly infinite patience as he attempted to convince her to see things his way, and it was a difficult combination to resist.

She had to agree with Dr. Cunningham in the final analysis. The truth was, there wasn't any good reason why she shouldn't listen to what the lawyer had to say, and there was no excuse for her to be as rude as Antonio Hernandez y Vega had been!

The day was cold and bright, and Amanda had dressed that morning with her luncheon engagement in mind. She wore a full-skirted suit in a blend of heather tweed between lavender and purple in tone and with it a swirling dark purple cape with a becoming stand-up collar. The previous night she'd gone over her favorite camel-colored boots with mink oil, and they both felt and looked good. Before leaving the school, she examined her makeup closely, then added a dash more violet eye shadow, a bit of rose-hued blush and tidied her chignon.

Dowdy, indeed!

She felt rewarded when she saw the definite expression of appreciation in Gregory Blake's eyes as he met her in the foyer of the small French restaurant just off Newbury Street he had chosen for their rendezvous.

The expression lingered after they had been seated in a booth toward the rear—which she was sure he must have requested, because it was definitely geared to privacy.

"Wine?" he asked. "Or would you prefer a Bloody Mary?"

"A glass of chablis, please."

"Shall we sip for a few minutes before we place our order?"

"Yes, if you like."

"I like," he said in a way that could be taken to have a dual significance, and she could not help but smile. He returned the smile, and she found it impossible not to like him. Too bad, she thought, that he was connected with Antonio Hernandez.

The waitress brought their wine, and Gregory raised his glass in a silent toast. Then he said, "Thanks for coming today, Amanda. You don't mind if I call you Amanda, do you?"

"No."

"Then maybe you'll call me Greg?" He didn't wait for an answer to this but went on to say, "Look, I can understand your turning me down yesterday. Tony can be very difficult—I don't deny that."

"Tony?"

"Surprised I'm on that familiar a basis with him?" he said.

"I hadn't really thought about it," she replied.

"Amanda, I've known Antonio Hernandez y Vega for a long time. He took a couple of years of business law at Harvard when I was at the law school myself, and we came to know each other very well. Tony was expected to learn how to handle the family businesses in Spain and Majorca, even though he was the younger of two brothers by quite a few years. Anyway, Tony is my closest friend . . . as well as one of my best clients. I represent only his American interests, but even so—"

He broke off, noting her expression. "Am I boring you?" he asked bluntly.

"No," she said. She picked up her wineglass, twirling it as she stared down into its pale amber depths. "I suppose what surprises me—what I wonder about—is why you should be telling me anything about Antonio Hernandez at all."

"I feel the need to come to his defense where you are concerned," Gregory Blake said. "Very quixotic of me probably, but I can't help wishing you wouldn't hold Saturday against Tony. You did throw him a curve ball, you know. He had expected some sort of middle-aged, potential *dueña* . . . ."

"I didn't throw him a curve ball deliberately," Amanda said quickly. "I was just as surprised as he was. I assumed he'd be an elderly, paunchy, ailing Spaniard trying to find someone to more or less take his high-spirited young niece off his hands."

Gregory chuckled. "I'll admit," he said, "that Tony doesn't exactly fit the description. I believe you told him so?"

"Yes, I suppose I did."

"Amanda," Greg Blake said earnestly, "I know Tony seems arrogant, aloof—even rude at times. But he is essentially a very private person—he always has been. He's also fair, kind and warmhearted. You didn't see that side of him on Saturday, did you?"

"Definitely not."

"Well, it's true he sometimes conceals those traits very well," the lawyer continued. "You see, he isn't trying to shirk his responsibility toward Cristina—his niece—in the least, and he isn't trying to get anyone to take her off his hands. He is deeply concerned about her future—for many reasons. He feels entirely responsible for her, and in fact I guess you could say he is. Her parents were killed in the same terrible accident in which Tony was partially blinded. Ever since then—nearly four years ago—Tony has retreated behind that eye patch he wears. He seems to have made a kind of symbolic wall out of it that stands between him and the rest of the world.

"I think," Gregory Blake added slowly, "that Tony whips himself mentally every morning and several times during the day and then again at bedtime. He is bitter—there is no doubt about that. He blames himself entirely for the accident. You see, the family lives in Manacor, where their pearl manufactory is located, but they also have a house in Majorca's capital city, Palma. One day they were driving from Palma back to Manacor across a very steep range of mountains when there was a freak hailstorm. Tony'd had a rough weekend—he says he was exhausted at the time—and he was at the wheel of the car. Also, he and his brother Juan had been having an argument. Anyway, the car skidded, and Tony—normally an excellent driver—lost control. They plunged off the road and into a ravine, and it was hours before they were found.

"Juan and Inez, his wife—Cristina's mother—almost surely were killed instantly. Tony was unconscious when they found him, and he has no memory of anything that happened from the moment just before the crash until he woke up in a hospital back in Palma. He had struck his head against the windshield and was suffering from a severe concussion. For a time it was feared he would be totally blind. Then the sight in his right eye gradually returned, until now he sees quite well with it. He still suffers from terrible headaches, though. That's why he's here in Boston. He's been consulting a leading specialist. There's a chance surgery might alleviate the pain—"

"And totally restore his vision?"

"No," Gregory Blake said. "Tony's left eye is... gone."

Amanda's throat muscles constricted, and she swallowed painfully. Gregory, eyeing her curiously, said, "Hey, you've gone white as a sheet! Take a sip of that wine."

She obeyed him, but even when she swallowed, her throat still felt strangely dry. "How old is Antonio Hernandez?" she asked.

"Not quite thirty-four."

"And so he was thirty when the accident happened?"

"About."

"And Cristina, his niece—how old is she?"

"Eighteen. Eighteen, beautiful and headstrong."

"She wasn't in the car at the time of the accident?"

"No, she was in school in Palma. A convent school...private, quite posh, as I understand it. Tony's family is very wealthy—wealth that goes back a long way. There's a title lurking in the background that he has the right to use but doesn't. Background nonetheless is very important to him, and he wants only the best for Cristina. Now, as it happens, she has fallen in love with a young man of whom he thoroughly disapproves. That's the prime reason he's bringing her to Florida. He wants to get her away from this boy before they become involved too deeply and nothing can be done to stop it."

"Even though she loves him?" Amanda asked.

"Tony is very modern in some ways, very old-fashioned in others," Gregory said. "Essentially he is very Spanish. Cristina has become his responsibility, and he's not about to fail at what he considers his duty. Part of this 'duty' is being sure she marries properly. I think Tony actually envisions her as the wife of a diplomat, and certainly he sees her being married to a person of very high social standing. That's one reason he's so anxious to have her learn to speak English fluently. It would be a great asset if later she's to move in international circles."

"He does think of everything, doesn't he!" Amanda observed, and Gregory Blake shot her a surprised look.

"You really don't like him, do you?" he said then. "Well, that's your prerogative of course, Amanda. But I do have to say Tony is sincere in his actions. He really believes he's following the best course in regard to Cristina. You can't question his motives."

"I'm questioning the possible results," Amanda

said. "It seems to me your friend Señor Hernandez is exhibiting a feudal mentality, and I don't think his plans can be expected to work in this day and age—even with a girl who's been brought up in a Spanish convent school."

"Do I detect an undertone of ultrafeminism?" Gregory Blake asked her.

"Not really. I do believe in equal rights for women, if that's what you're implying. However, I'm not always too enthused about the performances that sometimes go with trying to acquire them. I don't think it's right to try to mold someone who belongs in today's world into an ancient form. One of these days I imagine Señor Hernandez will get his comeuppance. . . and I rather hope he does!"

"Well, I don't agree with you," the lawyer said calmly. "At least I hope Tony won't come up against anything in line with what you're saying where Cristina is concerned. Really, he's devoted to her and has only her best interests at heart."

"Then he's misguided," Amanda said flatly.

The waitress had been hovering nearby, so now Gregory Blake said, "Truce, okay? They have a fantastic seafood quiche, incidentally. Does that appeal? Maybe with a tossed green salad?"

"Sounds perfect," Amanda said, and also agreed when he suggested they have a second glass of wine.

As if by mutual consent they veered away from the subject of Antonio Hernandez y Vega and found they had many other common interests. They admired the same kind of art and music, and as an accomplished skier, Gregory was pleased to hear this was a sport in which Amanda was beginning to take a real interest.

"So your brother has a lodge in New Hampshire," he mused. "Perhaps some weekend. . . ."

"Perhaps," she acknowledged. "Once I can get down a novice slope at least without breaking my neck."

"Maybe I could give you a bit of extra instruction," he said with a smile. "Once Tony goes to Florida I won't be coming to Boston as often as I have been lately, but I still prefer to do my skiing in New Hampshire and Vermont, and they do a good job of keeping the highways open for us winter sports enthusiasts."

Antonio Hernandez's name had come between them again, and this time it seemed to cast an odd kind of shadow. Gregory said thoughtfully, "Tony used to be a very good skier. Really expert. He far outclassed me."

She couldn't suppress the question: "Did he give it up?"

He nodded. "He had to. The accident did something to his sense of balance, and being blind in one eye doesn't help."

"I thought Majorca was rather tropical," she said. "Certainly no place for skiing."

"True, it is quite tropical. Tony did most of his skiing in the Swiss Alps, except when he was here in the States. He and I used to go off together then. Tony hasn't confined himself to Majorca, Amanda. He's spent an equal amount of his time in Spain, in Madrid, and he's traveled extensively in the bargain. Also, until the accident, he was one of those people who do many things well. He raced cars for one thing. He was also a very good tennis player. Those are two other activities he's had to give up. But all of that is minor in comparison to the overall effect the accident has had on his life...."

The words trailed off, and he smiled at her ruefully. "I'm sorry," he said. "We don't seem to be able to keep off the subject of Tony for too long, do we?"

This was true. Antonio Hernandez, even in absentia, was much too potent a force to ignore. Definitely he came between them. As far as Amanda was concerned, he was an unwelcome intruder, and she wanted to block him out of her mind. Yet she had the unhappy conviction it would be impossible to become really friendly with Greg Blake without Antonio Hernandez figuratively if not literally intervening.

And that was too bad. She liked Gregory Blake; she would have welcomed the opportunity to know him better. He was the sort of person her brother Keith would get on well with, too. Greg would fit in with Keith and his crowd.

Damn Antonio Hernandez y Vega, she thought fiercely, and not for the first time.

DR. CUNNINGHAM DID NOT ASK FOR an accounting of what had taken place at her luncheon with Gregory Blake, and again Amanda appreciated his wisdom. Obviously if there had been anything to tell him that involved the institute, she would have done so.

Late in the week her brother called to tell her skiing conditions were ideal in New Hampshire and suggested she come up to the lodge for the weekend. It seemed an especially good idea, because she wanted to get away from Boston and her thoughts of the arrogant Spaniard. An excursion to the snow country offered a perfect escape.

She asked Dr. Cunningham if she might take the following Monday off, and he agreed. So Saturday morning Amanda got her rather venerable Dodge Coronet out of the garage where she usually kept it and set forth.

New England had turned into a winter wonderland, and there was a serene purity and beauty to the snowy landscape that evoked a welcome feeling of peace. Furthermore, the roads were so well cleared that driving was easy. She had a horror of skidding, and just now skidding, like far too many other things, reminded her of Antonio Hernandez.

The weekend turned out to be wonderful. By the end of it, thanks to the expert teaching of Keith's instructors, she was actually venturing down the novice slopes, and Sunday night at the lodge they celebrated her progress with a bottle of champagne.

It was late Monday when she arrived back at her studio apartment, and she was physically very tired but more carefree mentally than she had been for a long time. Then, even as she opened the door, she heard the telephone ringing, and she had that quick feeling that comes close to being a premonition.

She picked up the receiver slowly, said a cautious hello and discovered immediately and without doubt who it was on the other end of the line.

"So you have finally decided to come home," Antonio Hernandez said sarcastically, his Spanish accent more evident than she had remembered.

"Was there some reason I should have come back sooner?" she said, trying to remain calm.

"I attempted to reach you all Saturday, all yesterday and all today," he answered, clearly exasperated.

"Oh? Was I supposed to sit at home and wait for your call?"

"No, you were not to do anything! It is I who have been concerned, because I go to Florida tomorrow and it is imperative I see you before I leave."

Amanda felt her throat constrict and thought, not without resentment, that this was becoming a distressfully frequent reaction where Antonio Hernandez was involved. She struggled to force out the single word, "Why?"

"Obviously I must speak to you," he replied impatiently.

"I don't see anything obvious about it."

"Mrs. Hughes, do not be obdurate!"

Obdurate now! Dowdy and obdurate.

"I don't think we have anything to say to each other, Señor Hernandez," she said crisply.

"But we do," he assured her. "Gregory mentioned he told you about my niece Cristina, and I wish to speak to you about her further myself. I wish to seek your advice."

"*My* advice?" Nothing could have surprised her more.

"Yes," he said. "Gregory has indicated it would be useful to me. I will not take much of your time, señora, but if you will permit me to call at your apartment in half an hour or so, I will appreciate it very much."

Amanda could not answer him immediately. The mere thought of seeing him was totally unnerving—

and yet so tempting she knew very well she was not going to be able to resist.

What harm could it do after all, she rationalized. It might even do some good insofar as Cristina was concerned, poor girl. If he would *listen* to what she had to say in that particular area, perhaps he'd give thought to the fact his ideas about handling a young girl were absolutely archaic. . . .

"Señora?" he asked.

"I will see you—but only for an hour or so," she said quite autocratically. "After that—"

"After that I am sure you must have a *compromiso* . . . an engagement, that is," he said suavely. "An hour, however, will be more than enough time for our meeting. *Hasta luego,* señora."

CHAPTER FIVE

AMANDA PREPARED for her next encounter with Antonio Hernandez y Vega as if she were getting ready to go to war. She took a quick shower, donned her attractive amethyst caftan and put on a pair of slender gold kid slippers. She brushed her hair into golden waves that touched her shoulders and made up very carefully, highlighting her eyes and smoothing lavender shadow on her lids, all of this with deliberate grim determination.

As a final touch she carefully anointed her wrists and the hollows in her neck with L'Air du Temps. This was a strange kind of battle dress, but at least she was going to show him that whatever else she might be she wasn't dowdy!

It was true she had dressed down for a long time. This effort, in fact, had gone beyond attire; she could see now that through the years of her marriage she had suppressed her own personality. She had seldom permitted herself to act the vibrant outgoing person she knew herself capable of being. She'd known instinctively that if she let herself go, the chasm in age between Gerard and herself would be all the more obvious to others.

She had modified everything about herself for Gerard's sake, and she knew she'd do it again under the same circumstances. She would be doing it still, for that matter, had Gerard lived.

Nevertheless she had not considered herself *dowdy*. She hated the word, damn it!

Just exactly what did *dowdy* mean anyway? She was about to seek the dictionary for a precise definition when she heard the doorbell ring, and she froze.

It took real effort to cross the room, turn the doorknob and face Antonio Hernandez, standing on her threshold. Her first glimpse of him didn't help, either. He looked like a dark and angry thundercloud.

"Were you really away?" he asked immediately. "Or was it simply that you chose to ignore your telephone because of me?"

This was too much! "You flatter yourself," Amanda said. "I can't imagine why you'd think I wouldn't answer the phone because you might be calling me. However, for your information, I was at my brother's. I didn't go until Saturday, though. You had quite a bit of time prior to that to get in touch with me if you were so anxious to do so."

"I was in the hospital," he said shortly.

Anxiety surfaced, and despite herself Amanda couldn't entirely suppress it. "An emergency?" she asked him.

"No, an appointment," he said quickly. "May I come in, Mrs. Hughes, or must we once again hold an entire conversation while we stand in a doorway?"

"Come in, of course," Amanda said, stepping back. But he did not at once cross her threshold. Instead he stood and looked down at her from that definitely imposing height of his, and she could feel her throat constricting again, only this time it was not from anger. Rather she felt herself swayed by him in a way that was completely unreasonable. Being so close to him gave her the oddest sensations, and she was aware of feeling inwardly shaken, as if every vein in her body were actually trembling.

From what, she demanded of herself? Certainly not from *desire*. How could one possibly desire a person she also detested?

The answer came unbidden. Human nature was a strange thing, and the sensual aspects of one's being were not to be trusted—that's all there was to it! It was entirely possible to be overwhelmingly aware of Antonio Hernandez as a man—a dangerously attractive man—while at the same time disliking his personality, his arrogance and everything he stood for.

She moved back and tried not to look at him directly, but this soon became impossible. She saw that his mouth was tight, as though there were a thin white line around his lips, and for an insane moment she thought he was going to take her into his arms. She glanced down to see his hands were actually clenched, as if he were trying to restrain himself. And the terrible part of it was, were he to draw her to him, she could not possibly resist him. She knew that. And she wanted to know what it would feel like to have his mouth press against hers, for he had a beautiful mouth, full and perfectly shaped. She wanted to know what it would feel like to have his hands move across her skin with caresses that would linger like tiny tongues of flame....

My God, Amanda! She nearly spoke aloud,

shocked at herself. Then she had the sensation Antonio Hernandez was capable of reading her mind as well as arousing her to an intensity of feeling that seemed absolutely indecent, given the circumstances. He nodded, a slight little nod that was somehow very foreign, and he smiled, a bitter twisted smile. There was irony in the lift of that fine-lined black eyebrow as he said, "After you, señora."

Chagrined, Amanda led the way into her studio living room and motioned him to a chair, but before taking one herself, she said, remembering her manners, "May I offer you a sherry? Or perhaps you'd prefer Scotch?"

"I would prefer Scotch, thank you."

She couldn't resist it. "Even though the sherry is Spanish."

He laughed. "Even though the sherry is Spanish."

She busied herself with glasses and bottles, her fingers fumbling slightly because she was so acutely aware of him. And she was afraid, as she gave him his drink, that if their hands touched in transit, she would drop the glass.

Fortunately this didn't happen. He took the Scotch from her with a grave, "Thank you," and then waited for her to sit down before he sat down himself.

Amanda had also opted for Scotch. Now she took a hefty swig of it, and it was lucky she swallowed before he spoke, because his first words thoroughly jolted her.

"So," he began, "I have a feudal mentality, do I?"

She bit her lip. "Of course Gregory Blake told you I said that," she replied.

"Yes," he confirmed, nodding, "of course he did. Why did you think he was so anxious to see you, señora? Oh, I do not deny he finds you attractive, but in this instance his prime motive was in his capacity as my attorney. I wished him to find out what you think of me."

She met his scrutiny directly. "Why didn't you ask me yourself?" she demanded.

"I suppose you would have told me the truth?" he asked, clearly skeptical.

"Yes, I would have, Señor Hernandez. I have nothing to lose, after all. You've already made your position in regard to me very clear, wouldn't you say?"

"I suppose I have," he agreed. "So, then, what is the truth, Señora Hughes?"

He was daring her, a strange sort of dare and a thoroughly annoying one. Determined not to let him provoke her, she said, "I don't know quite why you're baiting me...."

"Baiting you?" he asked, puzzled.

"It's what one does with a fish, Señor Hernandez, when one is trying to catch it. You're trying to get me to say I find you arrogant, overbearing and insufferable, aren't you? Very well, now I've said it. Does that satisfy you?"

As she spoke, she knew her cheeks were becoming flushed, her breath was coming faster and all her resolutions were going straight down the drain. This man had that kind of effect on her!

He did not answer at once, and when he did, his tone—to her surprise—was quiet. "I must give you credit for honesty in one way at least. You are not afraid to say what you think. In another way, however, you are like all women. I see your true self tonight, do I not, which makes the self you presented to me the other day a false one.''

"I don't know what you're talking about."

"But I think you must. You came to me the other day dressed as if you were going on a stage. To make a deliberate impression—that is what I want to say. Those ridiculous clothes you were wearing, that hat...."

"I beg your pardon," she said hotly, "but they were my clothes, and I wear clothes like that most of the time. If my wardrobe displeases you, I can't say I'm sorry about it because I'm not. I wasn't trying to make any impression on you at all. I felt I was qualified for the job you were offering, and I—"

"Yes," he interrupted. "In that I think I must agree with you. I believe I was mistaken. I think there is a good chance you are qualified for the job I am offering, after all."

She stared at him, not quite sure she was hearing him correctly.

His lips curved, mocking her. "Is it so difficult to believe I am capable of being convinced I may be wrong?" he asked her.

"Yes," she said, "it is."

He shrugged. "I do not suppose I can blame you for that," he admitted. "Our first meeting was a mutual shock. I was, perhaps, premature in my reaction."

"Gregory Blake has convinced you of that?"

"What a suspicious nature you have, señora! You are wrong in any event. Others do not convince me. I listen to them—true. Only a fool refuses to hear any-one else, and though you may disagree, I do not place myself in that category. But Gregory did, of course, speak to me about you after your luncheon together. It seemed to him that without even meeting Cristina you had a—how should I say it—an empathy for her. He told me he thought you would be good for her. Your youth, he said, would not detract from your ability to deal with Cristina. In fact, it is Gregory's feeling it would be an asset."

"Is it really?" she murmured, mocking now, too.

"So," Antonio said, disregarding this, "I went to speak to your Dr. Cunningham this afternoon."

She sat up straighter. "To the school?"

"Yes, of course to the school," he said impatient-ly. "*Dios*, do you think I am incapable of doing things for myself?"

"I rather thought you let Mr. Blake handle your mundane matters," she said, deliberately demure.

She caught his flash of anger, and his tone was cold. "There arrives a moment when one must make one's own observations and then decide upon ac-tion," he told her.

"And what have you decided, Señor Hernandez, if I may ask?"

"You definitely may ask, Mrs. Hughes, because my decision concerns you. I wish to employ you to teach Cristina English—conversational English espe-cially. I also want you to be a companion to her. She needs the guidance of a woman, even a young woman such as you."

"I suppose I should be flattered you might think me capable of guiding her," Amanda conceded, "but regardless of that I shall have to refuse you."

She awaited an explosion, but it didn't come. Instead Antonio Hernandez asked wearily, "May I have another drink?"

"Of course," she replied, hiding her bewilderment.

As she poured the Scotch for both of them, she glanced across at him, and to her surprise she saw he had leaned back and was resting his head against the top of the chair. He had closed his single eye, and looking at him now, she again felt the choking sensation that was becoming much too familiar.

Her slippers made no sound as she moved across the carpet so she was able to stand next to him, holding both of their glasses, and she found herself staring down unashamedly at the dark sweep of long lashes that fringed his cheek.

For the first time she noticed the lines of fatigue around his mouth and the pallor that underlay that slightly olive skin. The black patch he wore over his left eye was a large one; she could not help but wonder what it camouflaged. Had he been mutilated in the accident that had cost him an eye? She shuddered, a pang of pity for him stabbing her with a pain that was actually physical. It seemed so entirely wrong that he should be marred in any way, for there was a perfection to his classical features and to the deep raven hair that swept back from his broad forehead.

He was wearing a suit today that was so dark a blue it was nearly black, and it didn't take a fashion designer to know that both the material and the tailoring were expensive. His garb was casual to the extent that he also wore a very pale yellow turtleneck. His arms lay outstretched along the sides of the chair, and as she gazed at his hands, Amanda again felt that odd little inner trembling. His hands were beautifully formed and looked as if they could be the hands of a musician or perhaps a sculptor. A heavy gold ring adorned his right index finger. It was emblazoned with a crest. His family crest, no doubt.

He spoke, and she was so startled she actually jumped backward, nearly spilling their drinks. "Well," he demanded coolly, "have you analyzed me sufficiently?"

"Damn you," she said furiously. "You were playing possum!"

"I do not know the phrase," he said indifferently, "but I believe I get the meaning. Very well, then, why not, Señora Hughes? Do I not have the right to pretend occasionally as much as you do? Now you have scrutinized me and you are brimming with curiosity, are you not? Am I supposed to *like* that?"

"Please," she said, actually feeling ashamed, though she quickly told herself there was no reason at all why she should be. "I didn't mean—"

"It doesn't matter what you say you meant," he cut in. "Everyone who looks at me is curious about my eye—I know that. Affliction inevitably arouses curiosity...morbid curiosity, I might add. I am used to the stares by now."

"Señor Hernandez—"

"Let us forget it, shall we?" he suggested curtly. "As I have said, it does not matter. What does matter is whether you can be persuaded to change your mind about becoming the companion-teacher to my niece. Dr. Cunningham is in accord with your taking this position, I might add. I wished to engage your services for a year. He, however, suggests a trial period of three months. If, at the end of that time, the arrangement is mutually satisfactory, then it would be understood it continues for another nine months. By that time Cristina should be thoroughly conversant in your language...."

"Why don't you teach her English yourself?" Amanda interrupted. "You're thoroughly conversant in it."

"No, I am not—not in the same sense I mean," he corrected. "We have already been through that before. If it is the matter of your position here in Boston that concerns you, Mrs. Hughes, Dr. Cunningham assures me there will be an opening for you in his school whenever you wish to take advantage of it. So I would say you have security all the way around. ¿*Verdad?*"

"It isn't security that concerns me, Señor Hernandez," Amanda said. "Not at this stage of my life."

"Then what does concern you?" he asked her.

"You," she said bluntly. "I could not possibly consider working for you. Dr. Cunningham must have told you, I am sure, there is at least one more school here in Boston you could apply to for assistance. And Mr. Blake could find a number of channels in New York through which you might be helped...."

"May I remind you I am not incompetent?" he said coldly. "I am aware the Cunningham Language Institute is not the only facility in your country wherein one might find a suitable person to instruct Cristina. It is only that it is well recommended to me, and you might say I was fortunate with the first applicant...."

"Me?"

"Oh, for God's sake, yes, you!" he said irritably. "Do I have to get down on my knees, señora, and apologize for the way I received you initially? Does one have any right at all to second thoughts or a second chance in your opinion?"

He was frowning, and as she watched, he rubbed his forehead wearily and she remembered the headaches Gregory Blake had said his client suffered from.

Abruptly she asked, "Why were you in the hospital?"

He stared at her. "What?"

"I asked you—"

"I know what you asked me. Why does it concern you?"

"I wondered...."

He sighed. "At times," he said, "Gregory talks too much. I suppose he went into details of my health in an effort to enlist your sympathy for me?"

"I wouldn't put it quite that way."

"I was in the hospital for consultation. Tests. Nothing overwhelmingly dramatic, señora. For the present, nothing will be done. A waiting period is indicated, during which it is hoped that some of my problems will work themselves out of their own accord. It has been suggested this be a reasonably tranquil waiting period, so I have been advised that it would be advantageous for me to spend the next three months in Florida. Does that answer your question?''

It didn't really, but she knew he was not about to go into the specifics any further, so she merely nodded.

"I go to Florida tomorrow," he said, "as I told you on the telephone. I have arranged for two plane tickets, the second one for you. There will be enough time for you to finish up your affairs at the school, to pack and so on, as we are taking a night flight. I must be with my doctors in the afternoon, for a final check before they send me on my way. I will pick you up here in front of your apartment house at eight o'clock. All right?"

"Most certainly not!" Amanda exploded. "I don't think you've been hearing me, Señor Hernandez."

"Yes, señora, I have heard you," he said slowly. "I do not wish to listen to you, that is all. I mean to say it is so important to me you agree to help Cristina that I assure you I will not give up easily about this. I might add that in Florida you will not have to see very much of me. It is a large house we have, my quarters are quite separate and in any event I am supposed to spend a fair amount of time resting during these next three months. We can go our own ways, you and I...."

Amanda could not imagine living in the same house with him—no matter how large it might be— without being so intensely aware of his presence it would be impossible to forget he was physically within reach. She found herself also realizing she did not really want to go her separate way, and yet any other course would be a clear invitation to disaster.

Not that she was apt to be offered a choice of courses! He was making it evident to her, without being absolutely rude, that he had no desire for her company. The arrangement he was offering was purely a business one. In his eyes she would become "hired help," his niece's governess actually, hidden behind a slightly different title. And Amanda had no doubt that in Antonio Hernandez's world, servants were kept in their proper place. The line between the world to which he would be assigning her and the world he thought of as his own was not one he would be apt to cross.

What did she really have to lose, though, if she accepted his offer? How could one deny the possible pleasures to be found in living in Florida in a large house during the next few months and thus escaping the rigors of the New England winter, if nothing more?

"The thoughts whirling through your head are almost visible, Mrs. Hughes," Antonio Hernandez said. "Would you not, perhaps, share some of them?"

She made up her mind, knowing this quick decision was one to which she'd be held. "I think I will accept your offer," she said stiffly. "For a three-month trial period, however, nothing more than that."

"Bueno," he said with a nod. He stood up and, to her surprise, reached out to shake hands with her, and the touch of his flesh made her feel light-headed. "I am grateful, señora," he added.

She accepted this even though she felt inwardly certain he had never been truly "grateful" for anything in his whole arrogant life.

They moved toward the door, but before they reached it, Antonio Hernandez paused. Looking down at her, he said, "You are a very lovely woman, Mrs. Hughes. Had you looked in the first place as you do tonight, I think I would at once have found you irresistible. I must tell you, though, I was mistaken even then in calling you dowdy. You are most certainly not dowdy, Mrs. Hughes."

"Oh?"

"No." His mouth twitched, betraying an expression of combined amusement and devilry. He said, "When you left the other day, I went to the dictionary to seek this word *dowdy*—I had observed your reaction to my use of it. You had cause to be offended. You, of course, know the precise meaning?"

"You might refresh my memory."

"*Webster's International* defines *dowdy* as slovenly or ill-dressed. That is the first meaning. Surely you could never be called slovenly, and although I did not like those shapeless garments you were wearing when we first met, I cannot say you were ill-dressed, either. So you see," he continued, clearly enjoying this, "my English is not, after all, as fluent as you think. But I did discover another new word, *prim*, which I would say describes you nicely."

"*Prim?*"

"Yes," he said. "The definition says stiffly formal or demure. Then there is *prig*, which means one who makes a show of virtue."

"And so you consider me a prim prig, is that it?"

The minute she said this Amanda knew she had made a mistake. He was looking at her with a lazy amusement that at once made her bristle, and yet she

knew very well that were she to put on a show of out-
rage, she would only become a caricature of this
definition he had already worked out. His opinion—
and his choice of words, she added hastily—had no
validity at all! But that didn't help. Nor did it help
that at the moment he looked so intensely masculine. . . this to the point of distraction.

She thought, somewhat desperately, that it would
have been so much easier if he had been the elderly
and ailing Spaniard she had expected him to be.
Then, perhaps, she would have had to put up with
irascibility and maybe an occasional show of downright bad temper. As it was. . . .

"So you maintain you are neither prim nor a prig.
Shall we see about that?" he said.

Amanda answered stiffly, "I don't think we really
need see about anything, Señor Hernandez. This
whole discussion is quite pointless as far as I am concerned. I. . . ."

But she was not to speak further. While her heart
fluttered as if she were a Victorian valentine, dismayed and annoyed at her own weakness where this
man was concerned, he reached out strong arms to
draw her close to him with an insistence that clearly
brooked no argument.

He was only trying to prove a point—she knew
that. A very chauvinistic point in the bargain. But
this didn't seem to matter in the least. His lips descended to claim her mouth, and in one searing instant all of Amanda's worst fears were realized. She
was even more helpless than she had thought she
would be. . . and the terrible thing was, she didn't
even want to resist him! Although mentally she

fought him every inch of the way, physically she virtually melted into his arms as his firm fingers pressed the folds of the filmy caftan against her body and his touch molded her contours with an undeniable expertise. His hands explored onward with a well-practiced inquisitiveness, and his kiss became a torch sending fingers of flame through all parts of her body.

She met his caress with rising passion and a mounting sense of urgency all her own—an entirely new emotion to her. No man had ever evoked such a response in her before and she tried to summon reason with which to forestall his mastery, but her everyday logic had deserted her. It was not until she realized that in another instant he would be slipping the caftan off her shoulders and she would then be standing before him wearing nothing except for a wisp of a bra and matching panties that she rallied. But she was breathing hard as she thrust him away from her, and for a long unsteady moment she thought it was going to be impossible to gain back even a vestige of self-control.

Her chest was still heaving, her breath coming with difficulty, as she managed to say with surprising iciness, ''Just what are you trying to prove, Señor Hernandez?''

He was not breathing all that evenly himself, she noted with satisfaction. Still, after an instant in which she thought he might very well force his arms around her again, he replied with a politeness that at once aroused her suspicions, ''I was not trying to prove anything, Mrs. Hughes. I think it is you who were trying to show you are neither prim nor a prig, were you not?''

He smiled at her, an infuriatingly smug smile. Obviously he was entirely satisfied with his performance, having demonstrated his physical superiority. Again she felt as if she were about to choke, but this time the sensation stemmed purely from anger.

"You do find me amusing, don't you?" she challenged. "Well, I'm sorry to say I can't return the feeling. I don't think you were very funny at all, Señor Hernandez. In fact, you were completely out of line. You acted in very poor taste."

"Oh?" he said, that interrogating eyebrow lifting in a line of pure skepticism. "I can't say you seemed to object to my attentions, señora. Indeed, there was every evidence you were for a time reciprocating. Or do I again flatter myself?"

Her fury matched her ardor of a few moments earlier. She said tightly, "Leave, if you please. We have nothing further to say to each other."

He considered this with irritating deliberation. "No, I would say we probably do not," he agreed. "We will have time enough on the airplane to talk about Cristina and your future duties."

She stared at him. "You can't really think I would go to Florida with you after this, can you?" she demanded.

"Our small encounter?" he asked mockingly, and it was all she could do not to reach out and slap his lean olive cheek. "Señora, you are taking that little episode much too seriously, I assure you. I also assure you it will not happen again. You are enticing—very definitely you are enticing. But in the future I can promise I will exercise restraint. And I will find it entirely possible to keep my hands off you."

"So," she said, stung and trying not to show it. "This was merely what you consider a 'little episode,' señor?"

He nodded. "But certainly, señora. Or perhaps a better choice of words would be to say it was a test. I think you know what our next step would have been and so do I. Had you succumbed that easily, I must admit I would have had second thoughts about choosing you as a companion for Cristina. As it is, your show of virtue was without question sincere."

He had been moving toward the door as he spoke. Now he opened it, then touched his hand to his forehead in a brief salute. "Until tomorrow evening, Mrs. Hughes," he told her. "Please be ready promptly at eight."

CHAPTER SIX

THE RIDE OUT to Logan Airport with Antonio Hernandez was something Amanda could not face. In the middle of the afternoon she called the Carlton Plaza, then remembered, even while the phone in the eighteenth floor suite was ringing, he had told her he would be busy with several last-minute medical appointments. When the switchboard operator cut in, Amanda left a message saying she would meet Señor Hernandez at the air terminal that night near the main information desk.

As she packed, she expected the phone to ring at any moment, for she was sure her Spanish employer would be annoyed by her change in plans...his plans. He surprised her, however, by not phoning, and by the time she was ready to call a cab, she was wishing he had. And she was wondering what kind of reception she would get when she arrived at Logan.

It had already been a traumatic day for Amanda in many ways. She'd gone to the language institute at her usual time, only to find someone else conducting her Tuesday-morning class—and this had been a blow. Then she'd sought out Dr. Cunningham, intending to tell him her employment with Antonio Hernandez was off—very definitely off—but Dr.

Cunningham had forestalled her by expressing his pleasure over her having agreed to take the job.

"It will be excellent publicity for the institute," he told her, beaming. "The sort of person-to-person praise that counts more than anything else. I know you will do a fine job with your student in Florida, Amanda, and I can't tell you how delighted I am you will be representing us—even though it means losing you here for a while."

The director had rambled on, sketching out the arrangements he'd made for the handling of her duties while she was away, whether that was for three months or the entire year. When he had finished, she knew he had thought of absolutely everything, and it would only be upsetting the proverbial apple cart if she now announced she wasn't going to leave at all.

Once again Antonio Hernandez had won. But this, she told herself, was only the first round. The battle was not yet lost!

Several of the other teachers had insisted on taking her to lunch, and they had celebrated with a bottle of champagne. By the time she returned to her studio apartment, Amanda was feeling more than slightly fuzzy, and it was at about this point she'd decided she couldn't possibly bear being alone with Antonio Hernandez in a cab on the way to the airport. She simply was not up to sparring with him now—verbally . . . or in any other way.

There were a few details to discuss with the apartment-house manager and several other minor particulars that needed her attention, such as canceling delivery of the daily paper while she was away. But the list was minimal, because Amanda was so certain she would not be remaining in Florida past the three-month trial period she'd decided on keeping the apartment without even trying to sublet it. Actually, Gerard had left her quite well provided for. She had an independent income that, while not extraordinarily large, was enough to permit a comfortable life. She'd not had to work unless she'd wanted to, and the job at the institute had been therapy more than anything else. Now, as she packed, the irony occurred to her that this next engagement was going to be anything but therapeutic—that much was certain!

When she arrived at the airport, Antonio Hernandez was waiting, striding impatiently up and down the lobby floor and glancing frequently at his watch. A frown creased his handsome forehead, and he was annoyed. Very annoyed. It gave her a strange sense of satisfaction. She was unprepared, though, for his expression of stark relief when he saw her.

"So you are here," he said as if it really didn't matter. Amanda had a feeling of downright exultation, however, for she knew this indifference was, at least in part, assumed.

"Didn't you expect me to show up?" she challenged.

He shrugged. "I would not be so foolish as to make predictions where you are concerned, Mrs. Hughes," he told her. "Shall we have your luggage weighed in?"

"As you say, Señor Hernandez," she replied.

A porter had carried her two large suitcases into the terminal for her. Now Antonio Hernandez lifted them himself—and with an ease that surprised her. Then she remembered that according to Gregory

Blake, her employer had been quite an athlete up until the time of his accident. As she followed along, he took her luggage to the check-in counter, picked up her boarding pass, then said, "We have time for a cup of coffee if you wish."

"Sounds good to me," she said.

As they moved through the lobby to a coffee shop, Amanda was acutely aware of the glances being given them from all sides. She'd had no time in which to buy any new clothes for the trip, so she'd had to make do with what she already owned, delving into the boxes of stored summer things and wishing, as she sorted them out, they were all not quite so conservative in style. Still, she'd learned that touches of color, jewelry, added makeup, a belt cinched at the waist and similar little subterfuges could do a great deal for one's costume.

At the moment she was wearing a wool suit in an attractive beige and with it a cowled-neck blouse in a tone of pure yellow. She'd chosen amber jewelry for accents, hadn't bothered with a hat and had done her hair in a twisted coil that was quite becoming. At least, she thought, she looked neither dowdy nor prim!

It was the man at her side, though, who was responsible for a major part of the attention they were attracting. She knew he would feel those stares were not from admiration but out of curiosity over the black patch that covered his left eye, and this, she conceded, was partly true. What she suspected he didn't know was that the eye patch drew notice largely because it gave him an air of mystery. Mystery that served to enhance his dark striking looks.

He was wearing a perfectly tailored, charcoal gray

suit, with a shirt in the palest shade of coral, and a tie that combined gold, coral and deep gray in wide stripes. He moved with a grace characteristic of Latin men, his tallness giving him an added advantage, and he walked with his head held high, the aloofness and arrogance that seemed so much a part of him totally in evidence.

The coffee shop was crowded, but after a moment they found a booth. A waitress appeared, and he ordered two coffees without consulting Amanda about her preference. It was only after they had been left alone that he seemed to remember his omission. "Excuse me," he said. "Perhaps you would have preferred something a bit fancier? Maybe an Irish coffee, no?"

"Thank you for asking," she said, hoping that with this agreement she was still managing to convey the fact she would have liked to have been asked in the first place. "Black coffee will be just fine."

"Cream and sugar are permitted if you wish, señora," he said with a faint smile.

"Señor Hernandez—"

"Mrs. Hughes," he cut in, "must we disagree about absolutely everything?"

"No," she said, and was chagrined to find herself beginning to stammer. "That is—"

"Good," he finished. "I do not think that is necessary, either. But I am curious as to why you did not wait for me at your apartment?"

"I preferred to come out to the airport by myself," she answered bluntly.

"I see," he said, nodding thoughtfully. "Then my company is so totally disagreeable to you?"

She couldn't look at him. "It isn't that you are disagreeable. . ." she began.

"Then what is it, Amanda?"

Her eyes widened involuntarily at his use of her first name, and her throat began to constrict. He said her name so differently it—it did something to her. He pronounced it "Ah-mahn-dah," making it seem so soft and melodic and. . . .

"Do you object to my calling you 'Amanda'?" he asked now.

"No," she said nervously, "no, of course not. You may call me anything you wish. You are my employer, after all."

"I was not thinking of that," he said with a touch of ruefulness that surprised her. "It would seem to me that if we are going to travel together, to live together—"

"Please," she said.

"To live in the same house, I mean to say," he amended. "You must forgive my English. Anyway, it would seem to me we should be on a first-name basis. So please," he added, "call me 'Tony.'"

She looked at him now in disbelief. "I could not possibly call you 'Tony'!" she managed.

"Well, then, 'Antonio'?" he asked. "Only for God's sake, if you choose 'Antonio,' try not to say it as if it begins with a crawling insect! In Spanish the *a* is always broad."

"Very well," she said, "I'll call you 'Antonio,'" but once again she felt he was getting the upper hand, so she added, "Does that pronunciation satisfy you?"

"It is quite enchanting, Amanda," he said. "Ah,

here is our waitress with the coffees. You are sure you would not prefer something else?''

''Thank you, no.''

They were silent as they sipped from the steaming mugs, and shortly after they left the coffee shop their flight was called. It had been a while since Amanda had flown anywhere, and she tried to suppress her growing sense of excitement, an excitement edged with nervousness. She was sure Antonio would not only be amused but probably just a little disgusted with her, as well, for such a show of unsophistication.

Once aboard the plane she was surprised to find they were traveling first class, and the relatively spacious seats seemed downright opulent compared to what she remembered the tourist-class ones to be like. This was a first for her, although she supposed that Gerard might have chosen such accommodations had they ever flown anywhere together. Her previous flights had been with her father, when she had been much younger, and the practical Yankee streak in his nature had precluded such extravagances as first-class air tickets.

The interior of the plane was decorated in sun tones of orange, gold and coppery brown, and as she settled back against the soft upholstery and fastened her seat belt, Amanda sighed.

Antonio had ushered her with a gentlemanly motion of his hand into the window seat. Now he sat down on her left, and she could not help but wonder if he had deliberately chosen this arrangement so the ''good'' side of his face would be toward her. He had obviously noticed her sigh, for he said at once, ''You are not comfortable?''

"I am very comfortable," she told him.

"But a bit apprehensive, yes?"

Could she hide nothing from him, she wondered to herself. "Not really," she fibbed.

To her surprise his smile was gentle. "Do not pretend with me, Amanda," he said quietly. "Man is not in his natural element when he is flying. It is perfectly normal to be nervous, especially if it is something you are not used to. You have flown before, no?"

"Oh, yes," she admitted quickly. "I've flown before, but not for quite a long time."

"Then it is natural you should have some qualms, shall we say? The more frequently one flies, the more one becomes accustomed to it, until finally it becomes a casual way of transportation."

"I suppose you've flown a great deal?"

"Yes," he said matter-of-factly. "I have lost count of the number of times I have crossed the ocean, to say nothing of going about Europe. And for quite a long time I flew my own plane—mostly between Majorca and Madrid."

"But you don't fly anymore?"

"No," he said shortly. "No, I do not."

As he did not elaborate on this, she concluded, despite his outward air of total assurance, Antonio was very sensitive about his handicap. It was obviously not something he wanted to talk about, and she imagined the accident that had caused his partial blindness was an equally forbidden subject.

In the ensuing moments Amanda became completely involved in the takeoff. There was an undeniable stimulation to it, and she loved the feeling of the plane thrusting into the sky. Each flight, she felt, was akin to a new conquest.

When they were airborne and the Fasten Seat Belts sign had blinked off, an attractive stewardess appeared promptly and asked if they'd care for something to drink. And before Amanda could speak, Antonio caught her off her guard once again, ordering champagne.

For the second time in this rather astonishing day she was toasted. Antonio raised his glass and clinked it against hers, saying gravely, "To what I hope is the beginning of a sincere and productive association, Amanda."

She was touched, because he sounded as though he really meant it, and she found herself murmuring, "I hope so."

"*Salud, dinero y amor,*" he added. "A Spanish toast. Do you know it?"

"No, I'm afraid I don't."

"Health, wealth and love," he translated. "Three of the most important ingredients in life...though not, perhaps, in that order."

He left it at that, and she wasn't about to explore his remark with any comments of her own. Yet she found herself wondering which of these three things Antonio Hernandez really put first.

Health? Yes, she could imagine he would give a great deal to be restored to his original abilities. Certainly, she decided, he would place health first. He already had wealth—he had been born into wealth—so probably this factor would rank third.

That left love. Where did love reside in the scheme of Antonio Hernandez's life?

She was beginning to daydream on the subject of love when she suddenly realized he was pouring her a second glass of champagne. "Stop," she protested quickly. "That's too much!"

"No," he contradicted. "This will merely ease your nervousness. Very soon now we shall have something to eat, and although I cannot say the airlines very often earn gourmet points, there are times when food is good. Again, Amanda, *salud*."

"*Salud*," she responded.

He smiled—that faint smile of his—and it occurred to her she had yet to see him smile fully. Then he said, "Perhaps by the end of the year Cristina will have learned her English and you will have learned Spanish in return."

She started to tell him they were not going to have an entire year together, then thought better of it. At the moment they were getting along very well, and that was reason enough not to disturb the peace.

The stewardess brought their dinners and they spoke very little as they ate. When the trays were cleared away, Antonio pushed his seat back and leaned against it wearily. Amanda had the feeling one of his severe headaches was coming on, and she wanted so much to do something for him, were this the case. For a few minutes she was silent. Then she could not resist trying to help. "Could I get you anything?" she whispered.

That single dark eye, which had been closed, flew open, and she was afraid he was going to issue a sharp rebuff. Instead he said quietly, "No, *linda*. There is nothing to be done just now. Try to get some rest yourself."

The stewardess had passed out small pillows, and Amanda tucked one behind her head, but she couldn't really relax. She stared out into the darkness, and after a time she discerned the sparkling lights of a city far below them. It was a fairyland sort of scene, a crisscross of shimmering diamonds, but she saw nothing that identified the exact locale for her. After that there was only blackness, and finally she closed her eyes and began to drowse.

Actually sleeping was impossible, for Amanda was too intensely aware of the man beside her. There was a vibrancy about him, despite his fatigue, that intrigued her, and he was proving to be a constant surprise. New facets of his personality had emerged today, and he had been unexpectedly gentle with her at moments. There had been only a few touches of his usual arrogance.

She fluttered her eyelids and stole a quick glance at him. His face was turned toward her, and a strand of dark hair had fallen down over his forehead, giving him an uncharacteristic look of vulnerability. He was asleep now, and with the lines of tension gone, he looked surprisingly young—and so very handsome.

Amanda could feel her pulse throbbing, and her hands had turned clammy. It was then that the truth struck, and it struck with lightning speed.

She was, God help her, falling in love with Antonio Hernandez y Vega!

WHEN ANTONIO AWOKE, Amanda, now thoroughly awake herself, was in no doubt that he was suffering. He rang for the stewardess and requested some water, and when she brought it to him, he took two pills from a small vial he kept in his pocket and swallowed them.

"Please excuse me," he said then to Amanda, this with a wry smile. "I am afraid I am very poor company."

"There's no need to apologize," she answered. "Gregory told me a little about your headaches, and I only wish...."

"Yes?"

"I only wish I could do something about them."

"Wave a magic wand, perhaps?" he asked not unkindly. "I wish you could, Amanda. Or someone could. We will see, though, what these next three months in Florida bring. If the headaches do not begin to subside of their own accord by then, the possibility of surgery will have to be faced."

She looked up, startled. "Wouldn't it be better to face that now?" she dared to ask.

"Not really," he said. "You see, it would be rather delicate surgery with no guarantee of success. And there is always the risk involved...."

She stared at him so obviously aghast that he said quickly, "*Nina*, do not look like that! It may not be so bad. Possibly there will not be the need for any surgery at all. We simply have to wait and see."

Amanda could not find an answer for this, and fortunately the stewardess offered a reprieve, coming once again to ask if there was anything she could get them. Antonio sat up and suggested she might like a liqueur.

"Amaretto, perhaps?" he said. "Or would you prefer something else?"

"Amaretto would be fine," Amanda said.

He ordered this for her and, because of the medication he had taken, ginger ale for himself. As they sipped their drinks, she asked slowly, "Will you be able to rest in Florida? Rest completely, that is? I don't know whether it was Gregory or Dr. Cunningham who gave me the idea, but I thought you had business affairs there."

"I do," he said. "That is, I must decide what to do with my property. You see, Amanda, I have inherited a large tract of land, something like seven thousand acres."

"Seven thousand acres!" she stammered. "In Florida?"

"That is what I said at first. But as it happens, there are still many large land holdings in Florida, especially in certain sections. I realize, of course, that this is an exception these days, rather than the rule. Already, for that matter, I am being pressured to sell my land so it can be subdivided for various projects—industrial parks, condominiums, shopping centers...those sorts of things."

"But you don't want to do that?"

"I don't know yet just what I want to do," he admitted. "I have been there only once to see the property. It was last month, in fact. I have an elderly aunt who acts as a sort of *dueña* for Cristina, and I wanted to make an initial visit before I arranged for the two of them to come to Florida. Most of the land is in citrus groves, and they are not entirely unfamiliar to me. My family has owned orange groves in Spain, as well as almond and olive groves in Majorca."

"I thought your business was making pearls."

"Yes, in a way that is true," he said rather vaguely. "It was my brother who was supposed to be in charge of our pearl manufactory. Now, though, a cousin is handling that operation, and he seems to be doing very well with it. I hope he will continue in this capacity, or I may have to leave Florida sooner than I wish."

"Who manages this Florida property?" Amanda asked.

"An American," Antonio said. "His name is Roger Crane. You will become acquainted with him shortly, for he is to meet us at the airport. He was— how do you call it—the right-hand man of the relative from whom I inherited the property. The actual transfer occurred several months ago, but I have not been able to make the trip to the States any sooner."

"I see."

"It is complicated," Antonio said, "but also fascinating. You do not mind if I go on?"

"No, not at all," Amanda said.

"Well, then, the property in question has been in the hands of my family for many years. Originally it was a grant. That is to say, the king of Spain bestowed it on one of my ancestors who had evidently rendered favors to the crown. And there was much more land then—a vast number of acres...."

"Seven thousand acres sounds vast enough," she murmured.

"Yes, I agree. However, the original grant was substantially larger. Much of the acreage has been sold off through the years—and probably for very little money. You see, the land there, until late in the last century at the least, was not worth very much. And this was true because, as I found out when I started investigating the history of the area, Florida was as much of a real frontier as your Wild West."

"Cowboys and Indians?" she teased.

"Indians, yes," he said. "Hostile Indians. But I suppose one cannot blame them for their animosity toward my countrymen. The Spanish were the invaders, after all, and they were followed by the French, then the British and finally your own Americans, all seeking riches."

"I would say," Amanda ventured, "that your countrymen were the most avaricious of all, señor, when it came to the quest for gold. History documents that pretty well."

His eyebrow formed a noticeable arch. "So, Amanda," he said, "among your other accomplishments, you are a student of history, too?"

"The subject has always fascinated me," she admitted.

"Good, then," he told her, "because you should find Florida worthy of your study. I think most Americans today think of Florida only as a winter paradise, a vacationland for good suntans or a place for retirement. But behind those beachfront resorts, skyscraper hotels and general tropical opulence is a wild history. As I've said, it's as wild as your Wild West."

"That's true," she said, "and I hadn't realized it. But when the Spanish—your ancestors, probably— settled Florida, were they not able to civilize it? You know the way I mean?"

"Yes, Amanda," Antonio said, "I know what you mean, and no, they were not able to do so. It was a turbulent conquest—if indeed it can be called a conquest at all. As you say, it was the Spanish who first 'discovered' Florida. Ponce de León, to be precise."

"The Fountain of Youth man?"

"So history has named him. But that is not entirely accurate. Actually, he was after gold and other riches as much as he was trying to locate the youth-restoring waters he had heard about. It was in late March in the year 1513 when, as he sailed northwest from Puerto Rico, he saw what he thought was an island. Later this proved to be a part of the North American mainland.

"It was recorded at the time that de León and his men saw before them 'a beautiful view of many cool woodlands,'" Antonio continued. "This was at the time of the Pascua Florida—Easter, you call it, which we know as the Feast of Flowers. So he decided to name the new land Florida."

"That's rather lovely," Amanda said.

"Yes—" he nodded "—although there was not very much about Florida during the ensuing decades that could be called lovely. It was a jungle wilderness of impenetrable swamps, with alligators, poisonous snakes of all kinds and insects whose bite could bring disease. At the time of de León's first voyage, therefore, no attempt was made to do anything in the way of carving out a settlement.

"I might add that when he sailed south toward what is today called Cape Canaveral, he encountered a very strong current that was flowing in the opposite direction. This was the Gulf Stream, and its discovery was very important. Because it was, in effect, an ocean river. Our famous Spanish treasure fleets were able to use it as their main route back from the New World."

"Lucky for them," Amanda said.

"Yes, I suppose it was. Anyway, to go back to Ponce de León. He made a second voyage to Florida in 1521, and on that occasion he was killed by Indian arrows."

"I didn't know that," she said slowly.

"Ah, but it's true, Amanda," he told her. "In fact, many of the *conquistadores* met with disaster in their quests for treasure. Man is often paid off in a brutal fashion for his consummate greed. Hernando de Soto is another example. After helping Pizarro in the conquest of Peru, he decided to explore Florida for himself. When he landed at Tampa Bay in 1539, it is said he brought with him the best equipped army Spain was ever to send to the New World.

"De Soto had heard reports of great Indian gold stores, but he went on what one can only call a wild search in an attempt to find them. This adventure took him through the entire southeastern section of your country, until finally he died on the banks of the Mississippi, a man desolate in spirit because of his failure."

"And yet your people persisted, did they not?"

"Yes, they did. But they were continuously foiled by the Indians until—finally—they managed to settle Saint Augustine. That was in 1565. They built the Castillo de San Marcos there, which still stands. Pensacola, far to the northwest in the region called the Panhandle, was not founded until more than a century later. I believe the year was 1698."

"You have quite a memory for dates," she observed.

The faint smile returned. "It is recent homework I

have been doing," he confessed. "This aspect of history was totally unknown to me. Still interested?"

"Yes, very much so," she said, but then wondered if it wouldn't be better for him if he got some rest instead of talking to her. His face seemed lined with fatigue, and there was a definite pallor to his skin. Yet he also appeared more relaxed, although this, she surmised, was the effect of the medication he had taken.

Again it seemed as if he were able to read her mind. "Telling you these things helps me to take my mind off myself," he assured her. "Anyway, the pain has lessened. Shall I go on with your history course?"

"Yes," she said, possessed now with yet another new feeling for him. Absurdly she wanted to cry. To cry, or else to reach out. She wanted to draw Antonio Hernandez's dark head down to her shoulder; she wanted to hold him close to her, as if this in itself could bring him solace. She wanted to console him, to somehow be able to make up for his suffering, to spare him any further pain and....

"What is it, Amanda?" he asked her quietly.

"I—oh, nothing, really," she hedged.

"I have the strange idea you are worrying about me," he said. "Or am I flattering myself again?"

"No. That is... well, I am concerned about you," she admitted.

"Then I am flattered," he said. "You must not trouble yourself about me, though. I mean that, Amanda. I have this horror of being fussed over."

"As you wish," she said stiffly.

"Now I have hurt your feelings," he said, "and I didn't mean to do that."

"You haven't hurt my feelings, Antonio."

"Good. Then let us continue with our history lesson, okay?"

"Okay," she said, feeling an odd sense of relief.

"After the founding of Pensacola and during the first few decades of the eighteenth century, Spain was occupied with wars in Europe. At the conclusion of the Seven Years War, she lost Florida to England. Under British rule, Florida was divided into two parts. The entire peninsula became East Florida, and Saint Augustine was made the capital city. The Panhandle area became West Florida, with Pensacola as its capital. The British tried to attract settlers—especially from the American colonies—by offering land grants, and they were successful—to a limited extent. After the Revolutionary War, however, they decided, according to records, that Florida simply wasn't worth fighting over, and the land was restored to Spain.

"The Spanish returned to Saint Augustine in the early 1780s, by which time most of the British had departed. This second occupation met with nothing but trouble. Land grants were offered to outsiders who wished to colonize, and many Americans, including a good number of outlaws from Georgia and other states, poured in. It was during this period that my ancestor was given a grant. But I suppose you could say it was primarily a paper transaction. It was a long time before any member of the family actually came to take possession of the land.

"In the meantime Florida was beset with difficulties. Finally, in 1819, it was agreed that Florida would be ceded to the United States. The official change of flags took place in 1821.''

Antonio took a deep breath, then continued. ''At the time the United States acquired Florida in 1821, it was just about as wild and undeveloped as it had been when Ponce de León first sighted it.''

''After all that time,'' Amanda questioned.

''Yes,'' Antonio said, shrugging lightly. ''I think that is enough for a first dose, *linda*. Sometime later we can go on with the rest of the story.''

''What about your ancestor?'' she asked him quickly.

''What about him?''

''Well,'' she said, ''obviously the person to whom the original grant was given never even saw the land. I'm just curious as to when your family finally claimed it.''

''Less than a hundred years ago,'' he said, surprising her. ''The deed had been passed from generation to generation, in each instance belonging to the eldest surviving male. Finally it went to a descendant who was then living in Georgia. It was he who made the trip south to see what he had actually inherited, and when he saw what he had, he decided to move his family to this new area and make it their home.''

''He lived in *Georgia*?''

''Yes,'' Antonio said. ''He was a descendant of a Vega—this comes on my mother's side of the family—who had gone north when Saint Augustine fell to the British after the first Spanish occupation. The family subsequently lost a great deal in the American Civil War, for they were, of course, on the Confederate side. Their name has long since been changed to Field. Vega means field more or less. So it was Michael Field who eventually came south to take possession of the land, and through the intervening years a thriving citrus business was established. I understand that Hermosa Groves, as the property is known, is among the largest of the commercial groves in Florida today.

"For a time the raising of sugarcane was experimented with, but evidently someone decided there was more profit to be made in growing fruit. There was even a time when part of the acreage was converted into a ranch where thoroughbred horses were raised, although this was later sold off.

"Anyway," Antonio continued, "the property is to the northeast of Sarasota, perhaps an hour's drive from the Gulf of Mexico. You may know that still farther to the north, in the Ocala area, some of your country's finest thoroughbred horses are raised. Many of them have been winners at the Kentucky Derby, not to mention your other famous races."

"No," she admitted, "I didn't know that."

"Ah, Amanda," he teased, "you see how your education is progressing!"

"Yes, isn't it," she agreed. And indeed it was—in many and far more different ways than he was aware of!

CHAPTER SEVEN

AN AIRPORT WAS AN AIRPORT was an airport, Amanda decided. There was a concrete-glass-and-chrome anonymity about all of them, and Tampa International was no different in this respect.

Antonio had been silent during the last stage of their flight. She thought he had dozed for a time and so had taken care not to disturb him, but now she suspected he had merely been resting. When the moment had come to fasten their seat belts in preparation for landing, he had been fully awake.

It was nearly one in the morning when they arrived. "A late time for you," Antonio said as the plane was taxiing toward the terminal building. "I am sorry. An earlier flight would not have been possible today. The one before this left Boston not long after five o'clock, and I knew I would not be free by then."

She wished she could ask him more about exactly what had happened during the course of the afternoon's medical appointments, but despite the thaw in his manner toward her—during their trip, at least—she didn't quite dare do this.

Once inside the terminal he took her arm almost protectively, and again his touch was astonishingly provocative. She felt herself leaning toward him involuntarily and gazed up into a face she now found surprisingly austere. Then she realized Antonio was watching a rather stocky man with broad shoulders and reddish hair who was walking toward them.

"Crane," Antonio greeted him with a haughty nod, and she knew this must be the man who had been managing the Florida property. "Good of you to come out at this hour."

"My pleasure," Roger Crane said briefly.

Antonio performed introductions in a purely perfunctory fashion, and she noted his slight frown when the estate manager shook her hand, flashing an engaging and appreciative smile at her as he did so.

"Welcome, Miss Hughes," he said. "It will be good to have you at Hermosa Groves."

She could not suppress a smile, because Hermosa was a Spanish name and Roger Crane had sounded the *h* in it. She was reminded of her instruction in the correct pronunciation of Hernandez.

Before she could speak, Antonio intervened to say, "It is *Mrs.* Hughes, Crane." He did not elaborate on this but added, "We had better go and claim our luggage."

This was done quickly, and they walked out into a star-studded night that seemed so tropically warm to Amanda. She had left a frigid, snow-cloaked Boston, and now the air was soft, the breeze caressing, the full moon a pale shade of citron.

Roger Crane, who had gone ahead of them, now drove up to the airport entrance, and the luggage was transferred into a large station wagon that was light yellow in color and had the Hermosa Groves insignia emblazoned on its side in deep orange.

"We've a drive of about an hour," he told Amanda, speaking over his shoulder as he started the car. Antonio had automatically opened the rear door of the wagon for her and then taken his own place in the front passenger seat. "Nice night, isn't it?" Roger Crane now added.

"Heavenly," Amanda agreed.

"We had a cold snap last week," he told Antonio. "We were afraid of a severe freeze for a couple of days there, and some of the groves farther north did suffer. Our fruit is okay, though."

Antonio did not reply to this, and after a moment Crane said, "This your first trip to Florida, Mrs. Hughes?"

"Yes, it is."

"It's a different way of life," he said. "Different pace, too. You learn to suit yourself to the climate, I guess you'd say."

"You're a native Floridian, Mr. Crane?"

He laughed. "No," he said. "Actually, I'm a Californian. I came here ten years ago to manage Hermosa Groves, and I can't say I've ever been sorry I made the move."

"What about your family?"

"My parents live out on the Coast. Santa Barbara," he said. "I've got a brother in Bakersfield. Aside from that, I'm alone. No attachments, Mrs. Hughes."

It seemed to her Antonio stiffened, but he made no comment. Then, after a moment, he asked, "Has there been any word from my aunt or my niece?"

Crane nodded. "Pablo had a phone call from Madrid yesterday," he said. "They plan to fly over next week. I think they go to New York and then transfer to a flight for Tampa.''

"So," Antonio said, "Pablo will, of course, have the details."

"Yes. The call came through to the office and I had it transferred up to the house. Let's say there was a language barrier."

Antonio did not reply to this, either. Despite the warmth of the night—this in contrast to Boston—Amanda shivered. There was a coldness about Antonio at the moment she couldn't quite fathom. She'd had the feeling from the very first moment of their meeting he didn't like Roger Crane, and she wondered why. The grove manager seemed a friendly outgoing sort of person, and in the bargain he had devoted the past decade of his life to Hermosa Groves, evidently doing this successfully if the Groves were among the largest of the citrus producers in Florida.

She also wondered who the "Pablo" was they had referred to. A relative, or perhaps a member of the household staff whom Antonio had brought with him from Spain or subsequently had sent for?

Thinking ahead, she realized bleakly that as Cristina Hernandez's companion, she would be expected to spend most of her time with the Spanish girl and probably the old aunt, as well. Obviously neither of them spoke English, and if the household help was also Spanish, she was going to be at a serious disadvantage—or so it certainly seemed to her.

She began to feel as if she were in definitely foreign territory, then reminded herself sharply that this was Florida, one of the fifty states and very much a part of her own native land. It would have been quite a different matter if the position Antonio was offering had involved going to Majorca or to Madrid. Then she would indeed have been entirely on his ground.

As it was, she stared despondently at the dark silhouette in front of her, his head held at such a proud angle, and she sighed. Antonio was so *damnably* unpredictable! He was a fascinating, even tender and gentle companion one minute, then an aloof, arrogant and hostile Latin the next. She could not pretend to begin to understand him!

His voice cut sharply across her thoughts. "Is something the matter, Amanda?" he demanded.

"No," she said quickly. "Why?"

"Such a deep sigh," he said. She did know him well enough to catch the edge of mockery to his tone. "I thought that a problem might have arisen."

"I'm a bit tired, that's all," she replied.

Roger Crane interposed. "I don't blame you, seeing how late it is," he said in that friendly expansive manner of his, and Amanda could literally see Antonio's shoulders tense up. "Don't imagine you got much rest on the plane. Least I never can manage to sleep on a plane myself."

"I do find it difficult," she admitted.

"We shall be at the hacienda shortly," Antonio said, and she caught the hint of frost in his voice. "The house, I suppose I should say."

Crane chuckled. "I think of it as a hacienda myself," he said, once again disregarding the proper use of Spanish and pronouncing the *h*. "I guess it's because the place is built in a Spanish style—"

"I would say pseudo-Spanish," Antonio interrupted. "At my first impression it reminded me of something they'd put up in Hollywood for a movie."

"It was Mr. Field's pride and joy," Roger Crane said softly. "His grandfather built the original structure right around the turn of the century. It was considered quite a palace hereabouts at the time, or so I've been told. Sort of a wilderness castle. Then, after his father died and he'd inherited the property, Mr. Field added to it himself. He was living alone on the place even then, but that's when he was planning to get married."

"What happened?" Amanda could not resist asking.

"His fiancée was killed in a train accident up near Pensacola," Crane said. "That was around the time of World War Two. Mr. Field had been deferred from the service because of some kind of ear problem he had, if I remember it right. Anyway, there are still a few old-timers around who knew him then. I guess after his girl died he locked himself up for months. Wouldn't see anyone."

"Spanish grief." Antonio muttered it so softly that Amanda barely heard him.

"What?" Roger Crane asked, but Antonio didn't repeat the comment. "After that," he continued, "Mr. Field kind of lost interest in the place for a while. That's when he sold off the ranch property, or we'd be raising some mighty fine thoroughbreds today. Finally he came around, though, and he put all his efforts into Hermosa Groves. He finished additions to the house, built the courtyard and the terraces and landscaped on down to the swimming pool. Not too many ever saw what he'd done. He wasn't much for inviting people in. I don't think he ever used the pool, matter of fact. By the time I came on the scene he was a man in his sixties and it was a long while since anyone had got close to him. He spent more time in the office than he did in the hacienda. He liked to call it the hacienda himself, incidentally.''

"It sounds as if he was a very lonely person," Amanda said softly, her eyes fixed on that dark head in front of her. Antonio, she suspected, feeling a slight wrench at the thought, was in danger of following the same pattern set by this distant relative from whom he had inherited the property. But Antonio's grief stemmed from a car crash on a remote mountain road in Majorca. . . .

"I think," Roger Crane told her now, "that Mr. Field had got over being lonely a long time before I came to know him. What I'd say about him is that he was a loner and he didn't want anyone else in his life—not close. He'd got used to going it alone—I'd say he'd developed a pretty thick skin. He could be all business, let me tell you."

"It runs in the family," Antonio said abruptly. Amanda saw Roger Crane glance quickly toward his new employer and knew he would be met by the blind side of the handsome visage, totally inscrutable with the black patch masking one eye. She could not help but feel a twinge of sympathy for the grove manager.

They were silent for the rest of the drive. Finally they turned off the main highway onto a secondary route and continued for several miles before taking another turn onto a narrower, evidently private road.

Amanda became conscious of an intensely sweet

perfume filling the air. It was a heady scent, and as she sniffed deeply, she peered out the windows and saw they were going through a section of trees planted so thickly they were like fragrant barricades on either side of the road.

"Orange trees?" she asked Roger Crane, wishing she could see them more clearly through the darkness.

"Mostly, through here," he said. "Grapefruit and lemon, too. We also have some experimental sections with mangoes, papayas and some of the really exotic fruit like carambolas, which came from Malaysia originally. We don't grow those special things for market—not on a large scale, anyway. Experimenting with different sorts of fruit was a hobby of Mr. Field's. He went in for a lot of things like that."

"The fragrance is heavenly," Amanda said, "but almost overpowering."

"I find it so sweet it is close to sickening," Antonio said tautly.

She didn't know what to reply to that but was spared the need of seeking words, because just then the house loomed up ahead of them, its lighted windows sparkling like jewels in this near-tropical night. She drew in her breath at the sight of it.

It was indeed a hacienda, and this in the finest sense of the word, if, that is, hacienda referred to a manor or a very special sort of dwelling. She found herself thinking she was going to have to get a Spanish-English dictionary and start learning precisely what some things did mean if she was going to begin to cope with her present situation at all.

Language-wise Antonio Hernandez had her at a total disadvantage.

Meantime she let her eyes feast on the house as they drew up in front of it. It seemed huge to her: shallow steps leading to an entrance that framed a massive wooden door, itself studded with large brass nails and centered with a huge ornate brass knocker. The knocker looked Indian in design, like an Aztec sun symbol, and perhaps it was, even though this was Seminole rather than Aztec territory. When the opportunity presented itself, she'd examine it carefully.

Antonio helped her out of the station wagon, moving with that same abruptness with which he'd been speaking. He was frowning and seemed irritated. She wondered if perhaps his headache had returned to plague him further.

Roger Crane started to pick up two of their suitcases, but Antonio halted him with an imperious wave of the hand. "Pablo will take care of the luggage, Crane," he said. "Thank you for meeting us. I will see you at the office in the morning."

For an instant the grove manager did not even attempt to suppress the flash of resentment that came across his face. Then it was gone. He smiled agreeably enough and said, "As you wish. It's been good to meet you, Mrs. Hughes. I'll look forward to seeing you again."

"Thank you," she said, and wished she could say more, because it seemed to her Antonio had been needlessly rude—this dismissal went beyond mere thoughtlessness. She sensed Roger Crane had expected to be invited inside after making the trip all the way to Tampa to pick them up, and probably he would have liked to have been offered a nightcap.

Now, though, even as he turned away, the front door of the hacienda opened and a slender man of medium height hurried down the steps.

As he came closer, it seemed to Amanda he could easily have posed as the matador on a Spanish bull-fight poster. He was slight—he could have been called thin except for a wiriness to his body that gave a sense of latent strength. His dark hair was thickly sprinkled with silver—too old now to be a bull-fighter, though she had no doubt he was still intensely agile. He moved in a sinuous way that was pure Castilian. His skin was deeply olive, his features aquiline, his eyes a jet black that encompassed her in a single flashing instant, and then he turned to say, *"Don Antonio, bienvenido."*

"Gracias, Pablo," Antonio said, glancing with an oddly intent expression at the station wagon, which was now edging out of the driveway. "Amanda, this is Pablo, my good right arm. Señora Hughes, Pablo. She is to be Cristina's teacher and companion."

Amanda saw the expression of pure incredulity that came to highlight Pablo's intensely Spanish countenance, but he quickly recovered, bowed and said, *"Encantado, señora."*

They were mounting the steps, and Antonio asked a question in fluent Spanish in which Amanda caught only the word Cristina. Pablo answered him with equal swiftness, and she stifled a sigh before it became audible. This small exchange again brought home to her the strangeness of her position here. She was virtually a foreigner in her own country!

They walked into a large square foyer that seemed to be made entirely of marble. It was furnished with carved mission-oak chairs having vivid red velvet cushions, and there was a variety of tables—including a long refectory table—all of which gave the room a very Spanish atmosphere.

They moved into a drawing room where the Mediterranean theme had been continued, using wrought iron, more of the carved wood and chairs and couches thickly upholstered in deep rust and antique gold. The decor was accented by splashes of florid orange and bright lemon in the many small decorative pillows, and there were large vases filled with masses of fresh flowers. These colors were repeated in the large oil paintings that ornamented the walls, and most of the paintings depicted scenes of Spain.

It was a room that should have been very livable; yet there was a perfection about it that made it stilted. It seemed like a room that had never been lived in, and from what Roger Crane had said about the late Mr. Field, Amanda imagined this was probably true.

Would it remain unused, now that Antonio owned the hacienda? She wondered about this and decided it wouldn't, because Cristina and the elderly aunt would be living here, too. Surely they would begin to meet people...would want to entertain. Or would they?

She stole a glance at Antonio, who was again conversing with Pablo in rapid Spanish, and now she was not at all sure about the probability of entertaining. He was there primarily to rest, he had told her, and his wishes would dominate—of that she was certain.

Again she found herself feeling sorry for Cristina. Her austere uncle was taking her away from her own country and, according to Gregory Blake, the man she was in love with. He was transporting her to this entirely new land where she knew no one and didn't speak the language. Yet Amanda had the strong feeling Antonio was not about to encourage any sort of social life for Cristina. She wondered if indeed he'd not already picked out a future husband for his niece. Perhaps a middle-aged Spanish diplomat to whom the girl could be wed once she had mastered colloquial English.

Now Antonio turned toward her, and a dark eyebrow went up inquisitively. "You look at me as if I am in disfavor," he commented. "Is it because I have been speaking my own language with Pablo? I apologize for this, as undeniably it is rude. But he has very little English, you see. . . . ''

"I understand that," she said stiffly.

"Ah, then it is something else I have done that displeases you? Dismissing Crane, perhaps?"

"That's none of my affair, Antonio."

"Isn't it?" he asked. "He would have liked to come in, to linger, to talk with you—of that I am sure. He did not attempt to conceal his admiration."

"Really, now," she said, trying to keep this light. "You're imagining things."

"Am I, Amanda? I do not know. For someone who wishes herself so prim, you have a strange effect on men. I cannot help but wonder if it is entirely uncalculated. First Gregory and now Crane. . . . ''

He was mocking her, and she hated it when he used this particular tone of voice. Now thoroughly annoyed, she said, "Look, you may not be tired, señor, but I am! If it isn't against your rules, I'd like to go to bed."

It was strange. She felt as if a rubber band had been stretching tight between them and now it had snapped. The tension seemed to dissipate, and he said disarmingly, "I am sorry, Amanda. No, don't look like that. I mean it. Pablo has gone to bring us each a drink—I took the liberty of ordering a Scotch and soda for you as well as for me—and a few small sandwiches. Then, I can assure you, you will be shown to your room. You will sleep better with a bit of food and drink."

Even as Antonio spoke, Pablo was coming back into the room carrying a tray, which he placed on a coffee table in front of one of the couches.

Once again Antonio spoke to him in Spanish, but this time Pablo turned to bow to Amanda and said, *"Buenos noches,"* before he left them.

"I have suggested he retire," Antonio told her when the man had gone. "He starts early in the morning, and I said I would show you to your room myself and also place our tray in the kitchen. In this climate one must be careful about attracting insects—something which holds true in any of the warmer places."

He was handing her a glass as he spoke, and although she hadn't thought she wanted anything to eat or drink, the Scotch tasted good to her, as did the ham and turkey sandwiches on very thin white bread Pablo had made for them.

"There will be a few days before Cristina and Tía Inez arrive," Antonio told her now. "This will permit you a period in which to become acclimatized. I only trust you will not be bored. There is a fairly good library here in the house. All in English,'' he added hastily with a smile. ''My late relative had a wide range of taste in reading material. But then I suppose that when he was not involved in the operation of the groves, he spent much of his time with his books. He belonged to all of the popular book clubs, so there is a good deal of the new, as well as a fine selection of the classics. You should be able to find a book to divert you, if you wish. Also, there is a piano in the room he used as a library. Evidently he played. Do you?''

''Some,'' Amanda admitted. Actually she had taken lessons for years. Although she was out of practice, she loved to play the piano and under ordinary circumstances would have relished having an instrument around. These, though, were not ordinary circumstances—she could not imagine even attempting to play the piano in front of Antonio.

''Then we shall have the piano tuned,'' he told her, ''so that you may enjoy it.''

''That isn't necessary,'' she said quickly.

''Why not, Amanda? If you have musical talent, you are very fortunate. I do not and wish I did. To play an instrument is one of the best forms of relaxation. But then I am lecturing you again. You do not like my lecturing, do you?''

''Antonio....''

''You have had quite enough tonight—and enough of me,'' he surprised her by saying in answer. He rose and held out a hand. ''Come,'' he said. ''I will show you to your room.''

She ignored those tantalizingly outstretched fingers, knowing what his touch would do to her, and after a second he shrugged. Then he led the way back into the foyer and up a curving stairway with a wrought-iron railing to the floor above. A corridor extended in either direction from the head of the stairs and he turned to the right, leading her a short distance and then down yet another corridor at a right angle to the first one.

The walls were white stucco and the woodwork very dark. This same theme reappeared in the room into which Antonio ushered her. The room itself was very large and beautifully furnished in the same sort of carved mission oak she'd seen downstairs in the foyer. The bed was enormous and looked wonderfully comfortable. There was a dressing table, a massive chest of drawers, end tables, occasional chairs and a floor-to-ceiling sliding window. Antonio showed her this now, and she saw it led out onto a balcony where there was a small wrought-iron table and two matching chairs.

"Your bathroom is through the door on the right," he said. "I believe that is everything."

He stood before her, tall, dark, inscrutable. . . and devastating, and he reached out a tentative finger to tilt her chin slightly, gazing down at her with an intensity she found very disconcerting. She thought for a moment he was going to bend and kiss her, and her pulse began to pound in anticipation of her own response. But after a second that seemed to stretch, he took his finger away and moved back, and again he shrugged, that slight and disturbingly foreign shrug. She had thought this spelled indifference, but now she was not at all sure.

"Sleep well, *linda*," he said softly. "Sleep late, too, if you are able to do so. You will have your hands full once Cristina gets here, so enjoy your rest while you can."

With this he left her, closing the door behind him gently, and as she stared at its dark wood, Amanda wished, with an urgency that surprised her, it would open again and he would cross the room to take her into his arms.

This time she would not pull away from him. No, she would let him undress her; she would let him. . . .

She wrung her hands, forcing herself to dismiss such thoughts as the fantasies they were. Then she took a quick bath, slipped into a filmy, pale yellow nightgown and slid between sheets that were cool and fresh.

But sleep was a long time coming.

CHAPTER EIGHT

IT WAS THE SUNLIGHT blazing a trail of light through Amanda's bedroom windows that finally awakened her. She sat up in bed, momentarily disoriented, for she had been dreaming of Antonio. She had been dreaming he had kidnapped her and had whisked her off to Spain. And as she looked around her room, it almost seemed as if her dream might have come true.

She got out of bed and padded across the thick, deep turquoise rug to the window, then pushed back both the glass door and the heavier turquoise-and-sapphire draperies that hung on either side of it.

She could not resist the temptation to step out onto the balcony, and as she did so, she gazed with pleasure at the sight that met her eyes. Ells had been built on either end of the rear of the hacienda, and her own room was in the right wing formed by one of those ells. The two wings were like arms, and with the main body of the house they enclosed all but one side of a square paved courtyard with a cascading fountain in the center. Brilliant potted flowers had been placed everywhere, providing splashes of vibrant color, and hanging plants adorned the shaded walkway that ran along the three sides of the house at the inside edge of this huge inner patio.

At the far end Amanda could see the terraces Roger Crane had spoken of the previous night. They descended like a series of very wide steps to a lawn that was a vivid green, and beyond it she saw what looked like a very large swimming-pool area—she got a glimpse of bright blue green water.

The hacienda *was* beautiful. Antonio could call it pseudo-Spanish if he liked, but she found it absolutely lovely. There was a poignancy in knowing that much of this enchanting place had been designed for a bride-to-be who had not lived long enough to experience her own wedding day.

What a tragedy his fiancée's death clearly had been to Mr. Field. And what a lonely man he must have been thereafter, especially once this place was finished in accordance with his dream—this no matter what Roger Crane had said about him.

As she gazed out toward the pool, a deep familiar voice said, "What a lovely vision!" and startled, she glanced down to see Antonio standing just beneath her window.

He was wearing snug-fitting black trousers and a stark white shirt open at the neck, and he perfectly suited this background, pseudo-Spanish or not!

She was so mesmerized by the sight of him it took her a moment to remember she was wearing only her filmy nightgown, and she had to suppress a startled, "Oh!"

Before she could speak, he laughed and said, "I am glad it is I who am seeing you like this, Amanda. I think I would be intensely jealous if it were anyone else! Will you join me for breakfast and would you like to have it out here on the patio?"

"Yes," she said. "Yes, to both, but you'll have to give me a few minutes to dress."

"*Seguramente,*" he said politely, inclining his head in that slight, rather formal sort of nod that like many of his gestures made him seem so intriguingly foreign to her.

She had unpacked hastily the previous night, but now as she glanced over her wardrobe with a critical eye, everything seeming somewhat drab and outmoded to her. Finally she put on a sleeveless lavender cotton dress and chose to arrange her hair in a ponytail tied with a piece of bright pink wool. White sandals completed the costume, plus pink lipstick, although it was too early in the day for eye makeup, she told herself. She only hoped she wasn't on the verge of looking either "prim" or "dowdy" as she went downstairs to meet Antonio.

The scent of orange blossoms wafted through the air the moment she stepped out onto the patio, and she knew the groves must be all around them and were simply blocked from sight when one was within this inner courtyard.

Antonio was sitting at a glass-topped table, and he rose to pull out a white wrought-iron chair for her. As she sat down his hand brushed her bare arm, and she closed her eyes tightly, glad he couldn't see her face, which was hidden to him from this angle. God, the effect he had on her! She must, she vowed, somehow manage to keep from even the slightest physical contact with him if she were going to maintain her equilibrium at all!

"You look very lovely this morning," he commented as he pulled up a chair opposite her and seated himself. "I like your—what is it they call that way of doing one's hair?"

"A ponytail," she said, and he nodded.

"You should perhaps give me lessons in American slang when you teach Cristina," he suggested. "It is very picturesque—it spices one's conversation. There is a vitality to American English that is like the Americans themselves. But then," he added, "I am not at all sure you would like to be my teacher, would you, Amanda?"

Amanda tightened her lips, knowing he was beginning to bait her once again. She was determined not to start the day by going through a mocking interchange with him. She hesitated, then plunged. "Antonio," she said firmly, "may I make a suggestion?"

She saw his questioning eyebrow rise, but he only said politely, "But of course."

"Let's omit the sparring contests, shall we? Let's try to, at any rate."

"Sparring contests?" he queried.

"I think you know very well what I mean."

There was a moment of silence, and then he smiled. She had wondered what it would be like to see him smile, really smile, and now she knew. She could feel her throat tightening and she swallowed hard, then was vastly relieved to see a buxom, dusky-skinned woman come out a side door carrying a heavily laden tray. One more second and she would have been in danger of flinging herself at Antonio, verbally if not physically. She *wanted* to fling herself at him, damn it! She wanted. . . .

Antonio, his voice suspiciously mild, said, "This is Hortense, Amanda. She is our very good cook, and she runs the hacienda, as well. Pablo only thinks he is in charge here. Hortense, may I present Mrs. Hughes."

"We're glad to have you here, Mrs. Hughes," Hortense said in a voice that was deep and wonderfully mellow. And Amanda at once responded to her. Also, it was a relief to know there would be someone else around who spoke English!

Hortense had brought them a pot of coffee and another pot full of steaming milk, plus an assortment of hot rolls, some butter and two varieties of tropical jam. There was also orange juice, which, she said, had been freshly squeezed and came from their own trees.

Amanda was sure she had never tasted a fruit juice quite so sweet and flavorful. As she sat back, sipping it, a sense of complete contentment came over her— something she had never really expected to experience with Antonio so near at hand.

But he, too, seemed relaxed. Again he flashed that heart-stopping smile at her, then asked, "Do you like *café con leche*?"

"I don't think I've ever had it," she had to confess.

"Perhaps as *café au lait*?" he suggested. "A combination of strong coffee and hot milk?"

"Yes." She nodded. "Of course."

"Then may I mix it for you?"

"Please."

He had a graceful way of using his hands, she noticed, and he had beautiful hands, for that matter. His fingers were long and slender; his hands were capable, adroit, and she already knew their touch.

Memory brought a wave of purely sensuous feeling sweeping over her. She'd had experience with their ability to caress, to....

"Sugar?" he asked as he poured the milk and coffee together into a cup, holding a pot in each hand and letting the two steaming liquids merge into an enticingly frothy beverage. "I would advise at least one full teaspoon. Sugar is essential with this sort of coffee."

She nodded again, and he added sugar to her cup, stirred and then handed the coffee to her, watching as she took her first sip.

"It is delicious," she told him.

"The best way to have it for breakfast," he said approvingly. "Later in the day I like my coffee very hot, and it should be a special blend, such as espresso. Weak coffee, in my opinion, should be abolished from the earth."

As he spoke, he broke open a roll, buttered it and then spread it liberally with jam. "Guava," he told her, indicating the jam. "An unusual flavor, but I find it very palatable."

So did she, and it occurred to her she and Antonio were starting out this day in a surprisingly agreeable manner.

She was wondering how long this was going to last when he said, "This sparring you spoke of...."

"Yes?"

"I do not know what comes over me with you, Amanda," he confessed. "It is true I seem to want to pique you, to see what you—"

He broke off and she leaned forward, because she wanted to hear more of this. Then she realized from the expression on Antonio's face they were no longer alone.

. She turned, expecting to see Hortense or perhaps Pablo. Instead it was Roger Crane who was crossing the patio. He came to stand by the table, looking ruggedly handsome himself this morning, in tan chinos with a matching shirt. He carried a wide-brimmed hat—almost a Texas-style sombrero—and his hair seemed especially reddish in the morning sunlight. Light blue eyes smiled down at her, even though it was Antonio whom he addressed first.

"Hope I'm not interrupting anything, Mr. Hernandez," he said. "I brought some oranges up to the house for Hortense. She wanted them for a special dessert she's going to fix. I thought I might as well bring them along myself, because I imagined you'd want me to drive you back to the office about now anyway."

"Thank you, but I will drive over myself later in the morning," Antonio said coolly.

The grove manager's surprise seemed genuine enough. "I didn't realize you drove a car," he said bluntly.

Amanda could feel Antonio stiffen. Then he said, his voice cold, "I have an International Driver's License, Crane. It was renewed before I left Spain. My vision was sufficient to meet the requirements, I assure you."

"I'm sorry," Roger Crane said. "I didn't mean any offense."

"I'm sure you didn't," Antonio said smoothly. "Thank you for bringing the oranges, and I will see you later."

It was a clear-cut dismissal, and it could hardly have been more direct. Amanda flinched, feeling sorry for Roger Crane, but he only turned to her now to say, "You look as if the Florida climate's agreeing with you, Mrs. Hughes. Sleep well?"

"Yes, thank you," she replied.

"I'd be glad to show you around the groves anytime it would suit you," he volunteered.

"Thank you," she said without venturing to look at Antonio.

The grove manager nodded and a moment later was gone, his heels clacking against the tiles as he made his way across the patio. Only then did Antonio exhale audibly, and Amanda glanced up to see his face was grim.

"You really dislike him, don't you?" she asked, without even pausing to think about the possible effect of posing such a question.

"I really don't know what I think of him. More coffee?"

"Please."

Antonio frowned as he poured. "It is a—what I think you call a 'gut feeling,'" he said then. "Maybe I use too strong a phrase—you can correct me, if so. Crane seems like a genuine sort of person, and I appreciate that. But he tends to speak of Hermosa Groves as if the place belonged to him. I have the feeling that perhaps he thought it was going to belong to him, and I wonder if this was a valid hope on his part or only a wish. In other words, I wonder if my uncle was trying to find a way to circumvent the terms of the original deed. The deed required that the land go to a person of Vega blood descended from the original Vega who was given the grant in the first place. Also, it was stipulated that the person receiving the property would be the eldest male in each new generation. Do you follow me?''

"So far," Amanda said.

"It is chance, of course, that has made me the one to inherit. My mother had a brother who would have been the one to claim the legacy had he lived. And as it happened, he left only daughters, which made my brother, Juan, the next in line. When he died, it fell to me.''

"Just what relation was Mr. Field to you?"

"A distant cousin. At one time we would have shared common grandparents. It is ironical in its way that he was the last of the 'American' branch of the family. You could say that on his death the deed reverted back to Spain, or at least to those of us left in the Spanish branch. Our stock, too, is dwindling. My brother had only Cristina. And I,'' he added, staring down at the coffee cup he held in his hand, "I shall not marry. So for me there will be no descendants.''

Amanda felt as if he had dropped a cold stone directly into her heart. She forced herself to go on sipping her second cup of coffee as if nothing had happened, but it took all her effort to keep her fingers from shaking. Why was he so sure he would never marry? She couldn't come out and ask him directly, but she had to know, and so she said, trying very hard to make the question sound casual, "Aren't you being rather dire, Antonio? You are a relatively young man, and surely you will marry one of these days and probably have at least three sons of your own."

He did not respond to her attempt at a light touch; his face was moody as he shook his head. And then he went on to say firmly, "No, Amanda. I would not ask a woman to share my life, and in any event, I have no heart for marriage."

A moment later he got up, and making what she saw was a determined effort to put the subject behind him, he said, "Come. Let us walk down to the pool. You like to swim?"

"Yes," she answered.

"A bit chilly today for it, I think," he said. "It seems warm here because the contrast is so great to the weather in Boston, and yet the air is actually quite cool, except when you are directly in the sun. We can be sure, though, that here in Florida these next months it will get only warmer."

They were moving out of the patio area and onto the first of the terraces as he spoke, and from here she could look down at the swimming pool, which was even larger than she'd thought, remembering the glimpse she'd had of it from her balcony. It was free form in shape, looking very much like an artist's palette, and there were chairs and tables and bright umbrellas spaced along the concrete apron. It was an inviting scene, and briefly Amanda let herself imagine what it would be like to be with Antonio in a place like this under other circumstances. It would be bliss, paradise, if they were lovers, for instance. . . .

"Watch it," he said as at this thought she nearly stumbled on the steps that led to the second terrace and his arm reached out to grab her elbow. She could feel herself quivering and was surprised when he muttered something in Spanish that was clearly an expression of pure irritation.

"I cannot see your face when you are on my left side—for obvious reasons," he said tautly, pulling her around so she was facing him squarely. "What is it, Amanda? Why are you trembling so? You have not caught some tropical bug in the short space of time you have been here, have you?"

"No," she replied nervously.

"Well," he said, "it is I who am supposed to have trouble with such things as depth perception on steps. Yet you are the one who nearly fell down. I have the feeling I have disturbed you again. Is it because I dismissed Crane so abruptly?"

Amanda had forgotten all about the grove manager. She shook her head. "No," she said. "It isn't that at all."

"Then what is it, for God's sake?"

"You," she answered weakly.

"*Me?*"

"Are you so surprised?"

"Yes, I am very surprised," he said, and his Spanish accent seemed more pronounced. "What is there about me that causes you to come close to spraining an ankle?"

"Sometimes when you speak as you do..." she began, and then shook her head despairingly. "I don't know how to put it to you, Antonio, without your getting huffy with me...."

"*Huffy?*"

"Out of sorts. But it upsets me when you say things like you just did...things with such a finality about them. It's ridiculous, for instance, for you to insist you will never marry, for you to act as if your entire life were behind you...."

"Oh?" he demanded. Then, to her astonishment, he laughed out loud, and the smile he gave her was downright wicked as he added, "Are you telling me you think I should marry, Amanda?"

"Yes," she said. "One day when you find the right person and...."

"Would *you* consider marrying me, Amanda?" he asked her much too mildly.

"Of course not! You know very well I didn't mean that at all. I...."

"What did you mean?" he persisted, moving closer to her, so dangerously close she felt as if he'd drawn her into the powerful aura of his presence and she was standing within his own magnetic field.

His arms went around her, and when she made a faint effort to pull back, he laughed again. "Careful, *linda*," he cautioned. "There is another step directly behind you, and if I do not hold on to you, you are likely to go over the edge."

I am much more likely to go over the edge if you do hold on to me, Amanda said to herself silently. Then she added audibly, "Oh, my God, Antonio!"

For his hands were not remaining still but were exploring, sliding downward over her hips as he claimed her mouth with his. His kiss was searing—there was nothing gentle about it—and it came to her he was a *conquistador*, this man. He had not actually ventured forth from Spain like the Spanish knights of old. Yet their blood was in his veins, and she had no doubt at all he was more than capable of staking a claim and then refusing to relinquish it.

It was not the first time she found herself unable to resist him, and Amanda had the sinking feeling it was not going to be the last, unless she got a much firmer grip on her emotions. And how did someone manage to do that, she asked herself almost hysterically, when a man like Antonio Hernandez was literally in the throes of staking a claim? Maybe not in quite the way his ancestors had done in this new country... but quite as effectively!

She wanted to push him away from her. No, she amended, being honest with herself at least; she really didn't want to push him away from her at all. And just now her own "wants" were not going to matter all that much. Not unless she really put a quick halt to what he was doing to her... rebuffing him so firmly, so finally, he just might never try again to take her in his arms...and to kiss her as he was kissing her now.

His fingers moved on in further conquest, while Amanda found herself actually swaying, as if he'd truly hypnotized her. Her dress fastened down the front, and she felt one long lean hand start to undo it while the other hand continued to explore the contours of her hips and then her waist, coming finally to her breasts. Now Antonio was able to undo her bra, as well, and his mouth descended to etch a pattern of kisses that seemed to burn through her bare flesh. Then his ardent lips covered the rosy tip of first one breast and then the other.

Amanda was so afire, so possessed by him, she was only dimly aware that he, too, was thoroughly aroused. But the evidence of his sexuality became obvious when he drew her close to him, his body beginning to move against hers in a sinuous rhythm that mixed torment and rapture into an incredible symphony the very essence of passion.

Amanda heard a low moan—and could not believe it was she who was moaning...yet knew it was. He said something in a hoarse low voice...something she knew was Spanish—yet was international in its meaning.

They merged...and the interruption that came created a kind of shock wave, forcing them apart so quickly Amanda barely heard Antonio's muttered imprecation and this time wasn't certain whether he was speaking in Spanish or in English.

Through eyes that were close to glazed she saw Pablo hurrying across the patio toward the steps, and she instinctively reached for her dress and drew it up around her, fastening it quickly, only hoping that Pablo was concentrating so much on other things he hadn't fully taken in this scene he was coming upon.

As if to confirm this, Pablo called out, *"¿Don Antonio?"*

Antonio groaned, and she could only dimly imagine the effort it was costing him to call back, *"¿Si?"*

Amanda caught the word, *"Teléfono,"* and gathered there was a phone call for Antonio, a phone call that must be very urgent, indeed, if one was to judge from Pablo's manner. Then, in reply to a question from Antonio, Pablo answered, the name heavily accented. "It is Señorita Edmond."

"Perdón," Antonio said to her astonishment, and at once headed toward the house without a backward glance, followed by Pablo.

She stood, stunned, looking after them. The telephone call was obviously important to Antonio, very important. Important enough, certainly, to make him seemingly forget that point of no return the two of them had been approaching a moment before Pablo's summons.

She wandered across to the swimming pool and stared down into its calm aquamarine water, the ripples moving lightly across its surface, gently fanned by a rising wind. Beyond a wide clearing at the far side of the pool the groves began—rows of trees stretching as far as she could see in every direction. Glossy dark green leaves sheltered vivid orange globes—the treasures with which these trees were laden. To her surprise there were delicate white blossoms as well as fruit on some of the trees, and the air was redolent with their sweet heady fragrance.

Beauty always moved Amanda, and her eyes feasted on the orange trees, the exotic palms planted closer to the house and the vines showering over the edge of the ell nearest the courtyard, these laden with cascades of bright flame flowers. Yet even all this glory could not distract her as a question became uppermost in her mind.

Who, she wondered, was Señorita Edmond?

CHAPTER NINE

AMANDA DID NOT SEE ANTONIO for the rest of the day. After a while she stretched out in one of the chaise longues near the pool and let the sun caress her face. She assumed Antonio was going to return to her once he got through with his phone call from Miss Edmond, whoever she might be, but as the minutes continued to tick by, she knew she was mistaken.

She had no wish to get a sunburn and she had not thought to bring any tanning lotion with her. Reluctantly she strolled back into the house through rooms that were cool and pleasantly shaded. She found the late Mr. Field's library and even took down a couple of books for later reading. Just now, though, she was not at all in the mood to read.

What was she in the mood for? She acknowledged ruefully that the only thing in the world she really wanted at the moment was Antonio Hernandez y Vega's reappearance on her personal scene. Yes, heaven help her, she wanted him to take her in his arms again...and finish what they had begun on the terrace.

She shivered and then paused in the middle of the book-lined room, a sense of deep shock coming over her. She had never considered herself a physical person—at least not in the purely sensual meaning of the word. Perhaps, she conceded, there was more than she realized of the prim New Englander in her. She was coming to know only too well that so-called primness could merely be a camouflage for something else. Still, this overwhelming feeling, this urgency she felt toward Antonio seemed quite *carnal* to her, and in her mind that very word carried with it a quality of indecency.

Perhaps because her father had, of necessity, been put in the position of doing the job of two parents, he had brought her up with an especially strict sense of moral value. Perhaps her father really had been a prim New Englander at heart—his was an earlier generation, of course. Regardless, she had always had a strong sense of restraint insofar as members of the opposite sex were concerned, a self-control that had been more than a little irritating to boys who had dated her in earlier years.

Then, of course, she had married Gerard. There had been a physical side to their marriage, but she had to admit that even during the most intimate moments in their bedroom he had never aroused her as Antonio Hernandez had this morning.

There had been no incipient volcanic eruptions in the lovemaking between Gerard and her. She wondered, in retrospect, if the experiences she and her husband had shared could, in truth, even be called lovemaking...certainly not in the same sense the word would have in context with a man like Antonio. This she knew, and the knowledge was shattering—as shattering as the impact Antonio had upon her. She had heard of people who simply...succumbed. People who, once having coupled, couldn't resist each other and the urges of their own, deeply basic feelings. She had never thought herself a person like that, but now she knew she had put herself on a slightly higher plane. More the fool, she! She had put this kind of emotional intensity under the heading of "lust," and there had always seemed to her something dirty about it. But, on the contrary, this overwhelming attraction between Antonio and her was a blazing thing, as clean, as pure, as molten gold.

Or, she thought, as she moved across the library to stand by the piano in the corner, it had been. On her part, at least. Antonio's abruptness in abandoning her to respond to a phone call from another woman was leaving in its wake staggering doubts where he was concerned.

She reached out to touch an ivory key, but she did not press it, even though she would have loved nothing better than to sit down and play... play anything that would extract from this self she didn't even recognize some of the emotions that were proving entirely too heavy to handle.

There was a chance, though, Antonio might appear any moment, and she still could not imagine playing... performing... in front of him.

She wandered on through the empty drawing room, the two books she'd taken from the library clutched under her arm. There were fresh flowers in all the vases, and she realized someone changed them daily. Probably Hortense.

She thought of going back to the patio, but the sun was at its zenith now. With her fair skin unprotected she'd be sure to get a burn. So she slowly made her way up the stairs and into her own room, and it seemed to her as she went that the house was totally empty—to the point of desolation. Silence echoed around her, and for no good reason at all salt tears stung her eyes. She didn't like this kind of loneliness.

Her bed had been made and the room tidied. Pablo? Or Hortense? If there were other members of the household staff, she'd yet to meet them.

Finally she settled down in an armchair and tried to read one of the books. But it was impossible to concentrate. She could think only of Antonio, and wondered why he had gone off as he had and why he had not come back.

She was startled by a buzzer and traced it to an intercom on the wall just inside the door. She pressed buttons and heard Hortense's voice.

"Miz Hughes? Are you about ready for some lunch? Mr. Hernandez sent word he won't be joining you today. . . he had to go out for a while. But I've fixed a mighty good chicken salad. There's some nice shade in the corner of the patio, if you'd like to have it there."

"Thank you," Amanda said. "I'll be right down."

The chicken salad was delicious, and Hortense hovered over her like a ministering angel, making sure she had iced coffee or iced tea—she chose iced tea—and plenty of hot biscuits and butter.

The solitary lunch finished, Amanda went back to her room, stretching out on her bed this time because she was unexpectedly weary—the climate probably, she told herself.

She napped, and to her surprise it was dusk when she awakened. She got up and showered and then dressed with special care, choosing a simple white sheath that she highlighted with a chunky turquoise necklace. She cinched the dress at the waist with a slim rope of gold kid.

She wore matching gold kid slippers and decided to wear her hair long. As she gazed into the mirror before leaving the room, she was pleased with her own reflection. The brief exposure to the Florida sun that morning had brought touches of a becoming rosy color to her face. Also, she was alive with a different sort of glow: the glow of anticipation. She could not wait to see Antonio again.

She soon found she was to be doomed to disappointment.

Pablo appeared as soon as she entered the drawing room, and they managed to communicate about a drink. He brought her sherry in a lovely etched-crystal glass. He started to tell her something about Don Antonio but after a moment gave up, and with a wry smile and helpless shrug he left the room. A minute later Hortense came in, still clutching a large pot holder. Obviously she had been interrupted in the midst of cooking something.

"Pablo wanted me to tell you Mr. Hernandez won't be having dinner here tonight," she said. Warm brown eyes enveloped Amanda in a sympathetic but sharp glance. "Too bad, your having to eat all alone when you've fixed yourself up so pretty," she added. "You should have company before much longer, though. I take it from Pablo Mr. Hernandez's niece and aunt will be here in a couple more days."

This was not particularly good news, but Amanda,

trying to mask her disappointment at Antonio's not joining her, only nodded, then asked curiously, "How do you manage to understand Pablo, Hortense?"

"I speak a little Spanish," the cook told her. "My husband's family came to the Tampa area from Cuba and I had to learn enough so I could talk with my in-laws. It's not very much like Pablo's kind of Spanish, but with the help of some sign language we make do."

Amanda laughed, and Hortense went on to say, "Dinner can be served anytime you want it, Miz Hughes. Maybe you'd like another glass of sherry first?"

"Thank you, no," Amanda said. "But am I to eat in that huge dining room all by myself?"

"Would you rather have your dinner on a tray in the library?" Hortense asked perceptively. "Then you could watch some TV, too."

"I'd like that much better," she admitted.

As it developed, there was nothing that especially interested her on television. She watched the rerun of a situation comedy while she ate the delicious dinner Hortense had prepared for her. The meal was composed of succulently broiled gulf shrimp in a tangy lemon-and-butter sauce; rice evidently cooked with saffron, for it was a distinct yellow color and had a lovely savory flavor; and ripe red tomatoes, these served just as nature had grown them—and they couldn't possibly have been improved upon in Amanda's opinion.

The special dessert Roger Crane had mentioned that morning proved to be an ambrosia, which combined slices of oranges with slices of grapefruit, lots of coconut, maraschino cherries and pecan halves. It was the perfect final touch to a meal that had never been designed to be eaten in solitary splendor, Amanda thought ruefully.

After a time she switched off the television and sat looking around the library, letting herself feel its atmosphere. It seemed to her the late Michael Field must have spent a lot of time in the room. There was a personality about it more distinct than that of the rest of the house. In addition to the well-filled bookcases, the television set and the piano, there was a stereo in one corner and a cabinet full of records nearby. Mr. Field seemed to have been as catholic in his musical tastes as he had been in his choice of reading material. He had a selection of everything from baroque through the romantic school and on to modern rock.

He piqued her interest, this distant relative of Antonio's who had spent his life—or most of it, certainly—there on the grove property and had been so ill-starred in love. If she remembered rightly, Antonio had said Michael Field had inherited Hermosa Groves from his father during World War Two or shortly before it. She didn't know how old he'd been at the time of his death, but if he'd been seventy or so, that meant he'd come into his inheritance at a young age. He must not have had any brothers, she decided—certainly not any who had survived him, or they would now be the owners of Hermosa Groves, since it passed in line from eldest male to eldest male. When she thought about it, though, it seemed no wonder to her he'd built the business to the point where it was a leader in a state noted for its citrus production. He must have devoted a major part of his life and most of his energy to Hermosa Groves, and looking around her now, she felt very certain somehow that a good bit of the rest of his time had been spent right there in that room with his books, his music... and his memories.

Again she walked over to the piano and touched one of the ivory keys, but this time she let the note sound, and when she heard it, the temptation became too great to resist. She sat down at the keyboard and let her fingers roam idly, and lovely tones cascaded out into the room. She put her heart into her music as she went from a waltz into a sonata and then into a romantic Latin piece, her confidence growing as she played.

She almost wished Antonio *would* walk in. She imagined him coming to stand in the doorway and felt as if he were actually watching her as time wore on. At one point she turned around to look, but there was no one there.

ANTONIO DID NOT JOIN HER for breakfast the next morning, and Hortense once again did the explaining, telling her he had been required to go to Tampa on business. Amanda frowned when she heard this, because this sort of behavior on his part seemed very much at variance with the instructions he had received from his doctors. He had been told to rest for the next three months in the hope of averting surgery. If he was dashing around the countryside and going into Tampa on business and such, he certainly couldn't be getting much rest!

Once again she ate a solitary luncheon, but at the

end of it Pablo came to say in a curiously stilted tone, "Señor Crane, señora."

Roger Crane appeared right on his heels, and admittedly Amanda was very glad to see him. She swiftly became conscious that Pablo was aware of the smile of welcome she was giving the grove manager, and she had the definite impression Pablo disapproved.

Nevertheless she asked her visitor if he would care to join her in a glass of iced tea, and when he assented, she pointed to her own half-filled glass, pointed toward Crane, then held up two fingers and said, "Pablo—*por favor*."

Despite himself Pablo smiled, and a moment later he brought two glasses of the beverage to the round glass table set out in the patio, to which Amanda promptly said, *"Gracias."*

"De nada, señora," Pablo returned, actually bowing as he spoke, and she had the feeling she'd gone up a notch in his estimation.

Roger Crane, leaning back in his chair, said, "This is a delightful spot, isn't it? I'm glad to see you're making use of it."

"Didn't Mr. Field?" she asked him.

"Very little," he told her. "He was usually up at the office or else out around the property most days till just about dark, and then he got up at the crack of dawn and started to work all over again. I guess you'd say he was a workaholic. But it paid off here at Hermosa Groves. This is one of the biggest citrus businesses in Florida, and that's saying something. Sometimes I wonder if Hernandez realizes what a gold mine he's fallen into."

"I don't suppose he's had time to really get into it," she hedged.

"No, I don't suppose he has," the grove manager agreed. He finished his iced tea and put down the glass. His hands, she saw, were square and brown, his fingers strong and sturdy. Entirely different hands from Antonio's. But then Roger Crane was an entirely different sort of man. He was wearing faded jeans today, tucked into fairly short boots, and a pale blue shirt opened at the throat. He looked tanned and healthy—he emanated vigor, in fact—and there was an essentially male appeal about him that was impossible to be unaware of. Roger Crane was not devastatingly handsome at first glance like Antonio, and of course he had none of the foreign aura that gave Antonio such a distinct air of mystery. No, he was not like Antonio at all. But, she felt, he would be a lot easier to understand, and it would be a relief to be with someone like him. There would be no wondering where the next dart was coming from with Roger Crane.

"Well," he said now, flashing an engaging grin in her direction, "it seems my employer won't have any need of my services this afternoon, so I thought it might be a good time to show you around a bit if you haven't anything else you have to do."

"Nothing at all." She smiled back. "I'm totally idle until Cristina Hernandez arrives here."

"Great," Crane applauded. "I brought along the Land Rover in the hope you'd be free. Thought about taking you around in the Jeep, but that's open, and I didn't want you to get too much sun all at once. As it is, do you have a shade hat of some kind?"

"No."

"That'll have to be remedied," he said. "If you're going to mosey around here very much, you'll need something on your head. Specially someone as fair as you are. Come to think of it, I've got an extra sombrero in the car if you need it. Mostly we'll just keep you in the shade, that's all."

He got to his feet and she followed suit, and then she wondered if she should go into the house and find either Pablo or Hortense to tell them she was going out for a while. There seemed no real need for this, though. She was supposed to be a free agent, after all, until her duties with Cristina started.

Cristina. Every time she'd thought of the girl lately, it had been with an increased feeling of dread. It had only begun to occur to her that Cristina might be as arrogant in her own way as her uncle was...a spoiled slip of a girl who was wild, headstrong, and who—with the language barrier thrown in—would prove to be an unpleasant handful to manage.

She suppressed a sigh. There was no chance of back-tracking now—she knew that only too well. Sooner than she wanted to she would have to confront Cristina. But with every day that passed there was less of that three months she had committed herself to left. She could not help but wish something would happen to detain Cristina and her aunt in Spain awhile longer!

Roger Crane had parked the Land Rover at the front of the house. As she climbed into it, she found the seat was already hot from the touch of the sun.

"Plenty of fire in that old orb," the grove manager commented as Amanda muttered an "ouch." "Not too much for you, is it?"

"No," she said, "not at all. Matter of fact, a little heat on my skin feels good. It was freezing in Boston."

"Never been to Boston," he confessed, "but now that I know a Bostonian, it's a mistake I can rectify. How long are you planning to stay around, Amanda—if I may call you Amanda?"

She nodded. "Till the middle of April or so," she said then.

"Wow!" he said. "Hernandez expects his niece to learn English pretty fast, doesn't he?"

"It's not that," she admitted. "We agreed to a three-month trial period."

"And you've already decided to go home when it's over?" he asked, his lips quirking at the thought of this.

Noting this, Amanda had the sudden conviction Roger Crane didn't like Antonio any more than Antonio liked him. This realization, in turn, was rather like a warning flag flashing in front of her, and she had the feeling she'd better be careful what she volunteered.

"We shall have to see when the time is up," she said. "It's a two-way street, after all—an arrangement like that, I mean."

"True enough," he told her, but there was more than a hint of curiosity in the glance he gave her.

They had turned out of the semicircular driveway that fronted the house, and now he took a side road that led directly into the groves. Almost at once Amanda found herself surrounded by oranges.

She had to laugh. "Before we go back, I've simply got to pick one of them," she confessed.

He chuckled. "As many as you like," he promised her. "I'll even turn my back when you do it. They say forbidden fruit is always the sweetest."

Forbidden fruit. An uninvited thought of Antonio sprang into her mind, and she thrust it away. That was a mental topic she definitely wanted to avoid.

Now she said with genuine enthusiasm, "They're so exotic! I mean, it's one thing to pick apples at home. But to see oranges actually growing out in the open like this is terrific!"

"It's a sight I've seen all my life," he replied casually.

"Well, it's a first for me," she said. "The fragrance from the blossoms is tremendous, isn't it? Almost overwhelming."

"In time you get used to it," he said, "like you do to most odors, pleasant as well as unpleasant. Now I notice it only if I get away from it for a while."

"It seems so strange to see some of the trees in blossom and others with fruit on them," she told him.

"Yes. I guess you could say oranges have their own crazy habits, and these are as different as one variety from another. Do you know anything about citrus?"

"Not much, really," she said. "When I was a little girl, I used to find an orange in my Christmas stocking. More recently I've pondered whether to buy oranges or tangelos or tangerines or maybe grapefruit in our local Massachusetts supermarkets. Aside from that, I guess oranges came originally from Spain. . . ."

He shook his head. "No," he told her, "they came from the Orient. Originally, they think, from the

Malay archipelago and then India. Then at some remote time they were carried into China, and it was in China that sweet oranges as we know them today were developed. We don't know just how old oranges are, but they were first mentioned in a written record something like twenty-six centuries ago.''

"That's incredible!"

"Yes, and there's evidence that lemons are even older," the grove manager told her. "Citron, too. There's supposed to be a mention of citron in Egyptian literature that dates back to about fifteen hundred B.C. The Europeans have liked it for its rind for centuries, and citron rind is still a pretty important part of the scene when it comes to cooking. Holiday cooking especially."

She nodded. "Fruitcake, plum pudding, mince meat."

"That's right," he said, and then continued, "To get back to oranges—when Columbus started out to find a passage to India and wound up discovering the New World, he brought along with him orange, lemon and citron seeds that he got in the Canary Islands en route."

"Then it was Columbus who should be given credit for bringing citrus to Florida?" Amanda suggested.

"Only in a broad sense," Roger said. "We have to give the Spanish credit for beginning the act where the raising of Florida citrus is concerned. Oranges have been grown in Florida for well over four hundred years.

"The theory is that it was the Indians who propagated oranges across the whole peninsula. They got them from the Spaniards, and they scattered the seeds as they ate them. In some sections here you can still find coppices of wild oranges, especially around some of the lakes and along the rivers. Remember the Indians used the waterways as prime means of transportation in the early days. I might say that the white settlers followed suit. Until railroads were built in Florida—and they were a long while coming—boats were the main way of getting from one place to another, whether on business or for pleasure.

"It wasn't until the English took over Florida from Spain about a dozen years before the American Revolution that oranges came into play commercially," he went on. "There was some commercial trading in them then, but actually it wasn't until Florida was ceded to the United States—in 1821—that the development of citrus groves really got going.

"Anyway," Roger concluded with satisfaction, "today the U.S. leads all other countries in the world in citrus production, and Californian that I am, I have to concede that Florida leads all the other states in the Union in this field. Florida, in fact, produces more citrus all by itself than any country in the world, except the U.S.A., of course."

Amanda smiled. "You remind me of Antonio," she couldn't help saying.

Both the surprised glance he shot toward her and the tone of his voice were laced with suspicion.

"*I*—remind you of Hernandez?" He was incredulous.

"You both seem to have the same kind of interest in history and statistics—and a keen memory for it, too," she said.

There was derision in the grove manager's short

laugh. "I'd say that's about where the resemblance ends," he told her. "I don't think you could find two people more different than Hernandez and me. He's had everything in his life handed to him on a gold platter, probably one studded with diamonds and pearls, at that. I've had to work for what I've got every step of the way. Frankly, Amanda," he added, "I don't have much use for Hernandez's type, though I don't suppose I should be telling you that. Naturally I'm trusting you to keep anything I say about him in confidence... and we are both Americans, damn it! If we didn't have anything else in common, we'd have that. I'd like to think, though, that we could get a lot more going between us...."

"Roger..." she began, but he interrupted her almost roughly.

"You're not falling for Hernandez, are you?" he demanded. "Christ, I hope not! You'd only be leaving yourself wide open for a busted heart!"

She had to agree with him there. She said, her voice tight, "I've known Antonio Hernandez only a few days." And as incredible as it now seemed to her, this was true.

"That doesn't necessarily count," Roger observed wisely. "The chemistry between a man and a woman is a funny thing. I don't think I have to tell you that. But with Hernandez...."

"Why do you dislike him so, Roger?"

"I suppose," he began, pulling the Land Rover over to a sheltered spot at the edge of the road, "it's because I don't feel he belongs here. Hell, Mr. Field worked his—that is to say, he just about literally worked himself into the ground. He was seventy-one when he died, but he was still in the prime of life except for his heart—it gave out on him one day while he was out here in these groves, keeping his personal touch on everything like he always did. Do you really think Antonio Hernandez would get dust on his feet coming out here? So far I've had a couple of phone calls from him, but he hasn't even shown up at the office to go over things with me. Yesterday he was called to Tampa, and he went back there again today. If you ask me, I bet he's brought over some Spanish chick and he's keeping her up there."

The glance he gave her now was much too discerning. "You don't like the thought of that, do you?" he demanded bluntly.

"I think you're making a premature judgment," Amanda said. "I was with him when he got the phone call that summoned him to Tampa yesterday. It seemed obvious it was a business call."

But had it been? She was protecting Antonio, and there was no reason for her to do that, she told herself fiercely. Still, she could not go along with Roger Crane's comments about their employer, either.

"I don't think Antonio Hernandez is quite the effete aristocrat you imagine him to be," she said slowly.

"You don't deny he is an aristocrat, do you?" the grove manager countered. "Okay, Amanda, what I'm saying is that people like him don't belong in this kind of a world, and I think I'm right about that. He has no business here!"

"He inherited the property, Roger," she reminded him.

"Yes, so he did," he conceded grimly.

Then he rallied to flash an unexpectedly charming smile in her direction. "Look," he said, "why are we wasting our time talking about Hernandez? I'd much rather know more about you."

"There isn't that much to tell," she said evasively.

He chuckled. "I don't buy that," he informed her. "I'd like to know, for instance, about that 'Mrs.' tagged on the front of your name."

"I'm a widow," she said.

He sobered. "I'm sorry, Amanda. Hell, I do ride into things roughshod sometimes! Forgive me, will you?"

"There's nothing to forgive, Roger," she said slowly. "My husband was sick for a long time before he died...it wasn't unexpected. Also, it has been a while. I'm getting over it."

I'm getting over it. Her own statement came as a shock to her now, and she was glad she'd whipped out her sunglasses a few minutes earlier, because they helped camouflage the expression on her face. She didn't want Roger Crane drawing any further conclusions today.

But she *was* getting over it. She had, in fact, *got* over Gerard's death in the sense that he and her marriage to him seemed very remote. A sense of loss once sharp had dulled, so that in memory he was like a beloved father figure.

I loved him, she found herself thinking, *but never as I could love Antonio. The love between Gerard and me was a pastel thing, whereas with Antonio it's vibrant, vivid, flaming with colors as intense as a summer sunset over the plains.*

Roger had started the Land Rover up again, and

now he said, "Let's stop by the office and I'll show you our center of operations. Then we can go by the house and get a cool drink."

"Fine by me," Amanda said as a fantasy of Antonio came to trespass on her thoughts once again.

CHAPTER TEN

THE AFTERNOON WORE ON, time passing so quickly Amanda was not even aware of its escape. Roger Crane was very interesting when he talked about citrus growing—he was not only experienced in the actual operation of the groves but had gone into in-depth studies of every phase of the subject, and she could not help but feel Antonio was very fortunate to have him as a manager.

The "office" proved to be a house—actually a low ranch-style house surrounded by the fragrant fruit trees. There were two typists busy at work in an outer office, and in Roger Crane's own office was a detailed relief map of the entire grove area, showing in miniature exactly what portion of the acreage was planted in oranges, lemons, grapefruit and citron, as well as in more experimental tropical fruit.

"We're lucky here at Hermosa to have a lot of land ideally suited for citrus production," Crane told her. "High hammock land is the best, and we've got a good share of it. Actually, in terms of altitude, 'high hammock' isn't all that high. Florida is flat country. The highest spot in the whole state is only about three hundred fifty feet above sea level, and that's over near Lakewood, in the center of the state.

"The kind of land gives an idea of the sort of soil drainage you can expect," the grove manager continued, "and in a place like Florida that's mighty important. Around here, on the lower west coast, there's a lot of soil that doesn't drain by itself—and that means the growers have got to put out a lot of cash for drainage or eventually they'll lose the trees.

"Another thing we have to fear is frost. There's a long period of time when we have to be on guard against killer frosts...all the way from the middle of November to the middle of March," he added, and then flashed her a rather rueful grin. "Hell, Amanda," he said simply, "I must be boring you to extinction."

"Anything but " she said. "It's fascinating, Roger."

"I think you're just an unusually good listener," he teased. Nevertheless he went on to explain many facets of citrus production to her, which she really did find interesting. For one thing, citrus stock was currently grown from seed, and there were seemingly infinite varieties of citrus and many types of oranges, in particular.

Roger also went into some rather technical details about the successful budding of oranges and confided that one of the best ways of determining whether a particular stretch of property would be a good site for an orange grove was to carefully observe the old groves nearby.

"In a good grove," he said, "you'll find the trees are pretty uniform in both height and spread." This led him to explain the importance of the proper way of spacing and planting the trees. The prime objective, he indicated, was not so much to get trees to bear fruit quickly as to let them develop to a good size so they'd have long productive lives.

"You just don't hurry in this business," he said. "You've got to have a lot of patience."

She had a feeling he was again referring to Antonio, and she had to admit Antonio did not give the impression of a man possessed of infinite patience. Yet this might be only an appearance. She did not know Antonio well enough herself to make a judgment in that respect—and certainly Roger Crane, didn't either.

Finally Roger glanced at his watch and said, "Hey! If we don't watch it, the cocktail hour will be past us! We'd better get along."

She followed him out to the Land Rover but paused before she climbed in. "You promised me I could pick an orange," she reminded him.

"Right, and you can," he said. "Matter of fact, I've got just the tree in mind for you. Come on."

He indicated the Land Rover, so she got in, and with the engine revving, they were off, dust whirling up around their wheels as they moved farther into the grove—to her surprise.

"Where are we going?" she asked, for she had thought they'd be returning to the hacienda.

"The house," Roger said over his shoulder. "My house, I guess I should say."

"I didn't realize you lived here on the property," she said.

He laughed. "I'm surrounded with oranges day and night," he told her.

A moment later they pulled up in front of another low, ranch-style house. Palms had been planted at the edge of the clearings on all sides, and the front of the house had been landscaped with a variety of shrubs, many of them having exotic and variegated leaves.

"You live here by yourself?" Amanda asked Roger as they both got out of the Land Rover.

He nodded. "Not bad for a bachelor, eh? I've never had time to do much with it, but it could be fixed up pretty nice. One of these years I might clear back a ways and build myself a swimming pool. It would be kind of nice to have one with a barbecue area off to one side. Right now I barbecue out on my back porch when I have people over. My specialty's barbecued ribs. One of these nights you're going to have to try them."

Before she could comment on this he said, "Okay, now you can pick your oranges. Come on over here." She followed him to a tree heavy with fruit. "These are pineapple oranges," he said, "and to my mind they're among the best we grow. They don't have a very long season—in fact, they're at their peak from about now until well into February—but they have a great flavor."

"Do they taste like pineapples?" she asked him.

"Not to me," he said. "There are a lot of reasons they were given that name, but I don't think anyone will ever prove out any of them. Evidently someone got the idea they had a pineapple taste, and then someone else said they smelled like pineapples. Actually, they are just very good oranges. Go ahead," he invited, waving his hand expansively. "Help yourself."

Amanda tugged and found herself holding a beautiful orange gold globe. Roger smiled and added, "Take more than one."

"All right," she said, picking another orange and then another. "There, three is enough."

"Isn't there some kind of musical piece about three oranges?" Roger asked her, still smiling.

"Yes," Amanda said. "Prokofiev, the *March for the Love of Three Oranges*. It used to be the theme of one of the TV programs—I think it was about the FBI."

"That's it." He nodded. "Well, then," he went on, "now that you've done your work for the day as a grove picker, I think you deserve a little liquid refreshment before I take you back to the hacienda. Okay?"

"Yes," she agreed, and followed him into his house.

A wide overhang helped to keep the interior shady, and so it was pleasantly cool inside. Roger, she saw, had brought a decided touch of his native California to his choice of decor. His large living room was furnished in a Western theme, with brightly colored Indian rugs, some excellent pieces of pottery and vivid woven hangings that looked dramatic against the stark white walls. She decided it was somewhere between Mexican and American Western in emphasis.

"Like it?" he asked as she settled onto a low couch.

"Very much," she said.

"Well," he told her, "like I said, it has potential. I'm no interior decorator."

"You have a good eye for color."

"I'm glad you think so. Look, would vodka and tonic suit you?"

"That would be fine," she said.

She placed the three oranges she had picked on the heavy wooden coffee table in front of the couch and gazed at them with satisfaction. Sniffing her fingers, she found they had the scent of the oranges on them, for the hot sun had brought the rind's bittersweet oil to the surface.

She felt sun-warmed herself, content and at peace, and the drink Roger brought her was exactly right—cold and tangy.

"This has been a very pleasant afternoon," she found herself telling him. "Thank you."

"It has been my pleasure," he told her. "And I'm not just saying that, Amanda. It's wonderful to have you here. I—"

He broke off as they both heard a car come to an audibly abrupt stop in front of the house.

Roger stood and glanced out the front window. "It's the station wagon Pablo usually uses," he said. "Must be a message from the front." Then he frowned. "What the hell?" he exploded.

The knock at the door was loud and forceful, and without another word to Amanda Roger strode across the room to answer the imperative summons. Then Antonio Hernandez seemed to fill the entrance, and it took only a glance toward him to make her well aware he was highly annoyed.

"Excuse the interruption," he said tightly. "I was looking for Amanda."

"Well," the grove manager said, his own voice equally taut, "You've found her."

"So I have," Antonio acknowledged. "Perhaps I should have telephoned instead of interrupting you. I was, however, concerned," he continued, now addressing her directly. "Pablo told me you have been gone since early afternoon."

Roger Crane stiffened. "I was showing her the groves," he said. "There is quite a bit to see."

"Many thousands of orange trees," Antonio agreed, his face inscrutable except for that tightening of his jaw—a telltale sign of tension she had come to recognize. "This was your day off, Crane?"

The grove manager flushed. "Not exactly, Mr. Hernandez," he said. "I haven't made it a habit to take days off—or vacations, either—on any kind of regular basis. I choose my free time when the workload permits it."

"And today the workload permitted it?"

"Yes, it did," Crane said evenly. "I had arranged my schedule to include conferences with you both yesterday and today, but it seems you were otherwise occupied."

"So I was." Antonio nodded. "And I suppose I should express my appreciation for your entertaining Amanda in my absence. If you have finished your drink, Amanda, I would suggest we leave now. Hortense will be prepared to serve us dinner very shortly."

She had not finished her drink, but she put it down on the coffee table and stood, picking up her three oranges as she did so.

"Thank you, Roger," she said, her voice low. "I found it a very interesting afternoon."

"Again, thank *you*, Amanda," he told her.

Antonio marched out to the station wagon ahead of her in stony silence and held the door for her while she got in. As he took his place behind the wheel, he glanced at the oranges in her lap and asked, "Why do you have those?"

"I wanted to pick an orange," she said, "and Roger suggested I pick these. Do you have any objections? If so, I'll turn them over to Hortense when we get to the hacienda."

"Don't be ridiculous!" he snapped as he turned the key in the ignition. Then he said, his tone softer, "You are angry at me, I see, for interrupting you as I did."

"Yes," she told him frankly, "I am. You had no right to descend like that—like some sort of avenging. . . ."

"Devil, rather than angel?" he suggested with a bitter smile. "Very well, I wanted you at the hacienda because there is news to tell you. Cristina and my Aunt Inez arrive tomorrow."

"What?" she demanded, thoroughly shocked by this.

"It is such a surprise?" he asked.

"Well," she said, "I didn't think they were expected for several more days at the least."

That quick, appraising, black glance swept over her. "And you are not pleased?" he challenged.

"It is not up to me to be either pleased or displeased," she said. "I suppose you could say I'm not as ready as I'd like to be. I'd hoped to have time in which to plan a program I can use with your niece."

"I do not think a formal method of instruction is

necessary," he told her shortly. "I thought I had already made that clear."

"One has to have some sort of a definite procedure in mind," she disagreed.

He frowned. "Surely you already have that," he told her. "You are, after all, professionally involved in the ESL program. I don't expect your work here to be a precise extension of it, but it would seem to me you must be fairly organized in your thinking on how to proceed with a new student."

That she was, of course. But, she thought dismally, she had never before faced having a new student like this one.

She sighed, and he said, "Ah, so many *suspiros*!"

"*Suspiros?*"

"Sighs," he explained. "I seem to provoke them in you." She sensed his hesitation, but then he went on to add, "Very well, I suppose I must say something about that, too. I told you in Boston—I would say it was a part of our agreement, in fact—that I would not get in your way once you settled into your work at the hacienda. This remains true, Amanda. I expect, though, that I will join you and my niece and my aunt for dinner—at least a good part of the time, yes. But aside from that I shall not inflict my presence on you. You will be quite free in your work with Cristina. I ask only that you remember she is young and naive. It is hoped she will be looking to you for guidance, as well as to learn a language I do not think she especially wishes to learn."

She sat bolt upright. "Well!" she exclaimed. "This is a fine time to be telling me that!"

"I think no secret has been made of the fact Cristina did not wish to come to Florida,'' he reminded her. ''She will be here at my insistence, and I don't suppose she can be blamed if she resents that.''

''And if she resents me?''

It was his turn to sigh. Then he said softly, ''I do not think she will resent you, Amanda. But we shall see.''

CHAPTER ELEVEN

DINNER THAT NIGHT was a trying experience. Antonio retreated into an aloofness Amanda couldn't penetrate, though admittedly she didn't try very hard to do so. Increasingly she felt he had placed her at a definite disadvantage. She was going to have to overcome all sorts of obstacles in dealing with Cristina—that much seemed obvious. On top of that she had to face living here knowing he was only a stone's throw away from her. Yet he might as well have been on another planet.

As they got up from the table, she was further discomfited when he asked, "Will you play something on the piano for me?"

"I'd rather not," she replied bluntly.

"Oh?" There was frost in his voice as that expressive eyebrow rose. "Pablo and Hortense both told me you played last night and you play very well. Is it so impossible for you to share this sort of pleasure with me, Amanda?"

"Very well," she said, but she was miserably self-conscious as she led the way into the library. He was following so close behind her she was afraid that if she paused for an instant, he'd bump into her, and she knew she simply could not bear that sort of contact right now.

What had happened since yesterday? Certainly the quick flaring response between them had been mutual in its intensity. Yet he had thrust her away from him to answer the summons of another woman.... She'd *never* forget the name Edmond, she told herself!

It was true, of course, that Antonio had told her in Boston they would have little contact with each other in Florida. He had intended to take a rest cure of sorts, and he had made it plain her time would be more than occupied by his niece.

But there had been a change between them—not at all a subtle change—beginning with a surprising rapport on the plane flight down. And since....

Thinking about this, she stood by the piano and stared absently at the ivory keys. His voice brought her up short.

"If it is such a tragedy for you to play some simple song for me, then perhaps I had better excuse you," he said.

"No," she said quickly. "I was... merely remembering something, that's all." Before he could comment on this she drew out the piano bench and in a moment was fingering a Chopin nocturne.

As she played she could sense his surprise, and it was a miracle, she decided as she played the last arpeggio, that she had not fumbled and missed notes. Antonio was leaning against the piano with a negligent grace that managed to emphasize every masculine line of his body, and this sort of proximity was unnerving.

She paused, wondering if he might indicate he'd had enough, but instead he said, "Again you have underestimated yourself, Amanda. You play extremely well. You have studied a great deal?"

"Yes," she admitted, "but it was years ago. As a teenager I had visions of grandeur for a time."

"The concert stage?"

"Yes."

"But you did not persist?"

"No. My life was involved a great deal in those years with my father's. When he took trips, for instance, I traveled with him, and we used to go off for long periods each summer to places in which there wasn't any chance for me to practice."

"You traveled widely with your father?" he asked. "Europe, perhaps?"

"No," she said. "We covered the United States and a fair bit of Canada. We had plans to go to England, but we never made it."

"A purely Anglo-Saxon itinerary, yes?" Antonio observed dryly. Then he added, "Play something else, will you?"

She was thinking, as her fingers found the keys again, that he was not Anglo-Saxon at all. He was so essentially Latin, so Spanish....

She found herself drifting into the lilting strains of "Spanish Eyes." It seemed to her it possessed a tempo geared to Antonio. There was a cadence about it reminding her of the grace that was such an inherent part of him, but there was nothing remotely effeminate about it. No, he was as basically masculine as anyone possibly could be, with a heart-tugging attraction....

She felt her eyes sting, and an immeasurable longing for him surged through her. Inwardly she cringed, because this driving emotion, which inevitably came to possess her when he was near, had an intensity she actually feared. She was not at all certain she could go on controlling it if they were to be alone together very often, especially in moments that could become as surcharged as this one was becoming—for her, at least. And it would be unbearably humiliating to reveal her feelings to him, to let him know how helpless she was before these onslaughts of sheer desire. He could spurn her so easily if he chose to do so!

Her fingers trailed into the final chords, and he said, "*Muy bonita*. What is the name of that piece, Amanda?"

" 'Spanish Eyes,' " she said, and was totally unprepared for his reaction.

He had rested his hand on the edge of the piano, and now she saw it clench. Then he said in a curiously muffled voice, " 'Spanish Eyes,' is it?" She realized with dismay that he had accented the plural, and his own single dark eye blazed down at her.

"Even in that I am inadequate, am I not, Amanda?" he demanded.

And before she could answer him, he turned on his heel and strode out of the room.

SLEEP WAS A STRANGER that night, even though Amanda told herself she was totally innocent as far as this latest contretemps between Antonio and her was concerned. He was being ridiculously defensive, and certainly he was entirely too sensitive about his affliction. This surprised her, because he always seemed so extremely sure of himself, even to the extent of arrogance on occasion, as she had good reason to know.

But she also knew there was no point in trying to say anything to him about the incident in the library. Certainly he must realize she had not deliberately chosen to play a piece whose title would provoke him. Now it occurred to her that the very fact he'd taken it as a kind of personal slur showed he must be as on edge as she was.

This was puzzling. Antonio had no reason to be edgy—none that she could fathom, anyhow. Even if her forthcoming meeting with Cristina proved to be a fiasco, she could see nothing that should put *him* on the defensive. The burden of failure, she thought dismally, would be entirely hers.

It was very late when she finally fell into an uneasy slumber, and as a result of this she overslept. She was further dismayed to find, when she awakened, that it was nearly ten, and she wondered why Hortense hadn't buzzed her on the intercom to summon her to breakfast.

She showered and then dressed quickly in yellow slacks with a matching top. She had already verified from her balcony that there was no one in the patio-courtyard, and so she ran down the stairs, going first to the dining room—which she found empty, also—and then on to the kitchen.

Hortense was sitting at a big round table thumbing through a magazine, and she looked up with an expansive smile. "Well," she said, "so our sleeping beauty has come to life again."

"Why didn't you wake me?" Amanda demanded.

"Mr. Hernandez said to let you sleep," Hortense told her succinctly. "He said you looked kind of worn out last night and you needed some rest. Seems to me," she added, peering at Amanda closely, "you didn't get enough of it, at that."

"I'm fine," Amanda said hastily.

"Then let's make you finer by putting some good food in you," Hortense said, getting to her feet. "I've got sweet rolls, and I'll scramble up some eggs for you in a minute."

Although she'd not thought she had any appetite at all, Amanda did full justice to the breakfast, then wondered what to do with herself next.

"Why don't you go down by the pool and get some sun?" Hortense suggested, as if she, too, were a mind reader. "It's still a mite cool for swimming, but there's plenty of good to be had from those old rays."

"I think I will," Amanda decided, and went back upstairs to get her book, her sunglasses and some tanning lotion, as well. She also changed into a pair of yellow shorts that matched the top she was already wearing, and then she made her way through the patio and down the terraces and found a comfortable chaise longue to recline on at the edge of the pool.

As she anointed herself with the tanning lotion, she tried to tell herself how very lucky she was. In Boston people were sloshing through snow and ice just now. It was probably bitter cold, and she imagined that at least half the population of Massachusetts would give a great deal to be where she was right at that moment.

This pep talk to herself was not a great success, though. At least in Boston she would have her work at the institute to occupy her and keep her mind off things. Wryly she substituted "Antonio" for "things."

She forced herself to concentrate on her book, but the warm sun soon made her sleepy, and she drowsed. Suddenly she was awakened by an accented voice saying sternly, "That is a good way to get a severe burn! What are you thinking of, Amanda?"

She glanced up, to meet Antonio's frown, and that was all she could read of his expression. He had not removed the black patch, but he was wearing oversize, very dark glasses that covered it.

"Come get into some shade," he ordered now. "The opposite side of the pool is better at this hour."

This was true enough. There were beautiful old live oaks on the lawn beyond the pool, and their shade extended, in late morning, along the far rim of the pool and the apron beyond it. So, like a child who has been chastised, she followed Antonio around the edge of the sparkling aquamarine water and subsided into another chaise longue.

He pulled up a similar chair beside her and stretched out in it, his long legs extended. He was wearing snug beige chinos and a short-sleeved yellow shirt that almost matched her own, and he was beginning to tan. . . he had that kind of skin, she conceded. The effect made him seem more handsome than ever, but the dark glasses only heightened that aura of inscrutability, and somehow this gave her the dismal conviction that she would never ever really come to know Antonio. Antonio, she decided, did not want *anyone* to know him!

Now, to her astonishment, he chuckled. "You look as if you would like to bite someone," he teased her. "Me, perhaps?"

"No," she said shortly. "I'd get indigestion."

To her further surprise, he smiled at this. "So I would be a bitter dose, yes?" he suggested. "Ah, *linda*, I...."

He broke off, the smile gone now, and she surveyed him for a long moment before asking, "What is it?"

"I apologize," he said slowly, "for the way I behaved last night. I do not know what came over me."

"Well," she said bluntly, "you should stop to think before you become so—indignant. Why you should imagine that I...." It was her turn to break off.

"That you would deliberately prod me about this?" he asked gently, touching the dark lens covering the patch over his left eye. "I didn't. That is, I know you would not do such a thing. You may have a quick tongue, *linda*, but you are basically a kind person. No, it is I who was prodding myself."

He lifted the dark glasses briefly before replacing them. Then, in a quick change of subject, he said, "You look to me as if you have a slight burn. This sun is intense, Amanda. You must take more care with the kind of skin you have."

"Yes, I suppose I must," she conceded. "You're lucky."

"Me?"

"Yes," she said. "You've started to tan already."

He nodded. "True, I have more resistance to the sun than you do, but I do not become all that dark. I have no *moro*—Moor—blood in me."

"Only pure, pure Spanish?" she ventured to ask.

"Yes, only pure, pure Spanish," he countered. "But then you are pure Anglo-Saxon, are you not?"

"I suppose I am."

He did not answer this but gazed reflectively toward the water and observed, "One could almost swim today."

"Yes," she agreed, but she was conscious of the fact that anytime they got onto a subject that might lead into discussion of any depth, Antonio was quick to change it.

Now she did a little subject changing of her own. "Are you going to Tampa to meet your aunt and your niece today?" she asked.

His mind, she saw at once, was on other things, but after a moment, he said, "No. Perhaps I did not mention it, but Gregory Blake is to meet them in New York and he will be flying down with them. Pablo is driving to Tampa to get them—he will leave directly after lunch. Their flight gets in late in the afternoon, so we will have dinner tonight more in accordance with the dining hour in Spain."

"And what is the dining hour in Spain?" she asked him.

"Anywhere from nine in the evening until midnight," he said. "We have, traditionally, a small breakfast, then a large *comida* in the middle of the day, and then another meal late in the evening. After the middle of the day dinner there is, of course, the siesta time...."

"I can see why, if the climate's like this," she said. "Especially after a large dinner. One becomes possessed of total inertia after just an average lunch. At least I do."

He laughed. "There is always the matter of getting acclimatized anywhere," he told her, "and like most

Americans you seem to try to rush it. That is not the way to live life, *niña*. You should learn to relax. In fact, I would say this time in Florida would be an ideal one for you in that respect. You can learn to vary your tempo, and this can only do you good for the rest of your life.''

She did not answer this. No need to tell him it was unlikely she'd ever be able to relax as long as he was anywhere in the vicinity!

After a time they strolled back to the hacienda, but once inside the patio Antonio told her he was going to continue on to the office and would probably have a sandwich lunch there with Roger Crane.

''So,'' he said in parting, ''get a siesta, *linda*. You are certain to be up late tonight.''

AMANDA DID TAKE A SIESTA. Then, late in the afternoon, Hortense brought a tray to her room with a cool fruit drink and some cheese and crackers.

''You can't be expected to keep going till all hours without anything in your stomach,'' Hortense said bluntly. ''Mr. Hernandez thought it would be a good idea for you to have this, and he wants you to come and join him for a drink in an hour or so. If that was convenient for you, he said.''

Solicitude, on Antonio's part, had come to have the effect of arousing her suspicions, and Amanda pondered about this latest invitation. His attitude tended to be like a pendulum. If it swung too far to one side, it inevitably took a similar course to the other, and today she just wasn't up to facing such mood variations. It was enough to know that the confrontation with Cristina was literally at hand.

Still, she conceded she could use a drink before this took place, and so she told Hortense to convey the message that she would be downstairs by six o'clock.

She looked over her wardrobe with a discouraged eye. One of these days she would have to manage to get into Sarasota for some shopping. That, she thought, would be the nearest place with any good stores—this conclusion having come from scanning a map of Florida she had found in the library. Bradenton was another choice, and for that matter Tampa was not that far away. She wondered how Antonio would feel about it if she asked him if she could accompany him on his next foray to Tampa but decided that if she had any sort of wisdom at all, this was a suggestion she wouldn't make. On the other hand, she wasn't sure how he would react if she asked Roger Crane to take her along the next time he went some place she might find a few dress shops.

For that matter, she'd be more than happy to drive herself. She had already ascertained that there were several cars and station wagons belonging to Hermosa Groves. She hesitated, though, to ask Antonio for the loan of one of them. There was a chance he might refuse—if only out of perversity—and she knew in advance this would only infuriate her. It was something she didn't want to risk just now...not with the major part of this three-month experiment still ahead of her.

Pablo would probably be pressed into service were she to ask for a car, and although she liked Pablo, communication was still much too difficult. Under other circumstances she might have suggested to Antonio that he give her some basic Spanish lessons.

This would have made sense—and would still make sense—because it wasn't just Pablo she was going to have to try to communicate with. There would be Cristina and the elderly aunt, as well.

She sighed and forced her attention back to her wardrobe. Again she was disappointed by its contents. Finally she opted to wear the white sheath, this time encircling her waist with a narrow burnt-orange sash whose color was picked up by some lovely old gold-and-amber earrings. She slipped on her gold kid slippers, then wondered what to do about her hair. It was a temptation to let it hang down in a golden fluff. Yet she felt she should look reasonably dignified for this first encounter with Cristina, and so she worked it into a rather intricate chignon that was most attractive but did make her look a bit older. At least she hoped so, she thought to herself.

Antonio was waiting for her in the drawing room. He was dressed more formally than he had been since they'd arrived in Florida, wearing snug black slacks and a beautifully tailored jacket—this in a nubby material in a tone of off-white. His shirt was white, and his tie narrow and black. On him this proved to be a devastating combination, and Amanda felt that if she looked at him very long, she might well have need of a pacemaker.

He greeted her by saying, "You have fixed your hair differently."

"Yes," she said demurely.

"It is lovely, but I prefer it better when you do not put it up," he told her, illustrating this statement by moving his fingers in eloquent and appropriate gestures. "What will you have to drink, *linda*?"

"Gin and tonic, please."

"*Bueno,*" he said, and turned to the small bar that had been set up in the corner.

He made drinks for both of them, and touching his glass to hers, he said, "*¡Salud!*" Then his lips curved in a mocking smile and he added, "Do not look so stricken, little one. You appear as if you are about to confront a dragon. Cristina is no dragon, for God's sake, if that is what you are worrying about."

"And your aunt?" she could not refrain from asking.

"Old and tired," he said. "She will wish only to rest in the Florida shade. She has had her days in the sun."

"She must have enough vitality to manage your niece," Amanda pointed out.

Antonio shrugged. "She plays the role of a *dueña*, yes," he said. "Now do you prefer to stay in here, or would you like to go out onto the patio? On second thought, perhaps we should stay in here. Your dress has no sleeves, and it will be cool there for you with the sun gone."

Amanda at once became conscious of her bare arms and was annoyed with herself. There was no reason to let every single word he said affect her like this! Still, both her self-consciousness and her restlessness increased as the minutes ticked by, and she was actually relieved to finally hear the great front door swing open and footsteps crossing the foyer.

It was Pablo who appeared first. He was grinning from ear to ear as he said something in swift Spanish that, Amanda realized, must have imparted to Antonio the fact that all had gone well at the airport and the others were there.

A second later a slim, dark-haired girl flung herself across the room and into Antonio's arms, and Amanda heard her exclaim, *"¡Tío! ¿Cómo estás?"*

She had not expected such exuberance on the part of Antonio's niece—not toward him, certainly, when it was he who was taking her away from both her country and her sweetheart. She tried not to stare and in any event could only get a glimpse of long and shimmering black hair, a dress in a shade of olive green and slim feet encased in very high-heeled black sandals.

Then Gregory Blake was crossing the room, both hands outstretched, and it was she he was approaching.

"Amanda," he said, and at least there was no mistaking the genuine note of warmth in his voice. "How great to see you again!"

At this the young girl turned slowly, and Amanda felt herself the target of two coal-black eyes. They seemed to sear her as they swept over her in assessment, obviously reaching the conclusion that there was nothing very much of importance there, for Antonio's niece now turned back to her uncle, laughing as she gazed up into his face and said something to him that brought a smile to his lips.

He had been hugging her even as she was hugging him, but now he disengaged his arms and took her by the hand. "Come," he said this in English, and led her toward Amanda. "Mrs. Hughes," he began formally, "my niece, Cristina Hernandez y Castillo."

Cristina Hernandez nodded and said stiffly, *"Tanto gusto,"* all trace of merriment gone from her face. It was not a classically beautiful Spanish face,

Amanda saw. Cristina's features were a bit too irregular to achieve perfection. Yet she was a very pretty girl. Pretty, young and. . . hostile.

Now Antonio looked over his shoulder, and Amanda turned to see a woman of medium height, whose excellent posture made her look taller, slowly coming toward them. She was dressed in black, and Amanda would not have been surprised to see a lace mantilla draped over her beautifully coiffed white hair, but her head was bare.

Antonio moved forward to kiss her gently on each cheek, exclaiming, *"¡Tía!"* as he did so. This time he beckoned Amanda forward, and she followed his bidding, hating it because she could feel her cheeks growing hot. She was afraid the older woman's keenly observant eyes would almost surely notice this surge of color.

"¡Tía! Inez," Antonio said now, *"Tengo mucho gusto en presentarle a la Señora Hughes.* Amanda, my aunt, Señora Inez Diaz de Hernandez."

Amanda felt as if she should curtsy but restrained the impulse. Then, to her surprise, Antonio's aunt reached out a thin, delicately veined hand and said in halting English, "I am pleased, señora."

This small attempt to speak her language touched Amanda—touched her, in fact, to the point where she actually felt tears sting her eyes. She didn't know what to say in return, and it was an awkward moment—quickly bridged by Antonio, who asked in English, "Where is Pablo?"

"I think he must have gone out to the kitchen," Amanda said, but at that moment Pablo reappeared in the doorway, and a quick interchange in Spanish followed. A moment later Cristina and her aunt left the room, following Pablo, and Amanda realized he was evidently going to show them to their own quarters.

Gregory Blake, however, lingered behind, and without being asked, Antonio made a drink for him and also replenished both Amanda's glass and his own.

"They will be gone for at least half an hour," Antonio said then. "We might as well sit down and be comfortable. I believe Hortense has put you in the same room you had the previous time you were here, Greg. You remember the way?"

"Yes." The lawyer nodded. "But it's not going to take me thirty minutes to get ready for dinner, so I'll have this first." He indicated his drink.

His smile touched Amanda again, but his question was addressed to Antonio. "How goes it, Tony?" he asked.

Antonio shrugged. "In what way?" he countered.

"Well," Greg Blake began, "I wondered how far you'd progressed—"

"Let us not discuss business," Antonio interrupted, and Amanda was left to wonder what it was he was trying to "progress" with.

"Okay," the lawyer said easily. "I'd say you both look a lot healthier than you did when you left Boston. Remarkable what just a few days away from winter can do."

"I don't know about that," Amanda found herself interjecting. "I think the northern climate is more stimulating. At least to me it is."

She said this with a certain defiance, and she didn't

dare look at Antonio as she spoke. She was speaking generally, she reminded herself, and if, damn it, he chose to take the remark personally, then that was his business!

Greg laughed and said, "Well, my own regret insofar as your not being in New England this winter is that we will have to postpone our skiing date at your brother's place for another year. Maybe—about next February—we could all get together up there. Tony could give both of us some pointers."

Antonio said shortly, "My skiing days are over," and to her surprise he went and poured himself another drink. A stiff one, too, she saw. "In any event," he added, returning to his chair, "I have no idea where I may be a year from now."

"Do any of us?" Greg asked pleasantly. "After just a cursory look at this place, I wouldn't blame you if you decided to settle here in Florida and leave the running of the family businesses in Spain and Majorca to your cousins. From what you've told me I'd say they could handle them. You could keep your fingers on the guidelines, of course, and maybe make a trip back once a year or so."

"Stop planning my future for me, Gregory," Antonio advised, and there was no hint of amusement in his tone. "You seem to forget that yours is a foreign country to me. I cannot see myself adapting to American life permanently."

Something thudded inside Amanda when he said this, even though she cautioned herself that she, too, should refrain from taking remarks personally. This worked both ways, after all. Nevertheless he certainly wasn't attempting to hide the impression he didn't especially like either America or Americans. Yet Gregory Blake was, by his own admission, one of his closest friends, as well as being a lawyer he trusted implicitly.

She thought Greg might be a bit affronted by this statement of Antonio's, but he only laughed, a pleasant easy laugh, and said, "What's turned you so sour tonight, Tony?" Then his smile faded, and there was genuine concern in his voice as he asked, "Not another of those headaches, is it?"

"No," Antonio said explosively. "I do not have a headache! *Por Dios* . . . ."

"Sorry," Blake said levelly. "Maybe I'd better confine myself to a conversation with Amanda. Has Tony shown you around the property yet?"

It was an unfortunate question, but before she could answer it Antonio said in a clipped tone that only made his accent seem all the more pronounced, "My manager undertook to show her the groves himself."

"Just a quick tour, really," Amanda put in hastily. "I find the trees so absolutely beautiful, and all that bright glorious fruit seems unreal." She sensed tension mounting, so she babbled on. "Mr. Crane was very kind, too," she said. "He gave me a veritable minicourse in citrus. There is quite a romance to it. . . ."

"A *romance*?" Antonio said, pouncing on the word.

"Yes. The history. Going back to the Orient, to Egypt . . . Columbus bringing the first oranges to the New World, then the Spaniards. . . ."

Amanda talked on, detailing the highlights of

some of the things Roger Crane had told her, but all the while she was aware that Antonio's face looked as if it had been carved out of stone. Gregory, on the other hand, was listening to her a bit more raptly than her discourse really called for. When finally Cristina and Antonio's aunt came back to join them, she felt reprieved.

Hortense had prepared a delicious chicken-and-rice dish as a main course, and Señora Hernandez complimented her on it, doing so via Antonio, who translated rather stiffly. Hortense smiled, and Amanda knew the recipe was probably one she had learned from her Cuban in-laws and had chosen deliberately because it would have a kinship with Spanish cuisine. Thus it would have the effect of making Antonio's aunt feel at home here from the very beginning. Hortense was a smart woman, Amanda thought ruefully, and she wished that in some ways she could emulate her!

Dinner over, they moved back into the drawing room for coffee, but the conversation was entirely in Spanish, as it had been for the most part during the meal itself. Both Amanda and Gregory had been apologized to by Antonio for this, but the apology didn't preclude her feeling like a total outsider. As she sipped her coffee, Amanda felt that Greg Blake must share the feeling.

Somehow Greg had wound up sitting near Cristina, while Amanda was sitting at quite a distance from him but near Aunt Inez. Finally she could dally over the coffee no longer, and addressing Antonio, she said, "If you'll excuse me, I'm quite tired."

He rose instantly and answered, "Of course,

Amanda,'' with an edge of formality to his voice she found rather icy.

She tried to be equally formal. "Will you please tell your aunt and your niece I have enjoyed meeting them and I regret very much that I cannot speak their language. Tell them, please, that in the days to come I shall do all I can toward bettering the communication between us," she said.

It seemed to her his expression softened as he translated her message and then bade her goodnight—although, she reminded herself, such a softening might be only wishful thinking on her part. With Antonio, one was never sure.

CHAPTER TWELVE

THE KNOCK WAS GENTLE, a soft rap, and at first Amanda thought it might merely be the wind rattling something, for there was a steady breeze coming in her bedroom window.

Then it sounded again, so she slipped out of bed, put on the filmy blue dressing gown that was hanging over a chair nearby and padded across the room to the door.

To her astonishment Cristina was on the threshold, and before Amanda could speak, the young girl put a finger to her lips. Her eyes were huge dark pools, mutely imploring.

"Please," she whispered.

"Come in," Amanda whispered back, and quickly closed the door behind her. Cristina, too, was barefoot, and she was wearing a lovely quilted satin robe in a cream tone that enhanced her dark coloring and made her look very pretty.

She's lovely, Amanda found herself thinking. *Very close to real beauty. She has the type of looks that will become even more striking as she grows older. I underestimated her last night.*

She sat down on the edge of her bed and motioned Cristina to the small velvet boudoir chair nearby that was upholstered in a soft shade of rose. But Cristina shook her head and, to Amanda's surprise, said in a heavily accented yet understandable English, "If you do not mind, for a minute I will stand."

Amanda nodded, completely baffled, and Cristina sighed. "Yes, it is not difficult to imagine what you must think," she confessed. "I admit my deception, Senora Hughes. I am a—what would you call it—a fraud."

Now the girl did sit down, and tears filled those huge dark eyes. "I put myself on your mercy," she said. "*Tío* would be furious...."

"Perhaps," Amanda conceded. "But we can hardly hope to conceal from him the fact that you already have quite a good command of my language, can we?"

We. The word struck her ears even as she said it. Last night she had thought that Cristina was entirely hostile toward her. Now she was beginning to realize that actually Antonio's niece had been frightened. That, perhaps, was one reason she had been so extravagant in her display of emotion toward her uncle, why she had laughed at dinner more than she should have and why she had avoided any attempts at an interchange with Amanda.

"As I say," Cristina told her, "Tío Tony would be furious. And he is able to become quite angry."

"Yes," Amanda said dryly. "I can imagine."

"He has brought me here with the wish to get me away from my *novio*—I think you must know that?"

"He indicated you'd been involved in a romance of which he doesn't entirely approve," Amanda said carefully.

"*¡Gracias a Dios!* You speak very clearly. And if

you will be a bit more slow, I think I will have little difficulty in understanding you,'' Cristina said. ''But. . . to do with my romance—my uncle does not even know Felipe. It is one of these stupid things between families. For a long time Felipe's family and mine do not get on well. The Córdobas own one pearl business, the Hernandezes another. Bad feeling comes, maybe, between Felipe's grandfather and my grandfather over—well, who knows what over? So many years have since passed. But when Tío Tony hears it is a Córdoba I am interested in, at once he says, 'no!' ''

Wryly now Amanda remembered telling Gregory Blake that in her opinion Antonio Hernandez y Vega had a feudal mentality. . . and Gregory had actually repeated this remark to Antonio, causing repercussions. Yes, definitely there had been repercussions.

Yet certainly the sort of attitude on her uncle's part that Cristina was describing was feudal. What else could it be called?

''Has your uncle ever met Felipe?'' she asked now.

''Perhaps once or twice socially.'' Cristina shrugged. ''But as I say, he does not know him. . . he does not know him at all. Further, he thinks Felipe is even now studying at the university in Madrid. But this is not the case. Felipe's mother is English, you see, so he speaks your language excellently. Also, he is high in his studies. He has been able to make a transfer here to the Columbia University in New York.''

''You're telling me he's going to be at Columbia?'' The plot, Amanda thought, was getting thicker and thicker.

Cristina nodded so emphatically her black hair seemed to swirl about her head. "Even now," she said. "That is why, you see, he has taught me."

"English?"

"*Sí*. We have had lessons and lessons for months and months. We write in English. We speak on the phone in English. When I arrange meetings with him, it is all English, English, English," Cristina said. "This has been an—what is the word—an obsession with Felipe. Because, you see, I am to meet him."

Amanda sat bolt upright. "In New York?"

"*Sí.*"

Amanda got to her feet without even realizing it and found herself glancing apprehensively over her shoulder. God, if Antonio should walk in on them now! Or if he should be lurking in the courtyard beneath her window at this moment and their voices carried enough so they could be overheard....

She muttered, "Excuse me," and actually went out onto her balcony, anxiously surveying the patio beneath her to be sure. But it was empty—which was to be expected. It was, after all, not quite seven o'clock in the morning.

Returning to the room, she sat down on the edge of the bed again and then came right to the point. "Cristina," she said, "you can't do this! I'm aware you don't know me very well, but even so I'm going to ask you to think of me, if not of yourself. If you were to go and join Felipe in New York, your uncle would have my head!"

"What?" Cristina said. "Señora Hughes, you do not possibly mean that. Tío Tony has a hot temper, yes, but such violence...."

"I don't mean it literally," Amanda amended. "It is a...well, I suppose you would call it a figure of speech. I am not saying he would really cut off my head, but the effect would be almost as bad. Do you understand what I mean?"

"Yes." Cristina nodded. "I do see."

"Then let's think about this," Amanda urged. "You will be in a great deal of trouble yourself if you go off to New York, and I have the feeling I might as well go and jump in the Gulf of Mexico. No," she added hastily as Cristina began to speak, "I don't mean that literally, either."

"I will never understand these figures of speech," Cristina remarked dolefully.

"I think you understand them well enough," Amanda told her. "Now suppose we both sit back and think this situation over. To begin with, you should know my position in this...."

"I do know," Cristina said. "You have been employed by my uncle to teach me English and to—" she smiled, and it was an enchanting smile "—to be a kind of young *dueña*, would you not say?"

"I didn't mean that sort of position," Amanda said. "That is to say, the word has more than one meaning. I'm sure you must encounter the same thing in Spanish. In the sense that I am using *position*, what I mean is where I stand in this whole situation."

"I see," Cristina acknowledged gravely.

"In Boston," Amanda said very slowly, very clearly, "your uncle made an arrangement with me to come to Florida on a trial basis for three months. What I mean is that we agreed I would come here for three months and work with you, and we would see how it went—how we progressed, that is. At the end of three months we would evaluate. Then, if he was happy with my services and I was happy in his employ, I agreed that I would stay for an additional nine months. That, of course, would make one entire year.''

Cristina paled. "A *year*?" she echoed.

Amanda nodded. "It seemed a very long time to me, too," she confessed. "For that reason, when your uncle wanted me to commit myself to the entire year, I would not agree to do so. We settled upon— decided upon—this three-month trial period. I think, though, he would be very difficult about it if I tried to leave any sooner, or else I would go right now, Cristina. . . .''

"*¡Por Dios, no!*" Cristina protested. "You cannot simply abandon me here!"

"I don't intend to 'abandon' you," Amanda said, touched by this. "I was only thinking that if I were to leave, it might make things easier for you."

"But, no!" Cristina said quickly. "My uncle would be certain to think I had done something to send you away."

"Perhaps not," Amanda replied. "Your uncle and I do not always. . . get along. It would be easy enough to convince him it was he—not you—who was sending me away."

"But you must not go away!" Cristina said imploringly. "I do not understand every word you say to me, señora, but your meaning I do get. Also, I feel you are very *simpática*. I am lucky it is you who are here. Last night I thought, *ah, she is no doubt going* to be very strict and...difficult. I thought this, even though you looked so beautiful. You did not in the least look strict and difficult, but I know Tío Tony. He would not have employed you unless you were in your work perfect.''

''I am definitely not perfect, Cristina—in my work or in any other way—and I think your uncle already has come to realize this.''

''No matter. He must be satisfied, or he would have dismissed you,'' Cristina said. ''Only now....'' The dark eyes became doleful. ''What are we to do, Señora Hughes?'' Cristina asked helplessly.

''For a starter,'' Amanda suggested, ''don't you think it might be an idea for you to call me 'Amanda'? I'm definitely older than you are, but I'm not quite the traditional age for a *dueña*. At least I don't think so.''

''You certainly are not, Amanda,'' Cristina said with a smile, pronouncing her name almost exactly as Antonio did—which caused Amanda's heart to feel as if it were about to flop over.

''Cristina,'' she began, deliberately thrusting such feelings aside, ''we must think carefully, and in my opinion there is only one thing to do as a beginning.''

''Yes.''

''We must make a pact with each other...a solemn promise...to see this through for the three-month period. Already some of that time has slipped by. It will be up around the middle of April, and even before you came here I decided, for reasons entirely of my own, that I shall conclude the agreement at that time. So there is no thought of your having to stay here a year to study English with me.''

"I see," Cristina said pensively.

"Further, I would advise you to be very discreet in contacting Felipe. I can't expect you *not* to contact him—just be careful, that's all. I expect phone calls would be your best way of communicating, though I can't imagine your uncle actually stooping to opening your mail...."

"He would expect Tía Inez to open it," Cristina said dully.

A feudal mentality, indeed! Amanda bristled, but she only said, "Well, then, it might be wiser for you not to risk letters. And I imagine you'll have to make most of your phone calls yourself. Outgoing ones, that is."

"Yes. Felipe and I realize that."

"You must promise me," Amanda continued firmly, "that you will not run off and meet him in New York during these next few weeks. I can't govern what you do once I've left here in April, but in the meantime...."

"In the meantime, Amanda, I shall make you that promise," Cristina conceded.

Amanda suppressed a sigh of intense relief. She had no wish to confront Antonio, were his niece to take off with the intention of joining her *novio* in Manhattan. No wish at all. Even though, she thought stubbornly, he'd have only himself to blame for it!

She said now, "About your English, Cristina?"

"Yes?"

"We can't possibly hope to hide your familiarity with the language from your uncle. Surely you can see that? Did you ever study English at all in the convent school?"

"Two years," Cristina said ruefully, holding up two fingers as she said this. "Mostly I learned to read a little. I learned how to say 'good evening' and 'thank you' and 'how are you' and 'where is the post office.' But Felipe used to laugh at my pronunciation."

"What about your uncle? Did he know you were taking English in school?"

Cristina's face sobered. "No," she said. "He was in the hospital for much of that time. He would be in the hospital, that is, and then they would let him come home for a time, but then he would have to go back to the doctors again. You see, he was very seriously injured in the accident in which my parents were killed. My parents and his fiancée."

Cristina's voice was very low as she related this, and Amanda, hating to arouse painful memories, would not normally have prodded. But this last statement jolted her, and the exclamation came from her lips involuntarily, "His *fiancée*?"

"*Sí*," Cristina said, looking up, her dark eyes seeming now like deep fathomless wells. "Elena Velasquez. She was a *madrilena*—from Madrid,—a very beautiful woman, very social...you know. They were to have been married within the month."

"I see," Amanda said, her throat gone dry.

"So it was a tragedy in many ways for my uncle," Cristina continued. "Before—even to me, young as I was—he seemed so young himself, so full of fun, so handsome. Since, he is...."

Cristina shrugged helplessly. "I do not know all the words in English to express this," she confessed. "My heart tears for him sometimes, though. What is so horrible, you see, is that he blames himself. But it was not his fault. There was a very big investigation...the car was...." Cristina made an expressive gesture that conveyed more eloquently than words could have how the car had been totaled. "But," she went on, "there was enough for examination. They found the brakes were defective. The chauffeur the family had at that time had been pocketing money that was supposed to be spent for the mechanical improvements. You understand me?"

"Yes."

"There was a sudden storm. The hail, I think you say. Such types of storms in Majorca can come with not much warning. Tío Tony could not keep the road. You know?"

"Yes. Cristina, please. This must be very difficult for you."

"I do not mind to talk to you about it," Cristina said, her piquant face solemn. "I think if you are to be with Tío Tony, you should know why he seems as he does now. He is partly blind, *pobrecito*—he has to wear that ugly black thing over his eye. Even worse are the pains that come to his head—there are times when he suffers a great deal. You see," she added slowly, "even though Tío Tony tries to spoil my romance with Felipe, I still love him very much. You can appreciate that?"

"Yes," Amanda said. "Yes, Cristina, I can appreciate it."

And so she could, she thought wryly, once Cristina had left her to return to her own room. She could especially "appreciate" it, because she loved Antonio Hernandez y Vega so desperately herself!

As she dressed, that statement of Cristina's about the fiancée kept intruding on her thoughts. Why, she asked herself, had it come as such a shock? A man like Antonio surely had never been designed to be a bachelor. She should have known there must have been at least one very important woman in his life to date and God knows how many with whom the relationship had been entirely physical. Now, perhaps, there was someone else coming on the scene to take the place of the beautiful Spanish fiancée who had died so tragically. Florence Edmond. Who was she? Did Gregory Blake know, she wondered? Amanda was sorely tempted to ask him, and yet was aware she couldn't possibly do this without danger that word of her curiosity would get back to Antonio, if only because Gregory might imagine his client-friend would be amused by it.

Once she had finished dressing, her room, spacious though it was, seemed confining to her, and so she wandered downstairs and out onto the patio—almost at once to be confronted by the person who was uppermost in her thoughts.

Antonio was wearing white cotton slacks this morning and a vivid blue shirt that emphasized his new tan. He came toward her along the opposite side of the patio, probably, she surmised, from his own room.

"So you are down early," he observed. "It is not quite eight. You did not sleep well?"

"Quite well," she said. "I'm accustomed to getting up early. I'm used to going to work, remember?"

"Then you should fall into the habit again easily,"

he said. "Cristina will no doubt sleep late this morning after her travels of yesterday, but I see no reason why you should not begin some preliminary instruction with her this afternoon. There is no need to be formal about it.... ''

Amanda hesitated. She and Cristina had already decided how they were going to handle the subject of Cristina's English, but they had agreed it was something they should do together. Nevertheless there seemed no reason why she shouldn't mention the fact she'd had an earlier visit from Cristina and they both wanted to meet with him later.

She was forestalled from doing this by Hortense's appearance—and decided it was just as well she held her tongue.

Hortense brought them the makings for *café con leche*, and Antonio did the honors, dexterously blending the hot coffee and the hot milk into a deliciously frothy mixture to which he added what he considered the right amount of sugar.

She couldn't fault his taste in this respect. In fact, she thought, she couldn't fault his taste in anything. Watching him and trying to be discreet about it as she did so, she found herself remembering Cristina's comment that prior to his accident he had been "so handsome." It did not seem to Amanda that Antonio could ever possibly have been more handsome than he was at this moment!

Now she saw the line of his jaw tighten, and he asked carefully, "Why such close observation, Amanda?"

"I'm sorry," she replied inadequately.

"I do not like people to stare," he told her flatly.

"Antonio, I was *not* staring. . . ."

"It is not like you to be other than honest."

"Oh, damn it!" she cried. She stood, coffee cup in hand. "I'm going to take this someplace where I can drink it in peace," she sputtered, thoroughly annoyed by his attitude. "You don't seem to be able to keep from making an—an issue out of every single little thing. . . ."

"Sit down," he commanded, but she held her ground.

"Stop giving me orders!" she countered, tight-lipped herself.

Unexpectedly he smiled, and Amanda found herself thinking that Cristina should see him now. It was a devastating smile, so totally charming she could not help but catch her breath.

"*Please* sit down, *linda*," he said then. "And please forgive me for. . . many little things. I will try to do better—that is a promise. Where you are concerned I am much too—"

He broke off, and she could not resist asking, "Too what?"

His smile deepened, and to her chagrin he said something in Spanish, then added, "You will one day perhaps have to learn to speak *my* language, *niña*. Ah, here comes Greg. Another early riser, yes? But then it is an American habit, is it not?"

She had no answer for this. She knew only that as far as she was concerned, she wished Gregory Blake had this morning lingered longer in bed this morning!

Cristina arrived next on the scene, and since no one acted as if he was expecting Señora Inez de Hernandez to appear, Amanda assumed she'd probably have a breakfast tray in bed.

Hortense suggested bacon and eggs and biscuits for everyone but was vetoed in favor of toast and guava jam. She obliged the orders and went away mumbling that they'd all better be prepared to eat a big lunch.

"She's a jewel," Greg commented once she'd left them.

"Yes, she is," Antonio agreed, but he spoke absently, and Amanda had the impression his mind was elsewhere. He was watching Cristina, and he was much too discerning. Amanda would not have been surprised if he already suspected Cristina's secret.

As they all got up from the table, Cristina uttered something to him in quick Spanish, and he looked both puzzled and a bit perturbed by it. He turned to Amanda and said, "I understand you and my niece wish to consult with me?"

"Very briefly," she told him.

He nodded, but he didn't seem pleased about this. "Shall we go into the library, then?" he suggested.

Once inside the library Amanda could not keep her eyes from straying to the piano. She doubted if she would ever again be able to play "Spanish Eyes." She could not resist glancing at Antonio, though she was certain he would not permit himself to reveal any trace of feeling, even if he, like her, was thinking of their small fiasco the other evening. But in this she was wrong. She surprised what she could only think of as a very vulnerable expression on his face. For a heart-stopping moment he looked across at her in a kind of mute agony. Agony—wasn't that a strong word for it? No, she decided, just now there *was* something agonized about Antonio. She had the frustrating impression he was trying to convey something to her, but she wasn't able to grasp what it was.

It was over in an instant, and she almost convinced herself she had imagined this strange flare-up of an odd sort of feeling between them. Almost—but not quite. And she felt oddly disturbed as Antonio indicated that she and Cristina should both take chairs. She sat on the edge of the seat, as tense and unsure of herself before him as an adolescent schoolgirl might be.

Antonio sat down, too, crossing his legs negligently and looking very much at ease. But was he really, Amanda wondered? So often he was not at all the person he seemed on the surface. She was coming to appreciate this more and more, but the knowledge only enhanced her feeling of helplessness. If she couldn't even begin to read him, how could she possibly hope ever to truly understand him?

He said gravely, "What is the problem, Amanda? Or should I perhaps ask Cristina?"

"There is no problem, Antonio," Amanda said, trying to choose her words carefully and already feeling at a distinct disadvantage before him. Why did he inevitably seem to do this to her, apparently without even trying to disconcert her?

"There must be a reason for Cristina's urgency in your both wishing to speak with me," he said, his words managing to convey a slight but definite rebuke.

"We've something to tell you," Amanda began, but now that the moment was at hand this was not nearly so easy as she had thought it would be when she and Cristina had discussed their plan upstairs in her bedroom. True, the deception—if, in fact, it really could be called a deception—was all on Cristina's part, not hers. Yet somehow she had become Cristina's ally—though God knows Cristina needed one!

Even now Cristina was looking at her anxiously, and so Amanda plunged in. "The fact of the matter," she said, "is that Cristina has quite a surprise for you."

The eyebrow rose first. Then he said coolly, "Indeed?" He turned to Cristina. *"Una sorpresa, niña?"* he asked her.

Cristina's cheeks turned scarlet, but her voice was steady as she replied in English, "Yes. I...I have studied the English, *tío*."

She spoke haltingly and her accent seemed even more pronounced than usual, but Antonio flashed her a glance of utter astonishment—in which there was little pleasure.

"So," he said, speaking in English himself, "exactly how have you done this?"

"In school I took two years," Cristina said slowly.

"I am aware of that. Two years in which you did not apply yourself and learned almost nothing at all. Just because I was in the hospital much of that time, little *sobrina*, do not think I did not know how your studies were faring. The sisters gave me regular reports."

"Tío," Cristina began, and then went into a flood of Spanish. Antonio immediately shook his head.

"No," he said. "Since it appears you are at least somewhat conversant with the language, we will speak in English, if only to make ourselves clear to Amanda." For a moment Amanda thought he was about to say, "Mrs. Hughes." "It is Felipe Córdoba who has been your real instructor, I suspect. Correct?"

Cristina was literally wringing her hands, and Amanda could not resist interceding. "Antonio," she said, "does it really matter how she learned the language, as long as she—"

"Yes," he said, interrupting her and managing to put her in her place with just a single word. "To me it matters a great deal. I am pleased Cristina has *begun* her study of English, and you will note I emphasize 'begun.' I am sure she is not proficient, and even I can detect that much needs to be done about her accent. What is important to me, however, is the deception that has been involved. Why did you not tell me about this immediately, Amanda?"

She stared at him, astonished to think he should be putting any sort of blame on her in this instance. And now it was Cristina who came to the rescue. The girl spoke in low passionate tones, her Spanish so fast it was totally incomprehensible to Amanda, even though she was beginning to catch a word now and then when Antonio and Pablo spoke together.

When she had concluded, Antonio was silent for a long moment. Then he said, "It would seem you have made a convert out of my niece, Amanda."

There was an accusatory note to his voice, and Amanda resented this. "I have not been trying to proselytize," she told him stiffly.

"I beg your pardon?" he asked.

She was as suspicious as he had been accusing,

because she could not believe there was a single word in the English language he didn't fully understand. He sensed this, for a wry smile twisted his lips and he said, "You give me too much credit. I have tried to tell you I am not so fluent as you think, but you seem to disbelieve me. Very well, then, I can guess at what you are indicating to me. You have not tried to put Cristina to your side, is that right?"

"I wasn't aware there were sides to take," Amanda said flatly, and at that moment she happened to glance directly at Cristina and was amazed. Cristina was leaning forward, and she was actually smiling as she followed this interchange between Amanda and her uncle with fascinated concentration. But when she caught Amanda's eyes on her, she swiftly sobered.

"You are both too much for me," Cristina said. "The language, that is. I get only the general meaning for the most part, but what I try to tell *tío*, Amanda, is that you are not—what is the word—you are not to blame. How could you be?"

How, indeed! Amanda thoroughly agreed with this and shot a glance of pure triumph toward Antonio, but he only shook his head. "She is not so gentle as she seems," he told his niece. "Are you, Amanda?" In a swift and graceful movement he stood, towering over both Amanda and Cristina, looking down at them in that indolent way that could serve as such a camouflage.

"So," he said. "It would seem to me there is nothing more to say. Perhaps I should even be thankful to Felipe Córdoba, Cristina, for starting you on the path to learning English—of a sort, anyway. Amanda can now get deeply into her own task of perfecting your use of her language, and I expect in a few weeks to hear you sound like a proper Bostonian.''

"Oh, come now, Antonio," Amanda began, because he really seemed serious about this. But she stopped short when he laughed.

"It is a beautiful day," he said. "You should both go to the pool and swim and enjoy the sun. However, Cristina, do not let Amanda stay too long in the direct sun. She is *muy rubia*, and she will therefore burn easily. *¿Comprendes?*"

"Sí, tío," Cristina said. "The sunburn."

"Your lessons can begin at the pool—or in it—as well as anywhere else," Antonio continued. "As I have said before, I see no need for formal sessions, not unless you feel they are indicated, Amanda. You, after all, are the teacher."

"Thank you," she said, intending the irony, and a small pang of pleasure swept through her as his mouth twitched.

"De nada," he told her politely, and Cristina actually laughed aloud.

"Tío," she said then, "will you join us at the pool? You, too, could use the exercise. To swim, I mean."

"Oh?" he questioned, but as Amanda held her breath, unable to suppress the hope that soared within her at the thought of spending the morning by the pool with him, he shook his head. It seemed to her, though, it was with a certain reluctance that he added, "I must go to Tampa today on a business matter, little one. But I shall be returning for dinner tonight, and I will expect a report from Amanda about your progress. So be a good girl."

A PERSONAL CLOUD infiltrated the day's sunshine for Amanda with Antonio's departure. However, Gregory Blake did join them at the pool, and they spent a pleasant morning swimming and sunning. Gregory participated in Cristina's English lessons and got them both laughing at his humor as he did so. For Amanda, however, something was definitely missing, and she yearned for the sudden reappearance of the tall dark Spaniard who had such a profound effect on her. There were moments when she came close to despising him, moments when he caused her to become possessed with pure annoyance, but even more moments when she knew—this with a kind of desperation—that she loved him. He aroused in her so many conflicting emotions that at times she didn't know where to turn, and when her thoughts began to whirl, her physical response to them was pure treachery. It was a shock to know how much she, as a woman, *wanted* Antonio. Prudish echoes of her New England heritage, perhaps—she had already admitted that. But no matter how she might will it otherwise, these days the fire of desire seemed forever to be simmering much too close to the surface for her. She knew very well it was going to take all the strength she could possibly muster to keep that potential inferno under control, and she was grateful for Cristina's presence. Having Cristina around would preclude encounters with Antonio on a one-to-one basis—encounters she was very much afraid she wouldn't be able to manage much longer without totally giving herself away.

Gregory was attentive, and once when he strolled back to the house to get them cool drinks Cristina said, "He—how shall I say it—he likes you, Amanda." Cristina managed to put a tremendous amount of meaning into the word *like*, but the strange thing was, Antonio's niece didn't seem pleased about this supposed feeling on the part of Gregory Blake. This was puzzling to Amanda, because certainly Cristina wasn't interested in the lawyer herself—not, that is, if she was even as remotely devoted to Felipe Córdoba as she claimed.

Cristina frowned and added a bit reluctantly, "He is very nice, Gregory, yes. But. . . ."

She did not elaborate on the "but," and Amanda's curiosity surged. Still, she knew without pursuing it that there was enough of Antonio in his niece to make questioning quite useless.

CHAPTER THIRTEEN

THE DAYS PASSED, and they were certainly very pleasant days. Yet there was a bleakness to them for Amanda, because she saw so little of Antonio.

She knew he had converted one of the rooms off the patio into an office of sorts, and many mornings he and Gregory Blake were closeted there. It stood to reason, of course, that it took a lot of time and effort to run a business empire as large as the Hernandez-family empire evidently was. However, Antonio had been told to come to Florida to rest, and she doubted he was getting very much rest at all.

The mystery of Florence Edmond was solved when she came to the hacienda one weekend as a guest. She was a stunning woman, in her early thirties, Amanda surmised, or in other words about Antonio's own age. She was tall and slim, with very clear gray eyes and chestnut hair she wore straight back from her forehead and arranged in a coil at her neck, giving her a Madonna-like appearance. Yet Florence was an attorney and, Amanda suspected, a very sharp one. From the scraps of conversation they had while they sipped predinner drinks in the drawing room, she gathered that Antonio had hired Florence at Gregory Blake's instigation especially to deal with certain business matters involving Hermosa Groves.

References to these matters were deliberately veiled, and once again Amanda had the sensation of being an outsider. Nor did it help when she found out that Florence Edmond's law offices were located in Tampa. Was it really necessary for Antonio to make as many trips as he did in order to consult his Florida lawyer? Although he played the part of a courteous host—and no more—while Ms. Edmond was a guest at the hacienda, this, too, was something to be wondered about.

By this time Amanda and Cristina had become more like two sisters than teacher-pupil, although as a pupil Cristina was proving to be very apt, indeed. Felipe had given her enough of a grasp of the English language so that she was learning by leaps and bounds, and under Amanda's careful tutelage she was making a determined effort to polish her accent. It was not an easy matter to twist one's tongue around unfamiliar sounds, but Cristina was trying— and trying very hard.

Cristina was in touch with Felipe, Amanda soon realized, because now and then she would disappear for a time and later emerge, usually from the direction of the library, with a self-conscious look on her pretty face that was not untinged with guilt. Amanda knew she must have been calling Felipe in New York on those occasions, and one afternoon it occurred to her that Antonio might very well question these calls once he got his phone bill. When she mentioned this to Cristina, however, the Spanish girl had a ready answer. Felipe had instructed her always to call him collect. Thus the call would not be put through at all if he happened to be out, and in any event there would be no record of any calls originating from Hermosa Groves.

Amanda had to smile at this. It did seem as if, in their plotting for the sake of love, Cristina and Felipe had thought of just about everything.

On a couple of occasions Amanda had deplored her wardrobe selection to Cristina, and the girl had promptly offered to loan her some of her clothes because the two of them were very much the same size and Cristina had closets full of all sorts of outfits. Amanda had been tempted, but their coloring was so different that there were few things of Cristina's, she felt, that would really look good on her.

To Amanda's dismay, Cristina took matters into her own hands about this. Right after lunch one afternoon, she sought out Amanda, who had gone to her room to write a letter.

"We can go to Sarasota and do shopping," she said exultantly. "Just hurry and get ready. You have cash money?"

Amanda was amused at her way of putting it, but she said only, "Yes. How are we going to get to Sarasota, though?"

"I have arranged the ride," Cristina said importantly, so pleased with herself and so excited at the prospect of this venture that Amanda could not help but catch some of her spirit.

"What about Aunt Inez?" she asked.

"*Tía* is taking her siesta," Cristina said impatiently. "Nor would she ever have any wish to go out in the afternoon heat."

This was true enough. The señora, Amanda had learned, suffered from a slight heart condition, and she rested quite a bit of the time. In fact, Amanda thought wryly, she rested as much as Antonio was supposed to rest and didn't.

"Come on," Cristina said, adding quickly, "we cannot expect him to wait forever."

Amanda assumed that by "him" Cristina meant Pablo, but she didn't ask. It could also be Gregory Blake who was going to Sarasota for some reason or perhaps even both of them. For that matter, she thought with a skip of her pulse, it could be Antonio.

She was completely disconcerted to see the Hermosa Groves station wagon parked in front of the door and Roger Crane standing beside it.

She had seen very little of Roger since the day she'd gone to his house with him for a drink and Antonio had appeared to whisk her away so peremptorily. She had been busy enough with Cristina so that she hadn't thought too much about it. Now she wondered if Roger had been keeping away from her deliberately or if Antonio possibly had something to do with this.

Cristina, at her side now, said, "Mr. Crane came to bring some fruit to Hortense this morning, and he tells me he is going to Sarasota. So I ask if we can go, too. I tell him we want to make the shopping."

Cristina was so pleased with herself Amanda didn't have the heart to suggest to her that this expedition might be a mistake. It was too late, anyway. Roger was welcoming her with an expansive smile, and a moment later she was wedged in the middle of the station wagon's front seat between Cristina and him.

"This is terrific," he said as they started out, and

she had to agree. She hadn't been away from the immediate vicinity of the hacienda since she'd arrived in Florida except for that single tour of the groves with Roger. Although she'd not felt any particular deprivation because of this, it would be good to get out to where there were stores and people. Everyone, she told herself, needed an occasional change of scene.

As for Antonio, he was getting plenty of changes of scene with his frequent trips to Tampa, and now that she had met Florence Edmond, Amanda was increasingly convinced there was as much pleasure as business involved in these trips. Florence was a very attractive woman, and she had looked at Antonio in a way lawyers didn't usually look at their clients—or so it seemed to her. They had spent a good bit of their time in his office off the patio, too. Had this been all business? Or—

She fought back thoughts she didn't want to entertain and was conscious of Roger's curious gaze.

"You just muttered something," he told her.

"What?" she asked.

"I couldn't quite catch it," he said, and laughed. "Perhaps that's just as well. I'd call it a private mutter. Amanda, you look terrific. Florida is certainly agreeing with you, even though I haven't had much to do with that, I'm sorry to say."

Amanda knew Cristina was straining her ears, determined not to miss a single word of this interchange if she could possibly help it.

Painfully conscious of this, she said, "I imagine you've been quite busy, Roger."

"It seems to me you're the one who's been busy," he countered. "I've asked after you a number of times, but your employer has always said you were 'occupied.' I even called twice, but I was told the same thing on both occasions by that man of his, Pablo.''

"I never got a message you'd called," she replied, her indignation sparking at this.

"No," Roger said dryly, "I didn't imagine so. For my part, I've had the feeling at moments that you're being kept prisoner there at the hacienda. That's not true, is it, Amanda? I wouldn't put it past Hernandez to try it.''

Roger spoke swiftly, and Amanda was not sure just how much Cristina could understand of what he was saying. She was also aware of the fact Roger assumed Cristina didn't speak English, then remembered they had talked together after all. Cristina had made the arrangement for this particular trip with Roger herself. Still, they could have said very little. And just now Roger was certainly in danger of saying too much!

She told him hastily, "I'll speak to Antonio. I'll ask him to instruct Pablo to be sure and call me to the phone in future. Of course, Pablo doesn't understand much English, so that could have been the problem.''

"I speak enough Spanish to get along," Roger said, and now she imagined he must have spoken Spanish to Cristina when they planned this excursion. "Anyway, I should think he could recognize the name Hughes.''

"Even so," Amanda hedged. Roger, apparently on the verge of another comment, changed his mind and lapsed into silence.

They had driven beyond the Hermosa Groves property—at least beyond the groves themselves. Amanda had no idea of how far Antonio's land stretched in this direction. Now she saw cattle grazing in the shade of widespread live oak trees, these with large gnarled trunks and canopies of small, dark olive leaves. Stands of tall Australian pines had been planted as windbreaks, and they swayed in the breeze also ruffling the fronds on the palms that would forever seem exotic to her. It made for a strange sort of pastoral scene to someone raised in the north.

Amanda was especially intrigued by the flocks of white birds hovering close to the cattle. "What are they?" she asked Roger.

"Cattle egrets," he said. "They live among the cattle."

"Egrets?" she echoed, surprised. "Didn't ladies used to have plumes for hats made from their feathers?"

He nodded. "These are land egrets, though. You're thinking mostly of the two water varieties, the American egret, which is actually a very large white heron, and the snowy egret, which is smaller. Both were endangered species for a time, but they've made quite a comeback. The cattle egrets came from Africa originally. They think they were actually blown across the Atlantic, borne on storm winds." He paused, then added, "The cattle hereabouts are mostly raised for beef, incidentally."

There was a note in his voice as he said this that made her ask, "Would you like to be a rancher, Roger?"

He laughed. "In a sense, I am," he told her. "This

particular ranch belongs to Hermosa Groves—it's part of the property. I don't have a hand in actually running it myself, but I do keep an eye on the overall management, particularly the income figures. Sometimes I've thought I wouldn't mind giving up citrus growing and getting entirely into ranching myself. I've even thought of getting into the horse business. I've loved horses since I was a kid, and I've done my share of studying about them. You should see those farms around Ocala where they raise the thoroughbreds. Really magnificent." He laughed. "I wouldn't mind raising a Derby winner myself," he confessed.

"Then perhaps you will," she told him.

"Where there's a will, there's a way?" he said, and then shook his head. "Nothing like that's in my cards," he noted with a trace of bitterness she found surprising, for Roger struck her as such a positive person. "Some people fall into that pot of gold I think we talked about once before, and they come up clutching a handful of diamonds to boot," he added. "But not me, Amanda. I've worked—and worked hard—for every damned thing I've got."

Roger wasn't saying anything *against* Antonio Hernandez, she realized. Why, then, did she sense he blamed Antonio for his own lack of wealth and position? She began to feel certain Roger had indeed thought he was going to inherit something from the late Michael Field. Not merely something—a great deal. The whole grove property? Did Roger actually believe the ten years of his life he'd put in at Hermosa Groves had entitled him to inherit the whole seven thousand acres when Michael Field died? This seemed more than a bit unrealistic, in her opinion.

Certainly when he'd come to work at the Groves as the manager, it couldn't have been with the thought that one day he'd own the whole thing—not in the beginning, at least. On the other hand, he'd known, of course, that Michael Field was alone in the world—as far as any *close* relatives were concerned. There was the chance, in fact, that Roger had never even been aware of the family in Spain or its members, who stood to inherit under terms that had become more like a promise, as time went on, from generation to generation...a tradition, an obligation, to pass the land from eldest male to eldest male.

Despite the decades that had intervened since his own family had maintained any connection with the Spanish branch at all, there still must have been something of Spain in Michael Field, something to make him honor this strange sort of covenant, as had the Fields—and the Vegas—who had gone before him. Were this not so, it seemed to Amanda it would have been possible to break such a chain—legally, if one wished to do so—and to leave the property to whomever one wished.

Yes, a touch of Spain must have lived on in Michael Field. Spanish blood. Spanish eyes, she found herself thinking, and winced again at the memory of that scene with Antonio in the library.

Roger asked abruptly, "What's worrying you, Amanda? You seem to keep going off into trances."

"I...I'm just taking everything in," she said a bit lamely. "This is such a new sort of country to me."

That was true. The sky today was a bright intense blue, patched only by a single, very white cloud. They had passed the ranch and were driving through a wooded area where there were mostly palms and live oaks, these draped with the clinging gray tendrils of Spanish moss that had about it a haunting quality even when touched by the sun. Thick clumps of low palmetto shrubs grew close to the edge of the road, their fan-shaped leaves looking very sharp. It would be almost impossible to make one's way through terrain such as this, and she said, "It's like a jungle."

"It *is* a jungle," Roger told her. "Full of snakes— and I mean poisonous ones—and insects of all sorts. And you'll find alligators in some of the swamps. They were in danger of becoming extinct not too long ago, too, but now, like the egrets, they've made a big comeback in Florida—and in Georgia. Lots of them up around the Okefenokee Swamp. Now that's a place you ought to go through sometime. Miles of wilderness and black water. You go through in a boat—have to have a guide, or you'll never find your way out. Once you get past the edges, it's like a huge insidious maze."

She laughed. "I think I'll stay out of it," she said.

He shook his head. "No danger when you're with someone who knows what he's doing, and the guides up that way know the whole swamp like the palm of their hands, incredible though it seems."

They were driving over a low bridge, and she stared down at a narrow river where the water ran black, the sun casting a silver sheen on it.

"That's scary enough for me," she said, pointing. "I'd hate to fall in."

"No fear," Roger said, and smiled across at her. "I'd rescue you in a twinkling, darling."

Amanda felt Cristina stiffen. Cristina had understood the endearment well enough, but it seemed pretty clear she didn't like it.

Again Amanda was puzzled by this, although just now there were other things that bothered her more than this rather strange reaction on Cristina's part. For one thing, she resented Antonio's evidently having told Pablo to deflect any telephone calls that came for her. And she had no doubt this had been done, though she couldn't understand why.

At least she couldn't entirely understand why. She was beginning to think there was a real reason for the hostility between Roger and Antonio, a reason that went past the fact they were two entirely different kinds of men and basically incompatible.

It seemed absurd to think Roger might dislike Antonio because he felt he'd done him out of an inheritance that should have been his. Yet Roger did seem to be both bitter and, in a way, vindictive, where Antonio was concerned. This disturbed her. Antonio, on the other hand, during the few times she'd seen the two men together, had certainly merited Roger's dislike by his own supremely arrogant attitude. If he had not been so scrupulously polite at the same time, he could have been accused of blatant rudeness, and she would not have blamed Roger if he had quit on the spot.

Why didn't he quit, for that matter, if he found it so impossible to work for Antonio? He had made it clear he was a bachelor with no ties. It seemed to her that during these ten years since he'd come to Florida to manage Hermosa Groves he might very well have saved up quite a bit of money, since he surely hadn't so far exhibited any tendencies toward a flamboyant life-style. His house, she knew, was Groves property—probably one of the additional benefits he received for living out on the groves that, admittedly, were in a relatively desolate area. At least, she surmised, it would be a good hour's drive to get anyplace that offered much in the way of excitement. Not that she really knew what Roger would consider excitement.

"You're doing it again," he chastised her. "Don't tell me you're so enamored of this west Florida scrub country that it's putting you in a dreamworld."

"I do find it fascinating," she said. "It's so different from anything I've known, Roger. Cristina, does it remind you of Spain?"

"No," Cristina said shortly, and glancing at Roger, Amanda saw his start of surprise. So then he hadn't realized Cristina knew any English! "My family comes from Andalusia," Cristina added rather sullenly. "We have behind us the mountains, the Sierra Morena. We have many hills that are—how do you say it—steep. On them we grow the olives—there are thousands of trees—and the almonds, too. It is a *tierra del sol*—that is to say, a land of the sun. . . like here. But our properties are in the valley of the Guadalquivir, so the land can be—what do I want to say—cultivated more easily. For the most part," Cristina finished rather sadly, "Spain can be very poor. But the people—they are so good. They make of the life the happiness with what they have."

Had Cristina understood more of Roger's conversation than she had thought she could, Amanda wondered? If so, was this a rather subtle way of telling him he should be grateful for what he had? She was not at all sure, and was relieved when Roger first complimented Cristina on her English and then included both of them in his conversation.

As they neared Sarasota, they frequently passed large areas set aside for mobile-home parks, some of them very attractive with wide entrances and exotic tropical plantings. Then there were condominiums—usually, Roger said, considerably more expensive than the mobile homes, although those, too, could sometimes command a surprising figure.

"We get the snowbirds," he said. "People who come down from the north to vacation in the winter. Then they decide they want to retire here. Coastal Florida especially has a high population of folks over sixty. Lots of these mobile-home parks—and some of the condos, also—won't even let you buy in them unless you're over sixty. Fifty-five, anyway. Then they've got strict regulations on top of that to keep youth out. No kids, no pets."

"But that is unnatural," Cristina protested.

"I suppose it's the way folks want it, or they wouldn't keep on making the rules that way," Roger told her.

To Amanda this seemed sad. Perhaps because she had been married to a man so much older than herself, she appreciated the value of an interchange between people of different ages and the sharing of feelings and experiences. It dismayed her to think of age shutting out youth. This, she thought, could only lead to a static sterile sort of life with very little vitality in it.

She said slowly, "I don't think I'd like to live like that."

Roger laughed. "You've got centuries ahead of you, beautiful, before you have to begin to think about such things," he assured her.

As they neared the city, he said, "Some of the best shops hereabouts are in the malls. They have huge malls that would keep you and Cristina busy for a week if you took in all the stores.... Look, I'll drop you off, and let's say I pick you up two hours from now. Then we can have a drink somewhere before we go back to the groves, okay? We'll set a specific place where we won't miss one another."

"What about you?" Amanda asked him.

"What about me?"

"I don't want to think of your just trying to mark time for the next two hours, Roger, while we splurge."

"I have a business appointment," he said. "That's what brought me to town."

Amanda was annoyed with herself. She knew she and Cristina had in effect "hitched" this ride, so obviously it was a trip Roger had already planned to take. "Very well, then," she said a bit stiffly. "Tell us where you want us to wait for you, and we'll be there on time."

"No matter," he grinned. "I know what it does to women when you set them loose in a place like this! I won't mind waiting. I never mind waiting for something that's worth waiting for."

They were swinging into the huge outside parking lot of the mall he had suggested as he said this, and Amanda thought she'd seldom seen so many cars in one place, even around Boston.

They selected a main entrance as a rendezvous

point. Then Roger said, "Stay inside, though, if you get there before I do. The heat's pretty blasting today."

Amanda realized the truth of this as soon as she stepped out of the station wagon. Roger had been using the air conditioner all the way, but he had kept it low enough so she'd not been conscious of any rush of cold air. It was like a furnace outside, and she felt as if she and Cristina would both bake before they got inside the shaded acclimatized inner court of the mall.

Roger had been right. This was a shopper's paradise, and she and Cristina went from store to store with the zeal of two youngsters let loose in a candy factory. The shops had all been decorated for Valentine's Day, Amanda saw, and Cristina exclaimed about this. "In Spain," she said, "it is always said that you Americans are so commercial about your holidays. But I do not agree with that. I like all of this—what shall I call it—sentiment."

Looking at an assortment of heart-shaped boxes in red, pink and white satin ornamented with flowers, gold arrows and plump smiling Cupids, Amanda said, amused, "Yes, I guess you could say that."

The thought came to her that she'd love to get a Valentine for Antonio. Something really outrageous. But today, at least, she wasn't feeling quite that bold.

Under Cristina's tutelage she bought two new bathing suits, one a slip of a bikini in a blue so dark it was almost black. She'd never owned anything quite so revealing before, and she wondered if she'd dare ever wear it, but Cristina only said insistently, "You have the beautiful body, Amanda, and this is the style."

She also bought three new dresses that would be suitable for dinners at the hacienda, all of them in glowing shades far brighter than the things she usually dressed in. Next came some casual clothes for simply lounging around.

Cristina, to Amanda's amusement, purchased a vivid pink T-shirt with a palm tree on it and "Sarasota, Florida" printed in large blue letters across the front. "In Majorca it will be the rage," she told Amanda. "I will save it for my return."

Her return. There would come a day, Amanda thought now, when Cristina—and Antonio—would be returning to Majorca, and she didn't like to think about it. She didn't like to think about it at all. In this short space of time she had become terribly fond of Cristina, and....

She shivered, and Cristina, watching her, said, "Let us get an ice cream. What do you say?"

"I say yes," Amanda agreed, and they found a shop that sold ice cream exclusively. They sat at a round table with fancy wrought-iron chairs, and the Tiffany-style lamps hanging overhead, with their rich, jewel-toned shades, completed the effect of a Victorian soda parlor.

They both decided to try a thick drink made with coconut ice cream, and it was delicious. "This is *so* good," Cristina said. Then she giggled. "For me it will go on the hips," she added, "but you can tolerate some more pounds, Amanda."

"Not too many." Amanda smiled. "If I eat much more of Hortense's cooking, I won't be able to get into the things I bought today."

"Yes." Cristina nodded. "Hortense, she is excellent, no?"

"Definitely."

"*Tío* feels he is very fortunate she stayed," Cristina said. "She worked for our relative, but he was American. *Tío* felt she would perhaps not wish to work for foreigners."

"But that's ridiculous," Amanda said a bit more sharply than she intended. "Your uncle assumes people have all sorts of prejudices, when actually...."

"Yes?" Cristina questioned.

"It doesn't matter," she replied rather grumpily. She didn't want to get into a discussion about Antonio with Cristina...of all people.

But Cristina would not let it go at that. "Do you dislike *tío*, Amanda?" she asked bluntly.

"No," Amanda said quickly. "What makes you ask such a thing?"

"I at moments have wondered. Also, one time I think one thing, one time I think another thing," Cristina continued somewhat vaguely. "Men are attracted to you, Amanda. Gregory. This Roger Crane. My uncle, as well."

"Your uncle is not attracted to me," Amanda said shortly.

"I do not agree," Cristina told her. "But," she added enigmatically, "what is that saying you have? The time will tell? We shall see. Yes, we shall see."

TWO HOURS PASSED much too quickly. It was with reluctance that Amanda and Cristina finally made their way to the spot at which they had agreed to meet Roger, to find he was already waiting for them.

He groaned in pretended dismay when he saw their bulging shopping bags and at once relieved them of the major part of their load, carrying it out to the station wagon for them. It was still blisteringly hot outside, and the sun was surprisingly high in the sky.

"Sets late here relative to Boston," Roger said, following Amanda's glance in the sun's direction. "We'll get the air going, and you'll cool off in a minute."

As he drove out of the parking lot, he said, "I thought we might cut over to a place on the waterfront and have a drink, if that's okay with you. You haven't really seen anything of Sarasota yet. Maybe one day we can make a trip over here just for sightseeing. There's the magnificent residence John Philip Ringling—the circus man—built here, and you can go through it—it's like a Venetian palace, I guess you'd say. And there are a lot of other things that would interest the two of you. Right now, though, I thought we'd stop at Marina Jack's."

This popular place was right at the edge of a marina from which both fishing and sight-seeing boats departed regularly, Roger explained. There was a restaurant on an upper level—a very good one, he told them—and a lounge on the lower level. They opted for the lounge and sat at a highly polished wooden table near a window, from which they could see the boats bringing in the day's catches.

Roger suggested *piña coladas* for both of them, and Amanda and Cristina agreed they were rather like alcoholic counterparts of the coconut-ice-cream drinks they'd had earlier. The setting seemed very exotic to Amanda, lush and tropical and curiously relaxing. Roger kept the conversation on a general plane, pointing out the bridge just to their north that led out to Longboat Key, one of a series of keys off the coast in that area.

"Beautiful homes, gorgeous condos and one of the most extensive and exclusive shopping areas anywhere around at St. Armand's Circle," he told them. "That's where I should have taken you. Well...next time. Past Longboat Key you get onto Anna Maria Island. All along these gulf keys are magnificent white sand beaches. You girls really should experience a slice of this kind of Florida life."

He had to explain the use of the word *slice* in this connection to Cristina, but once she understood she nodded in total agreement.

"To me that would be a very good thing to do," she said, and Amanda had the impression the wheels inside Cristina's active little head were beginning to turn.

Even she had no idea of how fast they could whirl once they got started!

CHAPTER FOURTEEN

THE EXCURSION TO SARASOTA had a very disturbing aftereffect, and later when she thought about it, Amanda realized she should have known how displeased Antonio would be by her going off with Roger Crane and Cristina's accompanying her.

Antonio took his responsibility as Cristina's guardian very seriously. She'd already realized this, but she'd not realized just how seriously until, the morning after their shopping safari, he called her into his office off the patio.

Cristina and Gregory had gone ahead to the pool, with Aunt Inez trailing along after them, saying she would sit in the shade of an umbrella and read for a time. Amanda had been about to follow, when Antonio told her he wished to see her. He did this quietly, out of earshot of the others, but he still surprised her by making it sound as if it were a command rather than a request.

To her further astonishment he laced out at her once they were alone in a way made all the worse by the cold-and-quiet tone of voice in which he told her she had totally violated his confidence. Cristina, he reminded her, was a girl accustomed to a carefully chaperoned life. She was, in fact, accustomed to the confines of a convent school. And at home her life had been similarly regulated. Girls from proper Spanish families—even in this allegedly liberated day, he continued icily—did not cavort in public bars and make exhibitions of themselves.

This was enough. Amanda could feel her own fury rising, and since Antonio was sitting behind a desk, she rose to glare down at him.

"Somehow," she said, nearly choking over the words, "you certainly have missed the boat!"

"I beg your pardon?" he inquired loftily.

"Don't expect me to translate for you!" she snapped. "You know damned well what I mean. Cristina is no innocent little convent flower, as I think you realize."

He had never looked more Spanish, more inscrutable, and he was the epitome of haughtiness. "Are you implying my niece is not a virgin?" he demanded.

"Oh, for God's sake!" Amanda said, disgusted by this. "You do have a one-track mind, don't you? No, I'm not implying anything in that vein about Cristina. I wouldn't know, nor do I care. What I mean to say is that she certainly doesn't behave like a sequestered little flower who has never seen the light of day beyond the convent wall. She is a normal, intelligent, totally lovely and lovable girl, and I cannot understand why you want to subjugate her."

"An example of my feudal mentality?" he suggested, and she didn't like the way he said it.

"Yes!" she stormed. "It is an example of your feudal mentality, and I've had enough of you. More than enough of you! You may be able to dictate to everyone around you in your own country, but you are not going to dictate to me. Consider our arrangement terminated as of this moment! I've violated it anyhow in your opinion—that's perfectly clear to me. If you no longer have confidence in me where your niece is concerned, then there's really nothing more to say, is there?''

There was a pause, a long pause. His face was totally expressionless, the black patch seeming more like a mask than ever. Then he shrugged and said, ''Very well. If that is the way you wish it.''

Amanda's heart seemed to turn to stone. She could feel the sudden cold hardness, and it brought in its wake a pain that was so sharply physical she had to catch her breath. There were a thousand things she wanted to tell Antonio, a million words she wanted to hurl at him, but she knew she could not say one of them without bursting into tears.

Blindly she made her way out of his office and across the patio and ran up the stairs to her room. Still possessed by a complete sense of shock, she flung herself down on her bed, her breath coming in deep gasps.

It was a long time before she rallied. Then she rolled over, staring up at the ceiling, and asked herself dully just what it was she had expected. Had she thought he would plead with her to stay? She should have known better. She should have known that with Antonio pride triumphed over everything else.

Damn, arrogant, stubborn Spanish pride!

After a time someone rapped on the door, and she thought of not answering, then realized that sooner or later she'd be found out anyway.

''Yes?'' she called.

Cristina came into the room, her eyes huge. "This cannot be true!" she exclaimed without preamble. "*Tío* says you are leaving. You cannot leave, Amanda!"

"You might say I've been dismissed," Amanda shot back.

"But that is not so," Cristina said, coming to sit on the side of the bed, wringing her hands in that way she had when she was really distraught about something. "*Tío* says this is your wish. It is not his wish."

"That," Amanda snapped, "is a lie!"

Cristina was on the verge of tears, but her dark eyes still snapped defiantly. "*Tío* does not lie!" she stated emphatically.

"Then let's say he twists the truth to suit himself," Amanda retorted.

The tears spilled over in Cristina's eyes, and looking at her, Amanda could feel her own eyes begin to sting. This, she told herself sternly, was absolutely ridiculous! There was no reason why either she or Cristina should settle down to cry their hearts out because Antonio Hernandez y Vega was totally... impossible.

"Cristina," she said more gently. "Please, be sensible about this. My leaving won't be the end of the world for you."

"But it will be," Cristina sobbed. "Among other things, if you go there will be no chance of a...a reunion between Felipe and me."

"There's no way I'd have anything to do with a reunion between you and Felipe, whether I stayed or not," Amanda said flatly. "You should know that."

"Then," Cristina said, sniffling but with a strange

little note of triumph in her voice, "you are after all loyal to *tío*!"

"You are getting things very mixed up, Cristina," Amanda informed her, enunciating each word carefully because she wanted to be sure the girl understood precisely what she was saying. No margin for error here. "In any event, this has nothing to do with you and Felipe. Your uncle feels I am not a fit companion for you."

Cristina stopped crying, and wiping her eyes, she replied, "That I do not believe."

"It's true, Cristina. He said so himself. That's when I offered to leave. . .and he told me I might as well go."

Antonio had not said exactly that, but it amounted to the same thing.

Cristina shook her head. "I cannot believe *tío* would make such a—suggestion," she said.

"Then ask him yourself," Amanda answered crisply, adding, "Please, Cristina, I really don't want to talk about it anymore. I've got to pull myself together and see when I can get a plane out of here back to Boston. I have to pack, I have to—"

"Did my uncle say to you he wished you to leave immediately?" Cristina asked indignantly.

"No. But I want to go as soon as possible. You can understand that, can't you?" Amanda implored.

"Yes," Cristina said thoughtfully, "Yes. I think I can."

Cristina left, and Amanda sank back onto the bed again. She knew she should get up and start making phone calls, but even that presented a problem. There was no phone in her room, and she didn't know whether there was one in any of the other upstairs rooms. She could only hope—perhaps when the family was at lunch—that she could sneak down to the library unobserved and use the phone there.

She pressed the intercom to the kitchen and was relieved when Hortense answered instead of Pablo. She and Pablo were communicating better than they originally had, but she had no wish to try out their Spanish-English method of interchange that day.

She told Hortense she had a headache and asked if she could simply have a sandwich, come lunchtime, brought to her room on a tray. Hortense at first clucked disapprovingly over this and said it would do her more good to come down and eat a decent meal, but in the end she agreed.

Lunch was usually served at half past one, but it was shortly before one o'clock when there was a rap at the door and Amanda, surmising that Hortense had decided to bring her tray up to her before serving the others, went to answer it.

Antonio stood on the threshold, holding a tray on which rested a platter of sandwiches, a dish of fruit salad and a large glass of iced tea.

"I told Hortense I would give you this," he said. His gaze swept her face. "You have been crying," he accused.

She had indeed been crying. It seemed to her, in fact, she'd been crying off and on for hours, and she was disgusted with herself. But she didn't answer this. She simply reached out to take the tray.

Only he wasn't about to relinquish it. He strode into the room, depositing it on a table near the window, and then he said, "Close the door, will you please?"

"Why?" she demanded.

"Because I wish to speak with you and I don't want any eavesdroppers—Cristina or anyone else," he replied darkly.

She pulled the door shut, asking as she did so, "What makes you think Cristina would be eavesdropping?"

"Because she evidently feels I have ruined her life, and so naturally she is going to be interested in hearing what we have to say to each other," Antonio said equably. "She was going to bring up your tray herself, but I insisted that I do it."

"Well, that was very kind of you," Amanda told him. "Now you've done it. So please leave, will you?"

"Not until we have resolved this stupid impasse," Antonio said, the muscle in his jaw twitching visibly. "What you told Cristina is not true. I did not ask you to leave here. It is you who said you wanted to leave, and I said that if that is what you wished. . . ."

"Spare me the quotes," Amanda declared wearily. "It amounts to the same thing, doesn't it?"

"No," he retorted, towering over her, and there was nothing inscrutable at all about his face at the moment. He looked like a walking thundercloud. "You are wrong to say I want you to go away from here. The truth is very much to the contrary."

She stared at him. "For God's sake, Antonio," she said finally, "do you remember our little scene in your office this morning? I'm not accustomed to having the riot act read to me in that manner."

"It was not my intention to read you—whatever it is you call it," Antonio said impatiently. His mouth tightened. Then he muttered under his breath, "*¡Madre de Dios!* What is it you do to me? Will it help the situation if I apologize to you, Amanda?"

She was surprised. She would have thought it out of character for Antonio to stoop to apologizing to anyone, especially in regard to a matter in which he had seemed so supremely self-righteous.

"If I thought you meant it, it might help," she said bluntly.

"Then let me assure you I do mean it," he told her. "I held my tongue last night when you and Cristina returned from your expedition, and it was my intention to... keep silent. But I did not sleep well, and the more I thought about it the more... the more annoyed I became."

"Annoyed?"

To her astonishment he actually flushed. "Well, more than annoyed," he admitted. "I do not know quite how to say to you what I felt, but I think it might have occurred to you that I might have liked to be the one to take you and Cristina on a shopping trip—just as I would have liked to show you over the groves myself when we first got here."

She was astounded. "You never suggested such a thing in either case," she reminded him.

"No. But that was not because it did not occur to me or because I did not wish to. I have been occupied with something that is extremely serious since I have been here," he said slowly.

"The headaches?" she demanded at once. "You haven't—"

"No, *linda*," he said quickly, his tone considerably more gentle. "It is nothing to do with me personally. Entirely a matter of *asuntos*—business affairs, that is. I do not wish to concern you with them. But my time has been taken up with matters I surely wish had never arisen. I have had no choice."

"And you haven't got any rest either, have you?" she queried.

He looked surprised at this, and he said, "Very little, I admit. I cannot rest until certain matters are taken care of, certain facts established. It is my hope this will be done before too much longer. In the meantime—"

"Do these matters concern Roger Crane, Antonio?"

She had not intended to pose the question—it had simply slipped out—and now she wondered how he would take it. She fully expected to be rebuffed.

But Antonio only said, "Yes, they do. What makes you ask that?"

"It seems to me there must be some reason for your—your evident animosity toward Roger," she answered frankly. "I think you're too fair a person to be that high-handed without reason."

"That what?" he asked her, and then smiled. "The language is picturesque, but sometimes your figures of speech confuse me unless I take a moment to attempt to make sense of them. It is a good word, though, *high-handed*, and yes, I suppose that has been my attitude. But I am pleased that at least you give me some credit for having a reason to act as I have. On the other hand, you like Crane."

He did not ask her a question; he made this a statement, and she did not know just what to say. But before she could speak at all, he continued, "It is clear to me you do, and I cannot blame you. He is attractive, a macho sort of man, and he would be good company."

Amanda shook her head. "Antonio," she said, "don't read more into things than there are to be read."

"Am I reading more into things?" he asked her. "I would like to think so, but I do sense a *simpatía* between you and Crane. That is your right, of course. It is not my right to choose your associates for you. Nor—and I admit it—should I have taken you to task this morning as I did. It was not merited. Cristina is not a child—I know that. She is flowering into womanhood, and I only hope she will become as lovely a woman as you are. That is one reason I so much value this companionship of yours with her—and why I urge you to reconsider, Amanda. Perhaps if you understand why I acted as I did this morning, you will decide not to leave."

"Oh?" She fell into his trap. "Then why did you act as you did?" she asked him.

"Jealousy," he said, that devastating smile coming again to transform his face. "You and Cristina are both very lovely young ladies. Can you blame me for wishing I had been your escort yesterday? Perhaps that is something we can make amends for on another occasion."

AMANDA ATE THE LUNCH Antonio had brought her and then promptly curled up on her bed and fell asleep. But it was a restless sleep, plagued by dreams that verged on the bizarre.

She had not given Antonio an answer to the question of whether she would reconsider staying at the hacienda, even though she felt certain he knew as well as she did that that was precisely what she was going to do.

Cristina had come back to the room to fetch her uncle for lunch, and Amanda wondered just how that particular encounter between them would have ended if she hadn't. Antonio had kept his physical distance, but once he had left she could not help wishing he had been more impetuous. It seemed to her all her worries, all her fears, could have been laid to rest had he simply taken her in his arms.

Cristina—evidently on instructions from her uncle—did not come to interrupt Amanda's siesta, but when Amanda sought her out later in the afternoon, the girl made no effort to conceal her eagerness to know what was going to happen next.

"You are not leaving, Amanda?" she questioned immediately.

There was no point in hedging. "No," Amanda said.

She had found her pupil in the library, valiantly trying to read a John Steinbeck novel. Now Cristina jumped to her feet, casting the book aside, and threw her arms around her teacher, hugging her so tightly Amanda said, "Whoa! You're cutting off my breath."

"But I am absolutely *encantada*!" Cristina exclaimed. "I have so many plans for us, Amanda. I have already spoken to Tío Tony and he has agreed."

"What has Tony agreed to this time?" they were asked as Gregory Blake strolled into the room, looking very attractive in a light green leisure suit.

"Tony said you were a bit under the weather," he added, addressing Amanda. "Feeling better?"

"Yes, thank you."

"She is fine—she is absolutely fine," Cristina said exuberantly. "Everything is absolutely fine!" she added, and Amanda could only wish her enthusiasm was catching. Everything was not really fine as far as she was concerned. She wished she knew what it was that was causing Antonio to disregard his doctors' orders. She also wondered what it was that involved Roger Crane and was evidently so serious it took a priority in Antonio's scheme of things and, she suspected, was responsible for Gregory Blake's being here at the hacienda.

She had no intention of bringing up any of this to Roger the next time she saw him. She didn't know why she felt she must maintain Antonio's confidence—even if the little he told her really had been told in confidence. Nevertheless Roger's own bitterness had been all too evident on the trip to Sarasota the previous day. She had no desire to fan a spark into a flame.

Aunt Inez joined them, having concluded her afternoon siesta, and the four of them actually managed to get together a table of bridge. It was a game that didn't demand any great knowledge of language, Amanda discovered. In fact, she soon found herself bidding in Spanish a good bit of the time. Her own bridge was rusty; she had played occasionally with Gerard and his friends, but usually only when they needed a fourth, as she was not as expert as the others. This held true now, too. But bridge was a challenging game; it demanded concentration, and so it served the purpose of keeping her mind off Antonio.

This was as well, because when he failed to appear at the cocktail hour she could hardly *not* begin thinking about him again. They had moved on into the dining room for dinner and were seated, when Pablo announced that Don Antonio had called but would not be joining them, as he was detained in Tampa.

Tampa again! It didn't seem possible to Amanda all of these trips could involve business...especially when she conjured up a vision of Florence Edmond—and this was something she was able to do much too easily.

They watched television for a time after dinner, Greg insisting this was something bound to improve Cristina's command of colloquial English, and finally they all went to bed. Amanda slept for a time, but she awakened to find she had thrown off the covers and was hot and uncomfortable. It had been very warm that day, but what bothered her most at the moment was the humidity, which was extremely oppressive. The bed seemed stifling to her, so she got up and went out onto the balcony. Yet even this did not have the desired effect.

Restless, she decided to go down to the kitchen to see if she could find some fresh fruit juice in the refrigerator. There was a whole pitcher of orange juice, she discovered, and she poured some over ice cubes in a large glass. It was refreshing, but, she thought wryly, she needed more than orange juice to calm her right then. She was tense, and although the weather might be a contributing factor, it was not entirely to blame. Despite his subsequent apology, that morning's session with Antonio had unnerved her. She didn't know how many of those scenes with him she could take. It was so easy for him to later turn on the charm as if it were a chandelier to be lighted at will—or so it certainly seemed.

She moved on into the drawing room, where the long glass doors that led out onto the patio had been left open, screened, of course. Still, there was a gentle breeze that was quite soothing. Sighing, she sat down to collect her thoughts. After a moment she stiffened, because she caught sight of a man walking across the patio. He seemed to be staggering, and she knew a moment of sheer panic. There was no moon that night; she could see only the dimmest outline—a deep shadow against shadow—and she stood, shrinking into the shadows beyond the windows herself, wondering what to do next, for he was coming in her direction!

Somehow she must get to a phone and call the police. But where were the police, she wondered. Hermosa Groves seemed, to her, to be out in the middle of nowhere. Yet she'd heard often enough that there was no place safe today from predators, from vandalism. . . .

The sliding screen was pushed back; the man stepped into the room, and Amanda first choked back a scream and then exclaimed, "Dear God! Antonio!"

He was as startled as she was, speaking first in fast and incomprehensible Spanish and only then saying, "Amanda? What the devil are you doing here?"

As he came close to her, she instinctively drew back, because he reeked of whiskey. Then she knew at once he sensed her withdrawal and resented it.

"So," he said roughly, the words very slightly slurred, "do I offend you, fastidious lady, because I stopped off in a tavern down the road?"

"I didn't know there was a tavern down the road," she replied evasively.

His laugh was harsh. "No," he said, "you presume you are in the wilderness. ¿*Verdad?* That is not so, I must tell you, Amanda. There is wilderness, yes, in this Florida. But there is also much civilization. Too much civilization! One is never too far from— someplace. In short, you do not have to go all the way to Sarasota to find a good dress shop. There are other centers closer, where, I think, you might have been equally satisfied."

As he talked, he was moving away from her, and now he switched on a lamp by one of the long low couches, and in its light she saw he looked strangely disheveled for Antonio. The ebony hair was rumpled, he was beginning to need a shave and he wore the sort of shirt that demands a tie. But somewhere he had dispensed with the tie and had unbuttoned the shirt, so that a good bit of his chest was bare. She gazed at his smooth, olive-toned skin, and that old feeling came over her. Her throat began to constrict, and she knew only too well that the best thing she could do was to take her orange juice and beat a hasty retreat.

But she also had a strong suspicion Antonio was not about to let her go all that easily.

To her dismay, she saw he was heading for the small bar in the corner. He fumbled for a glass, found ice in a thermal bucket and splashed whiskey over it without bothering to measure. It was only then that he turned to ask, "Will you join me?"

"Thank you, no," she said, indicating the glass in her hand.

"Fruit juice, yes?" he said. "I could not perhaps enliven it for you?"

"It's too hot to drink anything strong," she told him.

"You think so? I do not agree, *niña*," he said, coming toward her but stopping short to take a generous sample from his glass. "There are times when there is solace in alcohol. It is a *muleta*—how do you say it? It is a crutch. So tonight I am using the crutch. And you do not approve, do you?"

"Antonio...." she began, but he cut her off.

"Ah, do not attempt to talk to me as if you were my Tía Inez," he told her. "You use that approach entirely too often, *linda* Amanda, and I become tired of it. I do not want you as an aunt."

What did he want her as? Amanda nearly posed the question, the words trembling at the edge of her lips, but then she thought better of it. Antonio was apt to tell her he wanted her as a woman...and God knows she wanted him as a man!

This silent statement came as a shock to her, even though she knew she should have been well prepared for such self-revelation long before now. Antonio Hernandez had cast his spell on her from their first moment of meeting. Remembering that first moment, she also remembered how she had expected to find him aging and infirm, and an involuntary smile twisted her lips.

He was watching her with that attention that could be peculiarly unnerving because he was so intent, this perhaps due to the fact that his vision was, obviously, not all it should be. And he asked, "What is it you find amusing? Will you not share your joke with me?"

"There is no joke really," she said. "I was only—"

She broke off, and his impatience became obvious as again he exclaimed something in Spanish. Then he said, "This habit you have of not finishing your sentences is most annoying, Amanda—and strange, I would think, for someone with your teaching background."

Her "teaching background" had very little to do with her choice of words when she was around Antonio, Amanda thought wryly. Not much of anything within the norm as she knew it was valid when it concerned Antonio. Even now, when she was repelled by his drinking, she was still aware of his potent sensual magnetism, and everything within her cried out for him, for his closeness, for the sensation of being as one with him as a woman could be with a man.

At the same time, though, she was aware of the weariness etched on his face, and there seemed, too, a vulnerability to the rumpled hair, the need for a shave and the shirt carelessly unbuttoned so that she could see the fine matting of dark hair on his chest.

Antonio, in such an unfamiliar guise, was very stirring. Tenderness came to mix with an overwhelming sexual attraction, and this threatened to become a combination more lethal than anything she'd yet encountered. She could resist Antonio only so long as she kept her wits about her, and this was difficult enough at best when his impact was purely sensual. But when the chemistry that seemed to draw them together so mercilessly became combined with yet another element...a poignant, intensely moving element...the result was very apt to make a ripple seem like a tidal wave.

He was still staring at her, and he said, "What is it you do to me, Amanda? I seem to have asked you that question before, have I not? I have thought it not once but many times. Ah, *mi vida*, I did not expect ever to—how shall I say it—experience this sort of feeling. You are like the dawn to me, beautiful in its glowing colors, promising a day that will be unequaled in my life!"

He was moving toward her as he spoke, and she knew the result was inevitable. At the last instant, in fact, she found herself meeting him, and then his arms were around her and she felt herself drawn against the warmth and excitement of a rampant masculinity that provoked a response as urgent and immediate as it was involuntary. Then his mouth descended on hers in a claim for possession that forced her lips to part, his tongue plunging deeply, as if he were a *conquistador*, ready to plunder if need be, to take what he wanted.

Amanda had never been kissed this way before; she had never been claimed this way before. In one expert motion Antonio divested her of the short robe she was wearing, and very briefly he seemed shaken by the sight of her as she stood before him, wearing only the sheer yellow nightgown that plunged to a deep vee in front. The bodice was made of a wisp of fabric trimmed with lace, the shoulder straps ties of the same lace. In a single swift movement Antonio unfastened the ties, and she could feel the gown slipping downward.

Instinctively she reached to clutch it, but strong hands prevented her. He said, his voice so deep it actually seemed hoarse, ''You are so beautiful, Amanda...*corazón de mi corazón*. Do not hide yourself from me!''

Then, before she could do anything at all, he gathered her to him, but now his palms were molding her bare flesh. They roamed across her body with the finesse of a sculptor, and as he pressed close to her, there was no doubt at all in her mind of the sensations she had aroused in him or of his need for her.

They clung together, riveted by a stream of purely molten feeling, Amanda moving with him, responding to him, as if keyed to meet the mounting force of his passion. His fingers explored every part of her until she was quivering with an incredible ecstasy and everything within her cried out for the culmination of an act as old as man and woman.

Then something seemed to snap. She was barely aware of the fact they were on the couch, Antonio on top of her, for she had become part of a seething emotional caldron. But even as he groaned with his own desire, his mouth descending again and again to meet hers, she was assailed by the sickly odor of stale whiskey, and this time she recoiled.

She pushed him away so suddenly she took him completely by surprise, and in another instant she was standing, groping for her nightgown, slipping on her robe, white-faced and shaking.

Antonio sank back against the couch, his lips compressed to a narrow line. After a long moment he looked up at her, his own face surprisingly ashen, and he said something in swift Spanish, then shook his head as if in a daze and muttered, "What in God's name is the matter with you, Amanda? Surely you expressed no reluctance. Are you about to tell me your desire did not equal mine?"

"No," she said. "To my discredit."

"Then. . . ."

She looked at him, her throat so tight she could barely get the words out. "I could not have gone on living with myself if I had let you take me when you're. . .drunk," she said.

Stark fury darkened his face for an instant so brief that had she not known Antonio as she did, it would have escaped her. Then the mask slipped on and he was totally inscrutable, his voice pure ice as he said, "Drunk! You think I am drunk?"

"Oh, for God's sake, Antonio," she said wearily, "I *know* you are drunk. You were—staggering when you came in here."

"And that could not be because the room was in darkness and I was trying to walk quietly, as I did not want to arouse anyone?"

"Please," she said. "I smelled your breath. You were reeking."

"Yes, you could smell the whiskey, I am sure," he said, "because, little puritan, you had not had anything yourself. I told you I had stopped for a drink at a tavern nearby. I did not say how long I stayed there or how many drinks I had. You didn't ask that."

"Nor am I about to," she told him.

"Two drinks," he said nevertheless, and held up two fingers, as if to prove his point. "Half an hour and two drinks. Not enough to make one *borracho*, I assure you. I flatter myself that my capacity is a bit better than that. But to your sensitive nose I reeked, is that it?''

"Antonio...."

"Do not try to evade me, Amanda. *Por Dios*, you are always trying to evade me! I find you a coward," he added. "Yes, you do not have the courage of those stalwart Yankees from whom you descend. You do not have the courage—how do you say it— the courage of your convictions. Or are you merely afraid to give yourself to a man?" He glared at her. "After all," he said coldly, "it is not as if I were the first."

CHAPTER FIFTEEN

CRISTINA SAID, "Amanda, I cannot believe you are still in bed. Even Hortense told me to come up to see you."

Cristina was wearing denim shorts and a bright red tank top, and she was barefoot. Amanda, gazing up at her, had to smile. Cristina did not look in the least like a proper Spanish young lady but rather like a delightful gamine, and she wondered what Antonio thought of this.

Antonio. She had rushed out of the drawing room last night and up the stairs and had even locked her door—not that he was about to follow her! In the early hours, unable to sleep, she had got up and turned the key back, just in case Cristina decided to come in, as she often did. Now, she told herself, it was a good thing she'd done so, for Cristina, with her fertile imagination, would surely have conjectured about the door being locked.

Ribbons of golden sunlight were streaming through the window, and it was late. But she'd not been able to sleep for hours, and even now she felt tired, drained, not at all like getting up and facing the world. Especially the immediate world, in which Antonio played such a dominant part.

"Shall I bring you some coffee and rolls?" Cristina asked.

Amanda shook her head. "I'll get up. Matter of fact, I think I'll put my suit on and go for a swim before I have anything to eat."

"I will go with you," Cristina volunteered promptly.

Greg Blake joined both of them at the pool, and when they'd had enough of swimming, Cristina went back to the house and returned with tall glasses of chilled orange juice for all three of them.

Antonio did not make an appearance, but then Antonio seldom came to the pool area. She wondered if he was unable to swim or if he simply did not care for the water.

Where was Antonio? Tampa again, she supposed, but she soon found she was wrong about this. He joined them at lunch—much to her consternation. All morning she had been dreading the thought of facing him again. Now, when she saw him, she could feel herself flushing and was afraid her face was turning bright red and Cristina certainly and probably Aunt Inez and even Gregory would notice this.

Antonio, though, paid very little attention to her beyond a perfunctory greeting. He was so stiffly formal, in fact, it was difficult to believe he had been trying to seduce her on the couch in the drawing room not that many hours earlier. Trying to seduce? In all honesty she had to admit he'd not needed to try very hard.

Immediately after lunch he left them, saying, "If I am needed, I shall be at the ranch office. Would you meet me there, Greg, in half an hour or so?"

The lawyer nodded, but his face was sober as Antonio left, and after a moment he said, "I wish he'd let up on himself."

"What do you mean?" Amanda asked, the question slipping out. She'd been determined not to say anything about Antonio to anyone from there on in.

"He's driving too hard," Greg Blake said simply. "Tony always has to take the reins, if you know what I mean. I wish he'd leave this whole damned mess to Florence and me, but that's just not the way he is. He's been to Tallahassee twice to look into the state archives himself when he could perfectly well get someone else to do that. Then all the trips to Tampa...."

"To see Miss Edmond," Amanda said rather than asked.

"Yes, to see Florence, of course. But—".

"I think he is in love with her," Cristina interjected unexpectedly.

"What?" Gregory Blake asked blankly.

"*Tío*—I think he is in love with this Florence."

"Oh, come on now, Cristina," Greg protested. "Florence is a very attractive woman, I admit, but this is a business matter between them."

"One thing it can lead to the other thing," Cristina said archly.

"You," Greg Blake told her, "are an incurably romantic kid! Don't get a lot of ideas that—"

"She's probably right, Greg," Amanda found herself saying.

"You see?" Cristina retorted triumphantly. "She is, after all, the right age for *tío*. Fairly *vieja*."

Greg chuckled. "I don't think Florence would exactly relish that description," he said. "Look, what are you girls up to this afternoon? More pool siding?''

"I'm going to take a siesta," Amanda said firmly. "I didn't sleep well."

"Would you like to go riding?" Greg asked Cristina.

Her eyes widened. "You mean—with the horse?" she asked him.

He laughed. "Exactly. I've discovered Hermosa Groves still owns one small stable, and they've got a couple of mounts that would be perfect for us. Tony says you're quite an expert. I'm not, but perhaps you'd let me tag along with you."

Cristina flushed with pleasure. "I am not so expert," she said. "In Spain and in Majorca I ride quite a lot, it is true—"

"And you've won a lot of prizes," Greg finished for her.

"Oh, *tío* has been talking too much," Cristina said, but she was pleased.

"I pried it out of him," Greg told her. "Look, I'll go over to the office and Tony and I can get the business concluded. Then I'll be back for you—let's say in about an hour and a half. Would that be okay?"

"It would be perfect," Cristina assured him.

When he had left them, she said, "He is a nice man, Gregory Blake. He would be a nice man for you, Amanda, and it is clear he likes you."

"He's right, Cristina," Amanda said a bit grimly. "You really are an incurably romantic kid! Gregory and I have become friends, and I hope we shall remain so—I find him a very agreeable person. But just to set the record straight for you, I am not in love with him, nor is he in love with me."

"So," Cristina said, "it is Roger Crane, then?"

"No!" Amanda exploded. "It is not Roger Crane. It is not anybody!"

Cristina merely smiled at this, and Amanda went upstairs to take her siesta feeling decidedly annoyed at her pupil. Cristina was entirely too much of a matchmaker at heart!

Amanda was so tired—mentally, physically, emotionally—that this, combined with the Florida climate, had such a soporific effect she fell into a deep sleep. It was midafternoon when she awakened, and she was thankful, once she'd splashed her face with cold water, that she seemed to be getting some of her energy back.

It was a hot sultry day, but the thought of a solitary swim didn't appeal. She'd discovered that the library was one of the coolest rooms in the house— probably why the late Michael Field had chosen it as his own special place of refuge—and so she sought it out now, intending to curl up with one of the many good books that lined the shelves.

She was over the threshold and into the room before she saw that Antonio had got there ahead of her. He was not reading, however. He was sitting in a chair near the window, his head tilted back, and for a moment she was sure he was asleep.

She thought immediately of retreat. She thought so often of retreat where Antonio was concerned! But before she could take a step backward, he said, "If being in the same room with me is so distasteful to you, Amanda, I shall leave."

He sat up as he said this, and to her dismay she saw he looked almost haggard. A pallor underlay the olive tone of his skin, and there was a tautness to his mouth that shouted tension.

"Please," she said quickly. "If one of us has to leave, I will. But—"

She stopped, because she didn't know just what she wanted to say to him. She simply was not about to assure him that being in the room with him was not distasteful to her, for the memory of last night was much too clear. Not only that, he actually seemed to be suffering. The consequences of his own indulgence, she guessed.

Without worrying about possible repercussions, she said, "You have a headache, I suppose."

"You *suppose*?" he queried. "Would you care to elaborate on that?"

She shrugged. "You drank too much. Most people pay for it when they drink too much. One remedy, of course, is to drink some hair of the dog that bit you...."

"What?"

She had to laugh. "You can't take it literally," she said. "What it means is that if you've had too much whiskey to drink, perhaps a shot of whiskey will help you feel better."

"Oh, my God," Antonio groaned. "You Americans have a language entirely your own. I doubt I will ever be able to follow it. What you think is that I have the hangover?"

"A hangover, yes," she corrected.

"Then you are wrong, Amanda," he said, "wrong entirely. Obviously you did not believe me when I told you I was not drunk, so I will not repeat it. It seems to me, in fact, you would find it easier to forgive me if you thought I was drunk.... "

"It isn't a question of forgiveness, Antonio," she said.

"No? Then what is the question? Can you tell me that?"

She sat down in a chair across from him and gazed at him thoughtfully. She was unaware she had seldom appeared lovelier. She was wearing a sheath in a strawberry-and-cream shade of pink, this echoed in her lipstick and faint touch of blush. She'd acquired a good bit of color since being in Florida, her skin was tanned to a very becoming pale golden hue and the sun had also lightened her hair. Because of the heat, she'd piled her hair high on her head today, and it looked like a shimmering crown. She was aware Antonio was staring at her, but it didn't occur to her it might be because she was a visual feast to him and he couldn't wrench his gaze away from her.

"I—I want to be honest with you," she said. "I've always wanted to be honest with you, for that matter. I—I'm not at all like Latin women, Antonio—I realize that. I don't have much capacity for... for deception and intrigue."

"So," he said, "you think Spanish women are deceptive?"

Amanda shook her head. "That isn't what I meant. I think that dealing with men is a—a kind of game to them. Flirting is an art, and they learn how to practice it from childhood. I envy them in a way. Coquettishness is rather like their use of the fan... an entire language."

"You are speaking of an earlier age," Antonio said abruptly.

"Perhaps. But I still think women in many other parts of the world are much more skillful than we Americans are in the art of attracting men."

"Because you are so liberated?" he demanded.

"No. Liberation doesn't have much to do with what I mean. I think it is perhaps because we've always been on more equal footing with our men. We've not been put on pedestals as Latin women—women in your class, anyway—are apt to be. We've shared the good and the bad."

"And you would wish to share the good and the bad, Amanda?" he asked with an intensity that startled her.

"Yes," she said, because this was true.

He leaned back again, closing that single eye, and as Amanda looked at him, all the love she had for him came over her in such a rush of feeling it was as if she were being engulfed in an emotional tidal wave. This was not desire, though. Actually it went beyond desire, and she was not at all sure she could cope with the depths of this kind of emotion.

She yearned to go to him and put her arms around him—because it seemed to her he needed comfort at this moment.

But then wearily he stood, to say in a curiously quiet voice, "I think I shall go take a siesta myself. Excuse me, will you, Amanda."

He had been moving toward the door as he spoke, but just before he reached it, he turned.

"About last night," he began. "I was not drunk. You may believe that or not, as you wish. But it was not the right moment. It was not as it should have been between us. In that you were correct.''

THE AFTERNOON WORE ON. Greg and Cristina came back from their ride, both of them glowing and in exuberant moods that Amanda found very hard—in fact, impossible—to match.

They met in the dining room for drinks before dinner, with Aunt Inez joining them for her usual sherry, but Antonio did not appear. Pablo spoke to Cristina, who translated, saying that *tío* was resting.

"One of his headaches," she explained dismally, and Amanda felt a swift pang of shame. She had accused Antonio of having a hangover when actually he had been suffering from something completely beyond his control.

She hoped he would be well enough to join them for dinner, but apparently he elected to continue with his rest. Afterward, when Gregory suggested they get up a bridge game, there was no reason to refuse. But Amanda was hard put to keep her mind on the cards—and to understand Aunt Inez's Spanish-English bids, as well. It came as no particular surprise that night when the scores were finally tallied to find she was the loser.

The others went to bed, and she paid a quick visit to the library to get the book she hadn't bothered with earlier in the day. Then she climbed the stairs to her own room and tried to read. She could think only of Antonio, though. In fact, she ached when she thought of him, because she wanted so much to be able to do something for him.

It was still quite warm, with the high humidity

making the air oppressive. Amanda was on the verge of having a headache herself, and she stepped out onto the balcony. But there was no breeze at all.

The darkness seemed intense. No moon, no stars that night, and she felt surrounded by blackness. Then, looking across the patio to the lower level of the hacienda, she saw a dim light sifting through the windows of a room in which the curtains had been drawn. Antonio's room—of this she was sure. With a sense of anguish she pressed forward to stand against the balcony rail, wishing she had it within her powers to see through walls.

Suddenly she heard footsteps below her and saw a figure wearing a white coat come out of the shadows in the kitchen area and proceed toward those lighted windows. Pablo. She leaned forward and could make out that he was carrying a tray. And when he reached the room on the far side, he let himself in without knocking.

She waited, and soon Pablo came out again, and after a while the lights across the way flicked out. Still, even after she'd got into bed and turned out her own lights, Amanda could imagine Antonio, lying alone and in pain. It took all the willpower she could manage not to go to him.

CHAPTER SIXTEEN

DURING THE NEXT FEW DAYS it seemed to Amanda Antonio was deliberately trying to avoid her. He appeared on the patio or in the drawing room or in the dining room only when there were other people around.

One afternoon Roger Crane called her, and this time the call connected. When he asked her if she would have dinner with him the following night, she saw no reason why she should refuse, whether or not this displeased Antonio. So she accepted, but she didn't mention it to Cristina or even to Hortense until the following day, when she felt obliged to tell Hortense she would not be dining at home that evening.

Hortense did not seem very pleased about this, but it was impossible to know if this was because she, too, didn't especially like the grove manager or if she merely felt disappointed there would be one less person around to appreciate her very good cooking.

Amanda had suggested to Roger that he pick her up at six o'clock—this with the deliberate intention of getting out of the house before the others convened in the drawing room for predinner drinks. She decided, in fact, she would be waiting for him at the front door when he arrived so there would be no need for a confrontation, and she only hoped she could slip out without Antonio—or anyone else, for that matter—seeing her. Questions could come later!

She decided to wear one of the dresses she'd bought in Sarasota with Cristina, the one in a soft shade of lilac fashioned of a clinging sort of material that draped beautifully. She had an antique amethyst pendant that was a perfect foil for it, and because of the hot sticky weather, she twisted her hair up into a high arrangement that was extremely becoming.

Fortunately Cristina and Greg had gone riding again, Aunt Inez was still in her own room and Antonio was not to be seen when the time came to go downstairs. Amanda did so as noiselessly as possible, feeling ridiculously like a child about to do something she knew was wrong.

Roger was prompt. He pulled up in the Hermosa Groves station wagon precisely at six, and Amanda virtually flew down the steps to meet him, climbing into the car before he could get out and come around to open the door for her.

"Wow!" he said, appraising her. "I'm glad I decided we should go someplace special. I'm taking you to a spot on the way to Bradenton I think you'll like. Hawaiian—but both the food and the decor suit this climate."

"Sounds perfect," she said.

"I'm not sure anything could live up to you, the way you look tonight," Roger added, smiling. "That one of the dresses you bought in Sarasota?"

She nodded. "Cristina talked me into getting it. I'm not usually quite so extravagant in my clothes purchases."

"It was designed with you in mind," Roger told her.

He was looking his best that night in a tropical worsted suit of a soft cream shade, his open-throat shirt a deep coral. He could be disturbingly attractive, Amanda conceded—or would be if she had not already been captivated by someone else.

It seemed to her, as it had before, that in contrast to Antonio, Roger was an open book. She could not imagine him capable of deviousness—he simply didn't seem the type. And yet she had the distinct impression Greg Blake didn't really trust him any more than Antonio did.

Trust? Trust implied a lot of things, and it was not a word she'd thought of before in connection with the feelings between Antonio and Roger. Initially she had settled for a hostility, a mutual animosity. But if the long hours Antonio was putting in, both in Tampa and lately at the Hermosa Groves office, involved a matter of trust, then this was very perturbing.

And why had Antonio made trips to Tallahassee to search the state archives?

Amanda brought herself up short, remembering her excursion with Roger when he had accused her more than once of being in a trance. She made a determined effort to chat about a number of things, and it was not difficult to get him to talk about himself and his earlier life in California. It occurred to her after a time that they both seemed to be avoiding the topics of Antonio Hernandez and Hermosa Groves.

The Hawaiian restaurant proved to be fun. All of the guests were greeted with traditional "alohas" and garlands of paper-flower leis were flung around their necks. Drinks were served in ceramic coconut shells, and there was a floor show that was actually very good. This included hula dancers swaying remarkably gracefully in their make-believe grass skirts and a couple of outrageously funny comedians. One was a man, the other an enormous woman who called herself Honolulu Honey and who brought the house down with her jokes and her antics, to say nothing of her version of the hula.

It was not until they were on the way home that Roger touched upon the subject that—Amanda had the feeling—was uppermost in both their minds. He said, "I don't expect you to tell tales out of school, but do you have any idea what Hernandez is planning to do?"

"About what?" she asked, the question taking her sufficiently by surprise so that there was nothing contrived about her reply.

"I'd kind of like to know whether he's going to sell out," Roger said.

This was the last thing she had expected to hear.

"Not that I know of," she answered honestly.

Roger was staring ahead at the highway, and in the light from the dashboard she saw his jaw-muscle twitch. It occurred to her he was considerably more tense than he seemed; his easy manner was as much of a camouflage as Antonio's inscrutability.

"It's no secret there's a lot of interest in Hermosa Groves," Roger said now. "It's a prime piece of property. The Florida coast has been built up—both the east coast and the west coast—to the point where there's only one direction to turn, and that's inland.

The Groves is close to the lake region, and it's not that bad a drive to the gulf, especially with the road system getting bigger and better all the time. And the properties are perfect for development—condos, mobile-home parks, big shopping malls...the works."

A bell rang faintly. At one point—had it been on the plane on the way down—Antonio had said something about offers from developers. He had mentioned potential condominiums and shopping malls. Yet it didn't seem to her he had evinced any particular interest in the prospect of selling. It seemed to her he had indicated he had wanted to look into his inheritance very thoroughly before he did anything at all.

Now she said carefully, "How do you feel? About such a development, that is?"

Roger didn't answer this directly. He said instead, "Michael Field had the chance to sell out...and he would have died first. So okay, I guess you could say he did die first—before the pressure really got to him. Hermosa Groves was his life. If you ask me, he'd have fought to save the last citrus tree."

"Does that mean you feel the same way, Roger?" she inquired.

He slanted a long level glance at her. "I don't know just how the hell I feel," he confessed, "except to say Hermosa Groves has come to be about as important to me as it was to Mr. Field. I don't know if that answers your question. A lot depends on circumstances, on what happens.... Does the name Edmund Trent mean anything to you?"

She shook her head. "No. Should it?"

"He's got his finger in a lot of Florida pies," Roger said. "Done a lot of stuff out on the keys in earlier years. In fact, he's mostly concentrated on the west coast. Now he's moving inland. He's looking to gobble up properties like Hermosa Groves. It's hard to believe he hasn't approached Hernandez."

"I wouldn't know, Roger," she said frankly. "I know nothing of Antonio's business affairs."

"Does that mean you know a lot about his personal affairs?" Roger asked, and she didn't especially like his tone of voice.

"It means I work for him, just as you do," she said, "though obviously in an entirely different sort of capacity. I spend most of my time with Cristina—which is what I've been employed to do."

"And Hernandez runs the show, eh? I'd take him for a chauvinist," Roger said. "Seems to me that lawyer of his has been hanging around quite a while. Blake, from New York, and now he's got the woman lawyer from Tampa, as well. Doesn't it make sense there's something up?"

"Greg Blake is a friend, as well as a legal advisor," Amanda said.

Roger laughed. "Yes," he conceded, "and I imagine Florence Edmond has become quite a 'friend,' too."

They'd come to the road that led into the grove property, and Amanda was relieved at this. Again the night air was redolent with the sweet fragrance of the orange blossoms, and sniffing, she said, "I don't think I'll ever get used to their perfume. It's gorgeous. . .and overwhelming."

"So are you," Roger said, and to her dismay he

brought the car to a stop. He turned to her, and she knew that in another minute he'd have her in his arms. "Amanda..." he began.

"Roger, please," she said. *"Please!"*

"Hell, you don't have to beg," he told her roughly. "If you don't want me to touch you, for God's sake, I won't touch you. I—"

"You're taking it the wrong way," she said, and he shot her a smile without mirth.

"Am I?" he demanded. He started the car up again, and they moved slowly down the road through the acres and acres of carefully planted trees. "I get the feeling," he said tightly after a moment of silence, "you're Hernandez's property. I got that feeling the day he came stalking in my house and practically dragged you out of it. If that's the truth, I think it would be only decent of you to tell me. It's not my style to go after someone else's property."

Someone else's property. The mere words inflamed her.

"I do not belong to Antonio Hernandez or anyone else," she said in a tone that brooked no argument, and she did not hesitate to get out of the car once Roger had pulled up in front of the house.

Roger had incensed her. She knew she was probably taking his allusion to her relationship with Antonio too seriously, but it was not the first time he had galled her in this respect, and she decided that if he called again, she would tell him flatly she had no desire for a repeat performance.

The house was in darkness when Amanda entered it, except for a light in the foyer that obviously had been left on for her. She undressed quickly and went to bed, hoping Cristina would not hear her and come in, brim full of questions. And to her relief the girl did not appear.

IT WAS CLOUDY the next morning, dark clouds lowering ominously on the western sky. At breakfast Greg said they were expected to have thunderstorms later in the day, these following a northwest to southeast course across the state. Amanda thought privately she would welcome a storm. Several storms were needed, she decided, if the air was to be cleared. . . in a variety of directions!

When the sun did appear though, at least temporarily, they decided to go outdoors.

She realized she wouldn't be able to escape Cristina's questions entirely, and this proved to be true. Once they were down at the pool together, Gregory Blake having gone off somewhere that morning, Cristina said, "*Tío* told me last night you had a *compromiso*. It was with Roger Crane, was it not?"

"What did your uncle say I had?" Amanda demanded, not liking the sound of the word Cristina had used.

"A *compromiso*," Cristina repeated. "An engagement."

"I went out to dinner with Roger," Amanda said flatly.

"That is what I thought." Cristina nodded. "And you were late returning, were you not—I was asleep."

"Have you suddenly become my *dueña*, Cristina?" Amanda asked sharply.

Cristina's large eyes at once became doleful, and

she looked utterly crestfallen. "You must excuse me, Amanda," she said. "I do not intend to be curious. It is only that I . . . well, I care. . . ."

Amanda patted her arm. "It's okay," she said. "Come on. I'll race you the length of the pool."

They were both good swimmers, and they engaged in several friendly races before they finally pulled themselves up the ladder at the deep end to sit at the edge of the pool, their legs dangling over the side.

Then behind them that accented voice Amanda knew so well said, "I should have my camera with me."

Cristina swerved so quickly she would have fallen in the water except for Amanda's restraining arm. "¡Tío!" she protested.

Antonio laughed. "You both look very beautiful, wet hair and all," he told them.

He looked pretty terrific himself, Amanda thought, that tight feeling taking possession of her throat again. He was wearing white slacks and a black shirt open at the throat, and the pallor she'd noted the other day had vanished. He appeared vigorous and devastatingly handsome.

"I have asked Hortense to bring out iced coffee," he said, and to Amanda's surprise he stretched out to his considerable length on one of the chaise longues. Next he whipped out the oversized dark glasses he sometimes wore and put them on—this, as usual, only making his expression all the more difficult to read.

She followed Cristina across the pool apron and noticed that Cristina deliberately chose a lounge chair one chair removed from Antonio's, so she had little choice but to take the one in the middle herself. She sat on the edge of it, towel drying her hair, so tremendously aware of the dark gaze on her that her fingers actually shook.

Antonio said casually, "I have a surprise for both of you," and Cristina, who had already lain down, sat bolt upright.

"What I think, *tío*?" she demanded.

"Probably what you think, *niña*," he conceded with an indulgent laugh. "I have rented a place on Siesta Key for a week, as you requested."

"Oh, but you are an angel!" Cristina shrieked, leaping to her feet and rushing over to hug him exuberantly. "Amanda, is this not wonderful?"

"I don't know what you're talking about," Amanda said carefully.

"When we returned from Sarasota, I told *tío* we had only a glimpse of the Gulf Coast," Cristina said. "I told him I would love the chance for salt-water swimming and sunning on a real beach, and I thought you would like such a thing, too. I told him that very soon would be the time together, even if you decide to stay with us past April. It would become almost too hot then. At least so it seemed to me. So *tío* said he would see about it, and...he has!" she concluded, bestowing an adoring look upon her uncle.

"I feel as if I have been sanctified," he said dryly. "Cristina, you are soaking me with your wet bathing suit. Get up, will you!"

She did so, laughing delightedly. She was like a child who had made it through the candy-store window, Amanda thought, and wished that she herself could be so effervescent about something. At moments like this Cristina's spirits rivaled champagne.

A few seconds later Cristina announced, "I'll go get the coffee for us," and before either Antonio or Amanda could speak, she had started for the house.

After a moment Antonio said, "It is not against your wishes, is it, to go to the Gulf Coast with Cristina and Aunt Inez?"

So this was to be a trip solely for the women in the house! Amanda fought back disappointment and answered quickly, "No, of course not. It's very kind of you...."

"Spare me your politeness, Amanda," he said wearily. "There are times when I like to indulge Cristina, I admit, and also I think it might be good for you to get away from Hermosa Groves for a time."

He didn't elaborate on this, nor did he mention her engagement with Roger Crane the previous evening. Antonio was, in fact, strangely silent today, and she had the impression he didn't know what to say to her right then, any more than she knew what to say to him.

It was a relief to see Cristina hurrying across the patio area—and with Greg Blake in tow. Greg had put on a bathing suit, and he was carrying a tray with glasses of iced coffee for all of them.

Cristina obviously had already told Greg about the projected trip to the Gulf Coast, if, in fact, Antonio had not done so previously. Now Greg said ruefully, "I wish I were going out to Siesta Key with the two of you."

"And Tía Inez," Cristina reminded him demurely.

"And Tía Inez, of course." Greg grinned.

"Then why do you not come, Greg?" Cristina asked innocently, and Amanda saw Antonio frown.

"Because I have to go to Washington on business for your uncle, little one," Greg said.

Washington! It was Amanda's turn to frown. It seemed to her there must be some very serious matters involving Hermosa Groves if Gregory Blake was required to make a trip to Washington because of them. On the other hand, she told herself, other Hernandez business interests could be involved, for she had no idea exactly how many pies—American as well as European—Antonio had his fingers in.

After a time Cristina and Greg decided to swim, but Amanda declined to join them, having just anointed herself with suntan oil. Left alone with Antonio, she closed her eyes and feigned dozing. After a moment he said, a rough edge to his voice, "Is it really necessary to pretend so, Amanda? Is it impossible for us even to talk together peacefully?"

Her lips tightened. "That's a question you should ask yourself," she told him.

"You still do not believe I was not drunk that night in the drawing room, do you?" he accused her resentfully.

"Please, Antonio," she said wearily. "I don't want to talk about it."

"But I have apologized," he reminded her. "Good God, Amanda, what more do you want? Must I crawl on my knees to you?"

"You could lower your voice," she suggested. "Greg and Cristina will hear us and—"

"Greg and Cristina are making so much noise

splashing around like a couple of large puppies they will not hear anything," he said. "Nor do I give a damn if they do!"

Nevertheless Antonio did lower his voice as he spoke. But his tone was no less volatile. She had the feeling he was holding himself back with considerable difficulty. She glanced at him, and once again the oversized dark glasses made it impossible to gain any idea of what he might be thinking. Yet she sensed a latent anger about him. Was it directed at her, she wondered. And if so, why? What had she done now to annoy Don Antonio Hernandez y Vega? A short time earlier, while he had been talking about the proposed trip to Siesta Key, he had seemed in a thoroughly agreeable mood.

No doubt about it, Amanda thought dismally, she brought out the worst in him. . .and a good bit of the time he brought out the worst in her, as well.

He said unexpectedly, "You were curious when Gregory mentioned he was going to Washington on my behalf, were you not?"

"Yes," she admitted frankly, and Antonio expelled a long sigh.

"At least for once you do not fence with me," he said. "You know I have been to Tampa often?"

"Yes," she said dryly. This was something she was only too well aware of!

"Also, I have gone to Tallahassee, the state capital," he added.

"I know that Tallahassee is Florida's state capital, Antonio," she said a bit too patiently.

"Must you always be so quick to take offense?" he asked, equally patient.

"I didn't take offense. It's just that you tend to take it for granted that I—"

"That you what, Amanda?"

"Let's forget it," she said. "What were you going to say about Tallahassee?"

"I went to the state capital with Florence Edmond," he said.

"Oh," Amanda replied, very careful to keep her voice level and as toneless as possible.

"We did much preliminary work in Tampa," he said. "Now we have looked into the state archives in Tallahassee. But there is still another step to take, and that is why Gregory is going to Washington."

"I still don't know what it is you're talking about," she told him.

"I wondered about that," he said, and again she glanced at him quickly but met only a blank dark gaze. "What this involves, Amanda, is the original grant that was given my ancestor," he said then.

"The original grant?" she asked, puzzled.

"Yes, exactly. It is complicated—the matter of the Spanish land grants in your country. As a matter of fact, there was litigation involving some of the grants that went on in your courts for the better part of a century."

He turned slightly so that he was facing her more directly, and she had the feeling he was watching her with a special sort of intentness. "If I may go into history with you once again," he said, "I believe you know the United States acquired Florida from Spain in 1821."

"Yes." She nodded.

"Then let me elaborate a little more," he said. "As

I mentioned to you when we spoke of this on the plane coming down here, Spain had been in the throes of war for a number of years. It was something of a relief to King Ferdinand to get rid of Florida for five million United States dollars. East and West Florida were included in the sale, with all the buildings, the forts, whatever sort of structures there were on the land in these areas...with the exception of private property. Exact boundaries were set, and there were definite conditions to be met by both sides.

"The matter that was to cause the most trouble was the Spanish land grants. A treaty clause provided that all land grants made by the Spanish crown *before* January 24, 1818 were to be considered valid. They were to be ratified, and the persons who were then in possession of the land would have their titles to it confirmed. All grants made *after* January 24, 1818, however, were considered null and void.

"Well, as it happens, quite a few Spaniards had sold their land—to Americans, this is—after the January 24, 1818 date but prior to the Florida purchase of 1821. The new owners found their deeds were worthless. This is what provoked the rash of litigation that went on through the courts for many years."

"But what does it have to do with Hermosa Groves?" Amanda asked.

"I did not know precisely when my ancestor was given the grant that encompassed considerable acreage, including the present Hermosa Groves property," Antonio told her. "At least, I know vaguely, but not exactly. It was on the eve of leaving Boston this last time that Gregory told me there was trouble brewing, and it was at his instigation that I hired Florence Edmond to represent me in Florida.''

"What sort of trouble brewing?" Amanda queried, and even as she spoke a very ominous feeling came over her.

''I told you I had been approached by people who would like to buy the property and turn it into condominiums and shopping centers," Antonio reminded her. "There is a man named Edmund Trent, who has been the most persistent of the lot. He is an entrepreneur, and it is said that everything he touches turns to gold for his pocket...at the expense of others. I would not deal with him even if I were to make the decision to sell Hermosa Groves. But," Antonio added, "he will not easily take no for an answer. He has implied he has proof my deed is invalid because my ancestor was given his grant after that crucial date in 1818.''

"Is that true?" Amanda asked quickly.

Antonio shrugged. "We do not yet know," he said. His lips twisted into a smile that was pure mockery. "You seem so surprised, *niña*," he said, "which in turn surprises me. Has Roger Crane not told you any of this?''

Amanda did not have the opportunity to answer Antonio, because Cristina and Greg had left the pool and rejoined them at that moment. The conversation became general, but she felt all the while that Antonio was again watching her with a special intensity, and she had the oppressive feeling this was because he distrusted her.

Greg left for Washington the following day, and

two days later Amanda, Cristina, and Tía Inez left for Siesta Key. A brand new station wagon owned by Hermosa Groves had been commandeered for the trip, and Pablo had been appointed to drive them.

Antonio appeared at the door to see them off, but he seemed preoccupied and was brief in his farewells. He kissed Cristina on the cheek, kissed Tía Inez on the forehead, then hesitated when he came to Amanda, and for one heart-stopping moment she thought he was going to kiss her, too. But he said only, "Enjoy yourself, Amanda."

He sounded tired as he said it, and she could not resist answering, "I wish you were coming, too...."

She was about to add it seemed to her he was in need of a rest and some diversion himself, but at once that interrogating eyebrow shot upward and his lips curved into the mocking smile that had become much too familiar to her.

"You surprise me, *linda*," he told her.

CHAPTER SEVENTEEN

THE VILLA ANTONIO HAD RENTED on Siesta Key was a
delight. It was one of a series of villas of various
sizes, all with white stucco walls and red tiled roofs,
that were in turn part of a large condominium com-
plex directly on the Gulf of Mexico.

Theirs was the largest of the individual villas, and
it fronted the beach. One stepped from a large airy
"Florida room"—a porch, really, completely enclosed by louvered glass windows—onto sand as soft
and white as powdered sugar.

Cristina was ecstatic, and although Amanda
wasn't able to put thoughts of Antonio out of her
mind, she could not help but share some of her
pupil's enthusiasm.

After a day of doing nothing but lounging on the
beach and swimming in the milk-jade waters of the
gulf, she became so relaxed that Hermosa Groves
seemed a long way away. Even her problems with
Antonio faded, although there was still one little area
of pure hurt she couldn't quite get rid of. It really
had stung to think he could accuse her—at least by
implication—of already knowing about the dispute
over the date of the Vega grant. If he'd ever had any
confidence in her in the first place, this surely indicated he had it no longer. Now the fact that he had

not once mentioned her having gone out to dinner with Roger took on a new meaning. Antonio had evidently reached his own conclusions about the dinner and wasn't even bothering to verify them.

Antonio. She had been possessed by the man ever since she'd first met him, she told herself angrily, as she watched a big, marvelously ludicrous gray pelican soar out over the waves. The bird dived straight down, huge beak extended, to come up from the water a moment later, visibly swallowing.

One less fish, Amanda thought. Something was always gobbling up something else—or perhaps it would be more correct to say someone was always gobbling up someone else. In this instance someone named Edmund Trent was trying to gobble up Hermosa Groves and thwart whatever plans Antonio might have been about to make for the place himself.

She didn't want to think about it and was glad to agree with Cristina's suggestion that they take a walk. They went a long way up the beach, coming back to the villa with an assortment of shells they had found in the course of their excursion.

By the time they had lunch, Amanda was more than ready for a nutritious meal. Pablo was doing the honors as cook for them, and although he wasn't up to Hortense's standards, he was quite good. They feasted on gulf shrimp sizzled in butter with a sprinkling of paprika, hot French bread and a crisp tossed green salad, and even Aunt Inez complimented Pablo on his choice of menu.

It was a lazy day. They went back on the beach in the afternoon for another swim, had dinner, and then Aunt Inez and Cristina settled down to watch a musical program on TV, while Amanda curled up with a book out in the Florida room.

She heard the phone ringing from a distance and was surprised when Pablo came to tell her the call was for her. She was especially surprised when she heard Antonio's voice at the other end of the line.

"Amanda?" he asked, and her heart turned over so he had to pose the question a second time before she could answer him. Then she did so—so faintly that he quickly said, "Are you all right? Is there something the matter?"

"No, yes—that is, I'm fine," she said, her words tumbling over one another in confusion.

"Is it so exciting being there?" he asked, and he sounded amused.

Being at Siesta Key was wonderful but not exciting. Rather, it was hearing his voice that was exciting—but there was no way she was about to tell him so. She said carefully, "The villa is quite charming. There are three bedrooms. Pablo has the smallest one, then Cristina and I share the largest and Aunt Inez has a back corner one that is nicely shaded and exactly what she prefers."

He chuckled. "I didn't ask you for a floor plan, Amanda," he chided. "I am glad you like the place, though. Divert yourself. And Amanda...."

"Yes?"

He said something in swift Spanish—she caught the word *quiero*—and that was all.

"Antonio," she protested, "that's not fair!"

"Perhaps it is my way of telling you I wish you would learn a little of my language," he countered.

This statement stayed with her, and the next morning while they were sunning on the beach, she brought the matter up to Cristina.

"Do you suppose you could teach me just a few phrases?" she suggested, refraining from mentioning that the idea for all this had come from Antonio.

"I have been wanting to do just that," Cristina said. "But you and *tío* have been so busy thinking about my English...."

"Your English is improving amazingly," Amanda said.

"Yes." Cristina nodded. "I know it myself. Felipe will be very pleased."

There was something about the way she said this that caused just the faintest alarm bell to ring for Amanda, but she put aside the question of Felipe for the moment to pose a question of her own. "What does *quiero* mean?" she asked.

Cristina's eyes sparkled with mischief. "*Querer* means to want or to wish...or to love," Cristina said. "If one says *quiero* they are most apt to be saying 'I love.'"

I love. Had Antonio been telling her he wanted something? Or could he—possibly—have been speaking about love?

CRISTINA DID NOT EXPLODE her bombshell until they had been swimming and were lying out on lounge chairs, drying off. Then she said, "I can wait no longer to tell you, Amanda."

"Tell me what?" Amanda asked lazily.

"Felipe is here," Cristina said.

Amanda shot up into a sitting position so fast it

made her head reel. "What did you say?" she demanded.

"You heard me correctly," Cristina answered very soberly. "No, please do not look at me like that, Amanda. I cannot bear it to have you furious with me. I am everything you say I am—I admit it before you even say it at all. But...."

"I can't believe this!" Amanda said, her eyes narrowing. "You arranged this! You conned your uncle into renting a place out here and...."

"Yes." Cristina nodded. "I did. If it is a consolation to you, Felipe should not be here, either. He is stealing the time away from his studies."

"Well, I hope they find him out and kick him out of Columbia!" Amanda snapped.

"Amanda, please," Cristina said gently, "listen to me."

"There is nothing you can tell me that will change my mind about this," Amanda said flatly. "You can't see him, Cristina, and that's all there is to it."

"But we have planned this," Cristina said. "It has not been easy."

"I'll just bet it hasn't been easy!" Amanda agreed grimly.

"Look, dear Amanda, it has not made me happy to deceive you," Cristina said, and her huge dark eyes could not have been more doleful. "You should know one will do anything for love, though."

"*I* should know?" Amanda queried, her voice ragged. "Just what makes you think I should know?"

"Because if it were Tío Tony you would act as I do," Cristina said. "You do love Tío Tony, do you not? I have seen your face when you look at him and

know he is not watching you. I have also seen his
face—"

"Oh, shut up!" Amanda said irritably, and didn't
care in the least that tears filled Cristina's eyes and
began to spill down her cheeks. "You don't know
what you're talking about! Was it Greg or your uncle
who said you're just an incurably romantic kid?
Whichever, that's the truth of the matter. And I am
not about to have your uncle skin me alive by letting
you rendezvous with your friend Felipe. So you
might as well make up your mind to it. You are not
going to see him!"

"I am afraid it is too late for that," Cristina said.
"He is here, and. . . ."

"What do you mean, 'here'?" Amanda demanded.

"He approaches us even now," Cristina said, and
Amanda swerved to see a young man definitely walking in their direction.

Felipe Córdoba was tall—but not nearly as tall as
Antonio. For that matter, he did not look Spanish in
the least, not in the conventional sense, for he had
brown hair with a distinctly reddish cast and gray
green eyes.

But all of that Latin charm was supremely evident
as he came up to Cristina, Amanda conceded bitterly. She watched him grasp Cristina's hands, and the
contained excitement that emanated from both
Felipe and Cristina was tangible. It brought an odd
sort of pang to her, because it made her feel intensely
lonely and all of a sudden terribly aware of Antonio's
absence.

Cristina said between laughter and tears, "Amanda, this is Felipe. You know of each other already.''

"Yes, we do, don't we," Amanda agreed ironical-ly. "Mr. Córdoba, I can't say I'm glad to meet you. You're putting me in a very dreadful position."

He looked faintly puzzled. Then he said, "Cristina told me you were on our side."

"Cristina was fantasizing," Amanda said bluntly. "I'm not on anyone's side in this matter except my own. As you know, I'm employed by Cristina's uncle, and he would not be agreeable to this meet-ing."

"No," Felipe said easily, "you're quite right about that. Tony Hernandez would not be at all agreeable to this meeting."

He spoke without a trace of a Spanish accent but with a slight English one, and Amanda remembered Cristina saying his mother was English. Now he smiled, and she could easily see why Cristina had been captivated by him.

"There's some truth to that old saying about everything being fair in love and war," he remarked. "Cristina and I felt this was the one chance we'd have to meet for—God knows how long. It's not go-ing to be easy for the two of us to be—discreet, I'll grant you that. But I can swear to you we will be, because neither of us wants to make trouble for you. Cristina speaks to me about you every time she calls. She insists you've saved her life."

"Among other things," Amanda said wryly, "Cristina tends to be overly dramatic."

"Cristina is also here," Cristina pointed out, "and you both talk of me as if I were not visible."

"You are entirely visible, *querida*," Felipe told

her, "and even more beautiful than you were the last time I saw you. Amanda, I can be here only three days...I do not dare stay away from the university any longer than that. If I agree to see Cristina only when you are present, will you keep our secret?"

Amanda looked from one anxious young face to the other, and she could not suppress a rather wistful smile. She said, feigning considerably more reluctance than she felt, "Go take a walk down the beach for a few minutes while I think about it."

They were off in an instant, and she lay back on her lounge chair, conflicting feelings immediately beginning to wage war within her. She liked Felipe Córdoba. A snap judgment, perhaps, but she didn't think it was one she would be apt to revoke later on. Also, there was no doubt in her mind Felipe and Cristina were really in love with each other, and the thought of family interference under such circumstances galled her. The attitude of their respective families reeked of the sort of feudal mentality she'd already accused Antonio of, and it had no place in the world of today, she thought firmly. Lovers illstarred because of family feuds belonged in *Romeo and Juliet* with its age-old hate war between the Montagues and Capulets.

Well, echoes of Shakespeare should be limited to stage performances, Amanda decided. What harm could it do if Cristina and Felipe walked up and down the beach together for the next couple of days?

Felipe was right. More than she'd realized, she was on their side.

THERE WAS EXCITEMENT to being part of a conspiracy. As she went to bed that night, Amanda thought, to her amusement, that she actually thrived on intrigue. Romantic intrigue, anyway.

She, Cristina and Felipe had had a long talk on the beach, Amanda feeling relatively safe about this because she knew Aunt Inez and Pablo had gone shopping together—Aunt Inez had decided she wanted to explore the mysteries of an American supermarket.

Nevertheless there was a certain tension involved in having Felipe so near the villa—or there was, until she discovered Felipe and Pablo had never met.

"That," Amanda said upon learning this, "is a relief! Pablo would be right on the phone to Antonio!"

"Well, you see," Cristina explained, "it is because Pablo comes from Andalusia, and I have known Felipe only on Majorca. Until not so long before my parents were killed," she added, her voice faltering slightly on this, "I lived most of my time in Andalusia. Then we moved to Manacor on Majorca because my father was supposed to take charge of our pearl manufactory."

"And we met one day on the beach," Felipe continued. "When I found out she was named Hernandez, I was pretty desolate about it. I knew all about the family feud, but until I really got into it I didn't realize how deep those things could go." He scowled. "It is so damned ridiculous!"

"I agree," Amanda told him. "Totally out of date. And unfortunately I don't have the power to change Spanish tradition. That will be up to you two—if you think you can handle it.''

"We're going to handle it—one way or another," Felipe told her. "One of these years when she's not quite such a child," he added, looking down at Cristina fondly, "I'm going to marry this young lady."

Cristina nodded and pressed herself up against him, and watching them, Amanda again felt the wistful pang that left a very bleak sense of sadness in her heart. She rallied to say briskly, "All right. Let's get back to *now*. I don't like deceiving Tía Inez, but obviously we can't let her know you're here, Felipe."

"Obviously," he agreed.

"That means just daytime meetings on the beach, I'm afraid," Amanda said. "No evening...*compromisos*."

Felipe grinned widely. "You have my word," he agreed. "No evening *compromisos*!"

FELIPE'S FIRST DAY PASSED and then the second day, and as the hours ticked by, Amanda began to realize what a vast sigh of relief she was going to breathe when he left to return to New York. Twice Aunt Inez had decided to go for a beach stroll at precisely the wrong moment, and it had been entirely too hairy for comfort. Aunt Inez seldom went for beach strolls at all, and it seemed incredible she would decide to do so now. But such were the quirks of fate, Amanda conceded.

The third morning, she and Cristina walked up the beach to a refreshment stand, and by prearrangement Felipe met them there. That afternoon it seemed safe enough to let him come to the beach in front of the villa. Aunt Inez always took a long siesta in the afternoon, and Pablo was going into Sarasota to actually see his first American movie.

Amanda had had enough of the sun for one day, so she took a wide shade hat and dark glasses with her when she went back out to the beach with Cristina after lunch, and she carried along a paperback novel she'd bought. She read for a time and then was almost dozing when she was roused not only to instant but to frantic wakefulness.

"*Querida,*" Antonio said, "your feet are going to become lobsters."

Amanda had attached a small canopy to her lounge chair, but even so her feet were thrust out into the broad sunlight, and once again Antonio was right. She covered them quickly with a beach towel she'd brought along, and only then did she dare to gaze up at him.

The sight was almost too much for her. He was wearing black bathing trunks that molded his body like a second skin. His hair was raven in the sunlight, with a bluish tint to it, and he was looking at her in a caressing sort of way that would have been enough to make her swoon even if his being there in itself hadn't already made her feel as though she'd suddenly started spinning out through space.

For a moment she forgot all about Felipe and Cristina, who had gone for a walk down the beach. She was conscious only of Antonio. In fact, she was so overwhelmingly conscious of him that the gulf, the pelicans, the palm trees and the tall Australian pines that fringed the beach were all blotted out. She could have been anywhere.

He sat down with that usual grace of his on the chair normally occupied by Cristina, that dark gaze—for he was wearing the oversized glasses—giving him an advantage once again because it was so totally unrevealing.

There was a hint of amusement in his voice as he asked lazily, "Am I to assume your reaction means you are welcoming me, Amanda? Or would you prefer I had never left Hermosa Groves? You said the other day you wished I were coming. Did I read an invitation where you did not intend one, *linda*?"

An invitation! Dear God, *she* was an invitation in herself where Antonio was concerned. She looked at him and could only hope her face was not as transparent as she felt it must be. Everything within her seemed to have surged to the surface, and her longing for him, her *desire* for him, was an overwhelming ache.

Nothing else seemed to matter. Nothing else did matter! The truth of this swept over her, and she was staggered by its sudden revelation. She *loved* this man sitting across from her, gazing at her with an enigmatic smile curving his lips. She wanted to feel those lips on hers, she wanted to feel the warmth of his hands caressing her body and she wanted to know the closeness of his body...so close, so close, they would become intertwined, they would become one in as true a sense of the word as possible. She wanted to know a union with him of the body...and of the mind...and of the spirit. She wanted to be his. Utterly, completely, his.

She shivered, and he said, "You still have not spoken a word to me, Amanda. Is my appearance here such a shock to you?"

A *shock*? The word snapped her to a different sort of attention. Her thoughts swirled away from herself and her own emotions, and now she stared across at him in horror.

He saw the look in her eyes and she knew at once he'd misread it. He frowned. "It would seem," he said coldly, "that I made a mistake in coming here."

"Oh, no, Antonio," she said swiftly. "No. I . . . I'm very glad to see you."

It was spoken lamely—she knew that. But it was still true. It was true, at least, in the sense that she was very glad to see him for her own sake, because he was her world. Yet she wished she had the power either to spirit him away from there immediately or else send a telepathic message of warning to Cristina and Felipe, who were blissfully walking along the beach.

As if he were reading her mind, Antonio asked abruptly, "Where is Cristina?"

"Resting," Amanda stammered.

"Cristina, taking a siesta?" He raised an eyebrow at this. "The two of you must be leading quite a life! And Tía Inez? She is taking a siesta, too?"

"Yes." Amanda nodded.

"So," he began as he got to his feet, "I think I will take a swim. Will you come with me?"

She longed to go with him, but she did not dare do so. There was the chance she could intercept Cristina and Felipe while Antonio was in the water. Still, she hated so much to refuse his invitation that when she said, "I don't think so, thanks," the words perversely gave the impression of indifference.

"Very well," he said, and she had no doubt at all she'd displeased him.

He started across the wide expanse of white sand without another word, and Amanda watched him go with an ache in her heart. He made an arresting figure—he was a man who would forever stand out in a crowd. Just the way he held his head at that proud angle and the way he moved. There was a pantherlike grace to his walk.

The beach was wide at that point, and there was almost always a procession of walkers along the water's edge. That afternoon was no different. Still, she had no difficulty in distinguishing Antonio's figure, and she saw him wade into the light green water and wished desperately she were with him. He had never seemed to swim in the pool at the hacienda, and she had thought that either he didn't swim at all or was not doing so for some reason involving his eye.

Now she wondered if the reason he usually refrained from going in the water was simply because he didn't want to remove the eye patch in front of anyone and it would be awkward to try to swim with it on. She shivered as she always did when she thought of the eye patch—or rather what lay behind it. Was Antonio so mutilated he really didn't think anyone—she—could bear to look at his disfigurement? The thought made her ache, for it seemed to her a burden he shouldn't have to bear. No matter what was behind the eye patch, she told herself, she could accept it, because it was, after all, a part of him. And if it were something...terrible...she wanted to console him, to entwine her arms around him and in her way attempt to make up for his suffering.

Now as she watched, squinting against the sun in her effort to see more clearly, he cut through the waves. But it seemed to her his dark head was still above the water. Then there were simply too many people in the way—he was lost from sight to her—and she leaned back in the lounge chair and closed her eyes, wondering what in God's name she was going to do next.

The sensible thing would be to go after Felipe and Cristina, tell Felipe to get away as quickly as possible and order Cristina back to the house and bed so her uncle could come and see for himself she was taking a siesta! But now she tried to remember which direction Felipe and Cristina had started off in, to the right or to the left, and she drew a total blank. She had been immersed in her book when they'd left, and she hadn't paid any attention to them. They'd been gone quite a while, so perhaps they'd stopped at a small beach club down the way for something to drink. That would mean they'd gone to the left. But on the other hand. . . .

She shook her head helplessly, sitting up again and peering in every direction. Then her attention was arrested by Antonio, who had left the water and was walking back across the sand toward her.

He filled her mind as well as her eyes, and as he came closer, she saw drops of water glistening on his olive skin, and this had a strangely sensual effect on her.

His hair was dry, and this, too, had an odd effect on her. He'd had to swim with his head out of water because of the patch, and yet she'd seen the way he'd cleaved into the low rolling waves. She had sensed the latent power in his stroke even from this distance, and she knew he must have longed simply to let go, to plunge into the water even as she herself did, to revel in it. It was another restriction in Antonio's life, and it occurred to her he'd had far too many restrictions imposed on him in a variety of ways. Roger Crane could say what he liked about people who were automatically given the pot of gold at the end of the rainbow, but with gold there could sometimes come a price....

He was looking down at her, and he said, his voice quite cold, "Would you happen to have an extra towel with you, Amanda?"

"Yes," she answered quickly, and rummaged in her beach bag, then handed him one. She watched, fascinated, as he dried himself, her eyes lingering on the sculpted contours of his body. He was not Greek, she found herself thinking. Yet he very well could have been a Greek god....

But there was nothing reminiscent of Olympus as he said, "*Por Dios*, what is it with you? You are looking at me as if I am some sort of menace!"

He was. More of a menace than he realized. She swallowed hastily and started to say something... and then she stopped, her eyes widening in pure horror. Cristina and Felipe were coming toward her, hand in hand, completely oblivious to everything except themselves.

"You look as though you are seeing ghosts," Antonio observed wryly. He shifted to follow her gaze, turning all the way around to see what she was seeing because they were coming from the left—his blind side.

Then he muttered something under his breath that was the distillation of fury, and she shrank from the venom in the expression that crossed his face.

"Please, Antonio," she began, and he turned to her angrily.

"Never again say please to me about anything, Amanda," he commanded. "It is enough I trusted you. You might as well have stabbed me in the back!"

At that instant Cristina looked up...and she stopped in her tracks, still clutching Felipe's hand, her piquant face not nearly so frightened as purely miserable.

"*Tío,*" she said simply, but the misery came through in the single word.

"So," Antonio said, disregarding his niece and addressing the boy at her side, "you managed to find her, Felipe. With Amanda's assistance, I presume?"

"No," Felipe said. "This was arranged entirely by Cristina and me, Tony. There is no need for you to blame Amanda."

"How generous of you to protect her!" Antonio said, and Amanda had never heard him sound more sarcastic. "But surely you are not trying to tell me your appearance here is a surprise to her? No wonder you were so distressed to see me, Amanda."

"I was not distressed to see you, Antonio," she said, her voice very low.

"Oh, come," he said. "Must it always be that just when I feel I can begin to trust you, you prove to me you are both a liar and a cheat?"

It was Cristina who answered this, her voice trembling. "You have no right to talk to Amanda like that, *tío*," she told him bravely. "She is not a liar and she is not a cheat. You should apologize to her."

"You think so?" Antonio demanded, his tone dangerously controlled. "I shall discuss Amanda's involvement with her later, Cristina. At the moment I am more interested in you and Felipe."

Felipe suddenly looked older. He kept his grasp on Cristina's hand, and there was a new determination about him as he met Antonio's disturbing black gaze squarely. "Don't blame Cristina for this," he said levelly. "It was my doing. When I knew she was coming here, I decided to skip out from school and come down. I had to see her. I make no apologies for that. I love her—I think you know very damned well I love her. I also think the only thing you've got against me is that my family are longtime business rivals of your family and through the years have kept up a stupid feud started by God knows who a long time ago. I doubt there's anyone alive who could really tell you how or why it started. It seems to me that, Spanish pride or no Spanish pride, things like this are damned well out of date, Tony. I've always thought you were quite a person. You never struck me as the sort who would cling to outmoded traditions. But perhaps I'm wrong. If you are all *hidalgo*—nobleman—and living back in the Middle Ages, then I have misjudged you."

Antonio did not answer this, but his face looked as if it had been carved from stone, and Amanda shrank from the coldness of his fury. This glacial anger was far worse than a red-hot rage, and she didn't know how to handle it.

After a moment that seemed eternal he said crisply, "Go back to the villa, Cristina. And you, Amanda, please go with her. I wish to speak to Felipe alone."

At least he had said please. But this was little consolation as she trooped back to the villa with Cristina, whose dark eyes were now brimming with tears.

Once in the bedroom they shared, Cristina flung herself on her bed and began to sob. Amanda, sitting down on the edge of her own bed, only wished she could let herself go with Cristina's kind of Latin abandon. She needed the purging effect of tears. But she was curiously dry-eyed, and her heart had never been heavier.

Antonio had reason to be angry with her, to be furious with her—she had deceived him in condoning the meetings between Felipe and Cristina those past couple of days. But the meetings in themselves had seemed so absolutely harmless. Was Antonio so completely devoid of real feeling he couldn't appreciate what young love was like? Had he forgotten how terribly vulnerable young lovers were?

Cristina, sobbing, said, "He will send Felipe away and I will never see him again. And now I have also got you in so much trouble, Amanda. Tío is so angry with you. . . ."

"Yes, he is," Amanda agreed. "But that's my fault, not yours, Cristina. I went along with you, and I didn't have to. Also, I knew in my heart that if Antonio ever found out, he would be apt never to forgive me. But I still felt you and Felipe deserved the chance to—to simply walk on a beach together for a few hours and dream about your future.''

''Oh, Amanda!'' Cristina cried, this statement provoking a fresh torrent of tears.

''Stop crying, Cristina!'' Amanda said abruptly. ''Your eyes will be red for the rest of your life! In any event, there is no reason to let your uncle make you so miserable. The thing to do is for you to stand up to him. Wait until tomorrow, when things are calmer, and then tell him frankly how you feel about Felipe...just as I'm sure Felipe is telling him now how he feels about you. Your uncle may be ridiculously proud and arrogant, but I don't think he's totally unfair. He's—''

She stopped because of a certain expression in Cristina's eyes and turned to see Antonio on the threshold.

There was cruelty in his mocking smile, and that single dark eye seemed to bore a hole through her. ''Go on,'' he invited, ''I am what?''

''You are a damned eavesdropper!'' Amanda said hotly.

He laughed at this, a short mirthless laugh, but he advanced into the room, looking down at both Amanda and his niece from a height that seemed to be towering.

''You looked very—unsteady when you stood up outdoors,'' he told Amanda. ''I was afraid you were about to faint. The effect of the sun, no doubt. Anyway, I came in to see if you were all right.''

''How considerate of you!'' she said, her words dripping with sarcasm. ''It was not the effect of the sun, however...as you very well know.''

"You blame me for your giddiness?" he asked.

"Yes," she said, and then she realized this could be considered quite an admission, depending upon his interpretation of her answer.

She saw his fists clench, and the muscle in his jaw twitched. He actually took a step toward her, and it was all she could do not to meet him halfway. Something flowed between the two of them—it was like the current in a river—and she felt herself caught in it, whirled into a torrent of emotion. Antonio, she knew, in this particular moment at least, was as powerless as she was. He, too, was being swept along on a current that was becoming stronger and stronger.

She felt her knees going weak, and she moaned softly. Then she looked at Antonio, and something seemed to lock between them. He stood very still. She had the feeling he was using every ounce of willpower he possessed to regain control of himself.

In the stillness Cristina asked, "Where is Felipe?"

Antonio rallied. "He has gone to dress," he told her. "I must do the same. We are going to meet for a drink."

"You and Felipe?" Cristina demanded, amazed by this.

"Yes," Antonio said tightly. "My mentality, little *sobrina*, is not entirely feudal," he added, while Cristina stared at him in astonishment. But he did not look at Amanda as he said this.

ALTHOUGH ANTONIO HAD GONE to meet Felipe for a drink, signifying a willingness at least to discuss matters, Amanda was well aware she was not off the hook with him.

No matter what action he might take where Cristina and Felipe were involved, she had gone behind his back, and she knew only too well this was not something he would be apt either to forgive or forget. No, sooner or later he was going to take her to task—she was certain of it.

The summons came even faster than she expected. During the morning it had been agreed that, after seeing yet another American movie, Pablo would stop at a Chinese restaurant on the Tamiami Trail and bring back an assortment of different Oriental dishes for their dinner. Fortunately Pablo was so intrigued with the menu he bought too much, and so there was plenty for everyone.

Antonio was amused at the menu choice, and they all chuckled at the thought of Pablo managing to give any order at all in a Chinese restaurant when his English was so limited...though admittedly it had been improving daily since he had been working with Hortense.

"I think Hortense has been giving Pablo English lessons, just as Amanda has been giving them to me," Cristina observed as they polished off egg rolls, crisp fried chicken wings, delicate shrimp puffs, baked ribs marinated in soy sauce and an assortment of main-course dishes that included a delicious chicken concoction done with toasted sesame seeds and a lemon-flavored sauce.

Antonio finished devouring a rib and then noted cryptically, "I would say Amanda has been giving you a lot more than English lessons, Cristina."

"Tío—" Cristina began, sensing trouble.

But Antonio interrupted. "May I have some more

tea, please, Amanda?'' he asked politely, and she refilled his cup with fragrant jasmine tea, her fingers shaking so badly it was all she could do not to spill it.

When dinner was over, Antonio announced without preamble, ''I wish to speak to you, Amanda. Alone. I suggest we take a drive.''

Cristina started to say something, but he commanded, ''¡*Silencio, niña!* I am not going to eat her alive, you know.''

''Only because you're afraid you'd get indigestion if you tried it,'' Amanda mumbled under her breath.

And heard him mutter for her ear alone, ''True.''

CHAPTER EIGHTEEN

Antonio said, "I was fortunate to be able to rent a small place farther down the key. I think we will go there."

They were walking along a path at the side of the villa that led toward a parking space facing Midnight Pass Road, which traversed the entire length of Siesta Key, and Amanda managed to feign indifference sufficiently to say, "Very well."

He nodded, walking with a long stride she found almost impossible to keep up with. She saw he was using another Hermosa Groves car, the crest emblazoned on the side of the dark sedan parked in the first space, and now he went ahead and opened the door on the passenger side for her.

She felt very small as she sank into the car's deep plush upholstery, but she wished she could make herself even smaller. She wished, in fact, she had the power to wave a wand and become totally invisible. Such magic, she conceded ruefully, was about the only way she could possibly hope to evade Antonio.

He turned right as they came out of the driveway, and within a very short distance turned right again, almost immediately entering a fairly large courtyard that had been converted into several parking spaces. They were facing a two-story building that was very

Spanish in design and seemed to be composed of individual apartments. Outside staircases done in tiles led to the second-floor units, and the lighting was especially effective. Large Mexican tin ''cutout'' lamps had been used everywhere, focused so that even at night one could enjoy the sight of vivid purple bougainvillea splashed against the beige stucco. There were lemon trees in blossom, their fragrance scenting the air with a perfume as intoxicating as that of the orange trees at the Groves, and when Antonio indicated to her she should go up the flight of stairs to the right, Amanda saw hibiscus bushes growing at the edge of the staircase wall, their vivid red blossoms highlighted in the lamp glow.

There was a full moon that night, a silver disk in an indigo sky. The stair landing on the second story served as a small balcony, too, from which one could look out over the gulf, the water glittering like lengths of shimmering metallic material. Amanda found herself thinking this could be a tropical paradise and the night really made for love—except it wasn't love that had caused Antonio to bring her there.

No, she had no doubt he had brought her there to tell her she was through and to make arrangements for her departure as soon as possible. Probably he'd already checked the flights to Boston!

She watched him turn the key in the door of his temporary apartment, and he flipped a switch that lighted a lamp at the far end of the room. It was a pleasant room, large, with windows facing the moonlit gulf. The curtains were drawn back so that the view was terrific—a clump of palms studding the sand midway along the beach between the building and the silver-sheened water.

Antonio said formally, "Sit down, will you please?"

Amanda obeyed, moving reluctantly—like a child who knows that punishment is coming and doesn't want to face it. He walked over to a small ice chest in the corner, and she watched his back, which, turned to her now, seemed totally uncompromising. A moment later he crossed the room to hand her a glass with two cubes of ice and a generous measure of amber liquid in it. She tested and found he'd poured Scotch straight on the rocks, but just now she didn't mind—she needed all the fortitude she could get!

Antonio sat down in a chair directly opposite her, from which he could look her straight in the face. No chance of being partially eclipsed by his blind side, she thought dismally. He took a long swallow of Scotch before he spoke, and then he said, his voice tightly controlled, "You really don't give a damn about my feelings, do you, Amanda!"

This kind of accusation was not at all the sort of thing she'd expected to hear from him, and she wished only that she knew what to say in answer. Anything she could think of on the spur of the moment seemed inadequate. Antonio smiled, a nasty triumphant sort of smile, and observed, "I seem to have made my point."

"No," she contradicted, "you haven't. It's simply that I don't know how to answer you. You've placed me at a disadvantage...again. You seem to have a tendency to do that."

His laugh was scornful. "*I* place *you* at a disadvantage?" he challenged. "I should say it is very much the opposite, Amanda. You are entirely different from any woman I have ever known, and I've felt at a disadvantage with you from the moment you first walked into my hotel suite back in Boston."

She couldn't resist it. "Dowdy creature that I was?" she reminded him.

His gaze swept the full length of her, appraising her from the crown of her golden hair—which she'd brushed down so that it hung in waves around her shoulders—to the rather low scooped neckline of the lavender linen dress she was wearing—another of the dresses she'd bought in Sarasota with Cristina. The dress fitted beautifully, emphasizing the round curves of her breasts, then hugging her waist and flaring into a wide circular skirt. She was wearing slim, high-heeled sandals fashioned in bands of lavender, pink and fuchsia leather, and she'd put on some pink shell earrings she'd bought at a shop on Midnight Pass Road only the day before. They were unusual in design, giving a sort of swirl effect, and they had instantly attracted her eye. Her skin was a light golden tan now, and the lavender shade of her dress brought out tones of violet in her eyes. Her mirror had told her when she'd dressed that night there was a new sort of loveliness about her—she could recognize this without any sense of self-conceit. But now Antonio was looking at her in a way she found very disconcerting, and she felt herself flushing.

She saw his jaw tighten, and he sought comfort in the Scotch before he spoke. She sensed the tight rein with which he was keeping himself in check as he said, his voice *too* controlled, "You look like a woman in love. Who is it, Amanda?"

Everything within her yearned to say, "You." But she could imagine his skepticism were she to do so, to say nothing of the fact such a statement on her part—disbelieved—could be all that was needed to unleash the fury he was restraining with a difficulty that was becoming increasingly obvious. So she said only, "You misunderstand me, Antonio."

"No," he replied roughly, emotion flaring briefly despite his rigid self-control, "I do not think I misunderstand you at all. You have disappointed me, yes, that I admit—"

"I don't think I've done anything so terrible," she interrupted, and was a bit surprised at her own statement. "Cristina and Felipe are in love, and it would have been cruel to have made him go away without seeing a little of her. Their meetings have been entirely on the beach...under enough chaperonage, I think, to satisfy even you."

"You think so?" He stared at her. "It occurs to me you don't know me very well at all, Amanda, even though for a time I thought...otherwise. I am not speaking merely of Cristina and Felipe when I say you have disappointed me."

She shook her head. "You're talking in riddles, Antonio."

"No, I am not," he contradicted. "You merely do not wish to hear me. I am disappointed about Cristina, yes. You knew that one reason why I brought her here was to break up this romance with Felipe Córdoba. You knew that, and whether I was right or wrong in such an action, you agreed to take the position I was offering with that in mind. Am I right?''

"Yes," she admitted. "You are quite right."

"And yet," he said, "you sabotaged all of that without so much as a thought as to how I might feel about it."

"That's not true," she said. "Sabotage is a ridiculously strong word to begin with—"

"Then forgive my poor English," he interjected coldly.

"It is not a question of your 'poor English.' It is a matter of your jumping to conclusions about things," she told him. "Especially, I think, about things in which I seem to play a part. As for the situation involving Cristina and Felipe, I did think about how you might feel in regard to their seeing each other. I was concerned about it. . . and I didn't enjoy deceiving you, though I think even *deceive* is a very strong word for what actually happened. I've told you the way it has been and I don't think I need to say any more about it. I deplore your attitude, Antonio—I really deplore it!''

His eyebrow lifted. "*You* deplore my attitude!" he said, obviously exasperated. "*Por Dios*, Amanda, but you have a way of—what is it you say—of turning the tables around."

"That's not what I'm trying to do," she said. "You're acting as if I've committed some sort of crime. I call that overreacting on your part."

"Do you indeed?" he said with deceptive mildness. He stood and went back to the table in the corner, sloshing Scotch into his glass without bothering to add any more ice to it. When he had resumed his seat again, she saw that his mouth was tight, and that, in fact he looked miserable.

"I wish," he said, staring into the depths of the whiskey, his face averted from hers, "that it was not this way, Amanda. But what am I to think? I know very well that when I mentioned the name Edmund Trent to you it was not the first time you had heard it. That's true, is it not?"

She was totally unprepared for this. Her eyes were huge as she looked across at him, a sense of distress such as she'd never felt before overtaking her.

"What are you saying, Antonio?" she asked him.

He shook his head. "I am not sure I know myself," he admitted.

"Are you implying Roger Crane has taken me into his confidence in some way that's against you?" she demanded, furious he should even think such a thing.

"Has he?" Antonio asked softly.

She glared at him, anger mounting with white-hot swiftness. "No!" she said with a violence that surprised her. "I would not keep such a confidence, I would never promise to do so, don't you know that? Don't you think I have any loyalty at all where you are concerned?"

"Loyalty," he echoed. "Do you have any loyalty where I am concerned, Amanda? You surely did not show it in the case of Cristina and Felipe."

"We have been through that," she said shortly. "This is something entirely different. . . as you know very well. You are acting as if you think I might sabotage you. I—"

She stopped short, arrested by the expression on his face. It was an expression not so much of skepticism as of sadness, and it made her forget about everything except her urge to somehow comfort him.

Anger faded, and in its wake surged the love for him that had become such a part of her, ever present, ever true. She knew she must reach this man before unfounded suspicions destroyed even a part of something between them that was tender and wonderful and very precious...despite the sparks that almost always seemed to ignite when they had any real encounter.

"Antonio," she said slowly, "we should not do this to each other. You should know I could never possibly go against you...to the point of betrayal— with Roger Crane or with anyone else. And we should not forever be at each other's throats like this when we both know...."

She broke off, on the verge of making an admission she did not want to make...because it would be a revelation so great in impact it would be impossible ever to face him on a casual footing again. And further, for her to declare her love for him in this way, would imply she thought he returned it.

How in God's name have I ever managed to come even close to that conclusion, she asked herself dully.

She tried to think of something else that would finish off her treacherous sentence, but before she could do so, he asked softly, "What do we both know, Amanda? Tell me, *vida,* what do we both know?"

Then, before she could answer him, he was on his feet. It was as if he'd cast a hypnotic spell over her, and she, too, stood drawn toward him in a trance of his making, going to meet him halfway. His arms went around her, and she felt the soft cotton of his shirt against her skin. Then he was holding her close, terribly close, and she was immediately aware of the effect she'd had on him. He was thoroughly aroused, the male essence of him hard against her, until involuntarily her thighs parted so that he could move even closer, so that she could feel him that much more.

Her senses swam, her emotions swelled as if to consume her. His sensuality went beyond her wildest dreams and she could feel the nipples of her breasts harden as she thrust herself against him. His lips touched hers, the mere contact sending off voluptuous little currents, that forked through her body so that she was consumed with the urgency of her own desire. Then, as he moved against her in a slow undulating rhythm, she knew his desire more than matched her own.

He began to undress her very slowly, and each gesture, each movement of his hands, was a stimulating caress. She wore only a pale blue satin bra and matching panties beneath the lavender dress, and he removed first one and then the other with deliberate languor until finally she stood nude before him. Then he fixed his gaze upon her as, with equal slowness, he unbuttoned his shirt, then unfastened his belt so that his dark brown slacks slid to the floor.

His body was beautiful, muscular, perfectly formed, his manhood now triumphant. Again she met him halfway, for she could not possibly have kept away from him or the experiencing of a new kind of contact as skin touched skin in the most intimate way.

The bed seemed to rise to meet them, and as their lips clung together, his hands passionately explored her. Then, almost shyly at first but with a confidence that grew, she began to explore him, experiencing him as she had never experienced a man before... not even her own husband. Finally he murmured, "*Ay, querida,* I cannot wait any longer!" And suddenly he was plunging himself into her, becoming a part of her. But she was ready for him, and they mounted together into a climax that spiraled Amanda into an entirely different dimension. And when the ultimate moment was over, she still stayed within the orbit of his arms until he kissed away the tears that had come to fill her eyes and brim over.

It was a long and very tender time, and she only wished it could go on and on and on. In the aftermath of their lovemaking she lay beside him, absorbing his warmth and suffused by a precious sense of belonging to him as she had never belonged to another person.

But when—finally—she stole a look at him, his expression surprised her. His lips were tight, and he looked as if he were struggling with an emotion she couldn't define; the eye patch seemed large and very black against skin that suddenly had a pallor to it. Even at the height of their lovemaking he had not removed the patch. Now it began to seem like a symbol of his apartness—even though, God knows, he had been as much a part of her as she'd been of him during the glory of those transcending moments together. Yet regardless of *everything*, there was a solitary quality to Antonio. It possessed him even now, she thought sadly.

He said, his voice very low, "I had better take you back."

She didn't answer. She stood; then all at once she felt she couldn't bear to be before his gaze with nothing on. She scooped up her clothes and made for the bathroom, and her hands were shaking as she fastened on her bra, slipped on her dress, then combed her hair and hastily put on some lipstick.

He was standing at the window when she returned to the room, and he was fully dressed, staring out at the moonlit gulf. And there was a very bleak aura about his silhouette. It came to her there was something so curiously tormented about Antonio that there would always, always be a part of him held in reserve. Whereas she had given herself to him fully, so fully. . . .

He turned to ask, "You are ready?"

"Yes," she said, subdued. She walked ahead of him out of the apartment and down the steps, but then she paused for an instant, waiting for him. And when he joined her, she saw he held in his hand a red hibiscus he had plucked from one of the bushes that grew along the staircase wall.

He handed it to her wordlessly. Their fingers touched, and she was astonished at the effect of this contact. She felt as if, with the flower, he was transmitting a message to her he was unable to convey himself.

He let her off at the villa, asking her only to tell

Cristina he would talk to her in the morning. "She needs to worry a bit over the night," he added cryptically.

Amanda went inside to find Cristina and Aunt Inez deeply involved in a program on television that was actually in Spanish. She slipped into the bedroom and sat down on the edge of her bed, studying the hibiscus. It was a beautiful exotic flower. There were five, slightly fringed petals in a vibrant shade of red fanning out into a wide trumpet. Emerging from the center was a long stamen with a fuzzy yellow cluster running along the length of it, the end terminating in a miniature flower of sorts formed by five tiny red circles. She peered deeper, and there—in the very heart of the hibiscus—she saw five dark spots that looked like a star. And she stared down at them in fascination. It seemed to her they formed in a sense the star of her own destiny. And it had been given to her by Antonio.

She put the hibiscus in a glass of water and placed the glass on her bedside table. It was the last thing she gazed at before she turned off her light. But when she awakened in the morning, she found to her dismay that the flower had curled up, petal wrapping around petal, the star at the heart completely hidden from her sight.

Carefully she placed the glass on the windowsill, and during the course of the day she went back to her room every now and then to see if, perhaps, the blossom had reopened under the benediction of the sunlight streaming in through the windows. But the hibiscus stayed tightly furled, and as evening approached it was wilting. By late that night, when

Amanda finally went up to go to bed, the lovely flower was dead.

Antonio had gone back to Hermosa Groves earlier in the day, and they'd not even had the chance to speak to each other beyond a quick exchange of greetings. Now, as Amanda stared out over the dark, still waters of the gulf, she thought of him and his gift, and she had never before felt so desolate.

CHAPTER NINETEEN

THEY WENT BACK to Hermosa Groves at the end of the week, to find they had the hacienda entirely to themselves except for the presence of Hortense.

Hortense, bored by being alone with no one to cook for, had gone on a baking spree, and for the next few days they were regaled with key-lime pies, pecan pies, fresh-orange layer cake, fresh-coconut layer cake and an assortment of hot breads and cookies.

Antonio, Hortense told them, had gone away on business and said he'd be away for several days. Gregory Blake had phoned to tell Antonio he'd finished up everything in Washington and was back in New York. Thus it seemed obvious to Amanda that Antonio and Gregory were not planning to meet at the moment and she could think only that he was with Florence Edmond in Tampa.

This belief was reinforced when he returned toward the following weekend, bringing the woman lawyer with him. He and Florence spent the next two days closeted in his makeshift office, but when Amanda observed the way Florence gazed at Antonio at the dinner table, she could not bring herself to believe it was entirely business between the two of them, and she was thoroughly heartsick.

Cristina had been strangely subdued since their return to Hermosa Groves. She and her uncle had had a long private talk, Amanda knew. Cristina had emerged from it looking very solemn, and she had been disinclined to say very much about it. Amanda had not wanted to push her, but this did hurt a bit, because until then she had been so totally in Cristina's confidence. She could not help but wonder if Antonio had said something to his niece about her. Perhaps he had even indicated to Cristina she was not to be trusted.

When such thoughts came, she tried to dismiss them with the self-admonition that she was on the verge of becoming paranoid. But it was not easy to shut away that sort of conjecture.

Cristina did mention *tío* had given her his permission to write to Felipe. As a result the girl spent hours in her own room, covering pages of pale pink paper with the fine handwriting she had learned in the convent school. She also received her fair share of mail from New York and spent further hours reading Felipe's letters until Amanda was sure she must know every word by heart.

Occasionally Roger Crane phoned and asked Amanda to go out to dinner with him, but she consistently refused. She had the uneasy feeling Pablo reported all of these calls to Antonio, but at least Pablo was now telling her when a call came that was for her. For her part, Amanda was careful not to antagonize Roger and so was pleasant to him on the phone. She didn't quite know why she felt it was important to keep on a fairly good basis with him, but she did.

One night he teased that although she never said no to him, she also never said yes, and he was left hanging in a hive of "maybes." She always managed to leave the impression that the next time he called she might be free. She knew her stalling naturally annoyed him; still, he did keep calling, and, she told herself morosely, if things kept on as they were just then—if she kept feeling lonelier and lonelier—she just might accept Roger's next invitation and let the chips fall where they may as far as Antonio was concerned. If, that is, Antonio still gave a damn about whether she went out with Roger . . . or anyone else.

February merged into March, and as March progressed, it got hotter. There were some very pleasant days, to be sure, but others were scorching—an unusually hot winter that year—and it was too hot to sit out on the patio, especially in the afternoons. It was too hot even to linger very long around the pool. As for the water in the pool, it was lukewarm, and there was nothing invigorating about it.

Cristina said sadly she wished they were back at Siesta Key because there they would have breezes from the gulf and they could "become refreshed." Amanda agreed absently when Cristina said this, but privately she didn't think she could bear to go back to Siesta Key. Now when she thought of that final night with Antonio, she cringed from the sense of pure shame that flooded her. And she could not help but think about it, could not help but relive it, even though to do so was agony.

Also, the ugly thought had come to her that Antonio had taken her to his apartment with a single goal in mind. He had planned to seduce her, and he had done so deliberately. The idea that he had contrived everything that had happened between them, that he actually had *planned* for it to happen, aroused fury in her. But it was an impotent kind of fury, and her anger slowly turned to hate and the hate lingered, a painful and bruising thing.

He had taken Florence Edmond back to Tampa after her weekend at the hacienda, and he had not returned since. Amanda's pride forbade her coming out and asking any direct questions about where he had gone, and Cristina said only vaguely that *tío* was involved in a number of things that would keep him absent for a time.

This, Amanda told herself bitterly, she definitely believed! Antonio surely had all sorts of "involvements."

One day she woke up to realize that in exactly another month her trial period with Antonio would be up. She would be free to go then, and now she wondered how she could get through the next thirty days until the moment of what she was beginning to think of as her release finally arrived.

During the past weeks Cristina's English had improved tremendously and Amanda had learned a good bit of Spanish herself. It was an almost entirely phonetic language when it came to pronunciation—which made it relatively easy. One said things just as they were written, and if one remembered to always broaden the *a*, to say the *e* as if it were *a*, and the *i* as if it were *e*, an acceptable accent became a goal not too difficult to achieve.

The day she realized there was only a month left

before she would be leaving, Amanda decided it was time to formalize Cristina's instruction. . . time to get down to some of the fine points.

She told Cristina this after breakfast, and at once Cristina frowned. "But why, Amanda?" she asked. "I mean, why do you suddenly wish us to have lessons as if we are in a school? I even write half my letters to Felipe in English, and he says I am doing very well. And I speak entirely in English to you, except when Tía Inez is present."

"I know." Amanda nodded. "But we have only another month, Cristina. I think we should try to accomplish as much as possible during the course of it, and this means a more regular schedule than we've been following."

Cristina, she saw, was looking at her with genuine amazement. . "What is this you say about another month?" she demanded.

"My time will be up in mid-April," Amanda answered patiently.

"*Tío* said that you—that we—will be here for the entire year—or at least that you will be with me, wherever I am," Cristina contradicted.

"Your uncle is wrong," Amanda said quietly. "I'm going back to Boston the very day my three-month trial period is up."

"But you cannot, Amanda," Cristina protested. "You cannot do such a thing!" She hesitated. "Can it be you are so unhappy?" she asked.

Amanda nodded wearily. "Yes," she said, "I am unhappy. There's not much point in denying it. I—I don't belong here, Cristina, so the sooner I leave, the better."

"I see," Cristina said, and her large dark eyes were worried. "Then *tío* is right after all."

"Right about what?"

"No matter." Cristina shrugged. "Very well," she added with a sigh, "if you wish us to have formal lessons, then we will do so. What of your Spanish?"

"What of it?" Amanda asked.

"You wish that we should also have formal lessons in Spanish?"

"No," Amanda said wearily. "There wouldn't be much point."

That afternoon she and Cristina adjourned to the library, and for the next two hours Amanda tried to execute the curriculum she had planned so carefully. But Cristina's mind was clearly not on the English language. This first experiment in teaching on a considerably more precise level was a distinct failure, leaving, for Amanda, a feeling of frustration in its wake. She knew very well, as she went to bed that night, that Cristina had not tried to learn that day—she had not tried at all. She hadn't balked, really. She merely had been indifferent, impassive, in a way that was much too reminiscent of Antonio.

The night seemed airless. Amanda turned out the lights and drew back the curtains and opened everything in the room that could be opened, but still there was no breeze to relieve the oppressiveness. She dozed, then woke with a pounding headache, and there seemed no chance of getting back to sleep again. She took a couple of aspirin, but after forty-five minutes they didn't seem to have worked at all, and so finally she got up.

She went out onto the balcony. Again, no breeze, but she did get a glimpse of the pool—or rather its glistening water, caught by the silken shafts of moonlight. The thought of a swim became tremendously appealing. It would cool her somewhat, relax her and was the one way, she told herself, in which she could hope to get back to sleep that night.

She slipped on her black bikini and then made her way down the stairs, and in another moment she was moving silently across the patio. The whole terrain had become so familiar to her that the fact the landscape was partially obscured that night by clouds didn't really matter. She went down the terrace steps and was nearly at the pool's apron when she suddenly saw someone in the water and almost screamed in fright.

As it was, she bit back the scream and it emerged as a kind of moan, but this was enough to startle the occupant of the pool. In another instant he was climbing out of the water and coming toward her, and when she was it was Antonio, her pulse began to thud so furiously she almost became giddy.

He stood in front of her, tall and menacing, and she was sure he would be thoroughly annoyed—if not furious—at her having come to interrupt his midnight swim. Then a ribbon of moonlight slanted across his face, and the sight made her gasp.

"Oh, my God!" she said. "Your eye!"

He was not wearing the patch. In that single shaft of light his face was silvered, and she saw not one but two dark eyes staring down at her.

"What of my eye?" he demanded, a chill to his voice.

"I—I thought you had—lost it," she stammered, thoroughly shaken.

"And that behind the patch there would be only a gaping hole or worse?" he finished for her. "Are you disappointed, Amanda?"

He was so caustic. Each word he spoke seemed to be etched in acid, and she crumpled. She sank onto the nearest lounge chair and the tears came—a flood of tears. And even as she cried she was remotely aware of how long she'd been suppressing those tears, how often she'd held them back from him, even though it had taken every ounce of her self-control to do so.

She turned her face into the softness of the chair back and sobbed, hating herself for her weakness. Then she felt strong arms around her, and she heard him murmur in her ear, *"Ay, Amada mia, no llora. Qué te quiero, Amanda!"* The soft Spanish slurred into roughly edged English. "Amanda!" he commanded. "Stop it for God's sake, will you?"

She wanted to stop crying. She'd never wanted anything quite so much! But the tears, so long held back, continued to stream down her face. She'd understood what he'd said in Spanish. He had called her his love; he had told her he loved her! At least, she amended hastily, that's what she thought he had said. Yet she must have been mistaken, for God knows Antonio didn't *love* her. Lust for her maybe, but love...?

He muttered something in Spanish she didn't understand at all, and then his arms tightened and he said, "I suppose there is only one way."

In another second he had turned her tear-streaked

face toward his and his lips descended upon hers, and with his kiss she knew he once again had captured her. Her blood ran warm, and the giddiness that overtook her had nothing to do with the shock of seeing him again so suddenly—or of seeing his face...

His face. She pushed him away, staring up at the face she was seeing fully now for the first time. God, but he was handsome! The patch had added intrigue, but without it he was devastating. No woman in her right mind, she told herself, could possibly resist this sort of attraction. She dared to look at the eye that had been obscured for so long, and in this light at least, it seemed quite normal. But she could see, starting at the corner and going up just beyond his eyebrow, a jagged nasty-looking scar that had been hidden before by the patch.

He was watching her very closely, and he asked, "What do you think, Amanda?"

"I—I don't know what to think," she said softly.

He had released her and was sitting back surveying her, his smile grim. He touched the scar lightly, and he said, "This is what caused my problem...or most of it." He paused. "You are wondering if I see with my left eye, are you not?" he asked her.

"Yes," she admitted.

He shook his head. "I do not," he said, "or only so slightly it would be better if I saw nothing at all. I see just shadows with this eye. They form vague gray patterns that are very distracting. It is for this reason I was advised to wear the patch."

"But—but surgery might restore the sight in it?" she asked.

He shook his head. "That is unlikely," he told her. "They explained it all to me in Boston."

"You've been back to Boston?"

He nodded, then looked at her curiously. "Did not Cristina tell you?" he asked.

"No," she answered, "she merely said you'd be away for a while. But then... Cristina hasn't told me very much of anything since we came back from Siesta Key."

"That is my fault... in part," he allowed. "Also, Cristina feels, I believe, that sometimes to make a mystery out of something is to incite interest. She thought, no doubt, that if you wondered where I was...."

Amanda managed to refrain from commenting as Antonio seemed to wait. "She did tell me tonight that you are going back to Boston next month," he said then, his voice curiously toneless.

"Yes."

"It has been such a bad experiment, Amanda?"

"You should know the answer to that," she replied bluntly. "Please, Antonio, I don't want to talk about it... about us. But I do wish you'd...."

"Yes?"

"Tell me what they told you in Boston."

"My doctors?"

"Yes," she said impatiently, "your doctors!"

"Does it matter so much to you, Amanda?" he asked, sounding exasperated. "What happens with my eyes, that is? Is it not my problem?"

He spoke dispassionately, staring out at the waters of the pool as he did so, but he could not hide his underlying torment from her. She knew him too well—much too well. Regardless of anything else, they had exposed themselves to each other in the most intimate of ways. True, they had come together in a fusion of passion that was in a sense purely physical. Yet there had been a commitment beyond it, and she had become his, her sense of this lingering long after the ecstasy itself had passed into memory.

"Oh, my God, Antonio," she said now, thoroughly stung. "How can you ask me such a thing? How can you possibly think I could be indifferent...?"

"To my suffering?" he asked wryly. "No, I suppose you could not possibly be indifferent to that. You are the sort who would go and bind up a bird's broken wing, are you not, Amanda? I can see you as a sweet Sister of Charity, giving solace to the aged, the blind and the homeless...."

The gesture came inadvertently: she raised her hand and struck his cheek, the resulting slap sounding disconcertingly loud in the night's silence. Then, moving without really knowing what she was doing, she ran across to the pool and dived into the deep dark water. She surfaced and began to swim furiously—and almost at once was aware he had followed her.

She tried to outdistance him, but it was impossible. He came from behind, swooping her into his arms, and although she tried to wrestle herself out of his grasp, there was no getting away from him. She found herself standing, the water coming almost to her chest. He, too, was standing, although he was only waist deep—in every way, it seemed to her, he had the advantage over her.

He drew her close and then he kissed her, his lips claiming hers with a savagery that was stunning. But then gradually his embrace changed. What she feared was pure brute force became fired instead with passion, the passion merging with tenderness, until she was clinging to him. Her lips parted as his tongue probed her mouth, tantalizing her, spurring her toward a danger area she'd been in before—and was determined not to go to again.

Yet somehow this experience was different. There was a tremendous sweetness to his embrace, and in response her desire became coupled with an intensity of love for him that seemed to suffuse every cell in her body. And when suddenly he released her, she stood there in the water, staring up at him with an awareness that was inescapable. She loved him! Oh, God, yes, she loved him! But hers was not a love that could be donned today and cast off tomorrow. He had become a part of her, and she knew in a blinding instant of revelation that without him she could never again be complete: no matter where she went, a part of her would remain with him forever.

Her shock must have shown in her face, for he said gratingly, "Don't worry. Once was enough, Amanda. I had no right, there on Siesta Key. I have even less right now."

"Antonio," she began, but he cut her off.

"There is nothing for you to say to me," he told her, and as she watched him, the tears came again, to make a shimmering curtain before her eyes. He turned and swam the length of the pool and then pulled himself up the ladder at the far end.

She chose to use the steps in the shallow end, but once on the apron she did not pause. Even as she cried out, "Antonio," she was walking toward him. And he swerved in his path—for he had started toward the house—a dim silhouette to her because the moon was cloaked momentarily by a cloud.

"Wait!" she said, and was not at all sure he would heed her command. But to her relief he stood unmoving, until she had caught up with him.

"Antonio," she began but he raised a hand to stop her.

"Please, Amanda," he said. "I repeat, there is nothing you need say to me. I will not touch you again—I swear it to you. Nor will I try to keep you from going back to Boston next month. That is your right. There is only one thing I will ask of you."

"Yes?" she questioned.

But he shook his head. The moon was clear again, and they were both bathed in its radiance as he said, "Excuse me, please, but I've got to get something over this eye. I usually swim late at night because when there is not too much light, my eye does not bother me. But the moonlight seems as brilliant as a bright lantern. It dazzles me. . .in more ways than one, I suppose," he finished dryly. "Principally, though, the visual effect is enough to drive me slightly mad. I suppose you could call it a new sort of lunacy."

He started away from her even as he was speaking, but she moved with him. Again it was difficult to keep up with his stride, but she was not about to let the night end for them like that.

"What is it you wished to ask of me?" she persisted.

He paused for just a second, his hesitation obvious. Then he said, "We can talk about it in the morning."

CHAPTER TWENTY

CRISTINA, ANTONIO AND TIA INEZ were already in the dining room having breakfast when Amanda went downstairs the next morning. They were talking in rapid Spanish, and as she stood at the threshold of the room, she felt very much an outsider...an intruder.

Then she saw, to her surprise, that Cristina was excited; her dark eyes sparkled in a way they had not since the trip to Siesta Key. When she spotted Amanda, she exclaimed at once, "We have such a surprise for you! We are all going to Majorca together! Is that not terrific?"

Antonio groaned and said, "Cristina, couldn't you wait until I...explained things to Amanda? You must not be so presumptuous. You make it sound as if she has no choice in the matter."

"But you surely do want to come, do you not, Amanda?" Cristina asked, her smile fading.

Amanda sat down at the table without saying a word and accepted the cup of *café con leche* Antonio poured for her. As he handed it to her, their fingers touched, and Amanda flinched. Then she saw his jaw tighten.

He said, "It would seem to me, Cristina, that Amanda's silence answers your question."

Amanda managed to find her voice. "I can't very well answer a question that hasn't been posed to me," she pointed out.

"The fact of the matter is, I must go to Majorca on a brief trip," he explained to her. "There are some affairs I must attend to there before...."

"Yes?" she said as he broke off.

"Before very much longer," he finished, and it seemed to her he gave Cristina a warning look. "We will be gone only a week or so. At first Cristina did not wish to come at all, I might add—until I told her I hoped you would accompany us. It would be a change of scene, obviously. Of course Majorca is tropical like Florida. We have many of the same trees, the same palms...."

Amanda nodded, but she was concentrating on one thing only. "You want me to go to Majorca?" she demanded incredulously.

His smile was rueful. "It is not the end of the world," he pointed out.

"Of course not," she said sharply. "I do realize that, Antonio. It seems to me, though, it would be quite a needless extravagance to take me along on such a trip."

"I do not agree," he said. "There is a reason I wish Cristina to go with me. Otherwise you could, of course, both stay here. As it is," he added, glancing with a smile toward his aunt, "Tía Inez will remain here at the hacienda. She is very comfortable here, and there is no need to disturb her for such a short time."

It was too much. People simply didn't dash across the Atlantic to a Spanish island for a mere week or so. At least the people she knew didn't. But then her father's circle of friends had been composed almost entirely of intellectuals who, for the most part, didn't have much money. Gerard's friends, while more affluent, generally speaking, had been thrifty New Englanders who planned their travels with considerable care. They didn't just rush off....

Antonio, his voice strangely dull, said, "You do not wish to go, do you?"

For the first time that morning she raised her eyes and looked directly at him, and she felt a strange little quiver of apprehension. He was wearing the eye patch again, so that the scar over his left eye was camouflaged. Yet it seemed to her she could see it as it had appeared in the moonlight last night, and suddenly she was afraid.

"Antonio," she asked him, "why are you really going?"

"Why am I really going?" he repeated. "As I told you, I have business to attend to and certain things I wish to accomplish at this time."

"Before what, Antonio?" she continued.

He grimaced impatiently. "Before I can give my full attention to Hermosa Groves," he said. But she knew this was not the real reason at all. She knew he was deliberately holding back from her, and when she glanced toward Cristina, she clearly saw confirmation of this on her lovely young pupil's face.

"It is all right," he said then almost gently. "This was a request on my part, not a demand. Do not look so unhappy, Amanda. Cristina and I will manage. It is just that I hoped to have your company for her. Nevertheless...."

"Nevertheless what, Antonio?"

"We can speak of it later," he said evasively, but this time she was not going to let him off so easily.

Tía Inez rose to leave the table with a pleasant, *"Con permiso,"* and Cristina immediately followed suit.

"I have a letter to write," she said. "You do not wish to start my lessons just yet, do you, Amanda?"

"No," Amanda answered, her attention on Antonio. There was no reason why he shouldn't leave her at the table alone, and she had the idea this was precisely what he intended to do, but before he could move, she said, "Will you fix me another coffee, please? And why don't you join me?"

He glanced at her suspiciously as he drew both her cup and his own in front of him before concocting the frothy blend of milk and coffee, sugaring it and then passing her cup back to her. It was only then that she inquired, "Is this what you meant last night when you said you had something to ask of me?"

He nodded as he stirred his coffee. "Yes," he said. "But it is clear that the idea does not meet with your favor so... forget it, Amanda. I think it is time, in any event, that we stopped this... this farce between us. I cannot fault you for what you have done as Cristina's teacher—that is true. But you have already told her you plan to leave as soon as the trial period is up, and I have decided there is no reason for you to wait that long."

She had not expected this, and his statement came as a very cold shock. Along with it a warning flag waved, and she asked him cautiously, "Are you dismissing me, Antonio?"

"No," he said, still not looking at her. "That is not my intention at all. I am giving you your freedom, Amanda. That is what you want, is it not?"

"I told you I would stay three months and I intend to stay three months unless you fire me," she said, feeling her way along very carefully. "You haven't asked me yet whether I want to go to Majorca with you and Cristina. You've merely told me you're sure I don't.

"Well," she went on, knowing only too well she was sitting to the left of him and wishing he'd turn his head around to face her, "you are wrong. Anyone would be an idiot, wouldn't she, not to accept such an offer? A week in a Mediterranean paradise—did you really think I'd be able to resist it?"

Now he turned around slowly, and she said, "Of course I'll go to Majorca with you, Antonio."

CRISTINA WAS IN HER ROOM, but she was not writing a letter. She was not doing anything. Amanda discovered her pupil slumped in a chair by the window, staring at her hands, which were folded in her lap.

She sat down in a chair opposite Cristina, her knees suddenly feeling weak, and she asked with an asperity she didn't really feel, "Just what is this all about?"

Cristina raised huge haunted eyes and said in a voice trembling with emotion, "I think you know, Amanda."

"Do I?"

"I think you know that *tío* is going to be blind, and so he is trying to—to take care of everything first, before it happens."

Amanda had not expected this, and she stared at Cristina in horror. "Why do you say that as if you're so sure of it?" she demanded.

"Because that is what...is most apt to happen," Cristina explained. She saw the look on Amanda's face and added quickly, "I am not making this up. I am not trying to be dramatic!"

"I wish to God you were," Amanda commented bitterly.

"Also," Cristina said, "you must not tell *tío* I have told you this. You absolutely must not, Amanda. I am not keeping his confidence, and he would be furious with me. This time I do not think he would forgive me."

"His confidence? Did he tell you he didn't want me to know this?"

"Yes," Cristina conceded. "He says he thinks you would then feel you would be required to stay here, even for the whole year, out of a...." Cristina paused, obviously trying to translate something from Spanish into English. "I think you would call it a 'matter of decency,' " she finished.

"A sense of decency?"

"Yes, that is better."

"And he wouldn't want me to stay here?" Amanda persisted.

"No, I do not think he would want you to stay here...under such circumstances," Cristina said. "You know, do you not, that *tío* is very proud?"

"Oh, yes," Amanda replied wryly. "I do indeed know that!"

"It will be very difficult for him," Cristina said slowly. "I cannot bear to think of him...."

Amanda could not bear to think of it, either, and she swallowed hard. In another minute, she knew, both she and Cristina would be sobbing in each other's arms, and this wouldn't do anybody any good.

She said, "Cristina, you seemed very happy when I went into the dining room this morning."

"Yes, I was happy." Cristina nodded. "I was, anyway, trying to be happy. I was thinking what fun it would be for us to go to Marjorca together—I was not letting myself think past that. In fact, I believe I imagined it was a...how shall I say it...a bad dream—that would go away if we went to Majorca. Like a cloud...."

"Well, then, we shall see whether you're right," Amanda said. "I'm going with you."

"You mean this, Amanda?" Cristina's face seemed to light up. Then she added more soberly, "You have told *tío*?"

"Yes, I've told *tío*," Amanda answered dryly. "He did not seem to be overwhelmed with joy."

"Perhaps he thinks it would be better if he had not asked you," Cristina conjectured. "It will only bring you that much closer, and *tío*—"

"Yes?"

"I—I think *tío* feels he must not have anyone in his life," Cristina said quietly. "You understand me, Amanda?"

"Yes," Amanda said slowly. "I understand you."

Cristina was right, of course. If Antonio really was facing blindness, he would not want to let anyone into his life. No, he would want to go it alone. Somehow he would manage to hold his dark head high, that arrogant Spanish pride taking over. She had a vision of him making his solitary way with the aid of a white cane. He would be aloof and alone, daring anyone to intrude into his private world. And a wave of emotion came over her that threatened to swamp her.

She said hastily, "Cristina, what makes you so sure? Did the doctors in Boston tell Antonio this?"

"They have told him he must have the surgery," Cristina said. "The headaches have been getting worse and worse. He suffers a great deal, and without the surgery this will continue. He cannot go on in such a way. They know it, and he knows it. But it is a very delicate operation. They say it will very surely put out the little bit of sight he has in his bad eye. . . and there is a great risk he will lose the sight in his other eye, as well. If there was anything else they could do, they would not operate," Cristina continued, her face so strained that for a moment Amanda could imagine how she would look when she was forty. "*Tío* knows this, of course. He. . . ."

Cristina faltered and could not go on. But now Amanda could see why he had been the one to bring their embrace to an end in the pool last night, when she knew very well he had wanted her as much as she had wanted him. During those few moments they had clung together, that wonderfully masculine body of his had given her full proof of this.

Dear God, his pride! She knew she could never hope to convince him of the truth in the old proverb, "Pride goeth before a fall." No, Antonio was an expert at building walls around himself, but this time he'd build a wall so high, so strong, there wasn't a chance there'd be a chink in it. Nor would anyone, anyone at all, ever be able to scale it. . . .

She could imagine his reaction were she to go to him and say, "I love you, Antonio, and if you're going to be blind, I want to be with you. . . I want to help you."

How he would scoff at her; how he would throw what he'd insist was her pity right back in her face! She could visualize the upward thrust of those dark eyebrows, the unseeing jet eyes and the hands that would forever be groping in the dark, and she shivered.

Cristina said sharply, "Amanda! You are all right, Amanda?"

She was not in the least all right, but she only nodded and said, "Yes." And then she was conscious of Cristina's penetrating gaze.

"You love him, do you not?" Cristina said. "You love Tío Tony."

There was no use in pretending any further. She nodded again, possessed of a feeling of total helplessness, and she said, "Yes. I have. . . almost from the very beginning."

"Then," Cristina said, "there is perhaps hope after all. Maybe in Majorca. . . ."

ANTONIO WAS VERY QUIET on the flight across the Atlantic. Amanda sat by the window, and he was next to her. Cristina was in the row behind them, with the seat next to her unoccupied. Once again they were flying first class, and the stewardesses were lavishing all sorts of attention on Antonio. He was responding amiably enough, but as Amanda watched him, it occurred to her he was curiously unaware of his own charm. In fact, despite his overbearing behavior at times, he was not in the least conceited about himself.

He turned to her and handed her one of the glasses of champagne a stewardess had just brought them, and there was a sweetness to the smile he gave her that caught at her heart. He had been gentle with her during the past few days while they had been preparing for the trip, although once again he seemed careful to be alone with her as little as possible.

Could it be Antonio did not really trust himself when it came to keeping those surging emotions—in particular his feelings toward her—under control?

Now he said, "I wish we had the time to spend a few days in Madrid. You will see little more than Barajas—the airport, that is. Our flight for Palma will leave within an hour of our arrival, so we may be able to get a coffee, but not much more than that. For that matter, I wish we were going to be in Majorca longer, because there is so much there I would like to show you. We will stay in Palma tonight, but I think tomorrow we will go directly to Manacor. It is only a drive of fifty kilometers or so from Palma, but a part of it is quite mountainous, and the road is narrow. I would prefer we did not drive it in the dark."

He said this levelly enough, but she knew he must be remembering the terrible accident in which his brother, his sister-in-law and his fiancée had all been killed and he himself so severely injured. Certainly it had happened on that road.

In the library at the hacienda Amanda had found a comprehensive atlas, as well as an encyclopedia, so she had done her homework on Majorca. She had been surprised at the size of the island, which was the largest of the Balearic group. Majorca covered 1405 square miles, and some quarter of a million people lived in its very old and historic capital, Palma.

Now she asked, "Were you born in Majorca, Antonio?"

He looked at her, surprised. "No," he said. "I was born in Andalusia—in the middle of a lot of olive trees."

Cristina had spoken several times of the family estates in Andalusia, and Amanda said, "I suppose I should have realized that, since Cristina comes from there, too."

"Yes, she does," he said. "We are not too far from Seville—our properties, that is—and so it is natural that in my mind Seville is the greatest city in Spain." He smiled. "So much of what people think of as Spanish comes from Andalusia," he said. "Flamenco, the guitars, the beautiful senoritas with flashing eyes and roses in their teeth. . . ."

He was teasing her, she knew, and yet she could not help thinking of his fiancée, who must have been a very beautiful senorita herself.

"It is writers from other countries, such as your Washington Irving, who give the world an idea of Spain that actually depicts Andalusia," Antonio said now. "You have read his stories about the *Alhambra*?"

"Years ago," Amanda confessed.

"They are magnificent, " he said. "But you ask about my own association with Majorca. No, I was not born there, though I do have very early memories of the island. Juan—my brother—and I would go there often during our vacations from school. Manacor, where our pearl business is located, is only a few miles from Porto Cristo, and when I was a boy this was a relatively sleepy little village on the shores of the Mediterranean. Today the high rises—hotels, condominiums—have infiltrated there, as they have all along the Mediterranean coast. In fact, they have been going up more and more often throughout most of Europe, and I think this is rather unfortunate. They give an anonymity to the landscape that I find regrettable.''

''I agree,'' she said.

Antonio laughed. ''So,'' he observed, ''we do occasionally agree about something, do we, Amanda?''

He didn't seem to expect her to answer this—which was as well. Everything had been happening so quickly she'd not yet been able to get a grip on herself, and so at the moment she was poorly equipped for any sort of verbal fencing with Antonio.

His good humor persisted, however, all the way across the Atlantic. At the Madrid airport—another study in concrete, chrome and glass that, except for the signs in Spanish, could have been virtually anywhere, Amanda thought ruefully—they did have just enough time for a cup of coffee. Then they boarded another plane and commenced the final leg of their trip to Palma.

It was dusk when they arrived. ''We shall take a taxi to the house,'' Antonio told her. ''The staff knows we are coming, of course, but I asked that it be kept quiet from everyone else. I did not wish all sorts of friends and relatives descending. We shall have a simple dinner. It would be terrible to put you through a whole formal *comida*." He smiled. "I would not want you to experience an inquisition on your very first night in Spain," he added, and again she found herself speechless.

As they walked from the airport toward a waiting taxi, Amanda's initial impression was of windmills! Windmills, some of them atop round, pale beige block structures, some of them atop squares built of the same material.

"So many windmills," she murmured. "I've never seen anything like it."

"Yes." Antonio nodded. "The *molinos de viento*. They are a typical feature of the Majorcan landscape—you will see them all over the island. In earlier years they were essential to life here. They owe their existence to the lack of fresh water on the island. Water could not be used to generate power, and so the mills were built. And they were lifesavers for the island people. You will see that the sails are of different colors, and it makes quite a picture when they are turning. It is said," he added, "that despite the greater publicity the windmills in Holland have received, there is no other part of the world where as many windmills can be found as on *Mallorca*."

"Right in the middle of town facing the *Paseo Maritimo* is a place with huge windmills that are a part of the building itself," Cristina broke in. "It is very old, but today it is a nightclub called Es Jonquet. Perhaps, *tío*—"

"No," Antonio said shortly. "We will be in Palma only tonight, Cristina, and on our return I doubt if we will stop over at all—it will depend upon the timing of our flight back to the States.''

"But then there is so much Amanda will miss," Cristina wailed. "She should at least see the cathedral, *tío*. Even you couldn't object to that. The cathedral is magnificent, Amanda. Some say the stained glass windows are even more glorious than those of Notre Dame in Paris and other such famous Gothic churches. Also, its history is so romantic—"

"*Por Dios*, Cristina," Antonio interrupted irritably. "Do you think of nothing but romance?"

"You cannot deny this, *tío*," Cristina told him. "When King Jaime set forth in 1229 to seize Majorca from the Saracens, he promised the Queen of Heaven he would build the most beautiful cathedral in the world for her if he succeeded in his conquest...and he did. Work was not able to start on it until the reign of his son, Jaime the Second, but only a hundred years later it was already half done. This is very fast for cathedrals!"

"It is indeed," Antonio said dryly, then added, "Also, Amanda can at least get a glimpse of the cathedral from the taxi window. One can hardly miss it. And if there is time later, after we have finished in Manacor, she can visit it."

Truly one could not miss the cathedral, Amanda conceded, as Antonio ordered the taxi to slow down so she could get a really good view of it. It dominated Palma's skyline as it stood overlooking the clear blue waters of the Mediterranean, its many spires thoroughly Gothic in their magnificence.

Not far beyond the cathedral they took a turn to the right, and soon they were going down narrow cobblestoned streets. The walls of the houses that crowded in on either side of them appeared ancient. They came to a stop in front of what first seemed to Amanda the blank facade of a building, but then she spotted the black iron gate that had been set into it, the design so intricate one could barely see through it at all.

Almost at once the gate swung open and Antonio was being welcomed by a tall thin man dressed in black—a Palma version of Pablo, Amanda thought wryly. Then she and Cristina were being ushered inside the gate and she was standing spellbound in the most beautiful courtyard she had ever seen.

There were arches all around her, covering passages on every side. Straight ahead a magnificent stairway curved upward, flanked on both sides by huge stone pots filled with gloriously colored blossoms. There was an enormous stone fountain to one side and this, too, was flanked by pots of flowers. Several wrought-iron lanterns had been lit, and they cast a yellow glow that deepened with the growing twilight.

It was with a sense of total unreality that she followed Cristina and Antonio up the wide stairway to glimpse on the first of the upper floors a bit of what she suspected were vast rooms of incredible opulence. She felt as if she'd suddenly been whisked back several centuries, for this residence had such strong Moorish features.

Then they went up yet another flight of stairs, and Amanda was ushered into an enormous bedchamber whose walls were a very pale tone of ivory and whose decor had been executed in varying shades of rose and the richest of fabrics—velvet and satin and tapestry.

Cristina, used to this and therefore undaunted by it, said, "I am just across the way, Amanda. *Tío*, we are to have *comida* downstairs?"

"No," he replied. "I have arranged for a fairly light supper to be brought to the small drawing room up here in an hour or so. Roberto has laid a table in there for us. I thought this would be more agreeable for tonight."

"Very much so," Cristina agreed. "I shall go refresh myself and join you later, then."

It occurred to Amanda that Cristina seemed very anxious to leave them, and she looked around for Roberto, hoping he would appear with their suitcases or sherry or something, because the thought of being alone with Antonio just now was unnerving. Seeing this house—just one of his many residences—had brought home to her a fact that Hermosa Groves had not: Antonio was not merely rich, he was extremely wealthy. Indeed, she couldn't even imagine the vastness of such wealth, and it seemed just one more thing that put him completely beyond her.

Antonio's voice cut short her musings when he said gently, "Amanda, will you look at me, please?"

She slowly raised her eyes, to see he was smiling, but it was a sad smile. "You are lovely," he said. "It seems to me you have become lovelier with each passing day. Yet just now you seem so lost."

He had never spoken to her quite like this before, and she could feel her throat constrict, as it had so often during those first days after they'd met. Still, she found enough voice to say, "I suppose I do feel. . .somewhat lost."

He went on. "This house—it is magnificent, is it not? But you know, I did not have much to do with acquiring it. I inherited it, just as I did Hermosa Groves. . .and the pearl manufactory. . .and the estate in Andalusia. And yes, I also have a place in Madrid, *linda*, though just now I have leased it to a cousin because I have no use for it. These things came to me only because I have. . .survived. So there is not much pleasure to them. There can be a great emptiness to material things, *linda*, and a time in one's life when they are of no help at all, believe me."

Was he thinking of his eyes? She was, and she swallowed hard. What he said was true. All the wealth in the world could not guarantee his sight.

He reached out to touch her cheek, and his fingers were feather soft. "I would take you in my arms," he said, his voice husky, "but if I did so, I could never let you go. Oh, *querida mia* . . . ."

Unfortunately Roberto did choose to appear at precisely that moment, bringing her suitcase and Cristina's, and Amanda could glady have choked Pablo's Palma counterpart.

Dinner was not exactly what Amanda would have called simple. They were served a clear broth in which slices of avocado floated, then a course of grilled fish and then an excellent tournedos of beef, accompanied by broiled mushrooms and a delicious mixture of rice and peas. A crisp green salad came after this and then a smooth, wonderfully creamy custard topped with a burnt-caramel sauce. This, Antonio told her, was a very good version of flan and could be called the national dessert of Spain.

Choice wines were present throughout the meal, and the type of wine changed from course to course. They finished with small cups of espresso, and Amanda sweetened hers, at Antonio's insistence, with a full teaspoon of sugar. He was right. Sugar was necessary with this sort of coffee, and it was really ambrosia when prepared in the right way.

Almost immediately after dinner Antonio excused himself, and Cristina frowned as she watched him leave the room. "It is another of the headaches beginning," she said. "He has been having them more frequently. I am very worried about him, Amanda."

It was difficult to be consoling to Cristina, because Amanda was worried about him, too. And it was a relief when Cristina finally said she supposed they had better get to bed, since they would be starting out for Manacor in the morning.

CHAPTER TWENTY-ONE

MANACOR WAS A RELATIVELY short distance from Palma, but it seemed to Amanda the drive took forever. For one thing, the tension inside the car was thick and threatening. Amanda was painfully aware of the fact that somewhere along this road Antonio's terrible accident had taken place, and she was sure its memory was uppermost in his mind.

He had looked pale and strained that morning when he had joined both her and Cristina for a breakfast of *café con leche* and *ensaimadas*—big circles of a flaky pastry liberally sprinkled with powdered sugar. They were, Cristina explained proudly, a distinctly Majorcan treat.

Now, in the car, Antonio sat next to Roberto, who was driving, while she and Cristina were in the back. The car itself was huge and black and expensive. Roberto kept it shined to a high gloss, and the interior upholstery, a rich, pearl-gray velour, was immaculate.

Cristina kept pointing out sights along the way as they drove, but it was all Amanda could do to wrest her attention away from the proud dark head in front of her.

The first part of their route reversed the one they'd taken to the house the previous day. They passed the cathedral and beyond the city the airport, and for a time the mills were the predominant scenic feature. In this region the land had been terraced and irrigated, but before Palma was very far behind them there was a distinct change in the landscape. It became increasingly hilly, and except for some areas in which groves had been carefully planted, it seemed to Amanda the land was very barren.

"The trees are almonds," Cristina told her. "They flower in winter—in February, usually—and all over the island it becomes like a fairyland—a beautiful sight. Those others with the tops that are—what would you call them—thick, I think...those are fig trees. Many almonds and figs come from Majorca."

"And olives?" Amanda asked.

"There are olive trees, yes. In fact, some are very old. You will see some of them. They have huge trunks that are all twisted. It is said that some of them are a thousand years old."

Amanda nodded, impressed by the thought of such antiquity, but her eyes still lingered on Antonio. The road was becoming narrower and more twisting, and they were driving in a circuitous way over a series of undulating hills.

"They call these *garrigues*," Cristina said. "How would you say it? Minimountains, I guess. Nothing so high as one finds to the north on the road to Formentor—that is a whole separate range of real mountains. But even so, here it is quite rough in places."

Cristina was frowning, and Amanda saw she was tense, too. Then, to her horror, Roberto pulled over on the side of the road—where there was really not much of a side on which to pull over—and she knew that should a car come upon them from the opposite direction, it could not possibly pass.

"Don Antonio," Roberto began, and then added something in a spate of words absolutely incomprehensible to Amanda. This was another language, she realized, and one that sounded quite different from Spanish.

"He says he is ill," Cristina translated. "I do not understand all of it myself because he is speaking Mallorquí, a dialect of Cátalan. It is the real language of the island and is what the Majorcans speak among themselves. Fortunately *tío* understands it."

Antonio climbed out of the car and opened the back door. Then he said, "Will you come sit in front, Amanda, and let Roberto take your place? He is suffering from a dizzy spell. He said he should have told me in the first place these twisting roads affect him in this way. In any event, it seems I must drive."

He spoke with a flatness that had an oddly disturbing quality about it, and Amanda swiftly climbed out of the car and made the transfer to the front seat. She was barely aware of Roberto settling back into the place she had just vacated, for she was concentrating entirely upon Antonio. As he slid behind the wheel, she could see the muscles in his jaw twitch, and his mouth was tightly set. In a voice so low she could barely hear him he said, "I am not sure I can do it."

He was turning the key in the ignition as he spoke, and the powerful engine responded at once. Still, he did not shift into gear, and Amanda found the courage to say, "I can drive, Antonio. Actually, I'm a good driver. If you'll trust me, I'd be glad to take over for you.''

He shook his head. "These roads are miserable," he said, "and this is country with which you are entirely unfamiliar. I am especially apprehensive, I admit, because... because my life came to an end only a few kilometers down the way and I have not driven along here since.''

My life came to an end. The words seemed to echo in Amanda's head, increasing in strength like the rolling of a drum, until she wanted to clap her hands over her ears to shut them out. He was telling her that everything that mattered had ended for him when the car he was driving had crashed and his Elena had been killed. He was telling her that beyond that point there had been nothing, that everything between them had meant nothing....

He said quickly, "*Linda*, please do not look like that. It is not that I distrust you. I trust you very much, and I would surely trust you to drive me anyplace, anytime. But in this instance I am being a coward, do you not see? It is something I must do—I know that. Can you understand it?''

"Yes," she said slowly. And she did. "Also," she added, "once you've done it you'll have nothing more to be afraid of.''

"And you trust me to take the wheel, *niña*?''

"I trust you to do anything," she told him steadily.

He sighed. Then his hand moved the gearshift and the big car began to roll. Amanda sat at his side staring straight ahead, wondering just where it was the crash had taken place and if she'd know, somehow,

when they passed the spot. But Antonio drove with
an unswerving steadiness—if the accident's site was a
personal wrench, he did not reveal it—and before
long they were beyond the hilly area of the "minimountains."

As they were going down a steep hill Antonio said,
"We are almost to Manacor. This is Villafranca we
are passing through. The countryside around here is
famous for its wonderful melons."

He had spoken easily, and she felt relieved the tension had drained out of him. Then he said, "There,
right ahead, is Manacor," and she saw the spires of
the cathedral stabbing the blue silk sky.

Manacor was larger than she'd thought it would
be. Its red-roofed houses were clustered closely
together, and shops of all kinds lined the streets.

"About twenty-five thousand people live here,"
Antonio said, reading her mind. "There is quite a bit
of industry—cabinet making as well as the pearl
manufactories, though the pearl manufactories are
the most prominent and the most famous business.
There are a number of pearl factories, incidentally—
some better than others." He actually flashed her a
smile. "We, of course, like to think that ours rank
with the best of the Majorcan pearls," he admitted.
"We must manage to find time for you to go through
our factory. It is quite fascinating to watch the way in
which the pearls are made. Majorcan pearls are entirely manmade, you know."

"No," she confessed, "I didn't. I know only that
they are world famous."

He nodded. "In beauty," he said, "they rival the
natural fine pearls that are really true jewels. Some

think they are cultured, but that is not so. Cultured pearls are made by what I suppose might be loosely termed artificial insemination—this of an oyster, of course. Our pearls, as I've said, are manmade, but we use the finest natural essences available, derived from the marine species that live in these warm waters of the Mediterranean.''

He laughed. ''I have never before tried to translate this information about the pearls into English,'' he admitted, ''and I know I have omitted facts I should mention, but all of that you can learn later.'' Then he added under his breath, ''Thank you, *querida*.''

''For what?'' she asked, puzzled.

''For not going into a panic when I showed very clearly that I was afraid to drive,'' he said frankly. ''Now it is over, and that is to the good. You were right. I will not feel that way about it again. But I gained strength because you were sitting by my side. I could not have made a mistake because it would have been you, who are so highly precious to me, I would have endangered.''

His voice was so soft as he spoke these final words she had to strain to catch them and she was sure she was mistaken about what he was saying. But then, she told herself, even if she had heard him rightly there was the matter of language: *precious* might mean one thing to Antonio and something entirely different to her!

The house he took her to now was outside of Manacor on a road that, he said, continued on to the beachside community of Porto Cristo. Also, he added, they were within the proverbial stone's throw of the well-known Cuevas del Drach.

" 'The Caves of the Dragon,' " he translated, "or you could say monster, if you wished, though there is nothing at all monstrous about the caves...they are extremely beautiful. There are many caves in Majorca, especially in this region. We shall have to visit some."

Amanda did not comment, because privately she hoped this was something he would forget. She had a horror of subterranean places and recalled being thoroughly terrified once when her parents had taken her to some caverns in New York State—not far from Albany, if her memory was correct. Looking down into vast chasms had made her giddy and had prickled her skin with a fear she could still remember.

Well, Antonio had said there would be so much for him to attend to during their brief stay in Majorca that chances were there wouldn't be time to explore any caves at all—at least she hoped so!

Again the house to which he took her was beautiful. It was of pale pink stone, built around a courtyard in the traditional Spanish manner and reminded her very much of the hacienda at Hermosa Groves.

"I think of it really as Tía Inez's home," Antonio told her. "It was her husband who was in charge of our pearl business. My father was a partner in this enterprise, but he was primarily concerned with our olive groves in Andalusia. When my uncle died, it was my brother, Juan, who came here to take over. Now I have placed the business in the hands of a cousin—a nephew of Tía Inez's, on her side of the family. His name is Carlos López, and you will meet him and his wife, Teresa. I think you will like them."

This proved to be true. She met the Lópezes the

second night they were in Manacor, when Antonio invited a number of his friends and relatives to join them for dinner. Cristina acted as his hostess—and did so charmingly. The guests all appeared to be delightful people, even though most of them spoke very little English and Amanda's Spanish, although improving, still had a long way to progress before it reached a conversational level.

It was not until the following morning that Amanda realized this dinner party had had quite a significance. A relative of the Córdoba family by marriage had attended, it seemed, and this person, she discovered, had been one of Antonio's reasons for wishing to return to Majorca just then.

"*Tío* says it is ridiculous, this estrangement between Felipe's family and mine," Cristina said. "He spoke with Felipe for a long time at Siesta Key, as well as with me. He made us promise we would not see each other again until he could talk personally to Senor Córdoba, Felipe's father. Now the uncle of Felipe on his mother's side of the family, who was here last night, will arrange such a meeting—or at least make it more pleasant, shall I say?"

It was entirely too much for Amanda. Such intrigue in the name of romance was something beyond her realm. Yet she saw that Cristina really thrived on it. Cristina *was* very Spanish in this way, as was Antonio, for that matter. Still, it seemed to her Antonio also had a strong practical streak in his nature, and she'd come to the conclusion his thinking was not nearly as "feudal" as she'd thought at first.

On the day Antonio met with Felipe's father, she and Cristina were invited to lunch at Teresa López's

house. Amanda rather dreaded this because it would
be so entirely foreign to her. But at least everyone
there spoke Spanish rather than Mallorquí, so she
understood enough of what they were saying to answer a question or two now and then.

Teresa joined them the next morning when Amanda and Cristina went on a tour of the pearl manufactory. This had been arranged by Carlos López, who
met them when they arrived and then turned them
over to an assistant who was almost overwhelmingly
anxious to please them.

Watching the process by which the pearls were
made was nothing new to Cristina, but she enjoyed
Amanda's enthusiasm, and Amanda was frankly fascinated. Dozens of women, all of them clad in neat
pastel aprons, sat at long tables illuminated by cen-
tral fluorescent lights. Each was working on a different stage of the pearl-making process, and this
division of labor formed a kind of assembly-line production, yet one done by hand with loving care and a
strong sense of commitment. Those employed in the
preliminary steps were definitely artists. They were
using, as Antonio had said, the utmost in modern
technique, and only natural essences, the formula of
which was kept a closely guarded secret.

The end result was pearls that equaled those of the
rarest natural variety in both radiance and beauty.

Next they passed through an entire room where
necklaces were being strung by experts at this task,
and finally they came to an area that separated the
manufacturing part of the building from the show-
rooms, which were open to the thousands of tourists
who flocked to Majorca every year. A majority of

these visitors took home something made with the beautiful local pearls. A souvenir...or, as the Spanish put it, a *recuerdo*—a remembrance.

She wandered through the aisles lined with glass-covered cases, each containing an array of pearl jewelry seemingly more beautiful than the last, and she decided she would splurge on just one thing. She would wear it constantly, she promised herself, once she'd returned to Boston, and it would remind her forever of this trip to Majorca and of Antonio...as if she really needed anything to remind her of Antonio!

As she was leaning over a counter, debating whether to choose a necklace or a pin, that voice that caused such sudden disturbances in her said over her shoulder, "Do you like them, *querida*?"

"They are absolutely beautiful," she replied sincerely, for they were. Each necklace, each ring, each pin was an exquisite work of art.

"Which would you like?" he asked her.

"I don't know," she told him, preoccupied with the matter of making a choice. "I doubt if I could afford to buy more than just one thing, so I want to be careful...."

"Buy?"

She looked up to see his lips quirk, and there was no doubt he was amused. "Can you possibly think you could buy anything in this room? These pearls are mine—therefore they are yours."

Cristina had warned her not to admire anything too much when she went to Teresa López's house because of the old Spanish custom making it necessary for the owner of the object of such admiration to offer whatever it might be to the person who had praised it.

She had understood, but she had added laughingly, "You don't ever actually take anything from anyone, do you?"

Cristina said seriously, "No, it is merely a custom."

Now Antonio was telling her she could have all the pearls in the showroom if she wanted them, and she decided that this, too, was purely a Spanish way of expressing generosity. The pearls were not hers, of course, simply because he owned them. Nothing that was his was hers, especially the one thing she wanted most of all: his heart. That, apparently, belonged to a dead woman!

He said patiently, "Well, *linda*? Since you cannot wear them all at once, which would you like to take with you?"

"I haven't decided," she admitted. "I shall have to price one or two things and see if I've brought enough money with me."

She was immediately conscious of his annoyance. "I have told you, Amanda," he said irritably, "there is no such thing as your buying anything here. Must I make it even plainer that I want to make you a present?"

She knew they were being watched by every saleslady in the place not already busy with a customer and probably by Cristina, Teresa and their guides, as well, all of whom were standing a short distance away, looking at some necklaces. Her face flamed, and she said, "There is no need for you to give me a present, Antonio."

He swore softly, then said, "You must be the most stubborn woman in the entire world! *Dios*, Amanda, do I have to get down on my knees and beg you to let me bestow something upon you that belongs to me?" He turned, and at once there was a saleslady standing behind their immediate section of the counter. He spoke to the woman in a Spanish so swift Amanda could not understand a word of it.

In another instant, a black velvet mat with some of the loveliest jewelry she had ever seen displayed had been laid out in front of her.

"Try this," Antonio suggested, and picked up a slim gold chain on the end of which dangled a large, round, beautifully formed pearl the color of deep rich cream. "Here, I will fasten it for you."

She felt his fingers fumble with the clasp, and it occurred to her he was not as calm as he seemed. Then he stood back, and looking down at the pendant, the pearl positioned now just in the hollow of her throat, he said almost brusquely, "That is very lovely. I think, in addition to this, some small pearl earings to be worn with it. . . just the single pearl set in gold, nothing more. You agree?"

She nodded dumbly and then to her astonishment heard him add, "I should like, also, to select a ring for you, but rings, I know, have a connotation you might not be willing to accept. So that, perhaps, we should reserve for another time."

Amanda could only hope the saleslady didn't understand English. She also wished Antonio's face were not quite such a mask at moments like this. Despite his words he was looking at her with an expression that seemed almost deliberately blank.

The saleslady was speaking to him, and now he said, "You do not wish the pendant boxed, do you, Amanda? I would prefer that you wear it—if you have no objection. We can take the box with us. Would you like to wear the earrings, too?"

"No," she said. "I don't think so. Not just now."

"Then we will take them along," he said, and a moment later thrust a package into her hand. "If you will excuse me," he told her then, "I wish to speak to Cristina and Teresa."

He left her, and she stood by the counter, glancing after him, watching him move across the floor with that aloof grace she would always associate with him. He was wearing a business suit in a pale shade of gray. His shirt was of a slightly lighter gray, and his tie was rather somber, with wide bands of gray and black. But the combination on Antonio was devastating. Every eye in the place turned to watch him as he came back to her side, and Amanda could only nod weakly and follow him when he said, "Come along."

He led her through a rear doorway and into a small paved area, where she saw the black car they'd driven to Manacor parked near a lone palm tree that grew at the side of the building. Antonio held the door for her wordlessly and then took his place behind the wheel, and it was not until he'd driven out into the street that he said, "I thought we would go to Porto Cristo for lunch."

"What about Cristina?" Amanda asked.

"Cristina is going to lunch with Teresa. Carlos is taking both of them, as a matter of fact. Would you have preferred to be with them?"

"No," she said very softly, not daring to look at him.

"Good," he said. "I was afraid you were about to tell me there was no reason why I should take you to lunch. Does it not occur to you, Amanda, that I wanted very much to give you the pendant you are wearing and that I want to take you to lunch? In other words, that I want to be with you? Does that idea never cross your mind?"

He spoke with a controlled anger that surprised her, and then he said in a way that, for a moment, made him seem almost more American than Spanish, "I don't know what the hell it is you do to me!"

She could have returned the sentiment, but just now she had no intention of doing so. To confess what he did to her was more of an admission than she ever intended to make to him!

As they drove toward the Mediterranean coast, she began to relax, and it occurred to her she'd be entirely happy if only they could keep going like this forever. Her feelings were reinforced when they came to Porto Cristo. It was quite a resort, with a seawall behind the pretty beach, lots of people, lots of boats and a fiesta air that seemed to envelop everyone and everything. Despite the restaurants and hotels that vied for space along the waterfront and the high rises Antonio had mentioned, there was still a lot of charm to the town. She thought it would be fun to spend a holiday there...and could imagine the sheer delight of having Antonio to share it with her.

He took her to lunch in a hotel that fronted directly on the small street back of the seawall. Its windows, edged with green wooden boxes bright with scarlet geraniums, looked out over the harbor. Antonio realized she wasn't accustomed to a huge Spanish *comida* in the middle of the day, so they had only fresh anchovies, crisp fried, and a large green salad, finishing with a sinfully rich chocolate dessert and small cups of espresso.

Antonio seemed to have forgotten his annoyance with her over the pearls. Only once did he take note of the lovely pendant she was wearing, to say, "It is most becoming." Then he went on to speak of a variety of things, and she had the feeling he was working his way around to the subject he really wanted to discuss.

"You should be pleased to know I found Felipe's father a very understanding person," he said finally. "We are in agreement there is no reason why the younger generation should pay for the animosities of their elders. Next Christmas, when we are all in Manacor again, the engagement between Felipe and Cristina will be announced, and they will be married when he has finished his studies at Columbia."

Next Christmas, when we are all in Manacor again. Those words stood out above everything else he had said, despite her genuine delight for Cristina. But he was using *we* in a purely impersonal sense, she was sure. He did not mean it to include her. And also, by next Christmas—if Cristina was right in her dire predictions—Antonio's world would be a very dark one. As she thought of this, Amanda shuddered.

At once he asked, "Are you not pleased? I thought you would be very happy, Amanda. It is in its way a victory for you, is it not?"

"I *am* very pleased," she said, "but I don't see why I should consider it a victory for me."

"Well," he said, "you proved I was wrong, did you not? And not for the first time, I might add."

He did not elaborate on this, and after a moment he glanced at his watch and said, "We had better get going. I have other things to show you."

It did not occur to her that among the "other things" he intended to visit were the Caves of the Dragon, until, without much warning, they were actually pulling up at the parking lot near the caves' entrance.

"It does not take very long to visit the caves," he said as he guided her along. "I think you will find them as fascinating as I do. Such a subterranean world never ceases to enchant me. Incidentally, at least two hundred caves have been discovered on the island. To my mind, Las Cuevas del Drach are the most magnificent. They have been called *La Alhambra Subterránea*—which means the Subterranean Alhambra—because the formations are so indescribably beautiful. All of the columns, which are like a succession of enchanted forests, have been formed by drops of water whose dissolved minerals have been transformed and precipitated out. The process has taken centuries and centureis. I find it something of a miracle."

Amanda agreed. Yet she wanted desperately to draw back when it came time to pass through the entrance. Then it was too late—he had bought their tickets and was slipping two green paper receipts into his coat pocket. And he was urging her on, telling her a tour was starting and they should go along with it.

Almost at once the caves were beyond and below

them, and even at first glimpse she knew he had not overestimated their beauty. It was impossible not to be tremendously awed by this display of nature's pure magnificence, the stalagmites and stalactites incredible in their range of colors, from purest gold to deepest green, shot through with highlights of vibrant turquoise and cobalt blue.

There were names for many of the formations, and these were translated for her benefit by Antonio in a soft whisper. "A Snow-Covered Peak"—and here the columns were clustered together into what did indeed look like a summit in the Alps. "A Pagoda"—this in tones of beige and ivory and gold, singularly Oriental in its architecture. "The Fairies' Theater"—an enchanted gold bronze world of chamber upon chamber edged by the mineral columns; some thick, some thin, some spiraling.

Amanda remembered that in the cavern she had visited as a child they had taken an elevator that had let them off far down into the earth—an eternity below the surface, it had seemed to her. There was no elevator in the Dragon's Cave, though, and they descended via a series of shallow steps and ramps—some of them quite worn—with thin railings along their edges that were much too wobbly for her comfort. She found herself moving close to the cavern walls, which were cold and moist to her touch, and everywhere she looked, there were plunging depths that made her giddy despite their beauty. At one place it appeared to her she must be seeing all the way to the center of the earth itself, and she recalled hearing, as a little girl, that China would be on the other side if one started digging a hole in the ground and made it all the way through. If she were to fall over the rim and into that colorful pit that yawned beneath her, would she end up in China, she wondered. She had to suppress a laugh she was sure would verge on the hysterical.

As it was she trembled, and Antonio asked quickly, "What is it, *linda*?"

Her teeth had begun to chatter, even though she was trying to tell herself sternly it was absolutely ridiculous to be afraid. The caves were visited by thousands and thousands of people on a regular basis, they were beautifully illuminated and undoubtedly safe, and there wasn't any danger.

But simply telling herself this did no good at all. Her fear of heights, or perhaps in this instance her fear of depths, plus a growing sense of claustrophobia, were rapidly forming an apprehension that went beyond the norm, and she knew she wasn't going to be able to handle it much longer.

Her teeth were still chattering, and Antonio asked insistently, "What *is* it, Amanda?"

"Do we have much farther to go?" she asked.

"Not much," he said. "It takes about three quarters of an hour to get to the bottom, so we are well on the way."

There were people all around them, and in fact Amanda was slowing down the pace of the group. Yet she knew there was absolutely no chance to turn at this point and reverse directions. She was committed to going all the way. Her knees, though, were shaking so badly she was not at all sure she was going to make it, and she wondered if anyone had ever passed out in the middle of a guided tour before!

Antonio said, "*Linda*, maybe it is the lighting in here, but you look green! Are you sick?"

"No," she said shakily. "Just terrified."

"Terrified?" he repeated incredulously. "There is nothing to be afraid of, *querida*."

"I—I know that," she stammered. "But knowing it doesn't help. I have the feeling I'm going to plunge over the edge and I—I will dissolve if that happens. There will be nothing left of me."

"But there is no chance of your falling over the edge," he told her. He put his arm around her, drawing her close to him. "Look, dearest, I will hold you all the rest of the way," he said. "Meanwhile, just keep your eyes on a step at a time...do not look off to the sides and down, all right?"

"Okay," she murmured nervously.

"Let me tell you about the lake at the bottom," he said. "It is called Lake Martel, named for the famous French speleologist who discovered it. They say it is the largest underground lake in the world. It is, I believe, nearly one hundred eighty meters long and about thirty meters wide. It has been beautifully illuminated so one can see how very clear the water is. In fact, one can gauge the depth of the water by its color. If it is white, then it is very shallow—only about a meter. If it is green, it is perhaps three meters. And if it is pure blue, then it is deeper—about eight meters. Also, there will be a surprise for you when we come to the lake."

Amanda was not at all sure if she could take any more of his surprises, but she did gasp in awe at the sight of the lake and the magnificent chamber at its edge—a huge cave in itself...a veritable amphitheater of stone. There were folding chairs lined up in rows, making a concert hall of the place, and Antonio urged her to sit down. She was glad enough to do so because she was shaking all over, and as if reading her thoughts, he said, "It will not be so bad going back up, *linda*. I will hold your hand all the way, and if you do not look back—and you must not—there will not be any trouble."

She nodded and was just beginning to feel more confident when suddenly the lights blinked out!

She stifled a scream, her teeth biting into her lips as she did so, and Antonio said softly in her ear, "It is only for a moment, *querida*, to show what true darkness is."

He said this calmly enough, but he could not have chosen a worse description, for now it swept over her that Antonio was going to be blind and the darkness would be forever.

Tears came immediately to burn her cheeks, and it was all she could do not to sob. Then she felt his lips brush her neck, and he said, "*Querida mia*, right now let me be strong for both of us, will you?"

She didn't know whether he intended the double significance, but she had no doubts he was the stronger of them.

He said gently, "Look, *linda*," and her eyes traveled out across the water. From a recess far back in the cave, boats began to glide toward them, gondolas beautifully outlined in white lights. There were men in each of the gondolas, and as they neared, she saw they carried instruments. Suddenly they began to play, and the sweet music of violins and violas and cellos blended into a sound more beautiful than anything she had ever heard before.

It was a moment she would never forget—being with Antonio in this concert chamber far below the surface of the earth. His arm was around her, his head close to hers, so that the nearness of him and the sound of the music seemed to be one and the same.

He was right. She followed his instructions on the way back, and the ascent was not bad at all. As they walked across the parking lot toward his car, she said, "You may not believe this, but I honestly thank you for taking me."

"I do believe it, *linda*," he answered. "One has to suffer through many experiences to know the full essence of life," he added mysteriously, and once again she was left to wonder at precisely what he had meant.

CHAPTER TWENTY-TWO

AFTER THE AFTERNOON in the caves the remaining time in Manacor passed with such a rush that before it seemed possible they were driving back to Palma again. There was no time to visit the cathedral or do much of anything else, but when Cristina deplored this, Antonio only said that some things should always be saved for later.

He had been in a very agreeable mood during the entire course of their Majorcan island hiatus, and since the episode in the caves he seemed especially tender toward Amanda. Once they left Madrid, however, and were winging their way back across the Atlantic, he retreated into a moody silence that was not easily broached.

Amanda, sitting beside him, lapsed into her own silence. She was aroused from the muddle of her thoughts by the stewardess's asking her if she would like champagne.

Antonio answered for her. "Yes," he said, "I think she needs something festive about now."

He handed her a glass of cool amber liquid alive with shimmering bubbles and clinked his own glass to it. "*¡Salud, querida!*" he said, and forced a smile. Then he added wearily, "And excuse me. I am being very bad company, I know.

Perhaps you would prefer to sit with Cristina?''

"No," she said, then hesitated. She wanted to ask him about his eyes. In fact, it seemed to her she could not bear to go on any further without knowing all there was to know about what he had to face in the impending surgery. Now she could tell he was watching her closely, and she grasped for courage, then said, "When are you going into the hospital?"

She heard him draw in his breath. "What makes you think I am going into the hospital at all?" he responded evasively.

"Please," she said. "I don't suppose I can say I have a right to know, but it does seem to me...."

"It concerns you so much, Amanda?"

She turned a lovely tormented face toward him, and she said in little more than a whisper, "Do you really have to ask me that?"

He frowned. "I am not sure," he admitted. "Oh, yes, I'm aware you have a very tender heart and so you would be concerned about anyone...anything...."

"Antonio!"

"Very well," he said. "The date has not been set, but it will be some time in the spring. There are matters that must be settled first at Hermosa Groves."

"There is still trouble about the original grant?"

"Yes," he said. "I will know more, of course, once we are in Florida. And whichever way it develops, I want it decided before I have the operation."

She swallowed hard. "Antonio," she began, "about the operation...."

He winced, and there was no doubt it was from

pain. "Please," he said, "it isn't that I am trying to hold back from you, but just now...."

"Another headache?"

"Yes," he said, grimly, "another headache. I can only hope to God the operation will put an end to them!"

He sank back into his seat, closing that single dark eye that could be so disturbing, and she sat quietly at his side, her heart aching because there was nothing she could do for him.

Would there ever be a time when she could do something for Antonio? Would he ever *let* her do anything for him?

Questions without answers, she thought dully, and closed her own eyes, trying to relax as the miles sped by.

GREGORY BLAKE MET THEM at the airport in Tampa—to Amanda's surprise. But before they had driven very far, he turned into the parking lot of a large restaurant and said, "Let's go into the lounge here and have a drink. There are a couple of things I'd like to go over before we reach the Groves."

Antonio had taken medication twice en route across the Atlantic and he seemed to be feeling better, although he was still both pale and tense. But he assented, and they found a booth at the very end of the cocktail lounge, as far removed as possible from the loud rock band that was playing. "So we can hear ourselves talk," Greg said.

Greg lost no time in getting to the point. "It seems incredible, Tony," he said, "but your family was given its grant precisely on January 24, 1818. That was later to be the cutoff date, as you know, insofar as the Spanish land grants were concerned.''

"So," Antonio said, "this makes the grant invalid?"

Gregory shook his head. "I don't think so, and Florence doesn't, either. We hope we can settle all this right in Tallahassee without recourse to Washington. You see, it was a year or so after the Florida purchase in 1821 before Congress created a board of three commissioners to hold sessions alternately in Pensacola and Saint Augustine to examine the land claims.

"They had no idea at the time this would prove to be the most difficult thing of all to handle. This was especially true in East Florida—which at that time included the whole peninsula—because often there were no records at all, and when documents could be found, they were almost always in Spanish. Naturally it was easy enough to have the documents translated, but they soon found that similar terms have different meanings in different languages.''

Amanda silently attested to this. Didn't they, though!

"Some of the claims went back to the time the British had owned Florida. These had been issued in English first. Then they were reissued in Spanish at the time of the second Spanish occupation," Greg continued. "In East Florida a lot of the land hadn't even been surveyed, so the claims had to be located and the boundaries established accurately. The entire thing became a total mess. At that period the land laws in the United States were entirely too loose, and a lot of people tried to take advantage of this once

Florida became U.S. property. In short, there were a lot of false claims, a lot of fraud involving the origin of the grants, the number of acres they included and their locations. It took a long time to straighten all of this out, and it seriously hampered the orderly transfer of Florida from Spanish to American rule.

"The treaty of cession had made things clear enough. Anything granted by the king of Spain prior to January 24, 1818 would be considered valid and anything granted after that date would not. To add to the problem, several very large tracts of land came into focus, and they were in litigation for a number of years. Many Americans had purchased land from Spaniards after the January 24 date, and the question was whether these Spaniards had seen the handwriting on the wall and knew the transactions wouldn't be any good."

"I follow you so far," Antonio said, while Amanda listened intently.

"An example of this," Greg went on, "is the story of the Alagan grant. On February 6, 1818, King Ferdinand VII granted eleven million Florida acres to the Duke of Alagon. On May 29, 1819, the duke sold the land to one Richard A. Hackley. By that time the U.S. and Spain were already negotiating. In fact, the January 24, 1818 date had been privately settled upon. The question arose as to whether the Duke of Alagon had prior knowledge of this or whether he had sold the land to Hackley in good faith. There's also the chance that Hackley, knowing how lax his countrymen were about land laws, might have thought the new American government in Florida would overlook the date when it got right down to the wire. Anyway, Hackley later insisted the sale was valid, and he turned around and sold the land to a Colonel George W. Murray from New York. The result was that Murray's heirs and their associates kept the case going through the courts until 1905—and, believe it or not, at that late date the U.S. Supreme Court ruled the grant had indeed been invalid in the first place under the terms of the treaty.''

"So,'' Antonio shrugged, "what might they do to us?''

"Well,'' Greg said, "your family's original grant involved about sixty-eight thousand acres, and as you know, during the past few decades the land has been sold off until now you're down to the present seven thousand. There are a lot of owners involved today insofar as the original acreage is concerned, but that doesn't mean they wouldn't all stand to lose if it were decided that the grant was invalid. I'm not sure, if this happened, whether the land would be put up for auction by the U.S. But it does seem possible to me it would give someone with the right connections a chance to get in on the inside and perhaps grab quite a prize chunk of prime Florida territory. Florence is at work now finding out whether that January 24 date is legally the last date upon which a grant would be considered valid or whether we've got to accept the fact that only grants made *before* January 24 stand up in court. I'll be frank and say I'd hate to get into court on this one. Litigation could drag on for years.''

"I agree,'' Antonio said tersely. "So Florence is now on the final course with this?''

"Yes. We should have a definite opinion from Tallahassee in a day or so.''

Antonio nodded. "Then," he said, "we can only wait."

"True enough," Greg agreed wryly. "Now about Roger Crane...."

"Let us discuss him later," Antonio said, quickly lifting his glass and avoiding Amanda's gaze.

THE RETURN TO THE HACIENDA was something of a letdown. Jet lag possessed her, and Amanda slept through most of the following day. Though refreshed once again, it still was difficult to pick up the exact threads of the life she'd been leading before they'd been to Majorca. She tried to continue with her "formalized" English lessons, but Cristina was restless, and it had to be admitted they weren't making very much progress.

Antonio spent much of his time in his office with Greg, and on two different days they both made the trip to Tampa, evidently for consultation with Florence Edmond. Greg seemed very preoccupied, too, and Amanda began to feel he was beginning to think seriously that the grant was not going to hold up.

She wondered just what this would mean to Antonio—or if, in fact, it would mean very much to him at all. He had no family or any real roots in America, and he did not seem all that fond of either America or Americans, despite his friendship with Greg and what seemed to her an obvious interest in Florence Edmond as a woman, rather than an attorney.

They had been back nearly a week when, one night, she was awakened by something striking her bedroom window. There was a thud, then a moment later another thud, and with the second one she slipped out of bed and crossed the room to stare out at the patio, bathed in moonlight.

A man stood in the shadows beneath her balcony, and she assumed it must be Antonio. But then he spoke, and the accent was entirely American. "Come downstairs," he said, and she realized, to her astonishment, it was Roger.

"What are you doing here?" she hissed.

"Amanda, if you don't get the hell down here I'm coming up there!" he assured her roughly, the words slurring enough so she knew he had been drinking.

It seemed to her there was no choice. "All right," she told him hastily. "Just give me a minute."

It was a very warm night, but nevertheless she sought a robe that was not transparent. She didn't want any trouble with Roger! She sped down the stairs without even bothering to glance in the mirror and joined him in the shadows. And as he started to speak, she touched her fingers to her mouth.

"There are bedrooms all around this patio," she reminded him. "Keep your voice down, will you!"

"I don't give a damn if I'm heard or not," he told her, but he lowered his voice slightly. "Has that bastard you work for told you what he's done?"

"Antonio?" she asked, and he laughed shortly.

"I'm glad to see you accept my choice of words," he said harshly.

"Roger, you shouldn't be here," she began, but he cut her off.

"He's sacked me, Amanda. Fired me. I'm through at Hermosa Groves. Hasn't he announced it yet?"

She had not expected this. She'd known from the

very beginning there was hostility between Roger and Antonio. Yet it had seemed to her that the groves themselves proved he'd been an excellent manager through the years. They could not have been more beautiful, and the citrus they produced was top quality in a state famous for fine citrus.

"Why, Roger?" she asked, honestly distressed.

"Ask *him* why!" Roger retorted bitterly.

A voice came from the shadows, deep, accented, disturbing. "Yes," Antonio suggested, "why don't you do that, Amanda?"

Roger swerved, his face contorted. "Why don't you tell her yourself, Hernandez?" he demanded.

"Very well," Antonio said, crossing toward them and managing to position himself directly in their midst. "I have dismissed him, Amanda, because he has allied himself with this man named Edmund Trent, who, it seems, would go to any length to acquire Hermosa Groves. It is he who has stirred up all the trouble over the date of my family's grant. He hoped to force me to sell to him by making me think I would lose entirely if I persisted in holding the land. I admit it costs money to fight legal battles, especially in your country. I do not think he realized I would spend any amount to validate my claim—if that is what you wish to call it—rather than give in to people like him. . . and Crane."

"You are mistaken, Hernandez," Roger said, tight-lipped. "Oh, you're right enough about Trent. He figured you for a foreigner who didn't know the ropes, but he wasn't aware that everything you touch turns to gold. He thought he could force your hand. And yes, he tried to get me to go in with him. He promised me a cut of the profit if he put this deal over. But what you don't realize is that I've been trying to block him at every curve in the road. Hermosa Groves," Roger said slowly, "has been my life these past ten years. When I came here, the place was going downhill. You can look it up in the records if you like and prove that for yourself. Mr. Field was tired...he didn't really give a damn. But he trusted me...he put it in my hands, and we made a good thing with what was left. He was a great old man. I don't see how the hell you ever came to be related to someone like that...."

"You have been seen with Trent on several occasions," Antonio said. "You don't deny those meetings, do you?"

"Of course I don't deny them!" Roger answered savagely. "The day I took Cristina and Amanda to Sarasota we damn near ran into him when I went back to the mall to pick them up. I can tell you I held my breath. I could imagine how you'd take it if you found out I'd introduced your niece and your—"

"Yes?" Antonio asked, his tone purely dangerous.

"I don't know what the hell Amanda is to you," Roger conceded unhappily. "I only wish I did!"

Amanda tensed, wondering what Antonio was going to say to this, but he had turned as silent and still as a statue. Then Roger said, "I apologize, Amanda. Okay, so I shouldn't have come. But I wanted you to know...."

"Yes," she murmured. "It's all right, Roger. But go now, will you?"

He nodded, and Amanda walked, her knees wobbling, over to the nearest chair and sat down. After a time she heard a car motor start and she knew Roger had left them. Antonio was still standing in the same place—she didn't think he'd moved an inch. She turned toward him, her voice suffused with fury.

"I hope you're satisfied," she told him.

He moved toward her, taking a chair on the opposite side of the table she'd chosen to sit at, and he said, "If it is any consolation to you, I am not satisfied at all!"

"I suppose you got your precious grant confirmed," she said. "Well, now you can have the groves and everything else, too. *That* should satisfy you!"

"It does not satisfy me at all," he said, and then added, "Crane told you the grant has been upheld?"

"No, he didn't tell me. I don't think he even knows," she stormed. "You are so damnably suspicious, Antonio. . . ."

"Yes," he said levelly, "where you are concerned I *am* damnably suspicious, Amanda, though not, I am sure, for the reasons you think. And yes, the grant has been upheld. Florence and Greg got word back from Tallahassee this afternoon that the records make it clear all Spanish land grants given *on* or before January 24, 1818 are legal under American law."

"And so you own Hermosa Groves, and you can very well live happily ever after," she said bitterly.

"You think so, Amanda?" he asked her. "Aren't you forgetting a few things?"

She fell silent at this. . . because it was only too true. Her anger toward him dissipated, and she said slowly, "It's so unfair, that's all, what you did to Roger."

"You care so much about Crane?"

"Oh, for God's sake," she said impatiently, "there's nothing *personal* about it. I wish you'd stop reading meanings into everything I say. It just seems to me Roger has managed Hermosa Groves extremely well, and it's too bad your relative didn't show some appreciation in his will for this sort of service. Rather than to have simply dismissed Roger because of your nasty suspicious mind, I would think it would have made more sense to have given him a chance first to prove whether he was innocent or guilty."

"American fairness, yes?" Antonio asked wryly.

"Call it American fairness if you like," she retorted. "You detest Americans and America, don't you?"

"No," he said slowly, "I do not. I admire both your people and your country, Amanda. Greg is not my only American friend. I know many Americans whom I like very well. I may not agree with everything about your way of life and it may seem to me our Spanish life-style does have some advantages, but I am not one of those foreigners who detest the United States because it is a rich and powerful country.

"Its people have an incentive and a spirit for achievement that unfortunately was lost in Europe a long time ago. I think it is now beginning to come back again...perhaps as a result of your guidance, whether we like to admit it or not. I am not an American, Amanda. I will never be an American. But please don't make me any more narrow than I am."

He was outlined in moonlight as he spoke, and she saw him rub his forehead wearily. This made her realize he'd undoubtedly been feeling considerable pain—physical pain—as he went through the scene with Roger, and she felt a pang of contrition. Yet she was not about to take back anything she had said to him. He had it coming, damn it!

Then he said, "The time is almost up, Amanda. April, I mean. It is not that far away. I feel you have perhaps had enough. You have done very well with Cristina. She is surprisingly conversant in your language, although her accent leaves much to be desired. But then, I realize, so does mine. It seems to me," he finished, "that since you have stated you do not intend to remain here for the entire year, there is no reason to hold you any longer."

He could not have made his message more plain.

CHAPTER TWENTY-THREE

GREGORY TOOK CARE of the travel arrangements. Amanda wondered if he might fly as far as New York with her, but he booked her on a nonstop flight from Tampa to Boston.

He drove her to the airport, with a silent Cristina sitting between them in the front seat of the car. Cristina had ranted and railed and cried and tried to persuade and finally had flung out angrily, "How can you do this to *tío*?"

Amanda had answered bitterly, her heart aching, "I am going at his request, Cristina. You must understand that!"

But Cristina had only shaken her head violently, her black hair tumbling around her shoulders. "That, I cannot believe," she had insisted flatly.

There had been tears in Tía Inez's eyes as she kissed Amanda goodbye, and this had been a surprise. She had become fond of Antonio's aunt and knew that Tía Inez liked her in return, but she had not expected such a show of affection from the dignified older woman.

Antonio had not come to say goodbye to her at all, and this had hurt terribly. "Excuse Tony, will you?" Greg Blake had told her. "He had to go to Tampa earlier this morning. He said he would have taken you along, but it would have meant a long wait for you in the airport.''

Antonio in Tampa! This certainly meant he had gone to see Florence Edmond again, and since matters concerning the land grant were now settled, it seemed unlikely it had been on legal business. This time, Amanda decided, Antonio's trip was obviously for pleasure, and the mere thought of it stung her.

As Greg checked her baggage through to Boston for her and Cristina stood in glum silence at her side, she found it hard to believe things were ending like this. She and Antonio had become as close to each other as a man and woman could ever get. . .and not in the physical sense alone. There had been no doubt at all about how they affected each other *physically*. But they'd gone beyond that. There had been moments of such intense sweetness and closeness that she knew only too well she would never—should she live to be a hundred—ever be able to equal them or even approach them with anyone else.

Yet last night he must have known he would be going to Tampa in the morning, although when he had left them not long after dinner to go to his room, he had not said anything at all to her to indicate they would not be seeing each other again. It seemed to her this was needlessly brutal. Why did he feel the need to hurt her so much?

Greg said, ''We've time for a drink before they call your flight, Amanda? How about it?''

''Perhaps some iced coffee,'' she agreed, but she couldn't even finish that. She felt physically ill and wished she'd bought some motion-sickness pills for the trip. Possibly the stewardesses on the plane would be able to provide things like that. She'd ask, at least.

At the gate Cristina's eyes brimmed over with tears, and this was too much. Amanda began to cry herself, and Greg, dismayed, said, "Hey, girls! This isn't the end of the line. You'll be seeing each other again!"

It seemed like a very hollow promise, and Amanda was tempted to tell him so, but she held her tongue. It was too late really to say anything. Much too late.

She clung to Cristina and suggested unsteadily, "One of these days when you're in New York visiting Felipe, give me a call and I'll come down."

"Yes," Cristina said, clutching at even this little bit of hope. "Yes, oh, yes, *querida* Amanda."

Querida. The sound of this Spanish endearment stabbed her because it reminded her so much of Antonio. She swallowed hard and was afraid she was going to begin to cry all over again, and was glad when the announcement that it was boarding time came over the loudspeaker and she could leave Greg and Cristina behind her.

Her eyes were blurry with tears as she moved down the plane's aisle to find her seat. She'd assumed that on this return flight Greg would probably book her in the coach section, but he hadn't. Once again she was going first class all the way.

She was barely aware of someone moving into the aisle seat beside her. Then a man said, "Pardon, but you are sitting on my seat belt."

Amanda shut her eyes tightly and, close to desperation, told herself she'd have to do better than this! It was getting so that everything reminded her of Antonio. Even this stranger's voice had a tone deeply familiar, and he spoke with more than a hint of a Spanish accent. . . .

"Amanda," he said now, and she clenched her hands so tightly her nails dug into her palms. "For the love of God, *querida*, what are you going to do? Pass out on me?"

Only now did she open her eyes, convinced she *had* to be imagining all of this. But Antonio was indeed staring down at her, his handsome face a mirror of concern.

"Vida," he said, "I didn't mean to frighten you to death! I waited till the last moment to board the plane because I was afraid if you saw me, you'd be apt to try to get off."

"But you went to Tampa?" she murmured, her voice trembling.

"This *is* Tampa, *linda*," he reminded her. "Yes, I left early this morning because I had to stop at Florence's office to sign some papers. Greg told you that, I'm sure. But for the rest of the time I have—what do you call it—hung around. I think these have been the longest hours of my life."

At his elbow a stewardess said, "Fasten your seat belt, please, sir. And, you, miss."

"You really are sitting on a part of my seat belt," Antonio told her. "Here, let me help you with yours. *Querida*, your hands are shaking so. . . ."

There surely was no denying that! And as he fastened her belt for her, his fingers brushed her breasts, and she could hardly bear the intimacy of his touch. Just to be near him like this was torture—such torture she posed an agonized question capsuled into a single word.

"Why?" she asked him.

He understood what she meant. And as the plane began to taxi toward the runway, he said quietly, "Because I could not let you go, even though I had sworn to myself I would do so. I had convinced myself it would be better for you if I had the courage to—release you. Yet it seemed to me we have had some of our best conversations on airplanes, perhaps because there are no interruptions of significance. So I decided to try one more time. . . ."

"Yes?"

"Also," he said, "the operation has been scheduled."

"Antonio!"

"*Querida*, please," he said. "You look as if in another instant you will require first aid." A smile flitted across his lips. "I would not in the least mind giving it to you," he said. "Perhaps—especially—the mouth-to-mouth resuscitation! But since this flight will not be endless and there is considerable material to cover, I am going to tell you first about this surgery I face and the reasons for it. You must promise not to look at me like that, though."

She said, subdued, "You're a lot braver about it than I am."

"It would make a great deal of difference in my life to get rid of the headaches I've been suffering from these past four years," he said frankly. "I have got rid of everything else that has plagued me, except for these last physical matters. Our trip to Majorca did that, *linda*. On that drive to Manacor it came to me that an accident is an accident, and I finally accepted that what happened four years earlier really was not my fault. It would have been the same if Juan had been at the wheel.

"I spoke to people in Manacor, and I went to the garage that had examined the car for the police after the crash. It was as they said. There were mechanical defects I had no way of knowing about. And so, you see, I finally laid many ghosts to rest—ghosts that had tormented me all this time."

Again her throat constricted in that much too familiar way. And it still took courage—a lot of courage—to pose the question. "Even—even your fiancée?" she asked him.

"Yes," he said, "even Elena." He frowned. "It is difficult to say this to you," he said, "but ours was a very Spanish engagement, *linda*. She was beautiful, true. An exquisite person. She was also from the proper kind of family—our families had been close for years. There was everything right about such a match, and it was in great favor with all of the relatives. In the normal course of events we would have divided our time between Andalusia and Majorca, with trips in season to Paris and London and perhaps New York. She would have borne me sons who would have carried on the Hernandez name and all the traditions. . . ."

"You don't have to say any more," Amanda protested weakly.

"Ah, but I do," Antonio corrected her. "I am Latin enough to be fascinated by beautiful women, although need I say that this is a characteristic common to most men, Latin or not. Elena was quite an enchantress in her own way, and she knew how to flirt. All Spanish women know how to flirt. It was a game, our courtship, something like a ritual. We went through all the steps of it, and I do not deny I found this pleasant, even delightful. But she never challenged me. . .she never made me experience the variety of emotions that, until quite recently, I never knew existed. I would have never known what it was to love with Elena, and I hope you do not think I am disloyal to her memory when I say this.''

"No," she said. "No."

"*Querida*, look at me, for God's sake," Antonio urged. "What I am trying to tell you is that I never knew what love was until an American who disagreed with me about almost everything began to teach me not one but several lessons. I should say," he added, "that as a result of one of them, Roger Crane will continue managing Hermosa Groves. From now on he will be a real part of the enterprise. There will be a profit-sharing system, and I am also going to deed a section of the groves to him directly. It was to finalize these matters that I went to Florence Edmond's office this morning."

"And Roger agreed to take back his job?" she asked.

"Yes." Antonio nodded. "Not without some persuasion, of course. It was not very easy for me, because I think he is infatuated with you. And, I admit, I was blinded by jealousy toward him from the time you came to Florida. Prior to that I was suspicious of him because of the information about Edmund Trent's dealings that had been passed on to me by both Greg and Florence."

"There was never any reason for you to be jealous," she said slowly.

"No?" He laughed. "I will be jealous of you for the rest of my life, *querida*! You may Americanize me to a point—but when it comes to the woman I love, I warn you I am essentially Spanish."

The woman I love. Amanda shook her head as these words began to echo in her mind, and he said gently, "Why do you disbelieve me?"

Again she had to swallow hard. Then she said, "For many reasons. We live in different worlds, you and I."

"And you think there is no chance of our making a world of our own?"

"I don't know," she said quietly.

He was silent at this, and she stole a quick glance at him. He had leaned back and closed that one visible eye, and he looked very tired.

The plane had started down the runway, and now in a quick thrust of power it lifted from the earth to soar toward the clouds. There was a freedom to flight that never failed to move Amanda—a severance of the shackles that kept one earthbound. Men had soared through the skies to touch the moon, and they would, one day, go on to distant planets. Life— love—could go beyond limited horizons, but exploration of any sort took courage.

It would take courage to make a world with Antonio, because they *were* so different in their backgrounds, their traditions. Yet if he truly loved her, there would be nothing to limit them.

If he truly loved her.

He said, his voice very soft, "You have not answered me. At least I don't consider your saying, 'I don't know,' an answer. But I admit to you I am afraid to pose the question again. I know, believe me, that you have found me arrogant and chauvinistic. I know how foreign I seem to you...."

"No," she said, shaking her head.

"No, what, Amanda?"

"You are not 'foreign' to me," she said. " 'To be foreign to me' would mean I don't understand you, and I think I understand you better than anyone else in the world."

Antonio sighed, a very long sigh. She had the feeling he'd been holding his breath and had expelled it all at once. Then he said, "You could share your life between your own country and Spain? I am going to keep Hermosa Groves, so we would live there a part of the year and maybe a part of the year in Boston, as well. But...."

She waited, and she saw him frown again. Then he said, "I was not going to say anything to you until the operation was over and done with and I knew how I was—going to be. No, don't interrupt me, Amanda. I have to confess that I was, in fact, going to make an appeal to you. I have rented a house on Cape Cod overlooking the ocean, where I can convalesce during the summer—and that is the truth. I was going to ask if you would consider coming there just for that interval so Cristina could continue with her language studies."

"Antonio...."

"I did not think you would come simply because of me," he said, and she realized to her astonishment that he *was* telling the truth. "Then, when I sat down next to you here, I saw you are wearing the pearl I gave you in Manacor. Perhaps it was foolish of me, but that gave me hope.

"Nevertheless," he went on, holding up his hand as she was about to speak, "it is only fair to tell you about the surgery I face. Once again Cristina has been overly dramatic, I am afraid. She told me last night she'd said to you it is almost certain I will be blind after it."

"Antonio...."

"Dearest, do not look at me like that! Cristina was not making up a romantic tale in this instance, but it was her fear she was expressing, not the whole truth. You see, at the time of the accident I suffered a skull fracture. At that same time the optic nerve governing my left eye was severely damaged. But the right one—very fortunately—was not affected. The doctors in Spain told me in the very beginning that nothing could be done about my left eye—the optic-nerve damage could not be repaired. More recently, though, in Boston, they explained to me that my headaches are an aftermath of the skull fracture. It seems there is a persistent leakage of cerebral spinal fluid, and this is what causes these headaches that are sometimes so intense as to make life close to impossible.

"They do not guarantee that surgery will cure the problem, but this is a risk I am prepared to take," Antonio said. "As for my vision—the surgeons have convinced me the only relief that can be offered me is by severing the optic nerve—"

"But that will mean..." she interrupted.

He shook his head. "No," he said, "it will not mean total blindness. It will mean permanent blindness in one eye, true. But I will no longer have distorted shadows to haunt me, and I will no longer have to wear the patch. That in itself will be a blessing, for it will mean I will no longer be stared at wherever I go."

She was tempted to tell him that with his striking good looks it would take more than giving up an eye patch to keep people from staring at him wherever he went. But he went on speaking before she could say anything.

"It is not an easy matter to agree to have the sight in one of your eyes extinguished for all time," he said gravely. "I suppose I have clung to the false hope that something could be done to give me at least clear partial vision. In a lifetime one is given only two eyes...and they are very precious. So in holding off this decision, I have been a coward."

"You could never be called a coward, Antonio," she said, horrified at the thought of what he faced and yet so relieved—so vastly relieved—his entire world was not going to be plunged into eternal darkness.

His laugh was short, and there was a tinge of bitterness to it. "I have been a coward where you are concerned, too, Amanda," he told her. "From the very beginning I was so attracted to you I thought I would lose my mind! But there were moments when you made me more uncertain of myself than I have ever been before. Times when I was incredibly jealous of both Greg and Roger—as I suppose I shall be of any man who ever looks at you. And it seemed to me that the differences between us—from your viewpoint, I am saying—were too great to be surmounted. But, *linda* . . . ."

His words trailed off, and she was astonished to see an expression on his face that seemed very strange for Antonio. He was not at all arrogant in this moment, nor was he showing anything of that aloof, very Spanish mien he so often presented to the world. No, he was actually unsure of himself. There was a new humility about him, and it swayed her more than anything else possibly could have.

She had never tested any of the Spanish Cristina had taught her, but now she said tentatively, "Antonio?"

"Yes, *querida*?" There was a note of dejection to the question, almost as if he was certain she was about to tell him they were too far apart ever to come together again.

"*Te quiero,*" she said, and she saw his start of surprise. "*Te quiero, vida mia,*" she continued bravely, "*con todo mi corazón....*"

She saw his hand reach across the division between the seats and in a moment it was clasping her hands tightly, and he said, "Let me say it to you in English, *querida*...as I don't think I ever have before. I love you, darling...with all my heart...."

He leaned across the space between them, his lips seeking hers, and his kiss plunged her into a vortex of such emotion she didn't know how she could bear the remainder of the flight when she had to keep even this distance from him!

Beside him a stewardess said, "Would you care for champagne, sir?" And then, looking closer, she added hastily, "Excuse me."

But Antonio straightened quickly. "Yes, please," he said. "We shall both require champagne. We have quite a bit to celebrate!"

However, when they had toasted each other and

were sipping the frosty bubbling beverage that had never before seemed quite so festive to Amanda, his face sobered.

"I have neglected to tell you that a major part of the success of this operation to cure the headaches depends upon the convalescent period," he said.

"Oh?"

"Yes. For the first week I will be kept in the hospital, and it will be necessary for my head to be totally immobilized—it must be kept absolutely still. After that—for the next month, at least—I must lead a very sedentary life. No exertion at all...."

"Well?" she questioned.

"Well?" he echoed. "*Por Dios*, Amanda, how do you think I can bear to be sedentary around you even for an hour, let alone a day or a week or a month?"

She smiled. "With the rest of our life in which to catch up," she told him, "I can't see that it will be too great a problem."

And, as the plane streaked northward, Antonio said under his breath, "We have tonight, *querida*. I do not go into the hospital until tomorrow."

"Yes," she told him, her love overflowing. "We have tonight...and forever after."

SUPERROMANCE

Longer, exciting, sensuous and dramatic!

Fascinating love stories that will hold
you in their magical spell till the last page
is turned!

Now's your chance to discover the earlier
books in this exciting series. Choose from
the great selection on the following page!

Now's your chance to discover the earlier
books in this exciting series.

Choose from this list of great

SUPERROMANCES!

SUPERROMANCE

Complete and mail this coupon today!

Worldwide Reader Service

In the U.S.A.
1440 South Priest Drive
Tempe, AZ 85281

In Canada
649 Ontario Street
Stratford, Ontario N5A 6W2

Please send me the following SUPERROMANCES. I am enclosing n
check or money order for $2.50 for each copy ordered, plus 75¢ t
cover postage and handling.

☐ # 26   ☐ # 32   ☐ # 38
☐ # 27   ☐ # 33   ☐ # 39
☐ # 28   ☐ # 34   ☐ # 40
☐ # 29   ☐ # 35   ☐ # 41
☐ # 30   ☐ # 36
☐ # 31   ☐ # 37

Number of copies checked @ $2.50 each = $_____
N.Y. and Ariz. residents add appropriate sales tax $_____
Postage and handling $_____
                           TOTAL $_____

I enclose_____
(Please send check or money order. We cannot be responsible for ca
sent through the mail.)
Prices subject to change without notice. Offer expires November 30, 19#

NAME_____
                (Please Print)

ADDRESS_____APT. NO.___

CITY_____

STATE/PROV._____

ZIP/POSTAL CODE_____
                                    305560000

Share the joys and sorrows
of real-life love in the new
Harlequin American Romances!™

GET THIS BOOK
FREE as your introduction to
Harlequin American Romances
an exciting new series of
romance novels written
especially for the North American
woman of today.

Mail to:
Harlequin Reader Service

In the U.S.
1440 South Priest Drive
Tempe, AZ 85281

In Canada
649 Ontario Street
Stratford, Ontario N5A 6W2

YES! I want to be one of the first to discover the new
Harlequin American Romances. Send me FREE and without
obligation *Twice in a Lifetime.* If you do not hear from me after I
have examined my FREE book, please send me the 4 new
Harlequin American Romances each month as soon as they
come off the presses. I understand that I will be billed only $2.25
for each book (total $9.00). There are no shipping or handling
charges. There is no minimum number of books that I have to
purchase. In fact, I may cancel this arrangement at any time.
Twice in a Lifetime is mine to keep as a FREE gift, even if I do not
buy any additional books.

Name   (please print)

Address   Apt. no.

City   State/Prov.   Zip/Postal Code

Signature (If under 18, parent or guardian must sign.)

AR-SUB-1

AM 305